# Pilgrim's Progress In Modern English

# Pilgrim's Progress In Modern English

### John Bunyan

## Sovereign Grace Publishers, Inc.

P.O. Box 4998
Lafayette, IN 47903
http://www.sgpbooks.com

# THE PILGRIM'S PROGRESS IN MODERN ENGLISH

## CHAPTER 1

As I walked through the wilderness of this world, I came upon a certain place where there was a den. And I laid down in that place to sleep. And as I slept I dreamed a dream. I dreamed, and, behold, I saw a man clothed in rags standing in a certain place, with his face from his own house, a book in his hand, and a great burden on his back (Isa. 64:5; Luke 14:33; Ps. 38:4; Hab. 2:2). I looked and saw him open the book and read in it. And as he read, he wept and trembled; and not being able any longer to contain himself, he broke out with a lamentable cry, saying, "What shall I do?" (Acts 2:37).

In this plight, then, he went home. And he restrained himself as long as he could, so that his wife and children should not see his distress. But he could not be silent long, because his trouble increased. So, at length, he opened his mind to his wife and children. And he began to talk to them in this way: Oh, my dear wife, he said; and you the children of my bowels, I, your dear friend, am undone within myself because of a burden that lies heavily on me. And I am certainly informed that this city of ours will be burned with fire from Heaven; And in that fearful overthrow, both you my wife and myself, and you my sweet babes, shall miserably come to ruin, unless some way of escape which I do not yet see can be found, by which we may be delivered. At this his relations were greatly amazed; not that they believed that what he had said to them was true, but because they thought that some crazy distemper had gotten into his head. So, it drawing towards night, and they hoping that sleep might settle his brains, with all haste they got him to bed. But the night was as troublesome to him as the day. Therefore, instead of sleeping, he spent it in sighs and tears. So, when the morning had come, they asked how he was. He told them, Worse and worse. He also started talking to them again. But they began to be hardened. They also thought they could drive away his distemper by acting harsh and surly toward him. Sometimes they would deride him, sometimes they would chide him and sometimes they would quite neglect him. So he began to retire to his room, to pray for them and pity them, and also to grieve over his own misery. He would also walk alone in the fields, sometimes reading and sometimes praying. And so for some days he spent his time.

Now when he was walking in the fields one time, I saw that he was reading in his book, as he usually did, and being greatly distressed in his mind as he read, he burst out in the same way he had before, crying, "What shall I do to be saved?" (Acts 16:30,31).

I also saw that he looked this way and that, as if he would run. Yet he stood still, because (as I realized) he could not tell which way to go. Then I looked and saw a man named Evangelist coming to him. And he asked, Why are you crying? He answered, Sir, I see by the book in my hand that I am condemned to die, and after that to come to judgment. And I find that I am not willing to do the first, nor able to do the second (Heb. 9:27; Job 16:21,22; Ezek. 22:14).

Then Evangelist said, Why are you not willing to die, since this life is attended with so many evils? The man answered, Because I fear that this burden that is on my back will sink me lower than the grave and that I shall fall into Tophet (Isa. 30:33). And, Sir, if I am not fit to go to prison, I am not fit to go to judgment, and from there to execution. And the thoughts of these things make me cry.

Then Evangelist said, If this is your condition, why are you standing still? He answered, Because I do not know where to go. Then he gave him a roll of parchment. And there was written within it, "Flee from the wrath to come" (Matt. 3:7). Then the man read it, and looking at Evangelist very carefully, he said, Where must I flee? Then Evangelist said, pointing with his finger over a very wide field, Do you see that wicket-gate there? (Matt. 7:13,14). The man said, No. Then the other said, Do you see the shining light there? (Ps. 119:105; 2 Pet. 1:19). He said, I think I do. Then Evangelist said, Keep that light in your eye and go straight up to it so that you can see the gate; at

7

which, when you knock, it shall be told you what you shall do. So I saw in my dream that the man began to run. Now he had not run far from his own door when his wife and children, seeing him, began to call after him to come back (Luke 14:26). But the man put his fingers in his ears and ran on, crying, Life! Life! Eternal Life! So he did not look behind him (Gen. 19:17), but fled towards the middle of the plain.

The neighbors also came out to see him run. And as he ran, some mocked, others threatened, and some called after him to come back. And among those that did so there were two that were resolved to bring him back by force. The name of the one was Obstinate, and the name of the other was Pliable. Now by this time the man had gone a good distance from them. However, they were resolved to pursue him. And they did, and in a little while they overtook him. Then the man said, Neighbors, why have you come? They said, To persuade you to go back with us. But he said, That cannot be, not by any means. You live, he said, in the city of Destruction, the place where I also was born. I see it to be so. And sooner or later, dying there, you will sink lower than the grave, into a place that burns with fire and brimstone. Good neighbors, be content and go along with me.

Obst. What, said Obstinate, and leave our friends and our comforts behind us?

Chr. Yes, said Christian (for that was his name), because all that which you shall forsake is not worthy to be compared with a little of that which I am seeking to enjoy (2 Cor. 4:18). And if you will go along with me and hold it, you will receive the same as I myself. For where I am going, there is enough and to spare (Luke 15:17). Come away and prove my words.

Obst. What are the things you seek, since you leave all the world to find them?

Chr. I seek an inheritance incorruptible, undefiled and that does not fade away. And it is laid up in Heaven and safe there, to be given at the time appointed to those that diligently seek it (1 Pet. 1:4-6; Heb. 11:6,16). If you will, read that it is so, in my book.

Obst. Nonsense, said Obstinate, away with your book. Will you go back with us or not?

Chr.No, not I, said the other, because I have laid my hand to the plow (Luke 9:62).

Obst. Come then, neighbor Pliable, let us turn back again and go home without him. There are a lot of these crazy-headed fools that once they take a fancy by the end are wiser in their own eyes than seven men that can give a reason.

Pl. Then Pliable said, Do not revile him. If what the good Christian says is true, the things he looks for are better than ours. My heart is inclined to go with my neighbor.

Obst. What! More fools still! Be guided by me and go back. Who knows where such a brain-sick fellow will lead you? Go back! Go back and be wise.

Chr. No, but do come with your neighbor Pliable. Such things as I have spoken of can be had, and many more glories besides. If you do not believe me, read here in this book. And for the truth of what is expressed in it, behold, all is confirmed by the blood of Him who wrote it (Heb. 9:17-22).

Pli. Well, neighbor Obstinate, said Pliable, I begin to come to a point. I intend to go along with this good man and to cast in my lot with him. But, my good companion, do you know the way to this desired place?

Chr. I am directed by a man whose name is Evangelist, to speed me toward a little gate that is before us, where we shall receive instruction about the way.

Pli. Come then, good neighbor, let us be going. Then they both went together.

Obst. And I will go back to my place, Obstinate said. I will be no companion of such misled, fantastic fellows.

Now I saw in my dream that when Obstinate had gone back, Christian and Pliable went talking over the plain, and this is the way they began their discourse.

Chr. Come, neighbor Pliable, how do you do? I am glad you are persuaded to go along with me. If even Obstinate himself had but felt what I have felt of the powers and terrors of what is yet unseen, he would not so lightly have given us the back.

Pl. Come, neighbor Christian, since there are none but the two of us here, tell me more now, what the things are and how they are to be enjoyed at the place where we are going.

Chr. I can better think of them in my mind than speak of them with my tongue. But, still, since you desire to know, I will read of them in my book.

Pli. And do you think that the words of your book are certainly true?

Chr. Yes, truly, for it was written by Him that cannot lie (Titus 1:2).

Pli. Well said. What things are they?

Chr. There is an endless kingdom to be inhabited, and everlasting life to be given us, so that we may inhabit that kingdom forever (Isa. 65:17; John 10:27-29).

Pli. Well said, and what else?

Chr. There are crowns of glory to be given us, and garments that will make us shine like the sun in the firmament of Heaven (2 Tim. 4:8; Rev. 22:5; Matt. 13:43).

Pli This is very pleasing; and what else?

Chr. There shall be no more crying, nor sorrow. For He that is owner of the place will wipe all tears from our eyes (Isa. 25:8; Rev. 7:16,17; 21:4).

Pli. And what company shall we have there?

Chr. There we shall be with seraphims and cherubims, creatures that will dazzle your eyes to look on them (Isa. 6:2; 1 Thess. 4:16,17). There you also shall meet with thousands and ten thousands that have gone before us to that place. None of them are hurtful, but loving and holy, each one walking in the sight of God and standing in His presence with acceptance forever. In a word, there we shall see the elders with their golden crowns, we shall see the holy virgins with their golden harps (Rev. 4:4; 14:1-5); and there we shall see men that were cut in pieces, burned in flames, eaten of beasts, drowned in the seas of the world, for the love they bore to the Lord of the place – all of them well and clothed with immortality as with a garment (John 12:25; 2 Cor. 5:2-4).

Pli. The hearing of this is enough to ravish one's heart. But are these things to be enjoyed? How shall we get to be sharers of them?

Chr. The Lord, the governor of the country, has recorded that in this book, the substance of which is this, If we are truly willing to have it, He will freely give it to us (Isa. 55:1-8; John 6:37; 7:37; Rev. 21:6,7; 22:17).

Pli. Well, my good companion, I am glad to hear of these things. Come on, let us change our pace.

Chr. I cannot go as fast as I desire, because of this burden that is on my back.

Now I saw in my dream that just as they had ended this talk, they drew near to a very miry slough that was in the middle of the plain. And not noticing it, they both fell suddenly into the bog. The name of the slough was Despond. Here, then, they wallowed for a time, being grievously smeared with the mud. And Christian, because of the burden that was on his back, began to sink in the mire.

Pli. Then Pliable said, Oh, neighbor Christian, where are you now?

Chr. Christian said, I truly do not know.

Pli. At this Pliable began to be offended and angrily said to his fellow, Is this the happiness you have been telling me of all this while? If we have such ill speed at our first setting out, what may we expect between this and our journey's end? If I get out again with my life, you shall possess the brave country alone, as far as I am concerned. And with that he gave a desperate struggle or two and got out of the mire on that side of the slough which was nearest to his own house. So he went away, and Christian saw him no more.

So Christian was left to tumble in the Slough of Despond alone. But he still tried to struggle toward that side of the slough that was furthest from his own house, and nearest to the Wicket-gate. But though he did, he could not get out because of the burden that was on his back. But I saw in my dream that a man came to him, whose name was Help. And he asked him, What are you doing there?

Chr. Christian said, Sir, I was told to go this way by a man called Evangelist, who directed me also to the gate over there, so that I might escape the wrath to come. And as I was going there, I fell in here.

Help But why did you not look for the steps.

Chr. Fear followed me so hard that I fled the nearest way and fell in.

Help. Then he said, Give me your hand. So he gave him his hand, and he drew him out. And he set him on sound ground, then told him to go on his way (Psalm 40:2).

Then I stepped up to him that plucked him out and said, Sir, why, since this place is the way from the city of Destruction to that gate, is this place not repaired, so that poor travelers might go there with more safety? And he said, This miry slough is such a place as cannot be repaired. It is the descent where the scum and filth that goes with conviction for sin continually runs. And that is why it is called the Slough of Despond. For still, as the sinner is awakened about his lost condition, many fears and doubts arise in his soul, with discouraging apprehensions, all of which get together and settle in this place. And this is the reason this ground is so bad. It is not the pleasure of the King that this place should remain so bad (Isa. 35:3,4,8). His laborers by the direction of his Majesty's surveyors have been employed about this patch of ground for more than sixteen hundred years, if perhaps it might have been repaired. Yes, and to my knowledge, he said, at least twenty thousand cartloads have been swallowed up here. Yes, millions of wholesome instructions that have at all times been brought from all places of the King's dominions (and they that can tell say that they are the best materials to make good ground of the place), if it might have been repaired by such. But it is still the Slough of Despond, and it will be so when they have done all they can.

True, there are by the direction of the Lawgiver certain good and substantial steps placed even through the very middle of this slough. But at that time when this place spews out its filth, as it does when the weather changes, these steps can hardly be seen. Or if they are seen, men through the dizziness of their heads step to the side of them. And they they are mired down on purpose, even though the steps are there (1 Sam. 12:21). But the ground is good when they are once inside the gate.

Now I saw in my dream that by this time Pliable was home at his house. So his neighbors came to visit him. And some of them called him a wise man for coming back. And some called him a fool for endangering himself with Christian. Others mocked at his cowardliness again, saying, Surely, since you began to explore, I would not have been so low as to have given up because of a few difficulties. So Pliable sat ashamed among them. But at last he got more confidence, and then they all turned their stories and began to deride poor Christian behind his back. And so much for Pliable.

Now as Christian was walking alone by himself, he saw one at a distance coming across the field to meet him. And they happened to meet just as they were crossing each other's way. The gentleman's name that met him was Mr. Worldly Wiseman, who lived in the town of Carnal Policy, a very great town, and also near the one Christian came from. This man, then, meeting with Christian, and having some knowledge of him (for Christian's journey from the city of Destruction was much talked about, not only in the town where he lived, but also it began to be the gossip in some other places), Mr. Worldly Wiseman then having some opinion of him, by seeing how laboriously he went, by observing his sighs and groans, and the like, began thus to enter into some talk with Christian.

*World.* Good fellow, why are you going away in this burdened manner?

*Chr.* A burdened manner indeed, as much as I ever believe a poor creature had! And since you ask me where I am going, I will tell you, sir, that I am going to that Wicket-gate before me. For there, as I am informed, I shall be put into a way to get rid of my heavy burden.

World. Do you have a wife and children?

Chr. Yes, but I am so loaded with this burden that I cannot take that pleasure in them as I did formerly. It seems to me as if I had none (1 Cor. 7:29).

World. Will you listen to me if I give you advice?

Chr. If it is good, I will. For I am in need of good advice.

World. I would advise you, then, that you with all speed should get rid of your burden. For you will never be settled in your mind until then, nor can you enjoy the benefits of the blessings which God has given you until then.

Chr. That is what I seek, even to be rid of this heavy burden. But I cannot get it off by myself. Nor is there any man in our country that can take it off of my shoulders. So I am going this way, as I told you, so that I may be rid of my burden.

World. Who told you to go this way to be rid of your burden?

Chr. A man that appeared to me to be a very great and honorable person. As I remember it, his name is Evangelist.

World. I curse him for his advice. There is not a more dangerous and troublesome way in the world than the one into which he has directed you. And you will find this if you are guided by his advice. You have met with something, I see, already. For I see the mud of the Slough of Despond is on you. But that slough is the beginning of the sorrows that go with those that go on in that way. Hear me. I am older than you. In the way you are going, you are likely to meet with weariness, painfulness, hunger, perils, nakedness, sword, lions, dragons, darkness; to be short, death and what not. These things are certainly true, being confirmed by many testimonies. And should a man so carelessly throw himself away by listening to a stranger?

Chr. Why, sir, this burden on my back is more terrible to me than are all these things which you have mentioned. No, it seems that I do not care what I meet with in the way, if it is possible I can also meet with deliverance from my burden.

World. How did you come by this burden in the first place?

Chr. By reading this book in my hand.

World. I thought so. And it has happened to you as to other weak men who have meddled with things too high for them and have suddenly fallen into your distractions. These distractions not only unman men, as I see yours have done to you, but they run them into desperate ventures to obtain they know not what.

Chr. I know what I desire to obtain. It is to be eased from my heavy burden.

World. But why will you seek for ease this way, since so many dangers go with it? Especially since (if you but had the patience to listen to me) I could direct you to the obtaining of what you desire without the dangers that you will run yourself into in this way. Yes, and the remedy is at hand. Besides, I will add that instead of those dangers, you shall meet with much safety, friendship and contentment.

Chr. Sir, I beg you to open this secret to me.

World. Why in that village there (the village is named Morality) there lives a gentleman whose name is Legality, a very judicious man and a man of very good name. He has the skill to help men take off such burdens as yours from their shoulders. Yes, to my knowledge, he has done a great deal of good this way. Yes, and besides, he has skill to cure those that are somewhat crazed in their wits with their burdens. To him, as I say, you may go and be helped at once. His house is not quite a mile from this place. And if he should not be at home himself, he has a handsome young man for a son, whose name is Civility, who can do it (as I say) as well as the old gentleman himself. There, I say, you may be eased of your burden. And if you are not of a mind to go back to your former home (as I indeed would not advise), you may send for your wife and children to come to you in this village, where there are houses now standing empty, one of which you may have at a reasonable rate. Provisions there are also cheap and good. And that which will make your life the more happy is this, that there you shall certainly live beside honest neighbors, in credit and good fashion.

Now Christian was somewhat at a standstill. But he soon concluded, If this is true which this gentleman has said, my wisest course is to take his advice. And with that, he spoke further in this way.

Chr. Sir, which is my way to this honest man's house?

World. Do you see that high hill there?

Chr. Yes, very well.

World. By that hill you must go, and the first house you come to is his.

So Christian turned out of his way to go to Mr. Legality's house for help. But, behold, when he had come near the hill, it seemed so high. And, also, that side of it which was next to the road hung over so much that Christian was afraid to go further, for fear that the hill would fall on his head. So he stood still there and did not know what to do. Also his burden now seemed heavier to him than while he was in his way. Also there came flashes of fire out of the hill, which made Christian afraid that he would be burned. So here he sweated and quaked for fear. And now he began to be sorry that he had taken Mr. Worldly Wiseman's counsel. And then he saw Evangelist coming to meet him. And as he saw him, he began to blush for shame. So Evangelist drew nearer and nearer. And coming up to him, he looked at him with a severe and dreadful face and began to reason with Christian in this way.

Evan. He said, What are you doing here, Christian? At these words, Christian did not know what to answer. So for the time he stood speechless before him. Then Evangelist said further, Are you not the man that I found crying outside the walls of the city of Destruction?

Chr. Yes, dear sir, I am the man.

Evan. Did I not direct you the way to the little Wicket-gate?

Chr. Yes, dear sir, said Christian.

Evan. How is it, then, that you are so quickly turned aside? For you are now out of the way.

Chr. I met with a gentleman as soon as I had gotten over the Slough of Despond, who persuaded me that I might find a man in the village before me who could take off my burden.

Evan. What was he like?

Chr. He looked like a gentleman. And he talked much to me and at last got me to yield. So I came here. But when I saw this hill, and how it hangs over the road, I suddenly made a stand for fear it would fall on my head.

Evan. What did that gentleman say to you?

Chr. Why, he asked me where I was going. And I told him.

Evan. And what did he say then?

Chr. He told me to get rid of my burden in a hurry. And I told him that it was ease I was seeking. And, I said, I am therefore going to that gate over there to receive additional direction as to how I may get to the place of deliverance. So he said that he would show me a better and a shorter way, one not so attended with difficulties as the way, sir, that you set me in. This way, he said, will direct you to a gentleman's house, and he has skill to take off these burdens. So I believed him and turned out of that way into this one, hoping I might be soon eased of my burden. But when I came to this place and saw things as they are, I stopped because I feared danger. But now I do not know what to do.

Evan. Then Evangelist said, Stand still for a while so that I may show you the words of God. So he stood trembling. Then Evangelist said, *"See that you do not refuse Him who speaks. For if they did not escape who refused Him that divinely warned them on earth, much more we shall not escape who turn away from Him who is from Heaven"* (Heb. 12:25). And he said, *"Now the just shall live by faith. But if any draw back, My soul shall have no pleasure in him"* (Heb. 10:38). He also applied them in this way: You are the man that is running into this misery. You have begun to reject the counsel of the Most High and to draw back your foot from the way of peace, even almost to the danger of everlasting ruin. Then Christian fell down at his feet as one who is dying, crying, Woe is me, for I am undone! Seeing this, Evangelist caught him by the right hand, saying, *"All kinds of sin and blasphemies shall be forgiven to men;" "Do not be unbelieving, but believing."* Then Christian again revived and stood up trembling, as at first, before Evangelist.

Then Evangelist went on, saying, Give more earnest care to the things that I shall tell you. I will now reveal to you who it was that deluded you, and also who it was that sent you. The man that met you is one Worldly Wiseman. And he is named, partly because he savors only of the doctrine of this world (1 John 4:5), and for that reason he always goes to church in the town of Morality; and partly because he loves that teaching best, for it is the best to keep him back from the cross (Gal. 6:12). And because he is of this carnal temper, he therefore seeks to pervert my ways, though right. Now there are three things in this man's counsel that you must utterly abhor: (1) his turning you out of the way; (2) his laboring to make the Cross odious to you; and, (3) his setting of your feet in that way that leads to the execution of death.

First, then, you must hate the fact that he turns you out of the way; yes, and your own consent to do it, because this is to reject the counsel of God for the counsel of a Worldly Wiseman. The Lord says, *"Labor to enter in through the narrow gate. For I tell you that many will try to enter in and will not be able...because narrow is the gate and narrow is the way that leads to life, and there are few that find it"* (Luke 13:24; Matt. 7:14). That is the gate to which I am sending you. This wicked man has turned you from this little wicket-gate and from the way to it, desiring to bring you almost to destruction. Therefore, hate the fact that he has turned you out of the way, and abhor yourself for listening to him.

Secondly, you must hate the fact that he labored to make the Cross offensive to you. For you are to prefer it before the treasures of Egypt (Heb. 11:26). Besides, the King of glory has told you that he who desires to save his life is the one that shall lose it. He also said that he who comes after him without hating his father, and mother, and wife, and children, and brothers and sisters; yes, and his own life also, he cannot be My disciple (Matt. 10:37-38; Mark 8:34, 35; Luke 14:26,27; John 12:25). Therefore, I say you must hate that teaching which will persuade you that the truth, without which you cannot have eternal life, is that which shall be death to you.

Thirdly, you must hate the fact that he set your feet in the way that leads to the execution of death. In order to do this, you must consider to whom he sent you, and also how unable that person was to deliver you from your burden. The one to whom you were sent for ease is named Legality, the son of a slave-woman, who is now in bondage with her children (Gal. 4:21-27). And, in a mystery, she is this Mount Sinai which you have feared will fall on your head. Now if she and her children are in slavery, how can you expect to be made free by them? This Legality, then, is not able to set you free from your burden. No one ever got rid of his burden by Legality, nor ever is likely to freed by him, *"No flesh shall be justified before Him by works of Law"* for by the deeds of the law no one living can be rid of his burden. So Mr. Worldly Wiseman is a stranger and Mr. Legality is a cheat. And as for his son Civility, in spite of his false smile, he is but a hypocrite and cannot help you. Believe me, there is nothing in all this that you have heard from these stupid men but a desire to cheat you out of your salvation by turning you from the way in which I had set you.

After this Evangelist called aloud to the heavens for confirmation of what he had said. And words and fire came down out of the mountain under which poor Christian stood, making his hair stand up in his flesh. And these were the words he heard, *"For as many as are of the works of the Law are under a curse – for it is written, Cursed is everyone who does not continue in all things which have been written in the book of the Law to do them"* (Gal. 3:10). Now Christian looked for nothing but death. And he began to cry out pitifully, even cursing the time in which he met with Mr. Worldly Wiseman, but still calling himself a thousand fools for listening to his counsel. He also was greatly ashamed to think that this gentleman's arguments, flowing only from the flesh, should have prevailed with him so much as to cause him to leave the right way. This done, he applied himself again to Evangelist in words and sense as follows:

Chr. Sir, what do you think? Is there any hope? May I now go back and go up to the Wicket-gate? Shall I not be abandoned for this and sent back from there ashamed? I am sorry I have listened to this man's counsel, but may my sin be forgiven?

Evan. Then Evangelist said to him, Your sin is very great, for by it you have committed two evils. You have left the way that is good, and you have traveled in forbidden paths. Yet the man at the gate will receive you, for he has good will for men. But, he said, be careful that you do not turn aside again, *"lest you perish from the way, when His wrath is kindled"* (Ps. 2:12).

Then Christian got ready to go back. And after he had kissed him, Evangelist gave him one smile and prayed that God would go with him. Then he went on with haste, speaking to no one by the way. And if anyone asked, he gave them no answer. He went like one that was all the while walking on forbidden ground and could not count himself safe until he had again gotten into the way which he had left to follow Mr. Worldly Wiseman's counsel. So in time Christian arrived at the gate. And over the gate was written, *"Knock, and it shall be opened to you"* (Matt. 7:8). So he knocked, several times, saying,

> May I now enter here? Will He within
> Open to sorry me, though I have been
> An undeserving rebel? Then shall I
> Not fail to sing His lasting praise on high.

At last a man named Goodwill, one of a serious face, came to the gate and asked who was there and from where he had come, and what it was he wanted.

Chr. Here is a poor burdened sinner. I come from the city of Destruction, but I am going to Mount Zion, so that I may be delivered from the wrath to come. Therefore, sir, I desire to know if you are willing to let me in, since I have been told that this is the gate by which I must go there.

Good. I am willing with all my heart, he said. And with that he opened the gate.

So when Christian was stepping in, the other gave him a pull. Then Christian said, What does that mean? The other told him, A little distance from this gate there is erected a strong castle, of which Beelzebub is the captain. From there both he and those that are with him shoot arrows at those that come up to this gate, hoping they may die before they can enter in. Then Christian said, I rejoice and tremble. And when he was in, the man at the gate asked him who directed him there.

Chr. Evangelist told me to come here and knock, as I did. And he said that you, sir, would tell me what I must do.

Good. An open door is set before you, and no one can shut it.

Chr. Now I begin to reap the benefit of my hazards.

Good. But how is it that you came alone?

Chr. Because none of my neighbors saw their danger as I saw mine.

Good. Did any of them know you were coming?

Chr. Yes, my wife and children saw me at the beginning. And they called to me to turn back again. Also, some of my neighbors stood crying and calling after me to return. But I put my fingers to my ears and so came on my way.

Good. But did not any of them follow you, to persuade you to go back?

Chr. Yes, both Obstinate and Pliable. But when they saw that they could not prevail, Obstinate went back, calling me names. But Pliable came with me a little way.

Good. But why did he not come through?

Chr. Indeed, we both came together until we came to the Slough of Despond, both of us suddenly falling into it. And then my neighbor Pliable became discouraged and would not adventure further. So he got out on the side next to his own house and told me that I should possess the brave country alone for him. So he went his way and I came on mine; he after Obstinate, and I to this gate.

Good. Alas! Poor man! Is the celestial glory of so little esteem with him that he does not count it worth running the hazard of a few difficulties to obtain it?

Chr. Truly, I have said the truth of Pliable. And if I should also tell the truth about myself, it appears there is no difference between him and myself. It is true, he went back to his own house, but I also turned aside to go into the way of death, being persuaded to do it by the carnal argument of Mr. Worldly Wiseman.

Good. Oh, did he light on you? Would he have you seek for ease at the hands of Mr. Legality? Both of them are cheats. But did you listen to him?

Chr. Yes, as far as I dared, I went to find out Mr. Legality, until I thought that the mountain that stands by his house would have fallen on my head. That is why I was forced to stop.

Good. That mountain has been the death of many and will be the death of many more. It is well that you escaped being dashed in pieces by it.

Chr. Why, truly, I do not know what would have become of me there if Evangelist had not providentially met me again as I was musing in the midst of my dumps. But it was God's mercy that he came to me again, for otherwise I would never have arrived here. But now I have come, such a one as I am, truly more fit for death by that mountain than to be standing talking with you. But, oh, what a favor it is to me that I am still admitted entrance here!

Good. We make no objections against any, regardless of all they have done before they come here, they are in no way cast out (John 6:37). So, good Christian, come a little way with me and I will teach you about the way you must go. Look before you. Do you see this narrow way? That is the way you must go. It was made by the patriarchs, prophets, Christ and His apostles, and it is as straight as a rule can make it. This is the way you must go.

Chr. But are there no turnings or windings by which a stranger may lose his way?

Good. Yes, there are many ways, and they are crooked and wide. But you may distinguish the right from the wrong, since the right only is straight and narrow (Matt. 7:14).

Then I saw in my dream that Christian asked him further, if he could not help him off with his burden that was on his back. For as yet he had not gotten rid of it, nor could he by any means get it off without help. But he told him, As to your burden, be content to bear it until you come to the place of deliverance. For there it will fall from your back by itself. Then Christian began to tighten his belt and get ready for his journey. So the other told him that when he had gone for some distance from the gate he would come to the house of the Interpreter, at whose door he should knock so that he might reveal excellent things to him. Then Christian took leave of his friend, and he again prayed that God would go with him. Then he went on, until he came to the house of the Interpreter, where he knocked again and again. At last one came to the door and asked who was there.

Chr. Sir, here is a traveler who was told by one who knows the Head of this house to call here for my profit. Therefore, I desire to speak with the master of the house. So he called for the master of the house. And, after a little time, he came to Christian and asked him what he wanted.

Chr. Sir, I am a man that has come from the city of Destruction and am going to Mount Zion. And I was told by the man who stands at the gate at the head of the way that if I called here you would reveal excellent things to me, things that would be helpful to me on my journey.

Inter. Then come in. I will show you whatever is profitable to you. So he commanded his man to light the candle, and he told Christian to follow him. And he brought him into a private room, where he commanded his man to open a door. And there Christian saw the picture of a very grave person hanging against the wall. And this was the way it looked: he had eyes lifted up to Heaven, the best of books in his hand, the law of truth was written on his lips, the world was behind his back; he stood as if he pleaded with men, and a crown of gold hung over his head.

Chr. Then Christian said, What does this mean?

Inter. The man whose picture this is is one of a thousand. He can beget children (1 Cor. 4:15); travail in birth with children (Gal. 4:19); and nurse them himself when they are born. And since you see him with his eyes lifted up to Heaven, the best of books in his hand, and the law of truth written on his lips, it is to show you that his work is to know and unfold dark things to sinners, even as you also see him stand as if he pleaded with men. And since you see the world as cast behind him, and that a crown hangs over his head, that is to show you that slighting and despising the things that are present for the love that he has to his Master's service, he is sure to have glory for his reward in the world that comes next.

Now I have shown you this picture first because the man whose picture this is is the only man whom the Lord of the place where you are going has authorized to be your guide in all difficult places you may meet with in the way. So pay attention to what I have shown you, and bear in mind what you have seen, lest in your journey you meet with some that will pretend to lead you right, but their way goes down to death. Then he took him by the hand and led him into a very large parlor, one full of dust because it was never swept. Then, after looking upon it for a while, the Interpreter called for a man to sweep it. But when he began to sweep, the dust began to fly about so abundantly that Christian almost was choked with it. Then the Interpreter told a girl that stood by to bring water and sprinkle the room. And when she had done this, it was swept and cleansed with pleasure.

Chr. Then Christian said, What does this mean?

Inter. This parlor is the heart of a man that has never been sanctified by the sweet grace of the gospel. The dust is his original sin, and inward corruptions have defiled the whole man. He that began to sweep at first is the law, but she that brought water and sprinkled it is the gospel. Now as you saw, when the first began to sweep the dust flew about so abundantly that the room could not be cleansed by him, but you were almost choked with it. This is to show you that the law, instead of cleansing the heart from sin (by its working) will in fact revive and put strength into sin and increase it in the soul, even as it discovers and forbids it. For the law does not give power to subdue (Rom. 5:20; 7:7-11; 1 Cor. 15:56). Again, as you saw the girl sprinkle the room with water, when it was cleansed with pleasure, this was to show you that when the gospel comes in the sweet and precious influences of it to the heart, then even as you saw the girl lay the dust by sprinkling the floor with water, so sin is vanquished and subdued, and the soul made clean, through believing the gospel. And it is consequently made fit for the King of glory to inhabit (John 14:21-23; 15:3; Acts 15:9; Rom. 16:25,26; Eph. 5:26).

And I saw in my dream that the Interpreter took him by the hand and had him go into a little room where two little children sat, each one in his chair. the name of the oldest was Passion, and the other's name was Patience. Passion seemed to be very discontented, but Patience was very quiet. Then Christian asked, What is the reason Passion is so discontented? The Interpreter answered, The governor asked him to wait for the beginning of the next year before he got his best things. But he wants them all now. But Patience is willing to wait.

Then I saw one come to Passion and bring him a bag of treasure, pouring it out at his feet. And he took them up and rejoiced in them, all the while laughing scornfully at Patience. But I watched only a little while until I saw he had extravagantly lavished all away, having nothing left but rags.

Chr. Then Christian said to the Interpreter, Expound this matter more fully to me.

Inter. These two boys are figures. Passion is the figure of men of this world, and Patience of the men of the world which is to come. For as you see Passion must have everything now, this year, that is to say, in this world. The men of the world are like this, they must have all their good things now. That proverb, 'A bird in the hand is worth two in the bush,' is of more authority with them than are all the divine testimonies of the good of the world to come. But as you saw, he quickly lavished all away and soon had nothing left him but rags. So it will be with all such men at the end of this world.

Chr. Then Christian said, Now I see that Patience has the best wisdom, and that many ways: (1) because he waits for the best things; (2) because he will have his glory when the other has nothing but rags.

Inter. No, you must add another, that the glory of the next world will never wear out, whereas these are suddenly gone. Therefore Passion had not so much reason to laugh at Patience simply because he had his good things first, but Patience will have to laugh at

Passion because he had his best things last. For the first must give place to the last, because the last must have his time to come. But the last gives place to nothing, for there is not another to succeed him. Therefore, he that has his portion first must have a time to spend it, but he that has his portion last must have it forever. So it is said of Dives, *"you fully received your good things in your lifetime, and Lazarus evil things also. But now he is comforted and you are suffering"* (Luke 16:19-31).

Chr. Then I perceive it is not best to covet things that are now, but to wait for things to come.

Inter. You speak the truth, for the things that are seen are temporal, but the things that are not seen are eternal (2 Cor. 4:18). But though this is so, yet since things present and our fleshly appetite are such near neighbors to one another; and again, because things to come and carnal sense are such strangers to one another; therefore it is true that the first of these may suddenly fall into amity, and that distance is so continued between the second.

Then I saw in my dream that the Interpreter took Christian by the hand and led him into a place where a fire was burning against a wall. And there was one standing by it, always throwing much water on it to quench it. Yet the fire burned higher and hotter. Then Christian asked, What does this mean?

The Interpreter answered, This fire is the work of grace that is worked in the heart. He that throws water on it to extinguish and put it out is the devil. But since you see the fire burn higher and hotter in spite of the water, you shall see the reason for that. So he took him around to the back side of the wall. There he saw a man with a vessel of oil in his hand, which he continually threw into the fire, but secretly. Then Christian asked, What does this mean?

The Interpreter answered, This is Christ, who with the oil of His grace continually maintains the work already begun in the heart. By this means the souls of His people prove to be gracious still, in spite of what the devil can do. And since you saw that the man stood behind the wall to maintain the fire, this is to teach you that it is hard for the tempted to see how this work of grace is maintained in the soul.

I also saw that the Interpreter took him again by the hand and led him into a pleasant place. There a stately palace was built, beautiful to behold. And Christian was greatly delighted when he saw it. He also saw certain persons walking on the top of it, who all were clothed in gold. Then Christian said, May we go in there?

Then the Interpreter took him and led him up toward the door of the palace. And behold, at the door stood a great company of men desiring to go in, but they dared not. A man also sat at a little distance from the door, at a table-side, with a book and his ink-horn before him, to take the names of those that should enter in. He also saw that in the doorway many men stood in armor to keep it, being resolved to do to the men that would enter what hurt and mischief they could. Now Christian was somewhat amazed. At last, when everyone started back for fear of the armed men, Christian saw a man of a very stout appearance come up to the man that sat there to write, saying, Set down my name, Sir. When he had done this, he saw the man draw his sword and put a helmet on his head and rush toward the door and the armed men. They laid upon him with deadly force. But the man, not at all discouraged, fell to cutting and hacking most fiercely. So after he had received and given many wounds to those that attempted to keep him out, he cut his way through all of them and pressed forward into the palace. Then there was a pleasant voice heard from those that were inside, even of those that walked on top of the palace, saying,

Come in, come in:
Eternal glory you shall win.

So he went in and was clothed with garments like theirs. Then Christian smiled and said, I truly believe I know the meaning of this. Now let me go away from here. No, said the Interpreter, not until I have revealed a little more to you. After that you shall go on your way. So he took him by the hand again and led him into a very dark room. And there sat a man in an iron cage.

Now the man looked sad. He sat with his eyes looking down on the ground, his hands folded together, and he sighed as if he would break his heart. Then Christian said, What does this mean? Then the Interpreter suggested he talk with the man. Then Christian said to the man, What are you? The man answered, I am what I once was not.

Chr. What were you once?

Man I was once a fair and flourishing professor, both in my own eyes and also in the eyes of others. Once I thought I was reasonably sure to gain the celestial city, and even then I had joy at the thoughts that I should get there (Luke 8:13).

Chr. Well, but what are you now?

Man I am now a man of despair. I am shut up in it, as in this iron cage. I cannot get out. Oh, now I cannot get out!

Chr. But how did you get into this condition?

Man I quit watching seriously over my soul. I laid the reins on the neck of my lusts. I sinned against the light of the word, and against the goodness of God. I have grieved the Spirit, and He has left me. I tempted the devil, and he has come to me. I have provoked God to anger, and He has left me. I have so hardened my heart that I cannot repent.

Then Christian said to the Interpreter, But is there no hope for such a man? The Interpreter said, Ask him.

Chr. Then Christian said, Is there no hope. Must you be kept in the iron cage of despair?

Man. No, there is no hope at all.

Chr. Why, the Son of the Blessed is very pitiful.

Man. I have crucified Him to myself afresh; I have despised His person; I have despised His righteousness; I have counted His blood an unholy thing; I have done despite to the Spirit of grace (Luke 19:14; Heb. 6:4-6; 10:28,29). Therefore I have shut myself out of all the promises. And now there remains nothing to me but threatenings, dreadful threatenings, faithful threatenings of certain judgment and fiery indignation. These shall devour me as an adversary.

Chr. For what did you bring yourself into this condition?

Man For the lusts, pleasures and profits of this world; in the enjoyment of which I promised myself then much delight. But now every one of those things also bite me; they gnaw me like a burning worm.

Chr. But can you not now repent and turn?

Man God has denied repentance to me. His word gives me no encouragement to believe. Yes, He Himself has shut me up in this iron cage, and all the men in the world cannot let me out. O eternity, eternity! How shall I wrestle with the misery that I must meet with in eternity!

Inter. Then the Interpreter said to Christian, Let this man's misery be remembered by you, and let it be an everlasting caution to you.

Chr. Well, this is fearful! God help me to watch and be sober and to pray that I may avoid the cause of this man's misery. Sir, is it not time for me to go on my way now?

Inter. Wait until I show you one thing more, and then you shall go on your way.

So he took Christian by the hand again and led him into a room where there was one getting up out of bed. And as he put on his clothing, he shook and trembled. Then Christian said, Why does this man tremble so? The Interpreter then told him to tell Christian the reason he did so.

So he began and said, Tonight, as I was sleeping, I dreamed. And behold, the heavens grew exceedingly black. And it thundered and lightened in a most fearful way, so that it put me into an agony. So I looked up in my dream and saw the clouds gathering at an unusual rate. Then I heard a great sound of a trumpet, and I also saw a Man sitting on a cloud, attended with the thousands of Heaven. They were all in flaming fire, also the heavens were all a burning flame. Then I heard a voice saying,, Arise, you who are dead, and come to judgment. And then the rocks were torn and the graves opened, and the dead that were inside came out (John 5:28,29; 1 Cor. 15:51-58; 2 Thess. 1:7-10; Jude

14,15; Rev. 20:11-15). Some of them were very glad and looked upward. And some sought to hide themselves under the mountains (Ps. 50:1-3,22; Isa. 26:20,21; Mic. 7:16,17). Then I saw the Man that sat on the cloud open the book and command the world to come near. Yet because of a fierce flame that issued out and came from before Him, there was a convenient distance between Him and them, as between the judge and the prisoners at the bar (Dan. 7:9,10; Mal. 3:2,3). I heard it also proclaimed to them that attended on the Man that sat on the cloud, Gather together the tares, the chaff and stubble, and throw them into the burning lake. And then the bottomless pit opened, just about where I stood. And out of its mouth came smoke and coals of fire in great abundance, with hideous noises. It was also commanded to those same persons, Gather My wheat into the garner (Mal. 4:2; Matt. 3:12; 18:30; Luke 3:17). And then I saw many caught up and carried away into the clouds (1 Thess. 4:13-18). But I was left behind. I also sought to hide myself, but I could not, for the Man that sat on the cloud kept His eye on me. And my sins came into my mind, and my conscience accused me on every side (Rom. 2:14,15). Then I awakened from my sleep.

Chr. But what was it that made you so afraid of this sight?

Man Why, I thought that the day of judgment had come and that I was not ready for it. But the thing that frightened me most was that the angels gathered up several and left me behind; also that the pit of hell opened her mouth just where I stood. And my conscience afflicted me; and, as I thought, the Judge had His eye on me continually, showing indignation in His face.

Then the Interpreter said to Christian, Have you considered all these things?

Chr. Yes, and they cause me both to hope and fear.

Inter. Well, keep all things so in your mind that they may be as a goad in your sides to urge you forward in the way you ought to go. Then Christian began to tighten his belt and to prepare himself for his journey. Then the Interpreter said, May the Comforter be always with you, good Christian, to guide you in the way that leads to the City. So Christian traveled on, saying,

> Here I have seen things rare and profitable,
> Things pleasant, dreadful, things to make me stable
> In what I have begun to take in hand;
> Then let me think of them and understand
> Why they were revealed to me; and let me be
> Thankful, O good Interpreter, to you.

Then I saw in my dream that the highway along which Christian was to travel was fenced on either side with a wall, and that wall was called Salvation (Isa. 26:1). So burdened Christian ran up this way, but not without great difficulty, because of the load on his back. And he ran this way until he came to a place that went somewhat upwards. And on that place a Cross stood; and a little below, in the bottom, there was a Sepulchre. So I saw in my dream that just as Christian came up to the Cross, his burden fell from his shoulders and from off his back, and it began to tumble and continued until it came to the mouth of the Sepulchre, where it fell in. And I never saw it any more.

Then Christian was glad and full of light. And he said with a merry heart, He has given me rest by His sorrow, and life by His death. Then he stood still awhile, to look and to wonder, for it was very surprising to him that the sight of the Cross should ease him of his burden in this way. He therefore looked, and looked again, even until the springs that were in his head sent the tears down his cheeks (Zech. 12:10). Then as he stood looking and weeping, behold, three Shining Ones came to him and greeted him with, si,"Peace be upon you." Then the first said to him, *"Your sins be forgiven to you;"* the second stripped him of his rags and clothed him with a change of clothing; the third also set a mark on his forehead and gave him a roll with a seal on it (Zech. 3:4; Eph. 1:13) which he told him to look upon as he ran, and that he should turn it in at the Celestial Gate. So they went away. Then Christian gave three leaps for joy and went on singing,

> Thus far I came loaded with my sin,
> Nor could anything ease the grief that I was in,
> Till I came here! What a place this is!
> Must here be the beginning of my bliss?
> Must here the burden fall from off my back?
> Must here the strings that bound it to me crack?
> Blessed Cross! Blessed Sepulchre! Blessed rather be
> The Man that there was put to shame for me!

I then saw in my dreams that he went on this way even until he came to a bottom. There he saw, a little out of the way, three men fast asleep,with shackles on their heels. The name of one was Simple, another Sloth, and the third, Presumption.

Then seeing them lying in this condition, Christian went to them to see if he might perhaps awaken them. And he cried, You are like those that sleep on the top of a mast (Prov. 23:34), for the Dead Sea is under you, a gulf that has no bottom. Awake, therefore, and come away. Be willing also, and I will help you off with your irons. He also told them, If he that goes about like a roaring lion comes by here, you will certainly become a prey to his teeth (1 Pet. 5:8). With that they looked at him and began to reply in this way: Simple said, I do not see any danger; Sloth said, Let me sleep a little more; and Presumption said, Every vat must stand on its own bottom. And so they laid down to sleep again, and Christian went on his way.

Yet he was troubled to think that men in that danger should so little esteem the kindness of him that so freely offered to help them, both by awakening them, counselling them and offering to help them off with their irons. And as he was troubled about it, he saw two men come tumbling over the wall, on the left hand side of the narrow way. And they quickly came up to him. The name of the one was Formalist, and the name of the other was Hypocrisy. So, as I said, they drew up to him. And he thus entered into discourse with them.

Chr. Gentlemen, from what place did you come, and where do you go?

Form. & Hyp. We were born in the land of Vainglory, and we are going for praise to Mount Zion.

Chr. Why did you not come in at the gate which stands at the beginning of the way? Do you not know that it is written, *"he that does not come in by the door of the sheepfold, but climbs up some other place, that one is a thief and a robber"*? (John 10:1).

Form. & Hyp. They said that to go to the gate for entrance was counted to be too far by all their countrymen; and that therefore their usual way was to make a short cut of it, and to climb over the wall, as they had done.

Chr. But will it not be counted a trespass against the Lord of the city where we are bound to violate His revealed will in this way?

Form. & Hyp. They told him that as for that he need not trouble his head about it; for what they did they had custom for it, and they could produce if need be testimony that would witness for it for more than a thousand years.

Chr. But will you be able to stand a trial at law?

Form. & Hypp. They told him that a custom that had stood for more than a thousand years would no doubt now be admitted as a thing legal by any impartial judge. And besides, they said, if we get into the way, what does it matter which way we get in? If we are in, we are in. You are only in the way, you who we see came in at the gate. And we also are in the way, we who came tumbling over the wall. In what way is your condition now better than ours?

Chr. I walk by the rule of my Master. You walk by the rude working of your imaginations. You are counted thieves already by the Lord of the way. So I doubt that you will be found to be true men at the end of the way. You came in by yourselves, without His direction, and you shall go out by yourselves, without His mercy.

To this they said little. Only they told him to watch out for himself. Then I saw that they went on, each man in his way, without much conversation with one another, except that these two men told Christian that as to laws and ordinances they had no doubts but that they would do them as conscientiously as he would. Therefore, they said, we do not see in what way you differ from us, except by the coat that is on your back, which we believe was given you by some of your neighbors to hide the shame of your nakedness.

Chr. By laws and ordinances you will not be saved (Gal. 2:16), since you did not come in by the door. And as for this coat that is on my back, it was given me by the Lord of the place where I go; and that was, as you say, to cover my nakedness. And I take it as a token of kindness to me, for I had nothing but rags before. And, besides, I comfort myself as I go in this way, thinking, Surely when I come to the gate of the City, the Lord of it will know me for good, since I have His coat on my back, a coat that He gave me freely in the day that He stripped me of my rags. And I have a mark in my forehead, which perhaps you have not noticed, which one of my Lord's most intimate associates fixed there in the day that my burden fell off my shoulders. I will tell you, too, that I was given a sealed roll then, to comfort me by reading as I go on the way. I was also commanded to turn it in at the Celestial Gate in token of my certain entrance after it. I doubt that you have all these things. And you lack them because you did not come in at the gate.

They gave him no answer to these things. but they looked at one another and laughed. Then I saw that they went on, except that Christian kept before them. And he had no more talk, except with himself, and that sometimes sighingly and sometimes comfortably. Also he would often read in the roll that one of the Shining Ones gave him, and he was refreshed by it.

Then I saw that they all went on until they came to the foot of the hill Difficulty, at the bottom of which was a spring. Also in that same place were two other ways, besides that which came straight from the gate. One turned to the left hand, and the other to the right, at the bottom of the hill. But the narrow way lay right up the hill, and the name of the ascending side of the hill is called Difficulty. Then Christian went to the spring and drank of it to refresh himself (Isa. 49:10-12). And then he began to go up the hill, saying,

> The hill, though high, I covet to ascend;
> The difficulty will not me offend;
> For I perceive the way to life lies here:
> Come, pluck up heart, let's neither faint nor fear.
> Better, though difficult, the right way to go,
> Than wrong, though easy, where the end is woe.

The other two also came to the foot of the hill. But when they saw the hill was steep and high, and that there were two other ways to go (and supposing also that these two ways might meet again with that way which Christian traveled, on the other side of the hill), they therefore were resolved to go in those ways. Now the name of one of those ways was Danger, and the name of the other was Destruction. So the one took the way that is called Danger, which led him into a great forest. And the other went directly up the way to Destruction, which led him into a wide field, full of dark mountains, where he stumbled and fell, and he arose no more. I then looked after Christian, to see him go up the hill. And I saw that he stopped running and began to walk, then went from walking to crawling on his hands and knees, because of the steepness of the place. Now about midway to the top of the hill was a pleasant arbor, made by the Lord of the hill for the refreshment of weary travelers. Christian then climbed in there, where he also sat down to rest himself. Then he pulled his roll out of his bosom and read in it to his comfort. He also now began to take a fresh look at the coat or garment which was given to him as he stood by the Cross. Pleasing himself in this way for a while, he at last fell into a slumber, and from there into a fast sleep, which kept him in that place until it was almost night. And in his sleep his roll fell out of his hand. And as he was sleeping, one came to him and awakened him, saying, *"Go to the ant, you sluggard; consider her ways and be wise"*

(Prov. 6:6). And then Christian suddenly started up and went quickly on his way. And he went quickly until he came to the top of the hill.

Now when he had gotten up to the top of the hill, two men came running with great speed. The name of the one was Timorous, and of the other, Mistrust. Christian said to them, Sirs, what is the matter? You are running the wrong way. Timorous answered that they were going to the city of Zion and had gotten up that difficult place. But, he said, the farther we go, the more danger we encounter. So we have turned and are going back again.

Mis. Yes, for just before us there are a couple of lions in the way, whether sleeping or waking we do not know. And we could not but think that if we came within reach that they would instantly pull us in pieces.

Chr. Then Christian said, You make me afraid. But where shall I flee to be safe? If I go back to my own country, it is prepared for fire and brimstone, and I shall certainly perish there. If I can get to the Celestial City, I am sure to be in safety there. I must attempt it. To go back is nothing but death; to go forward is fear of death, but with life everlasting beyond it. I will still go forward.

So Mistrust and Timorous ran down the hill, and Christian traveled on his way. But thinking again of what he had heard from the men, he felt in his bosom for his roll, that he might read in it and be comforted. He felt, but he did not find it. Then Christian was in great distress and did not know what to do. For he lacked that which usually relieved him, and that which would have been his pass into the Celestial City. So he began to be much perplexed here, not knowing what to do. At last he remembered that he had slept in the arbor that is on the side of the hill. And he fell down on his knees and asked God to forgive him for that foolish fact. And he then went back to look for his roll. But all the way as he went back, who could sufficiently set forth the sorrow of Christian's heart! Sometimes he sighed, sometimes he wept, and he oftentimes scolded himself for being so foolish as to fall asleep in that place which was erected only for a little refreshment from his weariness. So he then went back, looking carefully on this side and on that, all the way as he went, if perhaps he might find the roll that had been his comfort so many times in his journey. So he went until he came again within sight of the arbor where he sat and slept. But seeing it renewed his sorrow even more, by bringing up afresh the evil of sleeping to his mind. So he then went on wailing over his sinful sleep, saying, *"O wretched man that I am!"* that I should sleep in the daytime (1 Thess. 5:7,8; Rev. 2:4,5); that I should sleep in the midst of difficulty! that I should so indulge the flesh by using that rest for the ease of my flesh, when the Lord had only erected it for the relief of the spirits of pilgrims! How many steps I have taken in vain! So it happened to Israel. For because of their sin they were sent back again by the way of the Red Sea; and I am made to tread those steps with sorrow, when I might have trodden them with delight if I had not slept so sinfully. How far I might have been on my way by this time! I am having to tread those steps three times which I did not need to tread but once. Yes, now I am likely to be caught by darkness, for the day is almost gone. Oh that I had not slept!

Now by this time he had come to the arbor again, and he sat down and wept there awhile. But at last (as Providence would have it), looking sorrowfully down under the settle, he saw there his roll. He with trembling and haste caught it up and put it into his bosom. But who can tell how joyful this man was when he had found his roll again! For this roll was the assurance of his life and the acceptance token at the desired haven. So he laid it up in his bosom and gave thanks to God for directing his eye to the place where it lay. And with joy and tears he again began to travel on. But oh, how nimbly he went up the rest of the hill! Still, before he got up, the sun went down on Christian. And this again made him recall the vanity of his sleeping to his mind. And he again began to mourn within himself, O sinful sleep! How foolishly for your sake I am likely to be caught in the darkness in my journey! I must walk without the sun, darkness must cover the path of my feet, and I must hear the noise of the doleful creatures because of my sinful sleep! And he now remembered the story that Mistrust and Timorous told him, how they were frightened with the sight of the lions. Then Christian said to himself again, These beasts range in the night for their prey. And if they should meet me in the dark , how would I escape them? How would I escape being torn into pieces by them? So he went on his way. But while he was wailing over his unhappy miscarriage, he lifted up his eyes and saw there was a very stately palace before him. The name of it was Beautiful, and it stood by the side of the road.

So I saw in my dream that he hastened and went forward to see if it was possible for him to get lodging there. Now before he had gone far, he entered into a very narrow passage, which was about a furlong from the Porter's lodge. And looking very carefully before him as he went, he saw two lions in the way. Now, he thought, I see the dangers that Mistrust and Timorous were driven back by. (The lions were chained, but he did not see the chains.) Then he was afraid and considered also going back after them, for he thought that nothing but death was before him. But the Porter at the lodge, whose name is Watchful, seeing that Christian came to a stop, as if he would go back, cried to him, saying, Is your strength so small? (Mark 4:40). Do not fear the lions, for they are chained and are placed there for the trial of faith and to discover those who have none. Keep in the middle of the path and no harm shall come to you.

Then I saw that he went on, trembling for fear of the lions. But he carefully heeded the directions of the Porter. He heard them roar, but they did him no harm. Then he clapped his hands. And he went on until he came and stood before the gate where the Porter stood. Then Christian said to the Porter, Sir, what house is this? And, May I stay here tonight? The Porter answered, This house was built by the Lord of the hill, and He built it for the relief and security of pilgrims. The Porter also asked from where he came, and where he was going.

Chr. I have come from the city of Destruction and I am going to Mount Zion. But because the sun has now set, I desire, if I may, to stay here tonight.

Port. What is your name?

Chr. My name is now Christian, but my name at the first was Graceless. I came of the race of Japheth (Gen. 9:27), whom God will persuade to dwell in the tents of Shem.

Port. But how does it happen that you come so late? The sun has set.

Chr. I would have been here sooner, but being the wretched man that I am I slept in the arbor that stands on the hillside. No, even so, I would have been here much sooner if I had not lost my evidence while I was sleeping. I came without it to the brow of the hill, and then feeling for it and not finding it, I was forced with sorrow of heart to go back to the place where I had slept. There I found it, and now I have come.

Port. Well, I will call one of the virgins of this place. And if she likes you, she will bring you in to the rest of the family, according to the rules of the house.

So Watchful the Porter rang a bell, at the sound of which a girl with a serious but beautiful face came out of the door of the house. Her name was Discretion, and she asked why she had been called. The Porter answer, This man is on a journey from the city of Destruction to Mount Zion. But being weary and caught by the darkness, he has asked me if he might stay here tonight. So I told him that I would call you, and that after you had talked with him you will do what seems good to you, even according to the law of the house.

Then she asked him from where he came, and where he was going. And he told her. She also asked him how he got into the way. And he told her. Then she asked him what he had seen and met with in the way. And he told her. And at last she asked his name. So he said, It is Christian, and now I have so much the more desire to stay here tonight, because from what I see this place was built by the Lord of the hill for the relief and security of pilgrims. So she smiled, but the water stood in her eyes. And after a little pause, she said, I will call out two or three more of the family. So she ran to the door and called out Prudence, Piety and Charity. After a little more discourse with him, they brought him in to the rest of the family. And many of them meeting him at the threshold of the house said, Come in, you who are blessed of the Lord. This house was built by the Lord of the hill on purpose to entertain such pilgrims as you are. Then he bowed his head and followed them into the house. So when he had come in and sat down, they gave him something to drink. And they agreed that until supper was ready, some of them would like some particular discourse with Christian for the best improvement of the time. And they appointed Piety, Prudence and Charity to talk with him. And they began in this way:

Piety Come, good Christian, since we have been so loving to you to receive you into our house tonight, let us talk with you of all the things that have happened to you in your pilgrimage. Perhaps we may better ourselves in doing so.

Chr. With a very good will. And I am glad that you are so well disposed.

Piety What moved you at first to take up a pilgrim's life for yourself?

Chr. I was driven out of my native country by a dreadful sound that was in my ears; to wit, that unavoidable destruction would follow me if I remained in that place where I was.

Piety But how did it happen that you came out of your country this way?

Chr. It was as God would have it. For when I was under the fears of destruction, I did not know where to go. But providentially a man came to me as I was trembling and weeping, whose name is Evangelist. And he directed me to the Wicket-gate, which I would never have found otherwise. And so he set me into the way that has led me directly to this house.

Piety But did you not come by the house of the Interpreter.

Chr. Yes, and I saw such things there that the remembrance of them will stick by me as long as I live. I especially remember three things: (1) how Christ maintains his work of grace in the heart, in spite of all Satan can do; (2) how the man had sinned himself completely out of hopes of God's mercy; and, (3) also the dream of the one that thought in his sleep the day of judgment had come.

Piety Why, did you hear him tell his dream?

Chr. Yes, and it was a dreadful one to my mind. It made my heart ache as he was telling it. Still, I am glad that I heard it.

Piety Was this all you saw at the house of the Interpreter?

Chr. No, he took me and brought me where he showed me a stately palace. And I saw how the people that were in it were clad in gold. And I saw how an adventurous man came and cut his way through the armed men that stood in the door to keep him out. And I saw how he was told to come in and win eternal glory. And I felt within those things ravishing my heart. And I would have stayed at that good man's house for a year, but that I knew I had further to go.

Piety And what else did you see in the way?

Chr. Saw? Why, I went but a little further and I saw One, as I thought in my mind, hang bleeding upon a tree. And the very sight of Him made my burden fall off my back. For I groaned under a very heavy burden, but then it fell down off of me. It was a strange thing to me, for I never saw such a thing before. Yes, and while I stood looking up (because I could not stop looking), three Shining Ones came to me. One of them testified that my sins were forgiven me; another stripped me of my rags and gave me this embroidered coat which you see; and the third set the mark which you see in my forehead, and gave me this sealed roll. And then Christian plucked it out of his bosom.

Piety But you saw more than this, did you not?

Chr. The things that I have told you were the best. Yet I saw some other matters, such as when I saw three men, Simple, Sloth and Presumption lying asleep a little out of the way, as I came along, having irons on their heels. But do you think I could awaken them? I also saw Formality and Hypocrisy come tumbling over the wall, pretending to go to Zion. But they were quickly lost, even as I myself told them, but they would not believe. But above all, I found it hard work to get up this hill, and it was as hard to come past the lions' mouths. And, truly, if it had not been for the good man the Porter that stands at the gate, I do not know but that, after all, I might have gone back again. But I thank God

I am here, and I thank you for receiving me.

Then Prudence thought it would be good to ask him a few questions. And she asked his answer to them.

Pru. Do you not sometimes think of the country from where you started.

Chr. Yes, but with much shame and detestation. Truly, if I had been mindful of that country from where I started, I might have had opportunity to have returned. But now I desire a better country, that is, a heavenly one (Heb. 11:15,16).

Pru. Do you not still carry with you some of the things that you knew there?

Chr. Yes, but greatly against my will; especially my inward and carnal cogitations, with which all my countrymen, as well as myself, were delighted. But now all these things are my grief. And If I could but choose my own things, I would choose never to think of those things any more. But when I desire to do that which is best, then that which is worst is with me (Rom. 7:21).

Pru. Do you not sometimes find it as if those things were vanquished, the things which at other times are your perplexity?

Chr. Yes, but that is but seldom. Yet they are to me golden hours in which such things happen to me.

Pru. Can you remember by what means you find your annoyances at times as if they were vanquished?

Chr. Yes, when I think what I saw at the Cross, that will do it. And when I look at my embroidered coat, that will do it. And when I look into the roll that I carry in my bosom, that will do it. And when my thoughts become warm about where I am going, that will do it.

Pru. And what is it that makes you so desirous to go to Mount Zion?

Chr. Why, there I hope to see Him alive, He who hung dead on the cross. And there I hope to be rid of all those things that to this day are an annoyance within me. There they say there is no death (Isa. 25:8; Rev. 21:4), and there I shall dwell with the kind of company I like best. For, to tell you the truth, I love Him, because by Him I was eased of my burden. And I am weary of my inward sickenss. I would love to be where I shall die no more, and to be with the company that shall continually cry, Holy, holy, holy.

Then Charity said to Christian, Do you have a family? Are you a married man?

Chr. I have a wife and four small children.

Cha. And why did you not bring them along with you?

Then Christian wept and said, Oh! How willingly I would have done it, but they were all of them adverse to my going on pilgrimage.

Char. But you should have talked to them and should have tried to show them the danger of staying behind.

Chr. So I did. And I told them also what God had shown to me of the destruction of our city. But I seemed to them as one that mocked, and they did not believe me (Gen. 19:14).

Cha. And did you pray to God that He would bless your counsel to them?

Chr. Yes, and that with much affection. For you must think that my wife and poor children were very dear to me.

Cha. But did you tell them of your own sorrow and fear of destruction? For I suppose that destruction was visible enough to you.

Chr. Yes, over and over and over. They could also have seen my fears in my face, in my tears, and also in my trembling under the apprehension of the judgment that hung over our heads. But all this was not sufficient to prevail with them to come with me.

Cha. But what could they say for themselves as to why they did not come?

Chr. Why, my wife was afraid of losing this world. And my children were given to the foolish delights of youth. So, whether by one thing or another, they left me to wander in this manner alone.

Cha. But did you not with your vain life dampen all that you by words used to persuade them to come away with you?

Chr. Indeed, I cannot commend my life, for I am conscious to myself of many failings in it. I also know that a man by his behavior may overthrow what he labors to fasten on others for their good by argument or persuasion. Yet, I can say this, that I was very wary of giving them any occasion, by any unseemly action, to make them averse to going on pilgrimage. Yes, for this very thing, they would tell me that I was too precise, and that I denied myself as to things, for their sakes, in which they saw no evil. No, I think I may say that if what they saw in me hindered them, it was my great tenderness in sinning against God, or of doing any wrong to my neighbor.

Cha. Indeed, Cain hated his brother because his own works were evil, and because his brother's were righteous (1 John 3:12). And if your wife and children were offended with you because of this, they thereby show themselves to be implacable to good. And you have delivered your soul from their blood (Ezek. 3:19).

Now I saw in my dream that thus they sat talking together until supper was ready. So when they had made ready, they sat down to food. And the table was furnished with fat things, and with wine that was well refined. And all their talk at the table was about the Lord of the hill; namely, about what He had done, and why He did what He did, and why He had built that house. And by what they said, I saw that He had been a great warrior. And He had fought with and had slain him that had the power of death (Heb. 2:14); but not without great danger to Himself (which made me love Him the more).

For, as they said, and as I believed, said Christian, He did it with the loss of much blood. But that which put the glory of grace into all He did was this, that He did it out of pure love to His country. And, besides, there were some of them of the household that said they had visited with Him and had spoken to Him since He died on the cross. And they have attested that they had it from His own lips that He is such a lover of poor pilgrims that such love is not to be found from the east to the west.

And they gave an instance of what they said, that He had stripped Himself of His glory so that He might do this for the poor. And they had heard Him say and affirm that He would not dwell in the mountain of Zion alone. They also said that He had made many pilgrims princes, though by nature they were born beggars and had originated from the dunghill (1 Sam. 2:8). So they talked together until late in the night. And after they had committed themselves to their Lord for protection, they left to rest. They put the pilgrim in a large upper room with its window opening towards the sunrise. The name of the room was Peace. And he slept there until the break of day. And then he awoke and sang:

> Where am I now? Is this the love and care
> Of Jesus, for the men that pilgrims are,
> Thus to provide! That I should be forgiven,
> And dwell already the next door to heaven!

So in the morning they all got up. And after some more discourse, they told him that he should not depart until they had shown him the rarities of that place. And first they took him into the study, where they showed him records of the greatest antiquity. And, as I remember in my dream, they showed him the pedigree of the Lord of the hill, that He was the Son of the Ancient of days, that He came by that eternal generation. Here also was more fully recorded the acts that He had done, and the names of many hundreds that He had taken into His service; and how He had placed them in such habitations that could not be dissolved either by length of days or the decays of nature.

Then they read to him some of the worthy acts that some of His servants had done, how they had subdued kingdoms, worked righteousness, obtained promises, stopped the mouths of lions, quenched the violence of fire, escaped the edge of the sword, out of weakness were made strong, became valiant in fight and turned to flight the armies of the strangers (Heb. 11:33,34).

Then they read again in another part of the records of the house where it was shown how willing their Lord was to receive into His favor any, even any, though they in time past had offered great affronts to His person and proceedings. Here also were several other histories of many other famous things, all of which Christian could view – such as things both ancient and modern, together with prophecies and predictions of things that have their certain accomplishment, both as to the dread and amazement of enemies, and as to the comfort and solace of pilgrims.

The next day they took him into the armory, where they showed him all kinds of armor which the Lord had provided for pilgrims – such as sword, shield, helmet, breastplate, all-prayer, and shoes that would not wear out. And there was enough here to cover as many men for the service of their Lord as there are stars in the heaven for multitude.

They also showed him some of the engines with which some of his servants had done wonderful things. They showed him Moses' rod, the hammer and nail with which Jael killed Sisera; also the pitchers, trumpets and lamps with which Gideon put to flight the armies of Midian. Then they showed him the ox's goad with which Shamgar killed six hundred men. They also showed him the jawbone with which Samson did such mighty feats. And they showed him the sling and stone with which David killed Goliath of Gath. And also the sword was there with which the Lord will kill the man of sin, in the day that he shall rise up to the prey. They also showed him many excellent things besides these, with which Christian was much delighted. This being done, they went to their rest again.

Then I saw in my dream that on the next day he got up to go forward. But they asked him to stay until the next day also. And, they said, then if the day is clear we will show you the Delectable Mountains. This, they said, would further add to his comfort, because they were nearer the desired haven than this place where he was at present. So he consented and stayed.

When the morning was up, she took him to the top of the house and told him to look south. So he did. And, behold, at a great distance (Isa. 33:16,17), he saw a most pleasant mountainous country, beautified with woods, vineyards, fruits of all sorts, also flowers, with springs and fountains, very delectable to behold. Then he asked the name of the country. They said, It is Immanuel's Land. And it is as common as this hill is to and for all the pilgrims. And when you come there, from there you may see to the gate of the Celestial City, as the shepherds that live there will show you.

Now he thought of setting forward, and they were willing that he should go. But, they said, first let us go again into the armory. So they did. And when he came there, they dressed him out from head to foot with armor that had been proven, lest perhaps he should meet with assaults in the way. He being therefore thus armored, he walked out with his friends to the gate. And there he asked the Porter if he saw any pilgrim go by. Then the Porter answered, Yes.

Chr. Please, do you know him?

Por. I asked his name, and he told me it was Faithful.

Chr. Oh, said Christian, I know him. He is my townsman and my near neighbor. He comes from the place where I was born. How far do you think he may be before me?

Por. By this time he is below the hill.

Chr. Well, good Porter, the Lord be with you and add to all your blessings much increase for the kindness you have shown to me.

Then he began to go forward. But Discretion, Piety, Charity and Prudence desired to accompany him down to the foot of the hill. So they went on together, repeating their former discourses until they came to go down the hill. Then Christian said, As it was difficult coming up, so, so far as I can see, it is dangerous going down. Yes, said Prudence, so it is. For it is a hard matter for a man to go down into the Valley of Humiliation, as you are now, and not to slip by the way. That is why, they said, we have come out to go with you down the hill. So he began to go down, but very carefully. Still, he slipped a time or two.

Then I saw in my dream that these good companions gave Christian a loaf of bread, a bottle of wine and a cluster of raisins when he got down to the bottom of the hill. And then he went on his way:

> While Christian is among his godly friends,
> Their golden mouths make him sufficient mends
> For all his griefs; and when they let him go,
> He's clad with northern steel from top to toe.

But now, in this Valley of Humiliation poor Christian was hard put to it. For he had gone but a little way before he saw a foul fiend coming over the field to meet him: his name is Apollyon. Then Christian began to be afraid, and he gave some thought as to whether he should go back or stand his ground. But he considered again that he had no armor for his back. So he thought to turn the back to him might give him greater advantage, so that he could pierce him with ease with his darts. Therefore he resolved to be bold and stand his ground. For, he thought, If I had no more in my eye than to save my life, it would be the best way to stand.

So he went on. And Apollyon met him. And the monster was hideous to behold! He was clothed with scales like a fish (they are his pride); he had wings like a dragon, feet like a bear, and out of his belly came fire and smoke. And his mouth was like the mouth of a lion. When he had come up to Christian, he looked at him with a disdainful face and began to question him in this way:

Apol. From where did you come, and where are you bound?

Chr. I have come from the city of Destruction, which is the place of all evil. And I am going to the city of Zion.

Apol. By this I see that you are one of my subjects. For all of that country is mine, and I am the prince and god of it. How is it, then, that you have run away from your king? If I did not hope that you may do me more service, I would strike you now to the ground, with but one blow.

Chr. I was indeed born in your dominions, but your service was hard, and your wages were such that a man could not live on them. For the wages of sin is death (Rom. 6:23); therefore, when I had come to years I did as other considerate persons do; I looked for a way to better myself.

Apol. There is no prince that will so lightly lose his subjects, neither will I lose you. But since you complain of your service and wages, be content to return and I hereby promise to give you whatever our country will afford.

Chr. But I have given myself to another, even to the King of kings. So how can I with fairness go back with you?

Apol. You have acted according to the proverb, "You have changed a bad for a worse. But it usually falls out that those who have professed themselves to be His servants will after a while give Him the slip and return again to me. You do so too and all shall be well.

Chr. I have given Him my faith and have sworn my allegiance to Him. How then can I go back from this without being hanged as a traitor?

Apol. You did the same to me and yet I am willing to forget all if you will now only turn again and go back.

Chr. What I promised you was in my immaturity. And, besides, I believe that the King under whose banner I now stand is able to absolve me. Yea, and He will also pardon what I did when I complied with you. And, besides, O destroying Apollyon, to tell you the truth I like His service, His wages, His servants, His government, His company and His country better than yours. Therefore, please do not persuade me any further. I am His servant and I desire to follow Him.

Apol. When your blood has cooled, consider again what you are likely to meet with in the way that you are going. You know that most of His servants come to an ill end because they are transgressors against me and my ways. How many of them have been put to shameful deaths! And, besides, though you think His service to be better than mine, He never yet has come from His place to deliver any who serve Him out of their hands. But as for me, all the world very well knows how many times I have delivered, either by power or by fraud, those that have faithfully served me, from Him and His, though taken by them. And so I will deliver you.

Chr. His forbearing at present to deliver them is on purpose to try their love, to see if they will cleave to Him to the end. And as for the ill end you say they come to, that is most glorious in their account. Foras for the present deliverance, they do not much expect it. For they wait for their glory, and then they shall have it, when their King comes in His own glory and in the glory of His angels.

Apol. You have already been unfaithful in your service to Him. So, then, how do you think you will receive wages from Him?

Chr. In what way, O Apollyon, have I been unfaithful to Him?

Apol. You fainted when you first set out, when you were almost choked in the gulf of Despond. You attempted wrong ways to get rid of your burden, instead of waiting until your Prince had taken it off. You sinfully slept and lost your choice things. You were almost persuaded to go back when you saw the lions. And when you talk of your journey, and of what you have heard and seen, you are inwardly desirous of vainglory in all that you say or do.

Chr. All this is true, and you have left out much more. But the King I serve and honor is a merciful King, ready to forgive. But, besides, these infirmities seized upon me in your country, for there I sucked them in. And I have groaned under them, being sorry for them. And I have obtained pardon from my King.

Apol. Then Apollyon broke out into a grievous rage, saying, I am an enemy to this King. I hate His person, His laws and His people. I have come out on purpose to frustrate you.

Chr. Apollyon, be careful what you do. For I am in the King's highway, the way of holiness. Therefore, take heed to yourself.

Apol. Then Apollyon straddled himself over the whole breadth of the way, then said, I am totally unafraid in this matter. Prepare yourself to die. For I swear by my infernal den that you shall go no further. Here I will spill your soul. And with that he threw a flaming dart at Christian's breast. But Christian had a shield in his hand, with which he caught the dart and prevented any hurt from it. Then Christian drew, for he saw it was time to act. And Apollyon very quickly assaulted him, throwing darts as thick as hail. And despite all Christian could do, Apollyon wounded him in his head, his hand and in his foot. This made Christian give ground a little. Then Apollyon followed his work vigorously. But Christian again took courage and resisted as manfully as he could. This hot combat lasted for more than half a day, until Christian was almost worn out. For, of course, Christian was bound to grow weaker and weaker, because of his wounds.

Then Apollyon, seeing his opportunity, began to get up close to Christian and to wrestle with him, giving him a dreadful fall. And then Christian's sword fell out of his hand. Then Apollyon said, I am sure of you now. And with that he almost pressed him to death, so much so that Christian began to despair of life. But, as God would have it, while Apollyon was swinging his last blow to make a full end of this good man, Christian nimbly reached out his hand for his sword and found it. And he said, Do not rejoice against me, O my enemy! For when I fall, I shall arise! (Micah 7:8). And with that he gave him a deadly thrust, causing him to give ground, like one that had received his mortal wound. Seeing this, Christian swung at him again, saying, But in all these things we more than conquer through Him who loved us (Rom. 8:37,39; James 4:7). And then Apollyon spread forth his dragon wings and fled, so that Christian saw him no more.

In this combat, no one can imagine, unless he had seen and heard as I did, what yelling and hideous roaring came forth from Apollyon all the time of the fight. He spoke like a dragon. And, on the other side, what sighs and groans burst from Christian's heart! I never saw him give so much as one pleasant look all that time, until he saw that he had wounded Apollyon with his two-edged sword. Then, indeed, he looked upward and smiled. But it was one of the dreadfullest sights I ever saw.

And when the battle was over, Christian said, I will here give thanks to Him who had delivered me out of the mouth of the lion, to Him who helped me against Apollyon. And so he did, saying,

Great Beelzebub, the captain of this field,
Designed my ruin; therefore to his end
He sent him out harnessed; and he, with rage
That hellish was, did fiercely me engage:
But blessed Michael helped me, and I,
by dint of sword, did quickly make him flee:
Therefore to Him, let me give lasting praise,
And thank and bless His holy name always.

Then a Hand came to him with some of the leaves from the tree of life, which Christian took and applied to the wounds he had received in the battle. And he was healed immediately. He also sat down in that place to eat bread, and to drink of the bottle that was given to him a little before. And, being refreshed, he addressed himself to his journey with his sword drawn in his hand. For he said, I do not know whether some other enemy may be near. But he did not meet any other affront from Apollyon clear through this valley. Now, at the end of this valley was another one, called the Valley of the Shadow of Death. And Christian had to go through it, because the way to the Celestial City lay through the middle of it. Now this valley is a very solitary place. The prophet Jeremiah describes it this way, *"A wilderness, a land of deserts and of pits, a land of drought and of the Shadow of Death; a land that no one* (but a Christian) *passes through, and where no one lived"* (Jer. 2:6). And here Christian was assaulted even worse than in his fight with Apollyon, as you shall see.

Then I saw in my dream that when Christian had arrived at the borders of the Shadow of Death, two men met him there, children of those that brought up an evil report of the good land (Num. 13). Christian spoke to them as follows:

Chr. Where are you going?

Men Back! Back! And we want you to do so too, if you value either your life or your peace.

Chr. Why, what is the matter?

Men Matter? We were going that way that you are going. And we went as far as we dared. And, indeed, we were almost to the point where we could not come back. For if we had gone a little further we would not have been here to tell you of it.

Chr. But what happened?

Men Why, we were almost in the Valley of the Shadow of Death (Ps. 44:19), but fortunately we looked before us and saw the danger before we came to it.

Chr. But what have you seen?

Men Seen? Why we saw the valley itself, it's as dark as pitch. And we saw the hobgoblins there, and satyrs and dragons of the pit. We also heard in that valley a continual howling and yelling, as of a people under unutterable misery, sitting there bound in affliction and irons. And discouraging clouds of confusion hang over the valley. And Death always has his wings spread over it (Job 3:5; 10:22). It is absolutely dreadful, being utterly without order.

Chr. I still do not see by what you have said. But I see that this is the way to the desired haven.

Men Let it be that way. We will not choose it for ours.

So they parted. And Christian went on his way, still with his sword drawn in his hand, fearing that he might be assaulted. Then I saw in my dream that there was a deep ditch on the right hand, as far as the valley reached. It is that ditch into which the blind have led the blind down through the ages, with both of them miserably perishing there. Again, behold, on the left hand there was a very dangerous quagmire, into which even a good man, if he fell into it, could not find any bottom for his foot to stand on. It was into that quagmire that king David once fell. And no doubt he would have been smothered if he had not been plucked out of it by Him that is able (Ps. 64:14).

Here the pathway was also very narrow, so that good Christian was hard put to stay on it. For when he sought in the dark to keep out of the ditch on the one hand, he was ready to tip over into the quagmire on the other. And when he sought to escape the mire, without great carefulness he would be ready to fall into the ditch. So he went on, and I heard him sigh bitterly here. For besides the danger just mentioned, the pathway was also so dark that he oftentimes did not know where his foot would land when he lifted it up and set it forward. And about the middle of the valley, I saw the mouth of hell. And it was very near the wayside. Now, Christian thought, What shall I do? And again and again the flame and the smoke would come out of it, in such abundance and with such sparks and hideous noises, Christian was forced to put up his sword and take up another weapon (for these things did not care for Christian's sword, as did Apollyon). Taking up this new weapon, called All-prayer, he cried out in my hearing, *"O Lord, I beg You, deliver my soul"* (Ps. 116:4; Eph. 6:11).

He went on this way for a great while, and the flames still would reach out towards him. Also he heard doleful voices, and rushings to and fro, so that sometimes he thought he would be torn in pieces or trodden under like mire in the streets. For several miles one after another he heard these dreadful noises and saw these frightful sights. Then coming to a place where he thought he heard a company of fiends coming forward to meet him, he stopped and began to meditate as to what he had best do. Sometimes he had half a thought to go back. Then again he thought that he might be halfway through the valley. He also remembered how he had already vanquished many a danger, and that the danger of going back might be much more than that of going forward. So he resolved to go on. Yet the fiends seemed to come nearer and nearer. But when they had come up close to him, he cried out with a most vehement voice, *"I will walk in the strength of the Lord God"* – so they fell back and did not come any further.

I cannot forget one thing. I noticed that now poor Christian was so confounded that he did not know his own voice. And so I watched him, and just when he had come over across from the mouth of the burning pit, one of the wicked ones got behind him and stepped up softly to him, whispering many grievous blasphemies to him. And Christian truly thought they came from his own mind. And this was harder on Christian than anything he had met with before, to think that he would now blaspheme Him that he loved so much before. Yet if he could have helped it, he would not have done it, but he had not the discretion either to stop his ears or to know from where those blasphemies came.

When Christian had traveled in this disconsolate condition some considerable time, he thought he heard the voice of a man, as going before him, saying, *"Though I walk through the Valley of the Shadow of Death, I will fear no ill, for You are with me"* (Ps. 23:4). Then he was glad, for three good reasons:

1. Because he gathered from this that some who feared God were in this valley as well as himself.

2. For he perceived that God was with them, though in that dark and dismal state. Then, he thought, why not with me, though because of the hindrances in this place I cannot see it? (Job 9:11).

3. Because he hoped to have company with them, if he could overtake them.

So he went on, calling to the one who had gone before him. But that one did not know what to answer, for he also thought himself to be alone. And by and by the day broke. Then Christian said, He has *"turned the shadow of death into the morning"* (Amos 5:8).

Morning having come, he looked back (not that he desired to return, but to see by the light of day what hazards he had gone through in the dark. And he saw more perfectly the ditch that was on the one hand, and the quagmire that was on the other; also how narrow the way was which led between them. And now he also saw the hobgoblins, the satyrs and the dragons of the pit, but all were far away. For after the daybreak, they did not come near. Yet they were revealed to him, as it has been written, *"He reveals deep things out of darkness and brings to light the shadow of death"* (Job 12:22).

Now Christian was much affected with this deliverance from all the dangers of his solitary way. And though he feared them much before, he now saw the dangers more clearly because the light of the day made them conspicuous to him. And the sun was rising about this time, which was another mercy to Christian. For you must note that though the first part of the Valley of the Shadow of Death was dangerous, yet this second part which must yet be traveled was, if possible, far more dangerous. For from the place where he now stood to the end of the valley, the way was all along set so full of snares, traps, gins and nets; and so full of pits, pitfalls, deep holes and treacherous ledges; that if it had now been dark as it was when he came the first part of the way, even if he had possessed a thousand souls, they would have in reason been cast away. But, now the sun was rising. Then he said, *"His candle shines on my head, and by His light I go through darkness"* (Job 29:3).

In this light, then, he came to the end of the valley. Now I saw in my dream that at the end of the valley lay blood, bones, ashes and mangled bodies, even the bodies of pilgrims that had gone this way before. And while I was meditating upon the reason, I saw a little before me a cave, where two giants, Pope and Pagan, lived in days past. And it was by their power and tyranny that these men and their blood, bones and ashes lay there, having been cruelly put to death. But Christian went by this place without danger, at which I somewhat wondered. But I have learned much since then, that Pagan has been dead many a day. And as for the other, though he is still alive, because of his age and because of the many hard brushes that he encountered in his younger days, he has grown so crazy and stiff in his joints that he can now do little more than sit in his cave's mouth, grinning at pilgrims as they go by, and biting his nails because he cannot get at them.

So I saw that Christian went on his way. Yet, at the sight of the old man that sat at the mouth of the cave, he could not tell what to think, especially because he spoke to him, though he could not go after him, saying, You will never mend your ways until more of you are burned. But Christian was silent and set a good face on it. And so he went by without any hurt. Then Christian sang,

> O world of wonders! (I can say no less,)
> That I should be preserved in that distress
> That I have met with here! Oh blessed be
> That hand that from it has delivered me!
> Dangers in darkness, devils, hell, and sin,
> Did circle me while I this vale was in:
> Yea, snares, and pits, and traps, and nets did lie
> My path about, that worthless silly I
> Might have been caught, entangled and cast down;
> But since I live, let Jesus wear the crown.

Now as Christian went on his way, he came to a little ascent, which had been heaped up there on purpose so that the pilgrims might see before them. So Christian went up there. And looking forward he saw Faithful before him on his journey. Then Christian said aloud, Ho, ho! Wait, and I will be your companion. At that Faithful looked behind him. And Christian cried out to him again, Wait! Wait until I come up to you. But Faithful answered, No, I am going for my life, and the avenger of blood is behind me. Christian was somewhat moved at this, and he exerted all his strength in order to quickly catch up with Faithful. And he even overran him, so that the last was first. Then Christian vaingloriously smiled, because he had gotten ahead of his brother. But he was not taking heed to his feet, and he suddenly stumbled and fell. And he could not rise again until Faithful came up to help him.

Then I saw in my dream that they went very lovingly on together, having sweet discourse of all the things that had happened to them in their pilgrimage.

Chr. My honored and beloved brother Faithful, I am glad that I have overtaken you, and that God has so tempered our spirits that we can walk as companions in this very pleasant path.

Faith. I had thought, dear friend, to have had your company all the way from our town, but you started ahead of me. So I was forced to come this much of the way alone.

Chr. How long did you stay in the city of Destruction before you set out after me on your pilgrimage?

Faith. Until I could stay no longer. For there was a great talk soon after you had gone out, it being rumored that our city would shortly be burned down to the ground with fire from heaven.

Chr.What! Did your neighbors say that?

Faith. Even though there was a great talk about it, yet I do not think they firmly believed it. For in the heat of the discourse, I heard some of them speak deridingly of you and of your desperate journey (for so they called your pilgrimage). But I believed and I still do that the end of our city will be with fire and brimstone from above. And therefore I have made my escape.

Chr. Did you hear any talk of neighbor Pliable?

Faith. Yes, Christian, I heard that he followed you until he came to the Slough of Despond, where, as some said, he fell in, but he would not let it be known. But I am sure he was covered with that kind of dirt.

Chr. And what did the neighbors say to him?

Faith. Since he has come back, he has been had greatly in derision, and that among all sorts of people. Some mock and despise him, and hardly any will set him to work. He is now seven times worse than if he had never gone out of the city.

Chr. But why should they be so set against him, since they also despise the way that he left to come back?

Faith. Oh, they say, Hang him! He is a turncoat. He was not true to his profession. I think that God has stirred up even his enemies to hiss at him and to make him a proverb, because he has forsaken the way (Jer. 29:18,19).

Chr. Did you have no talk with him before you came out?

Faith. I met him once on the street, but he leered away on the other side, as one ashamed of what he had done. So I did not speak to him.

Chr. Well, when I first set out, I had hopes for that man. But now I fear he will perish in the overthrow of the city. For it has happened to him according to the true proverb, *"The dog has turned to his vomit again, and the sow has returned to her wallowing in the mire."* (2 Peter 2:22).

Faith. These are my fears of him too. But who can hinder that which will be?

Chr. Well, neighbor Faithful, let us leave him and talk of things that more immediately concern ourselves. Tell me now what you have met with in the way that you came. For I know that you have met with some things, or else it is a wonder.

Faith. I escaped the Slough that I saw you fall into. And I go up to the gate without that danger. Only I met with one whose name was Wanton, and he almost did me mischief.

Chr. It was good that you escaped her net. Joseph was assaulted by her, and he escaped her as you did. But it nearly cost him his life (Gen. 39:11-13). But what did she do to

Faith. You cannot believe, unless you know her, what a flattering tongue she had. She worked hard on me to cause me to turn aside with her, promising me all kinds of things.

Chr. But did she promise you the things that go with a good conscience?

Faith. You know that I meant all kinds of carnal and fleshly things.

Chr. Thank God that you have escaped her, for *"the abhorred of the Lord shall fall into the ditch"* (Prov. 22:14).

Faithh. But I do not know if I completely escaped her or not.

Chr. Why? I do not think that you consented to her desires.

Faith. No, not so as to defile myself, for I remembered an old writing that I had seen which said, *"her steps take hold of hell!"* (Prov. 5:5; Job 31:1). So I shut my eyes because I did not desire to be bewitched with her looks. Then she called me names, and I went on my way.

Chr. Did you not meet with any other assault as you came?

Faith. When I came to foot of the hill called Difficulty, I met with a very aged man who asked me what I was and where I was going. I told him that I am a pilgrim going to the Celestial City. Then the old man said, You look like an honest fellow. Will you be pleased to live with me for the wages which I will give you? Then I asked him his name and where he lived. He said that his name was Adam the First and that he lived in the town of Deceit (Eph. 4:22). I asked him then what was his work and what were the wages that he would give. He told me that his work was many delights and that this wages would be the inheritance he would give me at last. I then asked him what house he kept and what other servants he had. So he told me that his house was maintained with all the dainties of the world, and that his servants were those of his own begetting. Then I asked how many children he had. He said that he had but three daughters, their names being, *"the Lust of the Flesh, the Lust of the Eyes, and the Pride of Life"* (1 John 2:16). And he said that I could marry them if I desired. Then I asked how long he wanted me to live with him. And he told me it would be as long as he lived himself.

Chr. Well, and what agreement did you and the old man reach at last?

Faith. Why, at first I found myself somewhat inclined to go with the man. For I thought he spoke beautifully. But looking in his forehead as I talked with him, I saw there written, *"Put off the old man with his deeds"* (Eph. 4:22).

Chr. And what then?

Faith. Then it came burning hot into my mind that whatever he said or however he flattered, I would be sold for a slave when he got me home to his house. So I asked him to cease talking, for I did not desire to come near the door of his house. Then he reviled me and told me that he would send one after me that would make my way bitter to my soul. So I turned to go away from him. But just as I turned to go away from there, I felt him take hold of my flesh and give me such a deadly twitch that I thought he had pulled part of me after himself. This made me cry out, *"Oh, wretched man!!"* (Rom. 7:24). So I went on my way up the hill. But when I had gotten about halfway up, I looked behind me and saw one coming after me, swift as the wind. So he overtook me just about the place where the bench stands.

Chr. It was there that I sat down to rest myself, but being overcome with sleep I lost my roll out of my bosom there.

Faith. But, good brother, hear me out. As soon as the man overtook me, with but a word and a blow he knocked me down and laid me out for dead. For when I had come to myself in a little while, I asked him why he did this to me. He said it was because of my secret inclination toward Adam the First. And with that he struck me another deadly blow on the chest and beat me down backward. so I lay at his feet as dead, as before. And when I came to myself again, I cried to him for mercy. But he said, I do not know how to show mercy. And with that he knocked me down again. He would no doubt have made an end of me, but one came by and told him to quit.

Chr. Who was that that told him to quit?

Faith. I did not know Him at first. But as He went by, I saw the holes in His hands and in His side. Then I concluded that he was our Lord. So I went up the hill.

Chr. The man that overtook you was Moses. He does not spare any, nor does he know how to show mercy to those that transgress his law.

Faith. I know it very well now. It was not the first time that he has met with me. It was he that came to me when I lived securely at home, and he that told me that he would burn my house over my head if I remained there.

Chr. But did you not see the house that stood there on the top of the hill, on the side of which Moses met you?

Faith. Yes, and the lions too, before I came to it. But as for the lions, I think they were asleep, for it was about noon. And because I had so much of the day before me, I passed by the Porter and came down the hill.

Chr. He told me that he indeed saw you go by. But I wish that you had called at the house, for they would have shown you so many rare things that you would scarcely have forgotten them to the day of your death. But please tell me, did you meet no one in the Valley of Humility?

Faith. Yes, I met with one Discontent, who would willingly have persuaded me to go back with him again. He reasoned that the valley was altogether without honor. And he told me that to go there was the way to disobey all my friends, such as Pride, Arrogancy, Self-conceit, Worldly-glory, and others. And he said he knew that they would be very much offended if I made such a fool of myself as to wade through this valley.

Chr. Well, and how did you answer him?

Faith. I told him that although all these that he named might rightly claim kinship to me (for they were indeed my relations according to the flesh), yet since I had become a pilgrim they had disowned me. And I also have rejected them, I said, and therefore they were no more to me now than if they had not ever been of my lineage. And I told him that as to this valley, he had quite misrepresented the thing, for *"before honor is humility',"* and, *"a haughty spirit is before a fall."* I said, then, that I had rather go through this valley to the honor that was accounted to be so by the wisest, than to choose that which he esteemed most worthy of our affections.

Chr. Did you meet with anything else in that valley?

Faith. Yes, I met with Shame. But of all the men that I met on my pilgrimage, I think that he bears the wrong name. The others may have said nay, after a little argumentation and somewhat else. But this boldfaced Shame would never have done it.

Chr. Why, what did he say to you?

Faith. What! Why, he objected against religion itself. He said it was a pitiful, low, sneaking business for a man to pay attention to religion. He said that a tender conscience was an unmanly thing. And he said that for a man to watch over his words and ways and thus to tie himself up so as not to enjoy that liberty that the brave spirits of the times usually have would make that man the ridicule of the times. He also objected that but few of the mighty, rich or wise ones were ever of my opinion. Nor did anyone, either, before they were persuaded to be fools and to be of a voluntary fondness to risk the loss of all for nobody knows what (John 7:48; 1 Cor. 1:26; 3:18; Phil. 3:7-9). And he objected to the base and low estate and condition of those that were chiefly the pilgrims of the times in which they lived, and to their lack of understanding in all natural sciences. Yea, he held me to it at that pace as he objected to a great many more things than I can here relate. For instance, that it was a shame to sit whining and mourning under a sermon; and it was a shame to come sighing and groaning home; and that it was a shame to ask my neighbor forgiveness for petty faults, or to make restitution wherever I had taken from any. He also said that religion made a man grow strange to the great because of a few vices (which he called by finer names); while making a man to recognize and respect the lowly because of the same religious fraternity. And he said, Is this not a shame?

Chr. And what did you say to him?

Faith. Say? Why, I could not tell what to say at first. Yea, he put me to it so much that my blood came up in my face. This Shame brought it up and almost had beaten me completely off. But at last I began to consider that *"that which is highly esteemed among me is an abomination to God"* (Luke 16:15). And I thought again,that this Shame tells me what men are, but he does not tell me anything about what God is like, or how the word of God is. And I thought also that at the day of doom, we shall not be doomed to death or life according to the boasting spirits of the world, but according to the wisdom and law of the Highest. So, I thought, What God says is best, truly is best, though all the men in the world are against it. Since, then, God prefers His religion; since God prefers a tender conscience; since they who make themselves fools for the kingdom of Heaven are wisest; and since the poor man that loves Christ is richer than the greatest man in the world that hates him; then, Shame, depart from me, for you are an enemy to my salvation. Shall I entertain you against my sovereign Lord? How, then, would I look Him in the face when He comes? If I now am ashamed of His ways and servants, how can I expect the blessing? (Mark 8:38). But this Shame was indeed a bold villain. I could hardly shake him out of my company. Yes, he kept haunting me and continually whispering in my ear some one or other of the infirmities that attend religion. But at last I told him that it was useless for him to make any further attempt in this business, for the very things that he disdained were those in which I saw the most glory. And so at last I got past this persistent one. And when I had shaken him off, then I began to sing,

> The trials that those men do meet withal
> That are obedient to the heavenly call,
> Are manifold, and suited to the flesh,
> And come, and come, and come again afresh:
> That now, or sometime else, we by them may
> Be taken, overcome, and cast away.
> Oh, let the pilgrims, let the pilgrims, then,
> Be vigilant and behave themselves like men!

Chr. I am glad, my brother, that you withstood this villain so bravely. For as you say, overall I think that he has the wrong name. For he is so bold as to follow us in the streets, and to try to put us to shame before all men; that is, to make us ashamed of that which is good. But if he was not so audacious himself, he would never attempt to do as he does. but let us still resist him. For in spite of all his bravadoes, he promotes the fool, and no one else. Solomon said, *"The wise shall inherit glory, but shame shall be the promotion of fools"* (Prov. 3:35).

Faith. I think we must cry to Him for help against Shame, for He would have us be valiant for truth on the earth.

Chr. What you say is true. But did you not meet anyone else in that valley?

Faith. No, I did not. For I had sunshine all the rest of the way through that valley, and also through the Valley of the Shadow of Death.

Chr. It was good for you, for I am sure it fared far otherwise with me. Almost as soon as I entered that valley, I had a dreadful combat with that foul fiend Apollyon, for a long time. Yes, I truly thought that he would kill me, especially when he got me down and crushed me under him, as if he would have crushed me to pieces. For as he threw me, my sword flew out of my hand. Not only that, but he told me that he was sure of me. But I cried to God, and He heard me and delivered me out of all my troubles. Then I entered the Valley of the Shadow of Death, and I had no light for almost half the way through it. I thought I would be killed there, over and over. but at last the day broke and the sun rose, and I went through that which was left with far more ease and quiet.

And I saw in my dream that as they went on, Faithful happened to look over to one side and saw a man whose name is Talkative, walking at a distance beside them. For in this place there was room enough for them all to walk. He was a tall man, and somewhat more handsome at a distance than up close. Faithful addressed himself to this man in this way:

Faith. Friend, where are you going? Are you going to the heavenly country?

Talk. I am going to that same place.

Faith. That is good. Then I hope we shall have your good company.

Talk. I will gladly be your companion.

Faith. Then come on and let us go together, and let us spend our time in discoursing of things that are profitable.

Talk. To talk of things that are good is very acceptable to me, with you or with anyone else. And I am glad that I have met with those that incline to so good a work. For, to tell the truth, there are but few who care to spend their time in this way as they are traveling. Most choose rather to be speaking of things to no profit. And this has been a trouble to me.

Faith. Indeed, that is a thing to be lamented. For what things are so worthy of the use of the tongue and mouth of men on earth as are the things of the God in Heaven?

Talk. I like you wonderfully well, for your sayings are full of conviction. And I will add, what things are so pleasant and so profitable as to talk of the things of God? What things could be so pleasant, that is, if a man has any delight in things that are wonderful. For instance, if a man delights to talk of the history or the mystery of things; or if a man loves to talk of miracles, wonders or signs; where shall he find things recorded so delightful and so sweetly penned as in the Holy Scripture?

Faith. That is true. But it should be our design to be profited by such things in our talk.

Talk. That is what I said. For to talk of such things is most profitable. For by doing so a man may get knowledge of many things; such as, of the vanity of earthly things, and the benefit of things above. So it is in general, but more particularly, by this a man may learn the necessity of the new birth, the insufficiency of our works, the need for Christ's righteousness, etc. Besides, by this a man may learn what it is to repent, to believe, to pray, to suffer, or other things like them. Also, by this a man may learn what are the great promises and consolations of the gospel, to his own comfort. Further, by this a man may learn to refute false opinions, to vindicate the truth, and also to instruct the ignorant.

Faith. All this is true. And I am glad to hear these things from you.

Talk. Alas! It is the lack of this that causes so few to understand the need of faith, and the necessity of a work of grace in their soul, in order for them to have eternal life. But they ignorantly live in the works of the law, by which a man can by no means obtain the kingdom of Heaven.

Faith. But, if you will, heavenly knowledge of these things is the gift of God. No one attains them by human industry, or merely by talking of them.

Talk. I know all that very well. For a man can receive nothing except it be given to him from Heaven. All is of grace, not of works. I could give you a hundred scriptures for the confirmation of this.

Faith. Well, then, what is the one thing that we shall discourse upon at this time?

Talk. Whatever you like. I will talk of things that are heavenly, or things that are earthly, things that are moral, or things that are evangelical; things that are sacred, or things that are profane; things that are past, or things to come; things that are foreign, or things at home; things that are more essential, or things circumstantial; provided all is done to our profit.

Faith. At this, Faith began to wonder. And stepping up to Christian (who had been walking by himself), he said to him, but softly, What a brave company we have here! Surely this man will make a very excellent pilgrim.

Chr. Christian modestly smiled and said, This man, with whom you are so taken, will deceive you with this tongue of his, twenty times to those who do not know him.

Faith. Then do you know him?

Chr. Know him? Yes, I know him better than he knows himself.

Faith. Please, who is he?

Chr. His name is Talkative. He lives in our town. I wonder that you should be a stranger to him. But I know that our town is large.

Faith. Whose son is he? And where does he live?

Chr. He lived in Prating-row.   And he is known to all that are associated with him by the name of Talkative of Prating-row. And in spite of his fine tongue, he is but a sorry fellow.

Faith. Well, he seems to be a very handsome man.

Chr. He is, to those who do not have a thorough acquaintance with him. For he is best when he is away, near home he is ugly enough. Your saying that he is a handsome man brings to my mind what I have observed in the work of the painter whose pictures show best at a distance, but very near are more unpleasing.

Faith. But I am ready to think that you are joking, because you smiled.

Chr. May God forbid that I should jest in this matter (even though I smiled), or that I should accuse any falsely. I will give you a further discovery of him. This man is for any company and for any talk. As he now talks with you, so he will talk when he is on the ale-bench. And the more drink he has in his crown, the more of these things he has in his mouth. Religion has no place in his heart, or house or conversation. All he has lies in his tongue, and his religion is to make a noise with it.

Faith. Do you say so? Then I am greatly deceived in this man.

Chr. Deceived? You may be sure of it. Remember the proverb, *"They say, and do not,"* but the kingdom of God is not in word, but in power (Matt. 23:3; 1 Cor. 4:20). He talks of prayer, of repentance, of faith and of the new birth. but he knows only how to talk of them. I have been in his family and have observed him both at home and away. And I know what I say of him is the truth. His house is as empty of religion as the white of an egg is empty of taste. There is no prayer nor sign of repentance there. Yea, the animal, in his kind, serves God far better than he. He is the very stain, reproach and shame of religion to all that know him (Rom. 2:23,24). It can hardly have a good word in all that end of the town where he lives, through him. For the common people that know him say this, 'he is a saint away, and a devil at home.' His poor family finds it so. He is such a surly one, such a railer, such an unreasonable one ·with his servants, that they neither know how to act or how to speak toward him. Men that have any dealings with him say that it is better to deal with a Turk than with him, for they shall have fairer dealings with them. For if it is possible, this Talkative will go beyond them to defraud, deceive and overreach them. Besides, he brings up his sons to follow his steps. And if he finds in any of them a foolish timorousness (for this is what he calls the first appearance of a tender conscience), he calls them fools and blockheads. And then he will not employ them in much, or speak to their commendation before others. For my part, I am of the opinion that he has by his wicked life caused many to stumble and fall. And if God does not prevent it, he will be the ruin of many more.

Faith. Well, my brother, I am bound to believe you, not only because you say you know him, but because you also, like a Christian, make your reports of men. For I cannot think that you speak these things out of ill-will, but because it is even so as you say.

Chr. If I had not known him any more than you do, I perhaps might have thought of him as you did at first. Yes, if I had received this report from those who are enemies to religion, I would have thought it to be a slander — which often happens when bad men's mouths speak on good men's names and professions. But all these things, yea, and a great many more as bad, I can prove him guilty of by my own knowledge. Besides, good men are ashamed of him. They can neither call him brother nor friend. The very naming of him among them makes them blush, if they know him.

Faith. Well, I see that saying and doing are two things, and hereafter I shall better observe this distinction.

Chr. They are indeed two things, and are as diverse as are the soul and the body. So as the body without the soul is only a dead carcass, so mere talk, if it is alone, is also a dead carcass. The soul of religion is the practical part, *"Pure and undefiled religion before God and the Father is this, to visit the fatherless and widows in their affliction, and to keep oneself unspotted from the world"* (James 1:27). Talkative is not aware of this. He thinks that hearing and saying will make a good Christian. And so he deceives his own soul. Hearing is but as the sowing of the seed; talking is not sufficient to prove that fruit is truly in the heart and life. And let us assure ourselves that at the day of doom men shall be judged according to their fruit (Matt. 13:23). It will not be said then, Did you believe? But it will be asked, Were you doers? Or were you only talkers? And they shall be judged accordingly. The end of the world is compared to our harvest. And, as you know, men at harvest-time regard nothing but fruit. Not that anything can be accepted that is not of faith, but I speak this to show you how insignificant the profession of Talkative will be at that day.

Faith. This brings to my mind that of Moses, by which he describes the animal that is clean (Lev. 11, Deut. 14). He is one that parts the hoof and chews the cud, but not only the one that parts the hoof, or the one that only chews the cud. The hare chews the cud, but yet he is unclean because he does not part the hoof. And truly this resembles Talkative. He chews the cud, he seeks knowledge; he chews on the word, but he does not divide the hoof. He does not separate himself from the way of sinners. But, like the hare, he keeps the foot of a dog or a bear, and therefore he is unclean.

Chr. For all I know, you have spoken the true gospel sense of those texts. And I will add another thing. Paul calls some men (yea, and they were great talkers, too), sounding brass and tinkling cymbals. That is, as he expounds in another place, things without life, giving sound (1 Cor. 13:1-3; 14:7).

The things without life are those without the true faith and grace of the gospel. And, consequently, they are things that shall never be placed in the kingdom of Heaven among those that are the children of life, even though their sound, by their talk, is as if it were the tongue or voice of an angel.

Faith. Well, I was not so fond of his company at first, but I am sick of it now. What shall we do to be rid of him?

Chr. Take my advice and do as I tell you, then you will find that he will soon be sick of your company too, unless God shall touch his heart and turn it.

Faith. What would you have me do?

Chr. Why, go to him and enter into some serious discourse about the power of religion. And when he has approved of it, and he surely will, then ask him plainly if this thing is set up in his heart, his house and his life.

Then Faithful stepped forward again and said to Talkative, Come. How is it going now?

Talk. It is well, thank you. I thought we would have a great deal of talk by now.

Faith. Well, if you so desire, we will now fall to it. And since you left it to me to state the question, let it be this: How does the saving grace of God reveal itself when it is in the heart of man?

Talk. Then I see that our talk must be about the power of things. Well, it is a very good question, and I shall be willing to answer you. And take my answer in brief to be this: First, where the grace of God is in the heart, it causes a great outcry against sin there. Secondly, —

Faith. No, wait! Let us consider each one at a time. I think you should rather say, It shows itself by inclining the soul to hate its sin.

Talk. Why, what difference is there between crying out against sin and the abhorring of sin?

Faith. Oh, a great deal! A man may cry out against sin out of policy. But he cannot hate it except by virtue of a godly antipathy against it. I have heard many cry out against sin in the pulpit, who yet can live with it well enough in the heart, house and life. Joseph's mistress cried out with a loud voice, as if she had been very holy. But she would willingly in spite of that have committed uncleanness with Joseph (Gen. 39:11-15). Some cry out against sin in the same way a mother cries out against her child in her lap, when she calls it slut and naughty girl, and then falls to hugging and kissing it.

Talk. I see that you lie in wait to catch me.

Faith. No, not I. I am only for setting things right. But what is the second thing by which you would prove a discovery of a work of grace in the heart?

Talk. Great knowledge of gospel mysteries.

Faith. This sign should have been first. But, first or last, it is also false. For knowledge, great knowledge, may be obtained in the mysteries of the gospel and yet not be a work of grace in the soul (1 Cor. 13:2). Yea, if a man has all knowledge, he may yet be nothing; and so, consequently, he may be no child of God. When Christ said, *"Do you know all these things?"* and the disciples had answered, Yes, then He added, *"You are blessed if you do them."* He does not lay the blessing in the knowing of them, but in the doing of them. For there is a knowledge that is not attended with doing, *"He that knows his master's will and yet does it not."* A man may know like an angel and yet not be a Christian. Therefore your sign of it is not true. Indeed, to know is a thing that pleases talkers and boasters. But to do is that which pleases God. Not that the heart can be good without knowledge, for without that the heart is nothing. There is, then, knowledge and knowledge. There is a knowledge that rests in the bare speculation of things, and there is a knowledge that is accompanied with the grace of faith and love, and this sets a man to doing the will of God from the heart. The first kind of knowledge will serve the talker, but the true Christian is not content without the other kind: *"Give me understanding and I will keep Your law; yea, I will observe it with my whole heart"* (Ps. 119:34).

Talk. You are again lying in wait to catch me. This is not for edification.

Faith. Well, if you please, propound another sign how this work of grace discovers itself where it is.

Talk. Not I, for I see that we shall not agree.

Faith. Well, if you will not, will you allow me to do it?

Talk. You may use your liberty.

Faith. A work of grace in the soul reveals itself, either to him that has it, or to those who stand by. It is revealed to him that has it in this way: It gives him conviction of sin, especially of the defilement of his nature, and the sin of unbelief, for which he is sure to be condemned if he does not find mercy at God's hand, by faith in Jesus Christ (Mark 16:16; John 16:8,9; Rom. 7:24). This sight and sense of things works in him sorrow and shame for sin. And he finds revealed in him the Savior of the world, and the absolute necessity of closing with Him for life; which in turn reveals hungerings and thirstings after Him, and to these hungerings, etc, the promise is made (Ps. 38:18; Jer. 31:19; Matt. 5:6; Acts 4:12; Gal. 2:15,16; Rev. 21:6). Now, according to the strength or weakness of his faith in his Savior, so is his joy and peace, so is his love to holiness, so are his desires to know Him more, and also to serve Him in this world. But though it reveals itself to him in this way, yet it is but seldom that he is able to conclude that this is a work of grace — because his corruptions now, and his abused reason, make his mind to misjudge in this matter. Therefore, a very sound judgment is required in him that has this work before he can with steadiness conclude that this is a work of grace.

It is revealed to others in this way: First, by an experimental confession of his faith in Christ; secondly, by a life that answers to that confession, that is, a life of holiness (heart-holiness, and family holiness, if he has a family, and by holiness in behavior in the world), which teaches him generally to hate his sin, and himself for it, in secret; and he will suppress it in his family, and will promote holiness in the world (and that not by talk only, as a hypocrite or a talkative person may do, but by a practical subjection in faith and love to the power of the word). And now, sir, as to this brief description of the work of grace, and how it is revealed, if you have anything to object, then object (Ps. 50:23; Ezek. 20:43; Matt. 5:8; John 14:15; Rom. 10:9,10; Phil. 3:17-20). If not, then give me permission to propound to you a second question.

Talk. No, my part is not to object now, but to hear. Therefore, let me hear your second question.

Faith. It is this: Do you experience this first part of the description of it? And does your life and behavior testify the same? Or does your religion stand in word or tongue, and not in deed and in truth? Please, if you incline to answer me in this, say no more than that you know the God above will say Amen to, and also nothing but what your conscience can justify you in, *"for not he that commends himself is approved, but he whom the Lord commends."* Besides, to say that I am thus and thus, when my behavior and all my neighbors tell me I lie, is great wickedness.

Talk. Talkative then began to blush, but he recovered himself and replied, You come now to experience, to conscience, and to God. And you appeal to Him for justification of what is spoken. I did not expect this kind of discourse, nor am I disposed to give an answer to such questions, because I do not count myself bound to do it, unless you take upon yourself to be a catechizer. And though you should do so, I still may refuse to make you my judge. But, I beg you, will you tell me why you ask me such questions?

Faith. Because I saw you forward to talk, and because I did not know that you had anything else but notion. Besides, to tell you all the truth, I have heard of you, that you are a man whose religion lies in talk, and that your behavior gives this mouth-profession of yours the lie. They say you are a spot among Christians, and that religion fares the worse for your ungodly behavior; that some have already stumbled at your wicked ways, and that more are in danger of being destroyed by it. They say that your religion will stand together with an ale-house, covetousness, uncleanness, swearing, lying and the keeping of worthless company. The proverb is true of you which said of a whore that *"she is a shame to all women,"* so you are a shame to all professors.

Talk. Since you are so ready to take up reports and to judge so rashly, I cannot but conclude that you are some peevish or gloomy man who is not fit for discourse with me. Therefore, adieu.

Chr. Then Christian came up and said to his brother, I told you how it would be. Your words and his lusts could not agree. He had rather leave your company than to reform his life. But as I said, he is gone. Let him go, the loss is but his own. He has saved us the trouble of going away from him. For if he continues as he is (as I suppose he will), he would have been but a blot in our company. Besides, the apostle says that we should withdraw from such people (2 Thess. 3:6).

Faith. But I am glad that we had this little discussion with him. It may be that he will think of it again. However, I have been plain with him, therefore I am clear of his blood if he perishes.

Chr. You did well to talk so plainly to him as you did. There is but a little of this faithful dealing with men in these days, and that makes religion to stink so in the nostrils of many. For they are these talkative fools, whose religion is only in word, and they are debauched and vain in their lives. The fact that they are being so much admitted into the fellowship of the godly puzzles the world, blemishes Christianity, and grieves those who are sincere. I wish that all men would deal with such people as you have. Then they would either be made more conformable to religion, or else the company of the saints would become too hot for them.

Then Faithful said,

> How Talkative at first lifts up his plumes!
> How bravely he does speak! How he presumes
> To drive down all before him! But so soon
> As Faithful talks of heartwork, like the moon
> That's past the full, into the wane he goes;
> And so will all but he that heartwork knows.

So they went on talking of what they had seen by the way. And it made the way easy, otherwise, no doubt, it would have been tedious to them. For now they were going through a wilderness. And when they were almost out of the wilderness, Faithful happened to look back. And he saw one coming after them, and he knew him. Faithful said to his brother, Oh! Who is that coming yonder? Then Christian looked and said, It is my good friend Evangelist. And Faithful said, Yes, and my good friend too, for it was he that set me in the way to the Gate. Now Evangelist had come up to them and greeted them:

Evan. Peace be with you, dearly beloved. And peace be to your helpers.

Chr. Welcome, welcome, my good Evangelist. The sight of your face brings to my memory you kindness in the past, and your untiring efforts for my eternal good.

Faith. And a thousand times welcome, for your company, O sweet Evangelist, is most desirable to us poor pilgrims.

Evan. How has it fared with you, my friends, since the time of our last parting? What have you met with and how have you behaved yourselves?

Then Christian and Faithful told him of all the things that had happened to them in the way, and how, and with what difficulty they had arrived here at this place.

Evan. I am very glad that you have met with trials, but that you have been victors; and that you have in spite of many weaknesses continued in the way to this very day. I say that I am very glad,both for my own sake and for yours. I have sowed and you have reaped. And the day is coming when *"both he that sowed and they that reaped shall rejoice together"* that is, if you hold out, *"for in due time you shall reap if you do not faint"* (John 4:36; Gal. 6:9). The crown is before you, and it is an incorruptible one, therefore run so that you may obtain it. There are some that set out after this crown, and after they have gone far for it, another comes in and takes it from them, *"therefore, hold fast that which you have and let no one take your crown"* (1 Cor. 9:24-27; Rev. 3:11). You are not yet out of the devil's gunshot range, *"you have not resisted to blood, striving against sin."* Let the kingdom be always before you, and believe steadfastly concerning the things that are invisible. Let nothing that is on this side the other world get within you. And, above all, look well to your own hearts and to the lusts of it, for they are *"deceitful above all things, and desperately wicked"* (Jer. 17:9). Set your faces like a flint, for you have all power in Heaven and in earth on your side.

Chr. Then Christian thanked him for his exhortation, but he told him that they would like for him to speak further to them for their help the rest of the way. And this because they knew that he was a prophet, and that he could tell them of things that might happen to them, and things that would help them resist and overcome them. Faithful also consented to this request. So Evangelist began as follows:

Evan. My sons,you have heard in the words of the truth of the gospel, *"that you must through many tribulations enter into the kingdom of Heaven"* (Acts 14:22). And again, know that *"in every city bonds and afflictions await you,"* and therefore you cannot expect that you should go very long on your pilgrimage without them, in some sort or other. You have found something of the truth of these testimonies on you already, and more will immediately follow. For now, as you see, you are almost out of this wilderness. Therefore you will soon come into a town that you will see before you. And in that town you will be relentlessly surrounded with enemies, who will strain hard to kill you. And you may be sure that one or both of you must seal the testimony which you hold with blood, but *"be faithful to death, and the King will give you a crown of life"* (Rev. 2:10). He that shall die there, although his death will be unnatural, and his pain great, he will yet have the better of his fellow, not only because he will arrive at the Celestial City soonest, but because he will escape many miseries that the other will experience in the rest of his journey. But when you have come to the town, and when that which I have here related has been fulfilled, then remember your friend, and behave yourselves like men. And commit the keeping of your souls to your God in well-doing, as to a faithful Creator (1 Pet. 4:19).

Then I saw in my dream that when they had left the wilderness, they soon saw a town before them. And the name of that town is Vanity. And at the town there is a fair kept, called Vanity Fair. It is kept there all year long, and it bears the name of Vanity Fair because the town where it is kept is lighter than vanity; and, also, because all that is sold there, or that comes there, is vanity. This is as the saying of the wise, 'All that comes is vanity' (Eccles. 1:2,14; 2:11,17; 11:8; Isa. 40:17). This fair is not a newly-erected business, but a thing of ancient standing. I will tell you its history: Almost five thousand years ago, there were pilgrims walking to the Celestial City, as are these honest persons. And Beelzebub, Apollyon and Legion, with their companions, seeing by the path that the pilgrims traveled that their way to the city lay through this town of Vanity, they contrived to set up a fair here. In this fair would be all sorts of vanity. And it would last all the year long. Therefore, at this fair all merchandise is sold, such as houses, lands, trades, places, honors, preferments, titles, countries, kingdoms, lusts, pleasures. And all sorts of delights were sold here, such as whores, brothel-keepers, wives, husbands, children, masters, slaves, lives, blood, bodies, souls, silver, gold, pearls, precious stones, etc. And also at this fair, there is at all times to be seen jugglings, cheats, games, plays, fools, apes, knaves and rogues of every kind. Here also may be seen, and that for nothing, thefts, murders, adulteries, false-swearers, all of a blood-red color. And as in other fairs of less importance, there are several rows and streets under their proper names where such wares are sold. So here, in the same way, you have the proper places, rows, streets (viz. countries and kingdoms), where the wares of this fair are most quickly found. Here is the Britain-row, the French-row, the Indian-row, the Spanish-row, the German-row, etc., where several sorts of vanities are to be sold. But, as in other fairs, some one commodity is the chief of all the fair, so in this fair the wares of Rome and her merchandise is greatly promoted. Only our English nation, with some others, have taken a dislike to them.

Now as I said, the way to the Celestial City lies just through this town where this lusty fair is kept. And he that desires to go the the City must go through this town, or else go out of the world. The King of kings Himself, when here, went through this town to His own country. And it was on a fair-day, too. Yes, and as I remember, it was Beelzebub, the chief lord of this fair, that invited Him to buy of his vanities. Yea, he would have made Him lord of the fair if He would have done him reverence as He went through the town. And, because He was such a person of honor, Beelzebub had Him from street to street, showing Him all the kingdoms of the world in a little time, that he might, if possible, allure that blessed One to cheapen and buy some of his vanities. but He had no mind to the merchandise, and therefore He left the town without laying out so much as one farthing on these vanities (Matt. 4:8,9). This fair, then, is an ancient thing, of long standing, and a very great fair.

Now these pilgrims had to go through this fair. Well, so they did. But, behold, even as they entered into the fair, all the people in the fair were moved, and the town itself, as it were, gathered in a hubbub about them. And this was for several reasons: First, the pilgrims were clothed with clothing that was different from the clothing of any that traded in that fair. The people, therefore, gathered and stared at them. Some said they were fools (1 Cor. 4:9,19); some said they were crazy; and some said they were strange men. Secondly, they wondered not only at their apparel but at their speech. For few could understand what they said. They naturally spoke the language of Canaan, but they that kept the fair were the men of this world. So they seemed to be barbarians each to the other, from one end of the fair to the other. Thirdly, the merchandisers were amused to find that these pilgrims cared little for all their wares. They did not so much as care to look at them. And if they called on them to buy, they would put their fingers in their ears and cry, *"Turn away my eyes from beholding vanity"* (Ps. 119:37), then look upwards, signifying that their trade and traffic was in Heaven.

One happened, mockingly looking at the way the men acted, to say to them, What do you desire to buy? But they looked gravely at him and said, We will buy the truth (Prov. 23:23). At that, there was an occasion taken to despise the men the more. Some mocked, some taunted, some spoke reproachfully, and some called on others to strike them. At last things came to such a tumult and great stir in the fair that all order was confounded. And word was brought to the great one of the fair, who quickly came down. And he deputized some of his most trusted friends to take these men into examination, about whom the fair was almost overturned. So the men were brought to examination. And they that sat to judge them asked them where they came from, where they were going, and what they were doing in such unusual garb. The men told them that they were pilgrims and strangers in the world, and that they were going to their own country, which was the heavenly Jerusalem (Heb. 11:13-16); and that they had given no occasion to the men of the town, nor even to the merchandisers, to abuse them in this way. And they said that there was no reason for them to be hindered from their journey, except that when one asked them what they wanted to buy, they had said that they wanted to buy the truth. But they that were appointed to examine them did not believe them to be anything more than madmen, or else such as came to put all things into a confusion in the fair. So they took them and beat them, and they smeared them with dirt and then put them into the cage, so that they might be made a spectacle to all the men of the fair. They therefore lay there for some time, being made the objects of any man's sport, or malice, or revenge. And the great one of the fair was laughing at all that happened to them. But, the men being patient, not rendering railing for railing, but rather blessing and giving good words for bad, and kindness for injuries done, some men in the fair that were more observing and less prejudiced than the rest began to hold back and to blame the baser sort for their continual abuses of the men. These, then, in an angry manner, let fly at them again, thinking that these were as bad as the men in the cage. And they told them they seemed to be confederates, that they should be made partakers of their misfortunes. The others replied that for all they could see the men were quiet and sober, intending nobody any harm; and that there were many that traded in their fair that were more worthy to be put into the cage and pillory than were the men they were abusing. So, after many words had passed on both sides (the men behaving themselves all the while very wisely and soberly before them), they fell to some blows among themselves and did harm to one another. Then the two men were brought before their examiners again. And they were charged as being guilty of the late hubbub that had been in the fair. So they beat them pitifully, hanging irons on them and leading them in chains up and down the fair, as an example and terror to others, lest any should speak in their behalf or join themselves to them.

But Christian and Faithful behaved themselves still more wisely, receiving the ignominy and shame that was cast on them with so much meekness and patience that it won to their side several of the men in the fair (though but few in comparison to the rest). This put the other party into a still greater rage, so much so that they concluded that these two men must die. Therefore they threatened that neither cage nor irons would serve their turn, but that they should die for the abuse they had done, and for deluding the men of the fair.

Then they were ordered into the cage again, until further orders should be given. So they put them in and made their feet fast in the stocks. And here, also, the two men called to mind what they had heard from their faithful friend Evangelist. And they were the more confirmed in their way and sufferings by what he told them would happen to them. They also now comforted each other, that whoever it was that was to suffer, he should have the best of it. So each man secretly wished that he might have that preferment. But they committed themselves to the all-wise disposal of Him that rules all things, and they contentedly awaited in the condition in which they were, until they should be otherwise disposed of. Then a convenient time being appointed, they brought them forth to their trial, in order to condemn them. When the time had come, they were brought before their enemies and arraigned. The judge's name was Lord Hategood. Their indictment was one and the same in substance, though somewhat varying in form. And these were the contents: 'that they were enemies to, disturbers of, the trade; that they had made commotions and divisions in the town and had won a party to their own most dangerous opinions, in contempt of the law of their prince.'

Then Faithful began to answer that he had only set himself against that which had set itself against Him that is higher than the highest. And he said, As for a disturbance, I do not make any, being myself a man of peace. The parties that were won to us were won by beholding our truth and innocence, and they are only turned from the worse to the better. And as to the king you speak of, since he is Beelzebub, the enemy of our Lord, I defy him and all his angels.

Then a proclamation was made that they that had anything to say for their lord the king against the prisoner at the bar should appear at once and give in their evidence. So there came in three witnesses, Envy, Superstition, and Pickthank. They were then asked if they knew the prisoner at the bar, and what they had to say for their lord the king against him.

Then Envy came forth and said this: My lord, I have known this man a long time and will attest on my oath before this honorable bench that he is....

Judge Wait! Give him his oath.

So they swore him in. Then he said, My lord, in spite of his plausible name, this man is one of the vilest men in our country. He neither regards prince nor people, law nor custom, but does all that he can to possess all men with certain of his disloyal notions, which he in general calls principles of faith and holiness. And, in particular, I heard him once say that Christianity and the customs of our town were diametrically opposite and could not be reconciled. By which saying, my lord, he at once not only condemns all our laudable doings, but us in the doing of them.

Judge **Have you any more to say?**

Envy My lord, I could say much more, only I do not want to be tedious to the court. Yet, if need be, when the other gentlemen have given in their evidence, in order that nothing shall be lacking that will dispatch him, I will enlarge my testimony against him. So he was told to stand by.

Then they called Superstition and told him to look at the prisoner. They also asked him what he could say for their lord the king against him. Then they swore him in.

Super. My lord, I have no great acquaintance with this man, nor do I desire to have further knowledge of him. However, I know this, that he is a very pestilent fellow, having some discourse with him in this town the other day. For talking with him then, I heard him say that our religion was nothing, and one by which a man could by no means please God. Which saying of his, my lord, your lordship very well knows what necessarily will follow from it, that we still worship in vain, that we are yet in our sins, and that we finally will be condemned. And this is what I have to say.

Then Pickthank was sworn in. And they told him to say what he knew in behalf of their lord the king, against the prisoner of the bar.

Pick. My lord, and all you gentlemen, I have known this fellow for a long time. And I have heard him speak things that ought not to be spoken. For he has railed at our noble prince Beelzebub, and he has spoken contemptibly of his honorable friends, the Lord Old Man, the Lord Carnal Delight, the Lord Luxurious, the Lord Desire of Vainglory, my old Lord Lechery, Sir Having Greedy, and all the rest of our nobility. And he has also said that if all men were of his mind, if possible, there is not one of these noblemen that could remain in this town. Besides, he has not been afraid to rail upon you, my lord, who are now appointed to be his judge, calling you an ungodly villain, with many other vilifying terms like that, with which he has bespattered most of the ranking people of our town.

When Pickthank had told his tale, the judge directed his speech to the prisoner at the bar, saying, You renegade heretic and traitor, have you heard what these honest gentlemen have witnessed against you?

Faith. May I speak a few words in my own defense?

Judge Sirrah, you deserve to live no longer, but to be slain immediately at this place. Yet, that all men may see our gentleness toward you, let us hear what you have to say, vile renegade.

Faith. First, then, I say in answer to what Mr. Envy has spoken, that I never said anything but this, that what rule, or laws, or custom, or people were flat against the word of God are diametrically opposite to Christianity. If I have said anything wrong in this, convince me of my error and I am ready here to make my recantation before you.

Secondly, as to Mr. Superstition and his charge against me, I said only this, that in the worship of God there is required a divine faith. But there can be no divine faith without a divine revelation of the will of God. Therefore, whatever is thrust into the worship of God that is not agreeable to divine revelation cannot be done but by a human faith, which faith will not be profitable to eternal life.

Lastly, as to what Mr. Pickthank has said, I will avoid terms he used, such as railing, etc. But I say this, that the prince of this town and all his attendants, mere rabble, are more fit for being in hell than in this town and country. And so may the Lord have mercy on me!

Then the judge called the jury (who had stood by to hear and observe all this time), Gentlemen of the jury, you see this man about whom so great an uproar has been made in this town. You have also heard what these worthy gentlemen have witnessed against him. Also you have heard his reply and confession. It now lies in your hands to hang him, or to save his life. But yet I think it in order to instruct you in the law.

There was a law made in the days of Pharaoh the great, servant to our prince, that lest those of a contrary religion should multiply and grow too strong for him, their males should be thrown into the river. There was also an act made in the days of Nebuchadnezzar the great, another of his servants, that whoever would not fall down and worship his golden image should be thrown into a firery furnace. There was also an act made in the days of Darius, that whoever for some time called on any god but him should be cast into the lions' den (Exod. 1; Dan. 3; Dan. 6). Now the substance of these laws has been broken by this rebel, not only in thought (which is not to be allowed), but also in word and in deed (which therefore must be intolerable). Pharaoh's law was made on a supposition, to prevent mischief, no crime being yet apparent. But here a crime is apparent. As for the second and the third, you see that he disputes against our religion. And for the treason that he has already confessed, he deserves to die the death.

Then the jury went out, their names being Mr. Blindman, Mr. No-good, Mr. Malice, Mr. Love-lust, Mr. Live-loose, Mr. Heady, Mr. High-mind, Mr. Enmity, Mr. Liar, Mr. Cruelty, Mr. Hate-light and Mr. Implacable. Each one gave his private verdict against him among themselves, and afterwards they unanimously concluded to bring Faithful guilty before the judge. And first among themselves, Mr. Blindman, the foreman, said, I see clearly that this man is a heretic. Then Mr. No-good said, Away with this fellow from the earth! Yes, said Mr. Malice, for I hate his very looks. Then Mr. Love-lust said, I could never endure him. Nor I, said Mr. Live-loose, for he would always be condemning my way. Hang him! Hang him, said Mr. Heady. Mr. High-mind said, A sorry scrub! And Mr. Enmity said, My heart rises against him. He is a rogue, said Mr. Liar. Hanging is too good for him, said Mr. Cruelty. Let us dispatch him out of the way, said Mr. Hate-light. Then Mr. Implacable said, If I could have all the world given to me, I could not be reconciled to him. Therefore, let us quickly bring him in guilty of death. And so they did. Therefore he was presently condemned to be taken from the place where he was to the place from which he had come. And there he was to be put to the most cruel death that could be invented.

They therefore brought him out, to do with him according to their law. And first they whipped him, then they buffeted him, then they cut his flesh with knives. After that they stoned him with stones, then they pricked him with their swords. And last of all they burned him to ashes at the stake. So Faithful came to his end.

And I looked and saw there behind the multitude a chariot and a pair of horses waiting for Faithful. And as soon as his adversaries had dispatched him, he was taken up into it and immediately was carried up through the clouds, with the trumpet sounding as they went the nearest way to the Celestial Gate.

But as for Christian, he had some respite, being ordered back to prison, where he remained for a time. But He that overrules all things, having the power of their rage in His own hand, so worked it out that Christian escaped them for that time, going his way. And as he went, he sang, saying,

> Well, Faithful, you have faithfully professed
> Unto your Lord, with whom you shall be blest;
> When faithless ones, with all their vain delights,
> Are crying out under their hellish plights.
> Sing, Faithful, sing, and let your name survive!
> For though they killed you, you are yet alive.

Now I saw in my dream that Christian did not go forth alone, for there was one whose name was Hopeful (being so made by watching Christian and Faithful in their words and behavior in their sufferings at the fair), who joined himself to him and entered into a brotherly covenant with him, telling him that he would be his companion. So one died to bear witness to the truth, and another rose out of his ashes to be a companion with Christian in his pilgrimage. And Hopeful also told this to Christian, that there were many more of the men in the Fair that would take their time and follow after.

So I saw that soon after they had gotten out of the Fair, they overtook one that was going before them, whose name was By-ends. So they said to him, Where are you from, sir? And how far are you going this way? He told them that he had come from the town of Fairspeech, and that he was going to the Celestial City. But he did not tell them his name.

Chr. From Fairspeech? Is there any good that lives there? (Prov. 26:25).

By. Yes, I hope.

Chr. Please, sir, what may I call you?

By. I am a stranger to you, and you to me. If you are going this way, I shall be glad of your company. If not, I must be content.

Chr. This town of Fairspeech, I have heard of it. And, as I remember, they say it is a wealthy place.

By. Yes, I will assure you that it is. And I have very many rich relatives there.

Chr. Please tell me who are your relatives there, if a man may be so bold?

By. Almost the whole town. In particular, My Lord Turn-about, my Lord Timeserver, my Lord Fairspeech, from whose ancestors that town first took its name; also Mr. Smoothman, Mr. Facing-both-ways and Mr. Anything. And the parson of our parish, Mr. Two-tongues, was my mother's own brother by her father's side. And, to tell you the truth, I have become a gentlemen of good quality, yet my great-grandfather was only a waterman, looking one way and rowing another. And I got most of my estate by the same occupation.

Chr. Are you a married man?

By. Yes, and my wife is a very virtuous woman, the daughter of a virtuous woman. She was my Lady Feigning's daughter, so she came of a very honorable family. And she has arrived to such a pitch of breeding that she knows how to carry it to all, even to prince and peasant. It is true, we somewhat differ in religion from those of the strictest sort, yet but in two small points. First, we never strive against wind and tide. Secondly, we are always most zealous when Religion goes in his silver slippers. We love much to walk with him in the street, if the sun shines and the people applaude him.

Then Christian stepped a little aside to speak to his fellow Hopeful, saying, It runs in my mind that this is one By-ends, of Fairspeech. And if it is he, we have as true a knave as any living in these parts. Then Hopeful said, Ask him. I think he should not be ashamed of his name. So Christian came up with him again and said, Sir, you talk as if you knew something more than all the world knows. And, if I do not take my mark amiss, I believe I have half a guess who you are. Is your name not Mr. By-ends, of Fairspeech?

By. This is not my name, but indeed it is a nickname that is given to me by some that cannot stand me. And I must be content to bear it as a reproach, as other good men have borne theirs before me.

Chr. But have you never given any occasion to men to call you by this name?

By. Never, never! The worst that I ever did to give them an occasion to give me this name was that I always had the luck to jump in my judgment with the present way of the times, whatever it was. And it was my fortune to get it that way. But if things are thus cast upon me, let me count them a blessing. But let not the malicious load me with reproach because of it.

Chr. I thought that you were indeed the man that I heard of. And to tell you what I think, I fear that this name belongs to you more properly than you are willing that we should think.

By. Well, if you will imagine it, I cannot help it. You shall find me a fair company-keeper, if you will still admit me as your associate.

Chr. If you will go with us, you must go against wind and tide, which I see is against your opinion. You must also own Religion in his rags, as well as when he is in his silver slippers. And you must stand by him, too, when bound in irons, as well as when he walks the streets with applause.

By. You must not impose, nor lord it over my faith. Leave me to my liberty, and let me go with you.

Chr. Not a step further, unless you will do all that we propose to do.

By. I shall never desert my old principles, since they are harmless and profitable. If I may not go with you, I must do as I did before you overtook me, even go by myself, until some overtake me that will be glad of my company.

Now I saw in my dream that Christian and Hopeful left him, keeping their distance before him. But one of them looked back and saw three men following Mr. By-ends. And, behold, as they came up with him, they made a very low bow to him. And they also gave him a compliment. The name of the men were, Mr. Hold-the-world, Mr. Money-love, and Mr. Save-all, men that Mr. By-ends had formerly been acquainted with. For in their minority, they had been schoolmates together, being taught by one Mr. Gripe-man, a schoolmaster in Love-gain, which is a market-town in the county of Coveting, in the north. This schoolmaster taught them the art of getting, either by violence, fraud, flattery, lying, or putting on a guise of religion. And these four gentlemen had attained much of the art of their master, so that they could each of them have kept such a school themselves.

Well, when they had thus saluted each other, Mr. Money-love said to Mr. By-ends, Who are those on the road before us? For Christian and Hopeful were still within view.

By. They are a couple of far countrymen, who in their way are going on pilgrimage.

Money. Alas! Why did they not stay so that we might have had their good company? For they and we and you, sir, I hope, are all going on pilgrimage.

By. We are so, indeed. But the men before us are so rigid, and they love their own notions so much, and they also so lightly esteem the opinion of others, that however godly a man may be, yet if he does not jump with them in all things, they thrust him quite out of their company.

Save. That is bad. But we read of some that are righteous overmuch. And the rigidness of such men prevails with them to judge and condemn all but themselves. But please tell us on how many points did you differ?

By. In their headstrong manner, they conclude that it is their duty to rush on their journey in all kinds of weather. And I am waiting for wind and tide. They are risking all for God at a clap. And I am for taking all advantages to secure my life and estate. They are for holding their notions, though all other men are against them. But I am for religion in what, and so far as, the times and my safety will bear it. They are for Religion when in rags and contempt. But I am for him when he walks in his silver slippers, in the sunshine, and with applause.

Hold. Yes, and just wait there, good Mr. By-ends. For, for my part, I can count him but a fool who having the liberty to keep what he has, is so unwise as to lose it. Let us be wise as serpents. It is best to make hay while the sun shines. You see how the bee lies still in winter, stirring herself only when she can have profit with pleasure. God sends rain sometimes, and sunshine sometimes. If they are such fools to go through the first, yet let us be content to take fair weather along with us. For my part, I like that religion best that will stand with the security of God's good blessings to us. For who can image, if anyone is ruled by reason, that since God has bestowed on us the good things of this life, He would have us keep them for His sake? Abraham and Solomon grew rich in religion. And Job says that a good man should lay up gold as dust (Job 22:24). But he must not be such as the men before us, if they are as you have described them.

Save. I think that we are all agreed in this matter, and therefore there is no need for more words about it.

Money. No, there is no need for more words about this matter, indeed. For he that does not believe either Scripture or reason (and you see that we have both on our side), knows neither his own liberty nor seeks his own safety.

By. My brothers, we are, as you see, all going on pilgrimage. And for our better diversion from things that are bad, give me leave to propose this question to you: Suppose that a man, a minister, or a tradesman, etc., should have an advantage lie before him to get the good blessings of this life, yet so that he cannot come by them without at least in appearance becoming extraordinarily zealous in some points of religion that he did not meddle with before – may he not use this means to attain his end, and yet be a truly honest man?

Money. I see the bottom of your question. And, with these gentlemen's leave, I will try to shape an answer for you. And, first, to speak to your question as it concerns a minister. Suppose a minister, a worthy man, possessed by a very small benefice, yet has in his eye a greater, more fat and plump one, by far? He has also now an opportunity of getting it, yet it is by being more studious, by preaching more frequently and zealously, and, because the temper of the people requires it, by altering some of his principles. For my part, I see no reason why a man may not do this, provided he has a call to do so. Yes, and he may do a great deal besides, and still he will be an honest man. Why? First, His desire for a greater benefice is lawful. This cannot be contradicted since it is set before him by Providence. So then he may get it if he can, making no question for conscience' sake. Secondly, Besides, his desire after that benefice makes him more studious, a more zealous preacher, etc. So it makes him a better man, yea, it makes him improve his talents, which is according to the mind of God. Thirdly, as for complying with the temper of his people by deserting some of his principles in order to serve them, this shows that, (1) he is of a self-denying temper; (2) that he is of a sweet and winning deportment; and, (3) that he is more fit for the ministerial function. Fourthly, I then conclude that a minister that changes a small for a great should not be judged covetous for doing so. But instead, since he is improved in his talents and industry by it, he should be counted as one that pursues his call and the opportunity put into his hand to do good.

And now to the second part of the question, which concerns the tradesman you mentioned. Suppose such a person to have only a poor employment in the world. But by becoming religious, he may change his market, perhaps get a rich wife, or more and far better customers to his shop. For my part, I see no reason why this may not be lawfully done. Why? First, to become religious is a virtue, by whatever means a man becomes so. Secondly, it is not unlawful to get a rich wife, or more customers to the shop. Thirdly, Besides, the man that gets these by becoming religious gets that which is good, from them that are good, by becoming good himself. So then here is a good wife, and good customers, and good gain, and all these by becoming religious, which is good. Therefore, to become religious to get all these is a good and profitable design.

The answer made in this way by Mr. Money-love to Mr. By-ends' question was highly applauded by all of them. So they concluded that on the whole it was most wholesome and advantageous. And thinking that no one was able to contradict it, and because Christian and Hopeful were still within call, they jointly agreed to assault them with the question as soon as they overtook them. And this especially because they had opposed Mr. By-ends before. So they called after them, and they stopped and stood still until they came up to them.

But they decided as they went that not Mr. By-ends, but old Mr. Hold-the-world, should propose the question to them. And this because they supposed that their answer to him would be without the remainder of that heat that was kindled between Mr. By-ends and them, at their recent parting. So they came up to each other.

And after a short salutation, Mr. Hold-the-world asked the question to Christian and his friend. And he challenged them to answer it if they could.

Chr. Even a babe in Christ may answer ten thousand such questions. For if it is unlawful to follow Christ for loaves, as it is (John 6:26), then how much more hateful is it to God to make of Christ and religion a stalking-horse to gain and enjoy the world! Nor do we find any other than heathen, hypocrites, devils and witches that are of this opinion:

1. The heathen believe it. For when Hamor and Shechem desired the daughter and cattle of Jacob, and when they saw that there was no other way for them to get them except by being circumcised, they said to their companions, *"If every male among us will be circumcised in the way they are circumcised, shall not their cattle, and their goods, and every animal of theirs be ours?"* It was their daughters and their cattle that they sought to obtain, and their religion was only the stalking-horse they made use of to get them. Read

the whole story (Gen. 34:20-24).

2. The hypocritical Pharisees were also of this religion. They made long prayers for a pretence, but it was their intention to gain widows' houses. And it was greater condemnation that God gave them for their judgment (Luke 20:46,47).

3. Judas the devil was also of this religion. He was religious for the bag's sake, so that he might possess whatever was put in it. But he was finally lost, cast away, and is the very son of perdition.

4. Simon the wizard was of this religion too. For he desired to have the Holy Spirit so that he might get money by this. And his sentence from Peter's mouth was according to his desire (Acts 8:18-23).

5. Neither can I forget that the man that takes up religion in order to gain the world will also throw away religion for the sake of the world. For as surely as Judas became religious in order to gain the world, so did he also sell religion and his Master for the same. Therefore, when you answer the question affirmatively, as I see you have, and to accept such an answer as authentic is heathenish, hypocritical and devilish. And your reward will be according to your works.

Then they stood staring at one another, but they had nothing to answer Christian. Hopeful also approved of the soundness of Christian's answer. So there was a great silence among them. Then Mr. By-ends and his company staggered and kept behind, so that Christian and Hopeful should get ahead of them. Then Christian said to his friend, If these men cannot stand before the judgment of men, what will they do with the judgment of God? And if they are silent when vessels of clay deal with them, what will they do when they shall be rebuked by flames of a devouring fire. Then Christian and Hopeful went ahead of them again and continued until they had come to a delicate plain called Ease. Then they met with much contentment. But the plain was but a narrow one so that they were quickly beyond it. Now, at the furthest side of that plain was a little hill called Lucre. And there was a silver mine in that hill, which some of those who had formerly gone that way had turned aside to see, because it was so rare. But having gone too near the brim of the pit, the ground being deceitful under them, it broke in and they were slain. Some had also been maimed there and so could not be themselves again to their dying day.

Then I saw in my dream that just a little off the road, across from the silver mine, one Demas stood calling in a gentlemanly way for those passing to come and see. And he said to Christian and his friend, Ho! Turn aside here and I will show you something.

Chr. What can be so deserving that we should turn out of the way to see it?

Demas. A silver mine is here, and some are digging in it for treasure. If you will come, with a little effort you may richly provide for yourselves.

Hope. Let us go see.

Chr. Not I! I have heard of this place before now, how many have been slain here. And, besides, that treasure is a snare to those that seek it, for it hinders them in their pilgrimage.

Then Christian called to Demas, saying,

Chr. Is this place not dangerous? Has it not hindered many in their pilgrimage?

Demas It is not very dangerous, except to those that are careless. But he blushed as he spoke.

Chr. Let us not stir a step, but still keep on our way.

Hope. I will guarantee to you that when By-ends comes up, if he has the same invitation that we have, he will turn in there to see.

Chr. There is no doubt of it, for his principles lead him that way, and it is very likely that he will die there.

Demas But will you not come over and see?

Chr. Demas, you are an enemy to the right ways of the Lord of this way. And you have already been condemned for your own turning aside, by one of his Majesty's judges (2 Tim. 4:10). Then why do you seek to bring us into the same condemnation? Besides, if we turn aside at all, then our Lord the king will certainly hear of it. And He will put us to shame in the place where we desire to stand boldly before Him.

Demas cried again that he also was one of their brotherhood, and that if they would but wait a little he would also walk with them.

Chr. What is your name? Is it not the same by which I have called you?

Demas Yes, my name is Demas. I am the son of Abraham.

Chr. I know you. Gehazi was your great-grandfather, and Judas was your father, and you have walked in their steps. It is but a devilish trick that you are pulling. Your father was hung for a traitor, and you deserve no better reward (2 Kings 5:20; Matt. 26:14; 27:3). Assure yourself that when we come to the King, we will tell him of your behavior.

So they went their way. And by this time By-ends and his companions were coming within sight. And they at the first call from Demas went over. I do not know if they fell into the pit by looking over the edge, or if they went down to dig, or if they were smothered in the bottom by the damps that commonly arise there. But this much I observed, that they were never seen again in the way. Then Christian sang:

> By-ends, and silver Demas both agree:
> One calls, the other runs, that he may be
> A sharer in his lucre, so these do
> Take up in this world, and no further go.

Now I saw that just on the other side of the plain the pilgrims came to a place where an old monument stood close by the highwayside. When they saw this, they were concerned because it had a very strange form. For it appeared to them to be a woman transformed into the shape of a pillar. Therefore, they stood there looking and looking at it. But they could not tell for a long time what they should make of it. At last, Hopeful saw written above on the head of it an inscription in an unusual hand. But being no scholar, he called to Christian (for he was learned) to see if he could pick out the meaning. So he came. And after a little laying of the letters together, he found it to be this, *"Remember Lot's wife"* (Gen. 19:26). So he read it to his friend. And they both concluded that it was the pillar of salt into which Lot's wife had turned, because she had looked back with a covetous heart when she was leaving Sodom for her safety.

Chr. My brother! This is a timely sight. It came opportunely to us after the invitation which Demas gave us to come over to see the hill Lucre. And if we had gone over, as he desired us to do, and as you were inclined to do, my brother, for all I know we may have been made like this woman – a spectacle for those that shall come after us to behold.

Hope. I am sorry that I was so foolish. And I wonder that I am not now like Lot's wife, for what is the difference between her sin and mine? She only looked back, but I had a desire to go see. Let grace be adored, and let me be ashamed that such a thing ever should be in my heart.

Chr. Let us remember what we see here, for it will be our help in time to come. This woman escaped one judgment, not having fallen in the destruction of Sodom, but she was destroyed by another, as we see she was turned into a pillar of salt.

Hope. True, and she may be both a caution and example to us. She is a caution so that we should shun her sin. Or she is a sign of what judgment will overtake us if we do not heed this caution. Korah, Dathan and Abiram also, with their two hundred and fifty men, perished in their sin and thus became a sign or example to others to beware (Num. 26:9). But above all, I wonder how Demas and his fellows can stand so confidently yonder to look for that treasure which this woman sought, when they know that she was turned into a pillar of salt for merely looking back – and we do not read that she stepped one foot out of the way. And this especially when the judgment which overtook her made her an example within sight of where they are. For they cannot help but see her, if they would but lift up their eyes.

Chr. It is a thing to cause one to wonder. And it argues that their hearts have grown desperately wicked. And I cannot tell how to compare them, unless it be to those that pick pockets in the presence of the judge, or those that cut purses right under the gallows. It is said of the men of Sodom that *they were exceedingly great sinners,* because they were sinners in the plain sight of the Lord. And in spite of the mercies He had shown them, too, for the land of Sodom was at the time like the garden of Eden before (Gen. 13:10,13). This, therefore, provoked Him to be more jealous, and it made their plague as hot as the fire of the Lord out of Heaven could make it. And it is reasonable to conclude that there are some who will sin in His sight, just as these are doing. Yes, and that too in spite of such examples as are continually set before them to caution them to the contrary, so that they must be partakers of the severest judgments.

Hope. No doubt you have said the truth. But what a mercy it is that neither you nor I have been made such an example. This gives us occasion to thank God, to fear before Him, and always to remember Lot's wife.

Then I saw that they went on to a pleasant river, which David the king called *the river of God,"* but John called, *"the river of the water of life" (Ps. 46:4; Ezek. 47; Rev. 22:1).* And their path lay just on the bank of this river. So, then, Christian and his companion walked here with great delight. They also drank of the water of the river, which was pleasant and refreshing to their weary spirits. Besides, on the banks of this river, on either side, were green trees with all kinds of fruit. And they ate its leaves to prevent disorders and diseases that are common to those that heat their blood by traveling. On either side of the river there was also a meadow, curiously beautified with lillies. And it was green all the year long. They lay down and slept in this meadow, for here they could lie down safely (Ps. 23; Isa. 14:30). When they awoke, they again drank of the water of the river. And then they lay down to sleep again. So they did for several days and nights. Then they sang:

> Behold how these crystal streams do glide,
> To comfort pilgrims by the highway side.
> The meadows green, besides their fragrant smell,
> Yield dainties for them; and he who can tell
> What pleasant fruit, yea, leaves, these trees do yield,
> Will soon sell all, that he may buy the field.

So when they were disposed to go on (for they were not at their journey's end), they ate and drank and then departed.

Now I beheld in my dream that they had not gone far, but the river and the road were separated for a time, which saddened them. Yet they did not dare to go out of the way. Now the way from the river was rough, and their feet were tender because of their travels. So the souls of the pilgrims were much discouraged because of the way (Numbers 21:4). Still as they were going on, they wished for a better way. Then, a little in front of them, there was a meadow on the left hand side of the road. And there was a stile so that they could go over into it. Then they went to the stile to see. And, behold, there was a path running alongside the way on the other side of the fence. Then Christian said,

Chr. It is according to my wish. Here is the easiest going. Come, good Hopeful, and let us go over.

Hope. But what if this path should lead us out of the way?

Chr. Does it not go alongside the way? So Hopeful, being persuaded by his friend, went after him over the stile. When they had crossed over and had gotten into the path, they found it very easy for their feet. And as they looked before them, they saw a man walking as they did. And his name was Vain-Confidence. So they called after him and asked him where that road led. He said, To the Celestial Gate. And Christian said, Did I not tell you so? By this you can see we were right. So they followed, and he went on before them. But the night came on and it grew very dark, so that they lost sight of the one going before them. Then Vain-Confidence, not being able to see the way before him, fell into a deep pit (Isa. 9:16), which had been put there on purpose by the ruler of those grounds. For it was to catch vainglorious fools, and Vain-Confidence was dashed into pieces by his fall. Now Christian and his fellow heard him fall. So they called out to know what was the matter. But there was no one to answer. They only heard a groaning. Then Hopeful asked,

Hope. Where are we now?

But Christian was silent, suspecting that he had led him out of the way. And then it began to rain and thunder, and lightning flashed in a most dreadful manner. And the water rose quickly. Then Hopeful groaned and said,

Hope. Oh, that I had kept on my way!

Chr. Who could have thought that this path would lead us out of the way?

Hope. I was afraid of it at the very first, so I gave you that gentle caution. I would have spoken more plainly, except that you are older than I.

Chr. Good brother, do not be offended. I am sorry I have brought you out of the way and that I have put you into such imminent danger. Please forgive me, my brother, for I did not do it with an evil intent.

Hope. Be comforted, my brother, for I do forgive you. And also believe that this shall be for our good.

Chr. I am glad that I have a merciful brother with me. But we must not stand here. Let us try to go back again.

Hope. But, good brother, let me go first.

Chr. No, if you please, let me go first, so that if there is any danger I may be the first into it. For it was because of me that we have both gone out of the way.

Hope. No, you shall not go first. For your mind being troubled, you may again be led out of the way. Then to their encouragement, a voice was heard saying, *"Let your heart be towards the highway, and turn again to the way that you went"* (Jeremiah 31:21).

But by this time the waters had risen greatly, so that the way back was very dangerous. Then I thought this, that it is easier to go out of the way when we are in it, than it is to get back into the way when we are out of it. Yet they tried to go back. But it was so dark, and the flood was so high, that they were nearly drowned nine or ten times in going back. Nor could they, even with all the skill they had, get back to the stile again that night. So at last, falling under a little shelter, they sat down there until the day should break. But being weary, they fell asleep. And not far from the place where they lay, there was a castle called Doubting-castle. And the owner of it was Giant Despair. And it was on his grounds that they now slept. So he got up early in the morning and walked up and down in his fields, where he caught Christian and Hopeful asleep on his grounds. Then with a grim and surly voice, he commanded them to awaken. And he asked them where they came from and what they were doing on his gounds. They told him that they were pilgrims who had lost their way. Then the giant said, You have trespassed on me tonight by trampling in and lying on my grounds. Therefore you must go along with me. So they were forced to go, because he was stronger than they. They also had but little to say, for they knew that they were at fault. So the giant drove them before him. And he put them into a very dark dungeon in his castle, a nasty and stinking hole to the spirits of these men. They lay here from Wednesday morning until Saturday night, without one bit of bread, nor a drop to drink, nor any light, nor anyone to ask them how they did. So they were here in a bad way, being far from friends and acquaintances (Ps. 88:8). And Christian had double sorrow in this place, because it was through his ill advice that they had come into this distress.

Now Giant Despair had a wife, and her name was Diffidence. So when he had gone to bed, he told his wife what he had done, that he had taken a couple of prisoners and had cast them into his dungeon for trespassing on his grounds. Then he asked her what would be best for him to do with them? So she asked what they were and where they came from, as well as where they were going. And he told her. Then she counseled him to beat them without mercy when he should arise in the morning. So when he arose, he got a wicked crabtree cudgel and went down into the dungeon where they were. And he first fell to berating them as if they were dogs. Still, they gave him no word of distaste. Then he fell on them and beat them unmercifully, in such a way that they could not help one another, not even on the floor. Then he departed and left them there to condole their misery and to mourn under their distress. So all that day they spent their time in nothing but sighs and bitter lamentations. The next night his wife talked with him further about them. And hearing that they were still alive, she advised him to counsel them to commit suicide. So when morning had come, he went to them in the same surly manner as before. And seeing that they were very sore from the blows that he had given them the day before, he told them that since they were never likely to get out of that place, their only way to escape was to make an end to themselves. For why, he said, should you choose to live, since it is attended with so much bitterness? But they begged him to let them go. At that he looked ugly and he rushed in and would have no doubt made an end of them himself except that he fell into one of his fits (for he sometimes fell into fits in sunshiny weather), and he lost the use of his hands for a time. So he withdrew, leaving them, as before, to consider what to do. Then the prisoners consulted between themselves as to whether it was best to take his counsel. And so they began to say:

Chr. Brother, what shall we do? The life that we now live is miserable. As for me, I do not know if it is better to live this way, or if it is better to die, *"My soul chooses strangling rather than life"* (Job 7:15). And the grave is more easy for me than this dungeon. Shall we be ruled by the giant?

Hope. Our present condition is indeed dreadful. And death would be far more welcome to me than to forever live here. But yet let us consider that the Lord of the country to which we are going has said, "You shall not commit murder," not even to another man's person. How much more, then, are we forbidden to kill ourselves! Besides, he that kills another can but commit murder on his body, but when one kills himself he both kills body and soul at once. And also, my brother, you talk of ease in the grave. But have you forgotten the hell where murderers certainly go? For *"No murderer has eternal life."* And let us consider again that all the law is not in the hand of Giant Despair. As far as I know, others have been taken by him as well as we, and yet they have escaped out of his hands. Who knows but that God, who made the world, may cause Giant Despair to die, or that at some time or other he may forget to lock us in? Or it may be he may in a short time have another of his fits and may lose the use of his limbs. And if that ever happens again, for my part, I am resolved to take heart and to try my utmost to get out from under his hand. I was a fool that I did not try it before. However, my brother, let us be patient and endure for a while. The time may come when we may be given a happy release. But do not let us be our own murderers!

With these words Hopeful presently moderated the mind of his brother. So they continued together in the dark that day, in their sad and doleful condition. Then toward evening the giant went down into the dungeon again to see if his prisoners had taken his advice. But when he came there he found them alive. And, truly, they were barely alive now, what for lack of bread and water, and because of the wounds they received when he beat them. They could do little more than to breathe. But he found them alive. At which he fell into a grievous rage and told them that since they had disobeyed his counsel, it would be worse for them than if they had never been born. And they trembled greatly at this, and I think that Christian fell into a swoon. But coming to himself a little, they renewed their discussion about the giant's counsel, as to whether they had best take it or not. Now Christian seemed for doing it, but Hopeful made his second reply, as follows:

Hope. My brother, remember how valiant you were before? Apollyon could not crush you, nor could all that you heard or saw or felt in the Valley of the Shadow of Death. Think what hardship, terror and amazement you have already gone through, and are you now nothing but fears? You see that I am in the dungeon with you, a far weaker man by nature than you are. This giant has also wounded me as well as you, and he has also cut off my bread and water. And I mourn with you without the light. If we only but exercise a little more patience. Remember how you played the man at Vanity Fair, how you were neither afraid of the chain or the cage, nor even of bloody death. Therefore, let us bear up with patience as well as we can, at least to avoid the shame that a Christian ought not to be found in.

And when night had come again, and the giant and his wife were in bed, she asked him about the prisoners, whether they had taken his counsel. To which he replied, They are sturdy rogues. They choose rather to bear all hardships than to commit suicide. Then she said, Take them into the castleyard tomorrow and show them the bones and skulls of those you have already dispatched. And make them believe that before a week is past you will tear them into pieces, as you have done with their fellows before them. So when morning had come, the giant went to them again and took them into the castleyard to show them, as his wife had bidden him.

And he said, These were pilgrims like you once, and they trespassed on my grounds as you have. And when I desired it, I tore them into pieces. And so I will do with you within ten days. Get down to your den again! And with that, he beat them all the way there. So they lay there all day on Saturday in a sad condition, as before. And when night had come, and when Mrs. Diffidence and her husband the giant had gotten into bed, they began to talk of their prisoners again. And the old giant wondered why he could not bring them to an end either by his blows or his counsel. And then his wife replied, I fear that they live in hopes that some one will come to relieve them, or that they have picklocks about them by which they hope to escape. Then the giant said, If you say so, dear, I will therefore search them in the morning. But on Saturday, about midnight, they began to pray. And they continued in prayer until almost daybreak. And a little before it was day, good Christian, like one half amazed, broke out into this passionate speech:

Chr. What a fool I am, to lie this way in a stinking dungeon when I may as well walk at liberty! I have a key in my bosom called Promise, and I am persuaded that it will open any lock in Doubting Castle.

Hope. That is good news, good brother, pluck it out of your bosom and try it.

Then Christian pulled it out of his bosom and began to try to open the dungeon door. And as he turned the key, the bolt gave back and the door flew open with ease. Then both Christian and Hopeful came out. And going to the outward door that leads into the castleyard, he opened that door with his key also. Then he went to the iron gate, for that too must be opened. But that lock resisted strongly. However, the key did open it. Then they pushed the gate open in order to speedily make their escape. But when the gate opened, it made such a creaking that it awakened Giant Despair. And he arose hastily to pursue his prisoners, but he felt his limbs begin to fail because his fits came on him again. So he could not by any means go after them. Then they went on and came to the King's highway, and so were safe, because they were now out of the jurisdiction of Giant Despair.

Now when they had gone back over the stile, they began to seek ingenuously to devise a plan to put something at that stile to prevent those that should come afterwards from falling into the hand of Giant Despair. So they consented to erect a pillar there and to engrave on its side this sentence, 'Over this stile is the way to Doubting Castle, which is kept by Giant Despair, who despises the King of the Celestial Country and seeks to destroy His holy pilgrims.' Therefore, many that came afterwards read what was written and escaped the danger. And they sang as follows:

> Out of the way we went, and then we found
> What 'twas to tread upon forbidden ground;
> And let them that come after have a care
> Lest heedlessness makes them as we to fare;
> Lest they, for trespassing, his pris'ners are,
> Whose castle's Doubting, and whose name's Despair.

They then went on until they came to the Delectable Mountains, which belong to the Lord of that hill of which we have spoken before. So they went up into the mountains to see the gardens and orchards, the vineyards and fountains of water. And they also drank and washed themselves there, and they freely ate from the vineyards. Now there were shepherds feeding their flocks on the tops of these mountains. And they stood by the highway. So the pilgrims went up to them. And leaning on their staves (as was common with weary pilgrims when they stand to talk with any by the way), they asked, Whose Delectable Mountains are these? And whose sheep are these that feed on them?

Shepherd These mountains are Emmanuel's Land, and they are within sight of His city. And the sheep are also His, and He laid down His life for them (John 10:11,15).

Chr. Is this the way to the Celestial City?

Shep. You are right in your way.

Chr. How far is it?

Shep. Too far for any but those that shall truly get there.

Chr. Is the way safe, or dangerous?

Shep. It is safe for those for whom it is to be safe, *"but transgressors shall fall in it"* (Hos. 14:9).

Chr. Is there any relief for pilgrims that are weary and faint in this place?

Shep. The Lord of these mountains has given us a command that we should *"not be forgetful to entertain strangers' (Heb. 13:2), therefore the best of this place is before you.*

I also saw in my dream that when the shepherds perceived that they were wayfaring men, they also questioned them (to which they answered, as in other places), such as, Where did you come from? And, How did you get into the way? And, By what means have you so persevered in it? For only a few of them that began to come here show their faces on these mountains. But when the shepherds heard their answers, they were pleased with them, and they looked very lovingly on them and said, Welcome to the Delectable Mountains!

The names of the shepherds were Knowledge, Experience, Watchful and Sincere. And they took them by the hand and brought them to their tents. And they made them partake of all that was presently ready. And they said, We would like to have you stay here awhile and get acquainted with us; and even more, to solace yourselves with the good of these Delectable Mountains. Then they told them that they were content to stay. And so they retired to rest that night, because it was very late.

Then I saw in my dream that in the morning the Shepherds called up Christian and Hopeful to walk with them on the mountains. So they went forth with them and walked awhile, having a pleasing view on every side. Then the shepherds said to one another, Shall we show these pilgrims some wonders? So when they had decided to do it, they brought them first to the top of a hill called Error. It was very steep on the furthest side, and they told them to look down to the bottom. So Christian and Hopeful looked down and saw at the bottom several men dashed all to pieces by a fall that they had had from the top. Then Christian said, What does this mean? The shepherds answered, Have you not heard of those who were caused to err by listening to Hymeneus and Philetus (2 Tim. 2:17,18) in regard to the faith of the resurrection of the body? They answered, Yes. Then the shepherds said, Those that you see lying dashed to pieces at the bottom of the mountain are they. And they have continued unburied to this day, as you see, so that they might be an example to others that they should be careful how they climb too high, or how they come too near the edge of this mountain.

Then I saw them bring them to the top of another mountain named Caution. And they told them to look afar off. And when they looked, they saw what they thought to be several men walking up and down among the tombs that were there. And they saw that the men were blind, because they stumbled on the tombs sometimes, and because they could not get out from among them. Then Christian asked what it meant. The shepherds then answered, Did you not see a little below these mountains a stile that led into a meadow on the left side of the way? They answered, Yes. Then the shepherds said, A path goes from that stile directly to Doubting Castle, which is kept by Giant Despair. And pointing to those among the tombs, they said, These men once came on pilgrimage, as you are doing now, until they came to that stile. And because the right way was rough in that place, they chose to go out of it into that meadow. And there they were captured by Giant Despair, who threw them into Doubting Castle. And after they had been there awhile in the dungeon, the giant at last put out their eyes and led them among those tombs. And he has left them there to wander to this very day, so that the saying of the wise man might be fulfilled, *"He that wanders out of the way of understanding shall remain in the congregation of the dead"* (Prov. 21:16). Then Christian and Hopeful looked at one another and their tears gushed out. But they said nothing to the shepherds.

Then I saw in my dream that the shepherds brought them to another place, in a bottom, where there was a door in the side of a hill. And they opened the door and told them to look in. They looked and saw that it was very dark and smoky in there. They also thought that they heard a cry of some that were being tormented. And they smelled the odor of brimstone. Then Christian asked what it meant. The shepherds told them, This is a by-way to hell, a way that hypocrites choose, those like Esau that sell their birthright; or like Judas, that sell their Master. These are those that blaspheme the gospel with Alexander; or those that lie and dissemble with Ananias and Sapphira. Then Hopeful said to the shepherds:

Hope. I perceive that each of these has some sign of pilgrimage on them, as we have. Do they not?

Shep. Yes, and they held to it a long time too.

Hope. How far may they go on in pilgrimage in their days, even those that were so miserably cast away?

Shep. Some further, and some not so far as these mountains. Then the pilgrims said to one another, We need to cry to the Strong One for strength.

Shep. Yes, and you will have need to use that strength when you have it too.

By this time the pilgrims had a desire to go on. And the shepherds desired that they should. So they walked together towards the end of the mountains. Then the shepherds said to one another, Let us here show the pilgrims the gates of the Celestial City, if they are able to look through our perspective-glass. The pilgrims lovingly accepted the invitation. So they brought them to the top of a high hill called Clear. And they gave them the glass so that they could look. And they tried to look, but remembering that last thing the shepherds had shown them caused their hands to shake so much that they could not look steadily through the glass. Yet they thought they saw something like the gate, and also some of the glory of the place. Then they went away and sang:

> Thus by the shepherds secrets are reveal'd,
> Which from all other men are kept conceal'd
> Come to the shepherds, then, if you would see
> Things deep, things hid, and that mysterious be.

When they were about to depart, one of the shepherds gave them a map of the way. Another told them to beware of the flatterer. The third warned them to be careful that they did not sleep on enchanted ground. And the fourth bid them Godspeed. So I awoke from my dream.

Then I slept and dreamed again. And I saw the same two pilgrims going down the mountains along the highway towards the city. And a little below these mountains, on the left hand, lies the country of Conceit. And a little crooked lane comes into the way from that country. Then they met a brisk lad coming out of that country here, whose name was Ignorance. So Christian asked him from what parts he came and where he was going.

Ignorance Sir, I was born in the country that lies off there a little on the left hand, and I am going to the Celestial City.

Chr. But how to you think you will get in at the gate? For you may find some difficulties there.

Ignor. I will get in as other good people do.

Chr. But what have you to show at that gate so that the gate may be opened to you?

Ignor. I know my Lord's will, and I have been good. For I pay every man his own; I pray, I fast, I pay tithes and I give alms. And I have left my country for the place where I am going.

Chr. But you did not come in at the Wicket-gate that is at the head of this way. You came in here through that same crooked lane. And therefore I fear that whatever you may think of yourself, when the day of reckoning comes, you will have it laid to your charge that you are a thief and a robber, instead of getting admittance to the City.

Ignor. Gentlemen, you are total strangers to me. I do not know you. Be content to follow the religion of your country, and I will follow the religion of mine. I hope all will be well. And as for the gate you mentioned, all the world knows that it is a great distance from my country. I cannot think that anyone in all our parts so much as knew the way to it. Nor does it matter if they do or not, since we have, as you see, a fine pleasant green lane that comes down from our country, the next way into the way.

When Christian saw that the man was wise in his own conceit, he said to Hopeful, whisperingly, *"There is more hope for a fool than for him;" "When he that is a fool walks by the way, his wisdom fails him. And he says to everyone that he is a fool"* (Prov. 26:12; Eccl. 10:3). What! Shall we talk any further with him, or shall we go ahead of him now and thus leave him to think of what he has heard already? Then we can stop again for him later and see if by degrees we can do any good for him. Then Hopeful said,

> Let Ignorance a little while now muse
> On what is said, and let him not refuse
> Good counsel to embrace, lest he remain
> Still ignorant of what's the chiefest gain.
> God said, those that no understanding have,
> Although he made them, them he will not save.

Hope. I do not think that it is good to say so to him all at once. Let us pass by him and then talk to him again soon, even as he is able to bear it.

So they both went on, and Ignorance followed. Now when they had passed him a little way, they entered into a very dark lane. There they met a man whom seven devils had bound with seven strong cords. And they were carrying him back to the door that they saw on the side of the hill (Matt. 12:45; Prov. 5:22). Then good Christian began to tremble. And so did his companion Hopeful. And as the devils took the man away, Christian looked to see if he knew him. And he thought that it might be one Turnaway, who lived in the town of Apostasy. But he did not see his face clearly, for he hung his head like a thief that is caught. But when he had gone past, Hopeful looked after him and saw on his back a paper with this inscription, 'Wanton professor and contemptible apostate.'

Then Christian said to his fellow, Now I remember that which was told to me, of a thing that happened to a good man around here. The name of the man was Little-Faith, but he was a good man and he lived in the town of Sincere. The thing I was told was this, that at the entering in of this passage there is a lane called Deadman's-lane which comes down from Broadway-gate. It is so called because of the murders that are commonly done there. And this Little-Faith was on pilgrimage, as we are now. And he happened to sit down there and go to sleep. And it happened that at that time three sturdy rogues came down the lane from Broadway-gate. And their names were Faint-heart, Mistrust and Guilt, three brothers. And when they saw Little-Faith, they came galloping up with speed. And the good man had just awakened from his sleep and was getting up to go on his journey. So they all came up to him and with threatening language commanded him to stand still. At this Little-Faith looked as white as a sheet. And he had neither power to fight or to flee. Then Faint-heart said, Deliver your purse. But when he was slow to do it, hating to lose his money, Mistrust ran up to him and thrust his hand into his pocket and pulled out a bag of silver. Then he cried out, Thieves! Thieves! So then Guilt struck

Little-Faith on the head with a big club that was in his hand. And with that blow he knocked him flat on the ground. There he lay bleeding as one that would bleed to death. And all this time the thieves stood beside him. But at last, when they heard some were on the road, and when they feared that it would be one Great-Grace (who lives in the town of Good-Confidence), they took to their heels and left this good man to shift for himself. And after a while Little-Faith came to himself and got up and managed to scramble on his way. This was the story.

Hope. But did they take all that he ever had from him?

Chr. No, for they never ransacked the place where his jewels were kept. So he still kept those. But as I was told, the good man was much afflicted because of his loss, for the thieves got most of his spending-money. They did not get his jewels, and he had a little odd money left, but it was scarcely enough to bring him to his journey's end (1 Pet. 4:18). Yea, if I am not misinformed, he had to beg as he went in order to keep himself alive (for he was not permitted to sell his jewels). Yet, begging and doing all he could, he still went with many a hungry belly the most of the rest of the way.

Hope. But is it not a wonder that they did not get his certificate from him, that which he was to present in order to be admitted at the Celestial Gate?

Chr. It is a wonder. But they did not get it. Though they did not miss it because he was so cunning. For being dismayed at their coming on him, he had neither power nor skill to hide anything. So it was more by good providence than by his own effort that they failed to get that good thing (2 Tim. 1:14; 2 Pet. 2:9).

Hope. But it must be a comfort to him that they did not get this jewel from him.

Chr. It might have been great comfort to him if he had used it as he should. But they that told me the story said that he made but little use of it all the rest of the way, and that because of the dismay that he felt because they had taken his money away. Indeed, he forgot it a great part of the rest of his journey. And, besides, when it came into his mind at any time, and he began to be comforted with it, then he would get fresh thoughts of his loss and these thoughts swallowed up all his comfort.

Hope. Ah! This must have been a great grief to him.

Chr. Grief! Yes, indeed. Would it not have been so to any of us if we had been treated as he was, to be robbed and wounded too, and that in a strange place. It was a wonder he did not die with grief, poor heart! I was told that he scattered almost all the rest of the way with nothing but sad and bitter complaints; and he told all that overtook him, or those he overtook, where he was robbed, and how. And he told them who did it, what he lost, how he was wounded, and how he hardly escaped with his life.

Hope. But it is wonder that his great need did not cause him to sell or pawn some of his jewels so that he might have something to relieve himself during the journey.

Chr. You talk like one whose head is in the shell to this very day! For what should he pawn them? Or to whom should he sell them? In all that country where he was, there was not a soul who valued his jewels. Nor did he lack that relief which could have been administered to him from there. Besides, if his jewels had been missing at the gate to the Celestial City, he would have been excluded from an inheritance there (as he knew well enough). And that would have been worse to him than the appearance and villany of ten thousand thieves.

Hope. Why are you so tart, my brother? Esau sold his birthright, and that for a mess of pottage (Heb. 12:16). And his birthright was his brightest jewel. If he did it, why might not Little-Faith do it too?

Chr. Esau did indeed sell his birthright. And many others do so too. But by doing so they exclude themselves from the chief blessing, as did that wretched man. But you must put a difference between Esau and Little-Faith, as you would between their estates. Esau's birthright was typical, but Little-Faith's jewels were not so. Esau's belly was his god, but Little-Faith's belly was not so. Esau's need was in his fleshly appetite, but Little-Faith's was not so. Besides, Esau could see no further than to the fulfilling of his lusts, *"For I am at the point of dying, and what good will this birthright do me?"* (**Gen.**

25:32). But Little-Faith, though it was his lot to have only a little faith, was by that little faith kept from such extravagances, being made to see and prize his jewels more than to sell them as Esau did his birthright. You never read anywhere that Esau had faith, nor even so much as a little. So it is no marvel that where the flesh alone rules (as it will in that person where no faith exists to resist), that one will sell his birthright, and his soul, and all; and that to the devil of hell. For it is with such persons as it is with the wild ass who in her occasion cannot be turned away (Jer. 2:24). When their minds are set on their lusts, they must have them, whatever the cost. But Little-Faith was of another temper; his mind was on things divine; his livelihood was on things that were spiritual and from above. So why should he that is of such a temper sell his jewels in order to fill his mind with empty things (even if there had been someone who would have bought them)? Will a man give a penny to fill his belly with hay? Or can you persuade the turtle-dove to live on carrion, as the crow does? Though faithless ones can for the sake of carnal lusts pawn or mortgage or sell what they have, even themselves to boot, yet they that have faith, saving faith, cannot do so, even if their faith is a little faith. My brother, here is your mistake.

Hope. I acknowledge it. Still, your severe reflection almost had made me angry.

Chr. Why? I did not compare you to some of the birds that are of the bolder sort, who will run to and fro in untrodden paths with the shell on their heads. But leave that and consider the matter under debate, then all shall be well between you and me.

Hope. But, Christian, I am persuaded in my heart that these three fellows are only a company of cowards. Do you think they would have run at the noise of someone coming on the road, if it were not so? Why didn't Little-Faith pluck up a stronger heart? I believe he might have stood one brush with them and not to have yielded until there was no other remedy.

Chr. Many have said that they were cowards, but few have found it to be so in the time of trial. As for a great heart, Little-Faith did not have one. And, my brother, I see by you that if you had been the one concerned, you are only for a brush and then to yield. And, truly, since this is the height of your stomach now that they are at a distance from us, they might put you to second thoughts if they should appear to you as they did to him. But consider again that they are only journeyman thieves. They serve under the king of the bottomless pit. And he, if need be, will come to their aid himself. And his voice is like that of a roaring lion (1 Pet. 5:8). I myself have been assaulted, as Little-Faith was. And I found it to be a terrible thing. These three villains set upon me. And like a Christian, I began to resist. Then they only gave a call, and their master came charging in. As the saying goes, I would have given my life for a penny, except that, as God would have it, I was clothed with armor that had been proven. Yes, even though I was so dressed in armor, I still found it hard work to be manly.

Unless he has been in the battle himself, no one can tell what he will meet with in combat.

Hope. Well, but they ran, you see, when they only supposed that one Great-Grace was in the way.

Chr. True, they have often fled when Great-Grace has appeared, both they and their master. And that is no wonder, for he is the King's champion. All the King's subjects are not His champions. Nor can they do such feats of war as he, when tried. Is it right to think that a little child could handle Goliath as David did? Or can there be the strength of an ox in a wren? Some are strong and some are weak. Some have great faith and some have little. This man was one of the weak ones and that is why he went to the wall.

Hope. For their sakes, I wish that it had been Great-Grace.

Chr. If it had been he, he might have had his hands full. For I must tell you that though Great-Grace is excellent with his weapons, and though he has and can do well enough with them if he keeps them at sword's point, yet if Faint-heart, Mistrust or Guilt get within him, it will go hard with him and the will throw up his heels. And when a man is down, you know, what can he do? If anyone looks on Great-Grace's face, he will see there scars and cuts, which should easily demonstrate what I say. Yea, once I heard that he said (and that when he was in the battle), "We despaired even of life'." Did not those sturdy rogues and their fellows make David groan, mourn and roar? Yea, Heman, and Hezekiah too, though champions in their days, were forced to stir themselves up when they were assaulted by these. And even so, they had their coats soundly brushed by them. And once Peter willed to go and try what he could do. And though some say he is the prince of the apostles, they handled him so that they made him finally to be afraid of a pitiful little girl.

Besides, their king is at their whistle. He is never out of hearing. And if at any time they are put to the worst, he, if possible, comes in to help them. And it is said of him, *"The sword of his pursuer will not hold. The spear, the dart and the javelin, he counts iron as straw and brass as rotten wood. The arrow cannot make him flee; slingstones are turned into stubble by him. Darts are counted as stubble; he laughs at the shaking of a spear"* (Job 41:26-29). What can a man do in this case? It is true that if a man could at every turn have Job's horse, and if he had skill and courage to ride him, he might do notable things, for *"Can you make him afraid like a grasshopper? The majesty of his snorting is terrifying. He paws in the valley and rejoices in his strength; he goes on to meet the armed men. He mocks at fear and is not frightened. And he does not turn back from the sword. The quiver rattles against him, the glittering spear and the shield. He swallows the ground with fierceness and rage; neither does he stand still at the sound of the trumpet. He says among the trumpets, Ha, Ha! And he smells the battle afar off, the thunder of the captains, and the shouting"* (Job 39:20-25).

But for such footmen as you and I are, let us never desire to meet with an enemy, nor boast as if we could do better, when we hear of others that have been foiled. Let us not be tickled at the thoughts of our manhood, for such people commonly come to the worst when tried. Look at Peter, of whom I made mention before: he would swagger, and as his vain mind prompted him to say, he could do better and stand more firmly for his Master than all men. But who was so foiled and run down by these villains than Peter?

Therefore, when we hear that such robberies are done on the King's highway, it is becoming for us to do two things: First, to go out in full armor, and to be sure to take a shield with us; for it was for lack of that that he who lustily attacked Leviathan failed to make him yield (for, indeed, if that is lacking, he does not fear us at all). So that is why he who had such skill has said, *"Above all, take the shield of faith, by which you shall be able to quench all the fiery darts of the wicked"* (Eph. 6:16).

It is also good that we ask a convoy from the King, that He will go with us Himself. This made David rejoice when in the Valley of the Shadow of Death. And Moses was rather for dying where he stood than to go one step without his God (Exod. 33:15). Oh, my brother, if he will but go along with us, what need do we have to be afraid of ten thousand that shall set themselves against us? But without him, the proud helpers fall under the slain (Ps. 3:6; 27:1-3; Isa. 10:4).

As for me, I have been in the battle before now. And though I am alive, as you see, yet I cannot boast of any manhood, for it was through the goodness of Him that is best. I shall be glad if I never any more meet with such shocks, though I fear we are not yet beyond all danger. However, since the lion and the bear have not as yet devoured me, I hope God will also deliver us from the next uncircumcised Philistine. Then Christian sang:

> Poor Little-Faith! Have you been among the thieves?
> Were you robbed? Remember this, whoever believes,
> And gets more faith; then shall you victors be
> Over ten thousand — else scarce over three.

So they went on, and Ignorance followed. They then traveled until they came to a place where they saw a road coming into their road. And it seemed to lie as straight as the way which they should take. And here they did not know which of the two to take, for both seemed straight before them. So they stood still here to consider. And as they were thinking about the way, behold a man came to them, who was black of flesh but covered with a very light robe. And he asked them why they stood there. And they answered that they were going to the Celestial City, but that they did not know which of these ways to take. The man said, Follow me, for it is there that I am going. So they followed him in the way that now came into the road, which by degrees turned. And it turned them so far from the City that they desired to go to that in a little while their faces were turned away from it. Still, they followed him. But by and by, before they were aware of it, he led them both into a net, in which they were both so entangled that they did not know what to do. And then the white robe fell off the black man's back. Then they saw where they were. Therefore they lay there crying for some time, for they could not get themselves out. Then Christian said to his friend:

Chr. Now I see myself in an error. Did not the shepherds tell us to beware of the Flatterer? As it is in the saying of the wise man, so we have found it today, *"A man that flatters his neighbor spreads a net for his feet"* (Prov. 29:5).

Hope. They also gave us a map of directions about the way, so that we might more surely find it. But we have also forgotten to read in it and have not kept ourselves from the paths of the destroyer. Here David was wiser than we, for he said, *"Concerning the works of men, by the word of Your lips I have kept myself from the paths of the destroyer"* (Ps. 17:4).

So they lay in the net mourning within themselves. At last they saw a Shining One coming toward them with a whip of small cords in His hand. When He came to the place where they were, He asked them where they came from and what they were doing there. They told Him that they were poor pilgrims going to Zion, but that they had been led out of their way by a black man clothed in white. And they told Him how he had told them to follow him, since he was going there too. The the One with the whip said, It is Flatterer, *"a false apostle that has transformed himself into an angel of light"* (2 Cor. 11:14, 15; Dan. 11:32). So He tore the net and let the men out. Then He said to them, Follow Me so that I may set you in your way again. So He led them back to the way which they had left to follow the Flatterer. Then He asked them, Where did you stay the last night? They said, With the shepherds on the Delectable Mountains. He then asked them if the shepherds had not given them a map of directions for the way. They answered, Yes. Then He said, But when you were at a standstill you did not take out your map and read it? They answered, No. He asked them, Why? They said they forgot. Then He asked if the shepherds did not warn them to beware of the Flatterer. They answered, Yes, but we did not imagine that this fine-spoken man could be he (Rom. 16:17,18).

Then I saw in my dream that He commanded them to lie down. And when they had done so, He chastised them sorely, to teach them the good way in which they should walk (2 Chr. 6:27). And as He chastised them, He said, *"As many as I love, I rebuke and chasten; be zealous, therefore, and repent"* (Rev. 3:19). This done, He commanded them to go on their way and to be careful to the other directions of the shepherds. So they thanked Him for all His kindness and went softly along the right way, singing:

> Come hither, you that walk along the way,
> See how the pilgrims fare that go astray:
> They are caught in an entangled net,
> 'Cause they good counsel lightly did forget:
> 'Tis true, they rescued were; but yet, you see,
> They're scourged to boot: let this your caution be.

Now after a while they saw one coming softly from a distance, alone and all along the highway, to meet them. Then Christian said to his fellowsaint, Yonder is a man with his back toward Zion, and he is coming to meet us.

Hope. I see him. Let us be careful now lest he should prove to be a Flatterer also. So he drew nearer and nearer, and at last he came up to them. His name was Atheist. And he asked them where they were going?

Chr. We are going to Mount Zion.

Then Atheist fell into a very great fit of laughter.

Chr. What is the meaning of your laughter?

Ath. I laugh to see what ignorant persons you are, to take upon you so tedious a journey. And yet you are not likely to have anything but your travel for your pains.

Chr. Why do you think that we shall not be received?

Ath. Received? There is no such place as you dream of in this world!

Chr. But there is in the world to come.

Ath. When I was at home in my own country, I heard what you are now saying. And from hearing it, I went out to see. And I have been seeking this city these twenty years, but I find no more of it than I did the first day I set out (Eccl. 10:15; Jer. 17:15).

Chr. We have both heard and believe that there is such a place to be found.

Ath. If I had not believed, when I was still at home, I would not have come this far to seek it. But I have found none. And I would have found it, for I have gone further to seek it than you have. I am going back again, and I will seek to refresh myself with the things that I threw away because of the hope which I now see is nothing.

Chr. Then Christian said to his companion Hopeful, Is it true, this which the man has said?

Hope. Be careful, for he is one of the Flatterers. Remember what it cost us once already because we listened to this kind of fellow. What! No Mount Zion! Did we not see the gate of the City from the Delectable Mountains? Also, are we not now to walk in faith (2 Cor. 5:7)? Let us go on, lest the Man with the whip overtake us again. You should have taught me that lesson which I will now pound into your ears, *"My son, stop hearing the instruction that causes you to err from the words of knowledge"* (Prov. 19:27; Heb. 10:39). My brother, I say that you should stop listening to him and let us believe to the saving of our souls.

Chr. My brother, I did not put the question to you because I doubted of the truth of your belief myself, but to test you and to bring forth from you a fruit of the honesty of your heart. As for this man, I know that he is blinded by the god of this world. Let us go on, knowing that we have belief of the truth, and that *"no lie is of the truth"* (1 John 2:21).

Hope. Now I rejoice in hope of the glory of God. So they turned away from the man. And he went his way, laughing at them.

Then I saw in my dream that they went on until they came into a certain country whose air naturally tended to make one drowsy, if he came as a stranger into it. And here Hopeful began to be very dull and heavy in sleep. So he said to Christian, I am beginning to grow so drowsy now that I can scarcely hold my eyes open. Let us lie down here and take one nap.

Chr. By no means, lest we sleep and never wake again.

Hope. Why, my brother? Sleep is sweet to the laboring man. If we take a nap, we shall be refreshed.

Chr. Do you not remember that one of the shepherds told us to beware of the Enchanted Ground? He meant by that that we should beware of sleeping, *"Therefore let us not sleep, as others do, but let us watch and be sober"* (1 Thess. 5:6).

Hope. I acknowledge myself in fault. And if I had been alone here, I would have run the danger of death by sleeping. I see that it is true that the wise man said, that two are better than one (Eccl. 4:9). Until now your company has been my mercy. And you shall have a good reward for your labor.

Chr. Then, in order to prevent drowsiness in this place, let us fall into a good discussion.

Hope. With all my heart.

Chr. Where shall we begin?

Hope. Where God began with us. But you begin, if you please.

Chr. I will first sing you this song:

When saints do sleepy grow, let them come here,

And hear how these two pilgrims talk together;
Yea, let them learn of them in any wise
Thus to keep open their drowsy slumbering eyes.
Saint's fellowship, if it is managed well,
Keeps them away, and that in spite of hell.

Then Christian began, saying, How did you at first think to do what you are now doing?
Hope. Do you mean, how did I first come to look after the good of my soul?
Chr. That is my meaning.
Hope. I continued a great while in the delight of those things which were seen and sold at our fair, things which I now believe would have drowned me in perdition and destruction if I had continued in them.
Chr. What things were they?
Hope. All the treasures and riches of the world. Also I delighted in rioting, reveling, drinking, swearing, lying, uncleanness, sabbath-breaking, and what not — all that tended to destroy my soul. But at last I found by hearing and considering things that are divine, which indeed I heard from you, and also from beloved Faithful (who was put to death for his faith and good living in vanity fair) that *"the end of these things is death"* and that it was *"for these things' sake the wrath of God comes on the children of disobedience"* (Rom. 6:21; Eph. 5:6).
Chr. And did you fall under the power of this conviction at once?
Hope. No, I did not at once know the evil of sin, nor the condemnation that follows when one commits it. But when my mind at first began to be shaken with the word, I tried to shut my eyes against the light of it.
Chr. But what was the reason that you carried it to the first workings of God's blessed Spirit on you?
Hope. The reasons were these, (1) that I was ignorant that this was the work of God on me; I never thought that by awakenings for sin God at first begins the conversion of a sinner; (2), Sin was yet very sweet to my flesh, and I hated to leave it (3), I could not tell how to part with my old companions, their presence and actions were so desirable to me (4), the hours in which the convictions came to me were such troublesome and such heart-frightening hours that I could not bear so much as the remembrance of them on my heart.
Chr. Then, as it seems, you sometimes got rid of your trouble?
Hope. Yes, indeed. but it would come into my mind again, and then I would be as bad, no, worse than I was before.
Chr. Why, what was it that brought your sins to mind again?
Hope. Many things, such as, (1) If I but met a good man in the street; or, (2) if I heard anything read from the Bible; or, (3) if my head began to ache; or, (4) if I were told that some of my neighbors were sick; or, (5) if I heard the bell toll for some that were dead; or, (6) if I thought of dying myself; or, (7) if I heard that sudden death had happened to others; (8) but especially when I thought to myself that I must quickly come to judgment.
Chr. And could you at any time easily get rid of the guilt of sin when it came upon you by any of these ways?
Hope. No, not I. For then they took a faster hold on my conscience. And then, if I but thought of going back to sin (though my mind had turned against it), it would be double torment to me.
Chr. And how did you act then?
Hope. I thought I must try to mend my life. Or else I thought that I am surely to be condemned.
Chr. And did you try to mend it?
Hope. Yes. And I not only fled from my sins, but from sinful company too. And I took up religious duties, such as praying and reading, weeping for sin and speaking truth to my

neighbors, etc. I did these things and many others too many to relate here.

Chr. And did you think well of yourself then?

Hope. Yes, for a while. But at last my trouble would come tumbling on me again, and that over the neck of all my reformation.

Chr. How did that come about, since you were now reformed?

Hope. There were several things that brought it on me, especially such sayings as these, *"All our righteousnesses are as filthy rags;" "By the works of the law no one shall be justified;" "When you have done all these things, say, We are unprofitable"* (Isa. 64:6; Gal. 2:16; Luke 17:10). From which I began to reason with myself in this way: If all my righteousnesses are as filthy rags; if by the deeds of the law no one can be justified; and if, when we have done all, we are yet unprofitable, then it is but foolishness to think of Heaven coming by the law. I further thought in this way: If a man runs into the shopkeeper's debt for a hundred pounds, and after that pay for all that he shall get, still if his old debt stands still uncrossed in the book, the shopkeeper may sue him for it and throw him into prison until he shall pay the debt.

Chr. Well, and how did you apply this to yourself?

Hope. Why, I thought this way within myself: I have run a great way into God's book by my sins. And if I now reform it will not pay off that old score. Therefore I must still remember that in spite of my present reforms, I cannot be freed from that condemnation that I brought on myself because of my former transgressions.

Chr. A very good application, but please go on.

Hope. Another thing that has troubled me ever since my late reforms is this, that if I look narrowly into the best of what I do now, I still see sin, new sin, mixing itself with the best that I do. So now I am forced to conclude that in spite of my former fond conceits of myself and my duties, I have committed enough sin in one day to send me to hell, however faultless my former life may have been.

Chr. And what did you do then?

Hope. Do? I could not tell what to do, until I spoke my mind to Faithful. For he and I were well acquainted. And he told me that unless I could obtain the righteousness of a man that had never sinned, neither my own nor all the righteousness of the world could save me.

Chr. And did you think that he spoke the truth?

Hope. If he had told me this when I was pleased and satisfied with my own amendments, I would have called him a fool for his pains. But now, since I see my own infirmity and the sin which cleaves to my best performance, I have been forced to be of his opinion.

Chr. But when he first suggested it, did you think that there was such a man to be found, one of whom it might justly be said, that he never committed sin?

Hope. I must confess that the words at first sounded strangely. But after a little more talk and company with him, I had full conviction about it.

Chr. And did you ask him who this man was and how you must be justified by him? (Rom. 4; Col. 1; Heb. 10; 2 Pet. 1).

Hope. Yes, and he told me that it was the Lord Jesus, who dwells on high at the right hand of the Most High. And he said, So you must be justified by Him, even by trusting to what He has done by Himself in the days of His flesh, and that which he suffered when He hung on the tree. I asked him, further, how that Man's righteousness could be of such efficacy as to justify another before God. And he told me He was the mighty God, and that He did what He did, and died the death also, not for Himself but for me, to whom His doings, and the worthiness of them, should be imputed if I believed on Him.

Chr. And what did you do then?

Hope. I made my objections against my believing, because I thought He was not willing to save me.

Chr. And what did Faithful say to you then?

Hope. He told me to go to Him and see. Then I saw that it would be presumption to do so. But he said, No, for you are invited to come (Matt. 11:28). Then he gave me a book of Jesus' writing, to encourage me the more freely to come. And he said as to that book, that every jot and tittle of it stood firmer than the heavens and the earth (Matt. 24:35). Then I asked him what I must do when I came to Him. And he told me that I must beg on my knees (Ps. 95:6; Jer. 29:12,13; Dan. 6:10), with all my heart and soul, the Father to reveal Him to me. Then I further asked him how I must make my supplications to Him. And he said, Go, and you shall find Him on a mercy-seat (Exod. 25:22; Lev. 16:2; Heb. 4:16), where he sits all the year long, to give pardon and forgiveness to those that come. I told him that I did not know what to say when I came. And he told me to say something to this effect, *"God be merciful to me a sinner"* and, 'Make me to know and to believe in Jesus Christ, for I see that if His righteousness had never been, or if I do not have faith in that righteousness, then I am utterly cast away. Lord, I have heard that You are a merciful God and that You have ordained that Your Son Jesus Christ should be the Savior of the world. And also I have heard that You are willing to give Him to such a poor sinner as I am (and I am truly a sinner!). Lord, then take this opportunity and magnify Your grace in the salvation of my soul, through Your Son Jesus Christ. Amen.'

Chr. And did you do as you were told?

Hope. Yes, over and over and over.

Chr. And did the Father reveal the Son to you?

Hope. Not at first, nor second, nor third, nor fourth, nor fifth, no, not at the sixth time either.

Chr. What did you do then?

Hope. Why, I could not tell what to do.

Chr. Did you not have thoughts of leaving off praying?

Hope. Yes, and a hundred times over.

Chr. And what was the reason you did not?

Hope. I believed that what had been told me was true, that without the righteousness of this Christ all the world could not save me. And so I thought within myself that if I would quit, then I would die. And if I kept on, then I could but die at the throne of grace. And this came into my mind, *"Though it lingers, wait for it; because it will surely come. It will not be long"* (Hab. 2:3). So I continued to pray until the Father showed me His Son.

Chr. And how was He revealed to you?

Hope. I did not see Him with my bodily eyes, but with the eyes of my understanding (Eph. 1:18;19). And this is how it happened: one day I was very sad, I think sadder than at any one time in my life. And this sadness was because of a fresh sight of the greatness and vileness of my sins. And as I was then looking for nothing but hell, and the everlasting condemnation of my soul, suddenly I thought that I saw the Lord Jesus look down from Heaven at me and say, *"Believe on the Lord Jesus Christ and you shall be saved"* (Acts 16:30,31). But I replied, Lord, I am a great, a very great sinner. And He answered, *"My grace is sufficient for you."* Then I said, Lord, what is believing? And then I was shown that that saying, *"He that comes to Me shall never hunger, and he that believes on Me shall never thirst"* (John 6:35) meant that believing and coming were all one. He that came, then, that is he who ran out in his heart and affections after salvation by Christ, he indeed believed in Christ. Then the tears stood in my eyes. And I asked further, But, Lord, may such a great sinner as I am be indeed accepted by You and be saved by You? And I heard Him say, *"And he that comes to Me I will in no way cast out"* (John 6:37). Then I said, But, O Lord, how must I consider You in my coming to You, so that my faith may be placed right on You? Then He said, *"Christ Jesus came into the world to save sinners; He is the end of the law for righteousness to everyone who believes; He died for our sins and rose again for our justification; He loved us and washed us from our sins in His own blood; He is the Mediator between God and us; He ever lives to make intercession for us"* (1 Tim. 1:15; Rom. 10:4; Heb. 7:24,25). From all of this I gathered that I must look for righteousness in His person, and for satisfaction for my sins by His blood. And I saw that what He did in obedience to His Father's law, and in submitting to the penalty of it, was not for Himself, but for him that will accept it for his salvation, and be thankful. And now my heart was full of joy, my eyes were full of tears, and my affections were running over with love to the name, people and ways of Jesus Christ.

Chr. This was a revelation of Christ to your soul indeed. But tell me particularly what effect this had on your spirit.

Hope. It made me see that all the world, notwithstanding all the righteousness of it, is in a state of condemnation. It made me see that God the Father, though He is just, can justly justify the coming sinner. It made me greatly ashamed of the vileness of my former life, and it confounded me with the sense of my own ignorance. For before now there never came a thought into my heart that revealed to me so much the beauty of Jesus Christ. It made me love a holy life and to long to do something for the honor and glory of the name of the Lord Jesus. Yea, I thought that if I had now a thousand gallons of blood in my body, I could spill all of it for the sake of the Lord Jesus.

Then I saw in my dream that Hopeful looked back and saw Ignorance, whom they had left behind. Look, he said to Christian, see how far yonder youngster loiters behind?

Chr. Yes, I see him. He does not care for our company.

Hope. But I think it would not have hurt him if he had kept pace with us before now.

Chr. That is true. But I'll warrant you he thinks otherwise.

Hope. That I think he does. But, however, let us wait for him.

So they did. Then Christian said to him, Come away, man. Why do you stay so far behind?

Ignor. I take my pleasure in walking alone, even more a great deal than in company, unless I like the company better.

Then Christian said to Hopeful softly, Did I not tell you he did not care for our company? However, he said to him, Come up and let us talk away the time in this solitary place. Then directing his speech to Ignorance, he said, Come. How are you doing? How is it between God and your soul now?

Ignor. I hope well, for I am always full of good notions that come into my mind to comfort me as I walk.

Chr. What good motions? Please tell us.

Ignor. Why I think of God and Heaven.

Chr. So do the demons and condemned souls.

Ignor. But I think of them and desire them.

Chr. So do many that are never likely to come there, *"The soul of the lazy man desires, yet has nothing"* (Prov. 13:4).

Ignor. But I think of them, and I leave all for them.

Chr. I doubt that. For to leave all is a very hard matter. Yes, it is a harder matter than many are aware of. But why, or for what, are you persuaded that you have left all for God and Heaven?

Ignor. My heart tells me so.

Chr. The wise man says, *"He that trusts in his own heart is a fool"* (Prov. 28:26).

Ignor. That is spoken of an evil heart, but my heart is a good one.

Chr. But how do you prove that?

Ignor. It comforts me in hopes of Heaven.

Chr. That may be through its deceitfulness, for a man's heart may minister comfort to him in the hopes of something for which he has yet no ground to hope.

Ignor. But my heart and life agree together, and therefore my hope is well grounded.

Chr. Who told you that your heart and your life agree together?

Ignor. My heart tells me so.

Chr. You may as well ask your fellow if you are a thief. Your heart tells you so? Except the word of God bears witness in this matter, other testimony is of no value.

Ignor. But is it not a good heart that has good thoughts? And is it not a good life that is according to God's commandments?

Chr. Yes, that is a good heart that has good thoughts, and that is a good life that is according to God's commandments — but it is one thing to truly have these, and it is another thing merely to think so.

Ignor. Please tell me what you consider to be good thoughts, and what is a life that is according to God's commandments?

Chr. There are good thoughts of various kinds, some respecting ourselves, some God, some Christ, and some other things.

Ignor. What are good thoughts respecting ourselves?

Chr. When we pass the same judgment on ourselves which the word of God passes on us. To explain myself: The word of God says of persons in a natural condition, *"There is none righteous, there is none that does good"* (Rom. 3:10). It also says that *"Every imagination of the heart of man is only evil, and that continually"* (Gen. 6:5). And again it says, *"The imagination of man's heart is evil from his youth."* Now, then, when we think this way of ourselves, having understanding of it, then our thoughts are good ones, because they are according to the word of God.

Ignor. I will never believe that my heart is that bad.

Chr. Then you never had one good thought concerning yourself in your life. But let me go on. As the word passes a judgment on our hearts, so it passes a judgment on our ways. And when the thoughts of our hearts and ways agree with the judgment which the word gives of both, then both are good, because they agree to the word.

Ignor. Make out your meaning to me.

Chr. Why, the word of God says that man's ways are crooked ways, not good, but perverse (Ps. 125:5). It says that they are naturally out of the good way, that they have not known it (Prov. 2:15; Rom. 3:12). Now when a man thinks of his ways in this way — I say when he does so with understanding and with heart-humiliation — then he has good thoughts of his own ways, because his thoughts now agree with the judgment of the word of God.

Ignor. What are good thoughts concerning God?

Chr. Even (as I have said concerning ourselves) when our thoughts of God agree with what the word says of Him. And that is this, when we think of His being and attributes as the word has taught, of which I cannot at large discourse now. But to speak of Him with reference to us: When we think that He knows us better than we know ourselves, when we can see that He sees sin in us which we cannot see in ourselves, then we have right thoughts of God. Also when we think that He knows our inmost thoughts, and that our heart with all its depths is always open to His eyes; and when we think that all our righteousness stinks in His nostrils, and that He then cannot abide to see us stand before Him in any confidence, even in all our best performances, then we have right thoughts of God.

Ignor. Do you think that I am such a fool as to think that God can see no further than I? Do you think that I would come to God in the best of my performances?

Chr. Why, what do you think in this matter?

Ignor. To be brief, I think that I must believe in Christ for justification.

Chr. How? Do you think you must believe in Christ when you do not see your need of Him? You neither see your original sin nor your actual infirmities. but you have such an opinion of yourself and of what you do as plainly causes you to be one that never did see the necessity of Christ's personal righteousness to justify you before God. How, then, do you say, I believe in Christ?

Ignor. I believe well enough for that.

Chr. How do you believe?

Ignor. I believe that Christ died for sinners, and that I shall be justified before God from the curse through His gracious acceptance of my obedience to His laws. Put it this way, Christ makes my duties that are religious acceptable to His Father by virtue of His merits. And so I shall be justified.

Chr. Let me give an answer to this confession of your faith:

1. You believe with an imaginary faith. For this faith is nowhere described in the word.

2. You believe with a false faith, because it takes justification from the personal righteousness of Christ and applies it to your own.

3. This faith does not make Christ a justifier of your person, but of your actions; and of your person for your action's sake, which is a false faith.

4. Therefore this faith is deceitful, even the kind that will leave you under wrath in the day of God Almighty. For true justifying faith causes the soul to flee for refuge to Christ's righteousness, being sensible of its lost condition by the law. And this righteousness of Christ's is not an act of grace by which He makes, for justification, your obedience to be accepted with God. But it is His personal obedience to the law, in doing and suffering for us what the law required at our hands. I say that this righteousness will be accepted by true faith, and under its skirt the soul will be shrouded, and by it we will be presented as spotless before God and is accepted and acquitted from condemnation.

Ignor. What? Would you have us trust to what Christ in His own person has done without us? This conceit would loosen the reins of our lusts and permit us to live as we desire. For what does it matter how we live if we may be justified by Christ's personal righteousness from all, when we believe it?

Chr. Ignorance is your name, and as your name is, so you are. Your answer demonstrates what I say. You are ignorant of what justifying righteousness is, and equally ignorant as to how to secure your soul, through its faith, from the heavy wrath of God. Yea, you are also ignorant of the true effects of saving faith in this righteousness of Christ, which is to bow and win over the heart to God in Christ, to love His name, His word, His ways, and His people — it is not as you ignorantly imagine.

Hope. Ask him if he ever had Christ revealed to him from Heaven.

Ignor. What? You are a man for revelations! I believe that what both you and all the rest of you say about that matter is but the fruit of distracted brains.

Hope. Why, man? Chirst is so hidden in God from the natural apprehensions of the flesh that He cannot be savingly known by any man except God the Father reveals Him to him (Matt. 11:27).

Ignor. This is your faith, it is not mine. But I do not doubt that my faith is as good as yours, though I have not as many whimsies in my head as you do.

Chr. Please allow me to put in a word. You ought not to speak so lightly of this matter. For I will boldly affirm this, even as my good companion has, that no one can know Jesus Christ but by the revelation of the Father. Yes, and also that faith by which the soul lays hold on Christ (if it is a right faith) must be worked in us by the exceeding greatness of His mighty power (1 Cor. 12:3; Eph. 1:17-19). And I see, poor Ignorance, that you are ignorant of the working of that kind of faith. Then be awakened. See your own wretchedness and flee to the Lord Jesus. And by His righteousness, which is the righteousness of God (for He Himself is God), you shall be delivered from condemnation.

Ignor. You go so fast I cannot keep pace with you. You go on before me. I must stay behind awhile. Then they said:

> Well, Ignorance, wilt thou yet foolish be
> To slight good counsel, ten times given thee?
> And if thou yet refuse it, thou shalt know,
> Ere long, the evil of thy doing so.
> Remember, man, in time; stoop, do not fear:
> Good counsel taken well, saves; therefore hear.
> But if thou yet shalt slight it, thou wilt be
> The loser, Ignorance, I'
> The loser, Ignorance, I'll warrant thee.

Then Christian said this to his fellow:

Chr. Well, come, my good Hopeful, I see that you and I must walk by ourselves again.

So I saw in my dream that they went on speedily. And Ignorance came hobbling after. Then Christian said to his companion, I pity this poor man. It will certainly go ill with him at the last.

Hope. Alas! There are more than enough in our town in this condition. Whole families, yea, whole streets, even of pilgrims, are like this. And if there are so many in our country, how many do you think there must be in the place where he was born?

Chr. Indeed, the word says, *"He has blinded their eyes lest they should see, etc."*

But now we are by ourselves, what do you think of such men? Have they no convictions of sin at any time? And if so, do they not fear that their state is dangerous?

Hope. You are the oldest, you answer that question yourself.

Chr. Then I say that sometimes I think they may. But being naturally ignorant, they do not understand that such convictions are for their good. And so they desperately seek to stifle them, and they presumptuously continue to flatter themselves in the way of their own hearts.

Hope. As you say, I also believe that fear tends to the good of men, making them right at their beginning to go on pilgrimage.

Chr. It does without doubt, if it is right. For the word says so, *"The fear of the Lord is the beginning of wisdom"* (Job 28:28; Ps. 111:10; Prov. 1:7; 9:10).

Hope. How do you describe right fear?

Chr. True fear is revealed by three things, (1) By its rise, for it is caused by saving convictions of sin; (2) It drives the soul to lay fast hold of Christ for salvation; (3) It gives birth to a great reverence for God in the soul, and it continues in the soul, making it afraid to turn away from them either to the right hand or to the left; it will not allow a turning to anything that may dishonor God, break its peace, grieve the Spirit, or cause the enemy to speak reproachfully.

Hope. Well said. I believe you have said the truth. Are we now almost past the Enchanted Ground?

Chr. Why? Are you weary of this discussion?

Hope. Truly, no, but I want to know where we are.

Chr. We now have no more than two miles further to go in it. But let us return to our matter. Now the ignorant do not know that such convictions as tend to put them into fear are for their good. And that is why they seek to stifle them.

Hope. How do they seek to stifle them?

Chr. They think that those fears are worked by the devil (though indeed they are worked by God). And thinking so, they resist them, as things that directly tend to their overthrow. They also think that these fears tend to spoil their faith, whereas, alas for them, they are poor men with no faith at all! And so they harden their hearts against them. They presume that they ought not to fear, and so in spite of themselves they become presumptuously confident. They see that those fears tend to take away from them their pitiful self-holiness, and so they resist them with all their might.

Hope. I know something of this myself. For before I knew myself, it was so with me.

Chr. Well, for now we will leave our neighbor Ignorance by himself. Let us take up another profitable question.

Hope. With all my heart. But you still should begin.

Chr. Well, then, did you happen to know one Temporary in your community, about ten years ago, who was a forward man in religion then?

Hope. Know him? Yes, he lived in Graceless, a town about two miles from Honesty. And He lived next door to one Turnback.

Chr. Right. He lived under the same roof with him. Well, that man was much awakened once. I believe that then he had some sight of his sins, and of the wages that were due to them.

Hope. I agree, because my house was not more than three miles from him. And he would often come to me with many tears in his eyes. Truly I pitied the man, and I was not altogether without hope for him. But one may see that it is not everyone that cries, "Lord, Lord."

Chr. He once told me that he was resolved to go on pilgrimage, as we are going now. But all of a sudden he grew acquainted with one Save-self, and then he became a stranger to me.

Hope. Now, since we are talking about him, let us inquire a little into the reason for his sudden backsliding, and that of others like him.

Chr. It may be very profitable. But you begin.

Hope. Well, then, there are in my judgment four reasons for it:

1. Though the consciences of such men are awakened, yet their minds are not changed. Therefore, when the power of guilt wears away, that which provoked them to be religious ceases. Therefore they naturally turn to their old course again, even as we see the dog that is sick of what he has eaten, so long as his sickness prevails, vomit and throw up all. It is not that he does this of a free mind (if we may say that a dog has a mind), but because it troubles his stomach. But when his sickness is over, and his stomach is eased, his desires no longer being alienated from his vomit, he turns around and licks up all. And so it is true which is written, *"The dog has turned to his own vomit again"* (2 Pet. 2:22). So I say, being hot for heaven only because of the sense and fear of the torments of hell, then as their sense of hell and their fear of damnation chills and cools, so their desires for Heaven and salvation cool also. So then when their guilt and fear is gone, their desires for Heaven and happiness die. And they then return to their course again.

2. Another reason is that they have slavish fears that overmaster them. I speak now of the fears that they have of men, *"for the fear of man brings a snare"* (Prov. 29:25). So then, though they seem to be hot for Heaven as long as the flames of hell are about their ears, yet when that terror is over, they begin to think second thoughts. And they then think that it is good to be wise, and not to run the hazard of losing all for something they find doubtful. Nor can they see bringing themselves into unavoidable and unnecessary troubles, and so they fall in with the world again.

3. The shame that attends religion lies also as a block in their way. They are proud and haughty, and religion in their eye is low and contemptible; So when they have lost their sense of hell and the wrath to come, they return again to their former course.

4. Guilt, and the meditation on terror, are grievous to them. They do not like to see their misery before they come into it (though perhaps the sight of it at first, if they loved that sight, might make them flee where the righteous flee, and are safe). But as I hinted before, because they shun the thoughts of guilt and terror, therefore when they once get rid of their awakenings about the terrors and wrath of God, they gladly harden their hearts. And they choose such ways as will harden them more and more.

Chr. You are pretty near the business, for the bottom of it all is this, that they lack a change in their mind and will. And so they are but like the felon that stands before the judge. He quakes and trembles and seems to repent most heartily. But the bottom of it all is that he fears the rope, and not that he has any detestation for the offense (as is evident, for if you let this man have his liberty, then he will be a thief, and so a rogue, still. But if his mind was changed, he would be otherwise).

Hope. Now that I have shown you the reason they go back, now you show me how they go back.

Chr. So I will, willingly:

1. They draw off their thoughts, all that they can, from the remembrance of God, death, and judgment to come.

2. They then cast off by degrees all private duties, such as closet prayer, curbing their lusts, watching, sorrow for sin, etc.

3. Then they shun the company of lively and warm Christians.

4. Afterward they grow cold to public duty, such as hearing, reading, godly conferences, etc.

5. Then they begin to pick holes, as we say, in the coats of some of the godly, and that

devilishly, so that they may have some excuse to throw religion behind their backs (because of some infirmities they have espied in them).

6. Then they begin to adhere to and associate themselves with carnal, loose and wanton men.

7. Then they give way to carnal and wanton discourses in secret. And they are glad if they can see such things in any that are counted to be honest, so that they may the more boldly do it through their example.

8. After this, they begin to play with little sins openly.

9. And then, being hardened, they reveal themselves as they are. So, being launched again into the gulf of misery, unless a miracle of grace prevents it, they everlastingly perish in their own deceits.

Now I saw in my dream that by this time the pilgrims had passed over the Enchanted Ground. And they entered into the country of Beulah (Isa. 62:4-12; Song of Solomon 2:10-12).

The air was very sweet and pleasant in Beulah land. And so they rested and comforted themselves there for a time, the way lying directly through it. Yes, here they heard continually the singing of birds, and every day they saw the flowers appear in the earth, and they heard the voice of the turtle in the land. In this country the sun shines night and day, therefore this was beyond the Valley of the Shadow of Death, and also it was out of the reach of Giant Despair. Nor could those in this place so much as see Doubting Castle. Here they were within sight of the City they were going to. Also some of the inhabitants of it met them here, for in this land the Shining Ones commonly walked, because it was on the borders of Heaven. In this land also the contract between the Bride and the Bridegroom was renewed. Yea, *"as the bridegroom rejoices over the bride, so does their God rejoice over them."* Here they did not lack corn or wine, for in this place they found an abundance of what they had sought during all their pilgrimage. Here they heard voices from out of the City, loud voices saying, *"Say to the daughter of Zion, Behold, your salvation comes! Behold, His reward is with Him."* Here all the inhabitants of the country called them, *"The holy people, the redeemed of the Lord, sought out, etc."*

Now as they walked in this land, they had more rejoicing than in those countries which were more remote from the kingdom to which they were bound. And drawing near to the City, they had still a more perfect view of it. It was built of pearls and precious stones, and its streets were paved with gold, so that because of the natural glory of the city, and the reflection of the sunbeams on it, Christian fell sick with desire. Hopeful also had a fit or two of the same disease. So they lay by it a while, crying out because of their pangs, "If you see my Beloved, tell Him that I am sick of love."

But, being strengthened a little, and being better able to bear their sickness, they walked on their way. And they came yet nearer and nearer, where there were orchards, vineyards, and gardens with their gates opened to the highway. Now as they came up to these places, behold, the gardener stood in the way. And the pilgrims said to him, Whose beautiful vineyards and gardens are these? He answered, They are the King's, and they are planted here for His own delight, but also for the solace of pilgrims. So the gardener brought them into the vineyards, and he told them to refresh themselves with the dainties (Deut. 23:24). He also showed them the King's walks and harbors there, where He delighted to be. And they stayed here and slept.

Now I saw in my dream that they talked more in their sleep than at any other time in all their journey. And meditating thereabout, the gardener said to me, Why do you meditate about the matter. It is the nature of the fruit of the grapes of these vineyards to go down so sweetly as to cause the lips of those that are asleep to speak.

So I saw that when they awoke they addressed themselves to go up to the City. But, as I said, the reflection of the sun on the City (for the City was pure gold—Rev. 21:18; 2 Cor. 3:18) was so extremely glorious that they could not as yet behold it with open face. So they looked through an instrument made for that purpose. So I saw that, as they went on, two men in clothing that shone like gold met them, and their faces also shone like the light. These men asked the pilgrims where they came from, and they told them. They also asked them where they had lodged, what difficulties and dangers, what comforts and pleasures they had met with in the way. And they told them. Then the men that met them said, You have only two difficulties more to overcome, and then you are in the City.

Then Christian and his companion asked the men to go along with them. So they told them that they would. But, they said, you must obtain it by your own faith. So I saw in my dream that they went on together until they came within sight of the gate.

And I further saw that there was a river between them and the gate. But there was no bridge to go over, and the river was very deep. So at the sight of this river, the pilgrims were stunned. But the men that went with them said, You must go through, or you cannot come to the sight of the gate. The pilgrims then began to ask if there was no other way to the gate. To which they answered, Yes, but only two (Enoch and Elijah) have been permitted to travel that path since the foundation of the world, nor shall any other until the last trumpet shall sound. Then the pilgrims, especially Christian, began to be despondent in his mind. And they looked this way and that, but no way could be found by them by which they might escape the river. Then they asked the men if the waters were all of one depth. They said, No. Yet they could not help them in that way, for, they said, you will find it deeper or more shallow as you believe in the King of the place.

They then addressed themselves to the water. And as he entered, Christian began to sink. And he cried out to his good friend Hopeful, saying, I am sinking in deep waters, the billows are over my head, all His waves go over me. Selah. Then the other said, Be comforted, my brother, for I feel the bottom and it is good. Then Christian said, Ah, my friend, the sorrow of death has encompassed me. I shall not see the land that flows with milk and honey. And with that a great darkness and horror fell on Christian, so that he could not see before him. And also he here in a great measure lost his senses, so that he could neither remember any of those sweet refreshments he had experienced in the way of pilgrimage, or talk of them. But all the words that he spoke still tended to reveal that he had horror of mind and heart-fears that he would die in that river and never obtain entrance in at the gate. Here also, as they that stood by perceived, he was much in troublesome thoughts of the sins that he had committed, both since and before he began to be a pilgrim. It was also seen that he was troubled with frightening apparitions and evil spirits. For now and again he would intimate so much by words.

So Hopeful had much difficulty in keeping his brother's head above water. Yea, sometimes he would be submerged, then before long he would rise up again, half dead. Hopeful also tried to comfort him, saying, Brother, I see the gate, and men are standing by it to receive us. But Christian would answer, Tis you, Tis you they are waiting for. For you have been hopeful ever since I met you. And so have you, said Hopeful to Christian. Ah, brother, said Christian, surely if I was right, He would now arise to help me. But for my sins He has brought me into the snare and has left me. Then Hopeful said, My brother, you have completely forgotten the text, where it is said of the wicked, *"There are no bands in their death, but their strength is firm; they are not troubled as other men are, nor are they plagued like other men."* These troubles and distresses that you go through in these waters are no sign that God has forsaken you. But they are sent to try you, to see if you will call to mind that which you have before received of His goodness, and so live on Him in your distresses.

Then I saw in my dream that Christian was in meditation for a while. And Hopeful added these words to him, Be comforted, for Jesus Christ makes you whole. And with that Christian broke out with a loud voice, Oh, I see Him again! And He is telling me, *"When you pass through the waters, I will be with you; and through the rivers, they shall not overflow you"* (Isa. 43:2). Then they both took courage, and after that the enemy was still as a stone, until they had gone over. Christian then soon found ground to stand on, and so it followed that the rest of the river was but shallow. So they got over.

Now on the bank of the river, on the other side, they saw the two shining men again, waiting for them. Then having come out of the river, they greeted them, saying, We are ministering spirits sent out to minister to those that shall be heirs of salvation. So they went along towards the gate. Now, you must note, the City stood on a mighty hill. But the pilgrims went up that hill with ease because they had these two men to lead them up by the arms. Also, they had left their mortal garments behind them in the river, for though they went in with them, they came out without them. They therefore went up here with much agility and speed, though the foundation on which the City was framed was higher than the clouds. So they went up through the region of the air, sweetly talking as they went, being comforted because they had safely crossed the river, and they had such glorious companions to attend them.

The talk that they had with the shining ones was about the glory of the place. They told them that the beauty and glory of it was inexpressible. They said, There is *"Mount Zion, the heavenly Jerusalem, the innumerable company of angels, and the spirits of just men. made perfect"* (Heb. 12:22-24). They said, You are now going to the paradise of God, where you shall see the tree of life and eat of the never-fading fruits of it. And when you come there, you shall have white robes given you, and your walk and talk shall every day be with the King, even all the days of eternity (Rev. 2:7; 3:4,5; 22:5). You shall not see there again such things as you saw when you were in the lower region on the earth; there shall be no sorrow, no sickness, no affliction or death, *"for the former things have passed away"* (Isa. 65:16,17). You are now going to Abraham, to Isaac and Jacob, and to the prophets, men that God has taken away from the evil to come, and that are now resting on their beds, each one walking in his righteousness. The men then asked, What must we do in the holy place? They answered them, You must there receive the comfort of your toil and have joy for all your sorrow. You must reap that which you have sown, even the fruit of all your prayers, and tears, and sufferings for the King by the way (Gal. 6:7,8). In that place you must wear crowns of gold and enjoy the perpetual sight and vision of the Holy One, for *"there you shall see Him as He is"* (1 John 3:2). There you also shall serve Him continually with praise, with shouting and thanksgiving, whom you desired to serve in the world, though with much difficulty, because of the infirmity of your flesh. There your eyes shall be delighted with seeing, and your ears with hearing, the pleasant form and voice of the Mighty One. There you shall enjoy your friends again that have gone there before you. And there you shall with joy receive everyone that follows into the holy place after you. There you also shall be clothed with glory and majesty, and shall be put into a carriage fit to ride out with the King of Glory. When He shall come with sound of trumpet in the clouds, as on the wings of the wind, you shall come with Him. And when He shall sit on the throne of judgment, you shall sit beside Him. Yea, and when He shall pass sentence on all the workers of iniquity, whether they are angels or men, you also shall have a voice in that judgment, because they were His and your enemies. Also when He shall again return to the City, you shall go too, with sound of trumpet and be ever with Him (1 Thes. 4:13-17; Jude 14,15; Dan. 7:9,10; 1 Cor. 6:2,3).

Now while they were thus drawing towards the gate, behold a company of the heavenly host came out to meet them. And the two shining ones said to them, These are the men that have loved our Lord while they were in the world, and they have left all for His holy name. And He has sent us to bring them, and we have brought them this far on their desired journey so that they may go in and look their Redeemer in the face with joy. Then the heavenly host gave a great shout, saying, *"Blessed are they that are called to the marriage-supper of the Lamb"* (Rev. 19:9). Also at this time, several of the King's trumpeters came out to meet them, clothed in white and shining clothing. And with melodious and loud noises, they made even the heavens to echo with their sound. These trumpeters saluted Christian and his companion with ten thousand welcomes from the world. And they did this with shouting and sound of trumpet.

This done, they surrounded them, some going before, some behind; some on the right hand, some on the left (as it were to guard them through the upper regions); continually sounding as they went, with melodious sounds, in notes on high. So the very sight was to them that could see it as if Heaven itself had come down to meet them. Then they walked on together in this way. And as they walked, every now and then these trumpeters, even with joyful sound, by mixing their music with looks and gestures, would still signify to Christian and his brother how welcome they were into their company, and with what gladness they came to meet them. And now, as it were, these two men were in Heaven, before they came to it, being swallowed up with the sight of angels, and with hearing their melodious notes. Here also they had the City itself in view. And they thought they heard all the bells in it ring to welcome them to it. But, above all, the warm and joyful thoughts that they had about their own dwelling there, with such company, and that for ever and ever — Oh, by what tongue or pen can their glorious joy be expressed? So they came up to the gate.

Now when they had come up to the gate, there was written on it in letters of gold, *"BLESSED ARE THEY THAT DO HIS COMMANDMENTS, THAT THEY MAY HAVE RIGHT TO THE TREE OF LIFE AND MAY ENTER IN THROUGH THE GATES INTO THE CITY"* (Rev. 22:14).

Then I saw in my dream that the shining men commanded them to call at the gate. And when they did, some looked down from above, over the gate, even Enoch, Moses, Elijah, etc. And it was said to them, These pilgrims have come from the city of Destruction because of the love they bear to the King of this place. And then the pilgrims gave to them his certificate, which they had received in the beginning. Then they were carried in to the King. And when He had read them, He said, Where are the men? And they answered, They are standing outside the gate. Then the King commanded them to open the gate, *"that the righteous nation that keeps the truth may enter in"* (Isa. 26:2).

Now I saw in my dream that these two men went in at the gate. And, lo, as they entered, they were transfigured. And they were clothed in garments that shone like gold. Some also met them with harps and crowns, giving these to them; the harps for praise, and the crowns in token of honor. Then I heard in my dream that all the bells in the City rang again for joy, and they were invited to *"Enter into the joy of our Lord."* I also heard the men themselves as they sang with a loud voice, saying, *"Blessing, and honor, and glory, and power be to Him that sits on the throne, and to the Lamb, forever and ever"* (Rev. 5:13).

Now, just as the gates were opened to let in the men, I looked after them. And, behold, the City shone like the sun. And the streets were paved with gold. And many men walked in them, with crowns on their heads, palms in their hands, and golden harps to sing praises with.

Also some of them had wings, and they answered one another without intermission, saying, *"Holy, holy, holy is the Lord!"* which when I had seen, I wished myself among them.

Now while I was gazing on all these things, I turned my head to look back. And I saw Ignorance come up to the riverside. But he soon got over, and that without half the difficulty which the other two men met with. For it happened that there was then in that place one Vain-hope, a ferryman, who helped him over with his boat. So he, like the others I saw, went up the hill to come up to the gate. Only he came alone, nor did anyone meet him with the least encouragement. When he had come up to the gate, he looked at the writing that was above. And then he began to knock, supposing that entrance would be quickly given to him. But he was asked by the men that looked over the top of the gate, Where did you come from, and what do you want? He answered, I have eaten and drunk in the presence of the King, and He has taught in our streets. Then they asked him for his certificate so that they might go in and show it to the King. So he fumbled in his bosom for one and found none. Then they said, Do you not have one? But the man never answered a word. So they told the King, but He would not come down to see him, but He commanded the two shining ones that conducted Christian and Hopeful to the City to go out and take Ignorance, binding him hand and foot, and to carry him away. Then they took him up and carried him through the air to the door that I saw in the side of the hill.

And they put him in there. Then I saw that there was a way to hell, even from the gates of Heaven, as well as from the city of Destruction. So I awoke, and behold, it was a dream.

## CONCLUSION

Now, Reader, I have told my dream to thee,
See if you can interpret it to me,
Or to yourself, or neighbor; but take heed
Of misinterpreting; for that, instead
Of doing good, will but yourself abuse;
By misinterpreting, evil ensues.

Take heed also that you be not extreme
In playing with the outside of my dream;
Nor let my figure or similitude
Put you into a laughter or feud.
Leave this for boys and fools; but as for thee,
Do thou the substance of my matter see.

Put by the curtains, look within my veil,
Turn up my metaphors, and do not fail.
There, if you seek them, such things you'll find
As will be helpful to an honest mind.

What of my dross you find there, be bold.
To throw away, but yet preserve the gold.
What if my gold is wrapped up in ore?
None throws away the apple for the core;
But if you shall cast all away as vain,
I know not but twill make me dream again.

# THE PILGRIM'S PROGRESS

## PART II

### THE JOURNEY OF CHRISTIANA AND HER CHILDREN

#### *THE AUTHOR'S INTRODUCTORY VERSE*

Go, now, my little book, to every place,
Where my first *Pilgrim* has but shown his face.
Call at their door: if any say, Who's there?
Then you answer, CHRISTIANA is here.
If they invite you to come in, then enter
With all your boys; and then, as you know how,
Tell who they are, also from whence they came;
Perhaps they'll know them by their looks, or name:.
But if they should not, ask them yet again,
If formerly they did not entertain
One CHRISTIAN, a *Pilgrim*? If they say,
They did, and were delighted in his way,
Then let them know that these related were
To him; Yea, his wife and children are.

A while ago it was pleasant for me and profitable to you that I should tell you the dream that I had of Christian the Pilgrim, and of his dangerous journey toward the Celestial Country. Then I also told you what I saw concerning his wife and children, how they were unwilling to go with him on pilgrimage, how he was forced to go on his progress without them. For he did not dare to run the danger of that destruction which he feared would come by staying with them in the city of Destruction. So, as I then showed you, he left them and went his way.

Because of the multiplicity of business, I have been much hindered and kept back from traveling into those parts where Christian traveled. And so I could not until now gain the opportunity to make further inquiry about those he left behind. But having some concern lately that I should give you an account of them, I went down there again. And having taken up my lodging in a woods about a mile from the place, I slept. And I dreamed again. And as I was in my dream, behold, an aged gentleman came near where I lay asleep. And because he was to go some part of the way that I was traveling, I got up and went with him. So, as we walked, we fell into a discourse, as travelers usually do. And our talk happened to be about Christian and his travels. So I began to talk with the old man, saying, Sir, what town is that below? There is one on the left hand of our way. Then Mr. Sagacity, for that was his name, answered:

Sag. It is the city of Destruction, a populous place, but one possessed with a very ill-conditioned and idle sort of people.

And I said, I thought that was the city. I once went through that town, therefore I know that this report you give of it is true.

Sag. Too true! I wish I could speak truth in speaking better of those that live there.

I said, Well, Sir, then I see that you are a well-meaning man, and so one that takes pleasure in hearing and telling of that which is good. Please tell me if you ever heard what happened to a man of this town, whose name was Christian, who went on a pilgrimage up toward the higher regions.

Sag. Hear of him? Yes, and I also heard of the interference, troubles, wars, captivities, cries, groans, frights and fears that he met with and had on his journey. Besides, I must tell you that all of our country rings of him. There are but a few houses that have not heard of him and his doings. And many have sought after and have gotten the records of his pilgrimage. Yes, I think I may say that his hazardous journey has drawn many well-wishers to his ways. For though he was a fool in every man's mouth when he was here, yet now that he has left he is highly commended by all. But it is said that he lives bravely where he is. Yea, there are many that are resolved never to run his hazards, but their mouths water to have his rewards.

I said, They may truly think that he lives well where he is, for he now lives at and in the Fountain of life. And he has what he has without labor and sorrow, for there is no grief mixed with it. But please tell me what the people say about him.

Sag. The people talk strangely about him. Some say that he now walks in white (Rev. 3:4; 6:11); some say that he has a chain of gold about his neck; that he has a crown of gold; that he is encircled with pearls on his head. Others say that the shining ones, those that revealed themselves to him in his journey, have become his companions, and that he is as familiar with them in the place where he is as one neighbor is with another here (Zech. 3:7). Besides, it is boldly affirmed that the King of the place where he is has already bestowed on him a very rich and pleasant dwelling at court. And it is said that every day he eats and drinks, walks and talks with Him, and that he received the smiles and favors of Him who is the Judge of all in that place. And some expect that his King, the Lord of the country, will soon come into these parts and will demand the reason why his neighbors so lightly regard him (if they can give any reason), and why they had him so much in derision when they saw that he desired to be a pilgrim (Jude 14,15).

For they say that he now is so much in the affection of his King that his Sovereign is much concerned with the indignities that were cast on Christian when he became a pilgrim. And it is said that He will look upon all as if it were done to Himself. And it is no wonder, for it was because of the love that he had toward his King that caused him to venture as he did (Luke 10:16).

I said, I am glad of it. I am glad for the poor man's sake, because he now has rest from his labor (Rev. 14:13), and because he now reaps the benefit of his tears with joy (Ps. 126:5,6). And I am glad that he has gotten beyond the gunshot of his enemies, that he is out of the reach of those that hate him. I also am glad that the talk of those things is speculated upon in this country. Who can tell but that it may work some good effect on some that are left behind? But please, Sir, while it is fresh in my mind, do you hear anything of Christian's wife and children? Poor hearts! I wonder in my mind how they are doing.

Sag. Who? Christiana and her sons? They are likely to do as well as Christian did himself. For though they all played the fool at first and would by no means be persuaded by either the tears or entreaties of Christian, yet now second thoughts have worked wonderfully in them. So they have packed up and have also gone after him.

I said, That is better and better. But do you mean wife and children and all?

Sag. It is true. I can tell you of the matter because I was on the spot at the time and was thoroughly acquainted with the whole affair.

Then I said, It seems, then, that a man may report it for a truth.

Sag. You do not need to fear to affirm it. I mean to say that they are all gone on pilgrimage, both the good woman and her four boys. And as I see that we are going some considerable way together, I will tell you the whole of the matter.

This Christiana (which is the name she received from the day she and her children gave themselves to a pilgrim's life), after her husband had gone over the river, and after she could hear of him no more, began to have thoughts in her mind. First, she thought of how she had lost her husband, and how the loving bond of that relation had been utterly broken between them. For you know that nature can do no less, it must entertain the living with many a heavy thought in remembering the loss of loving relations. So, then, this cost her many a tear as she thought of her husband. But this was not all. For Christiana also began to consider within herself as to whether her unbecoming behavior toward her husband was not one cause that she never saw him any more; that this in some way was the reason he was taken from her. And thinking on this, swarms of thoughts came into her mind, of all her unkind, unnatural and ungodly behavior to her dear friend. And this clogged her conscience and loaded her with guilt. Also, she was much broken when she recalled the restless groans, the salty tears, and the wails of grief which proceeded from her husband. And she remembered how she had hardened her heart against all his entreaties and loving persuasions, that she and her sons should go with him. Yes, there was not a thing that Christian either had said or done to her while he was under his burden that did not return upon her like a flash of lightning. And it tore the lining of her heart to pieces when she thought of that bitter outcry of his, *"What shall I do to be saved?"* It rang in her ears most dolefully.

Then she said to her children, Sons, we are all undone. I have sinned away your father, and he is gone. He would have had us with him, but I would not go myself, and I kept you back from life also. And at that the boys fell into tears, crying out to go with her after their father. Christiana then said, Oh that it had been our portion to go with him! Then it would have been well with us, more so than what it is likely to be now. For as to the troubles of your father, I formerly foolishly imagined that they proceeded from a foolish notion that he had, or because he had been overrun with melancholy thoughts. But now I cannot get it out of my mind that they sprang from another cause, that it was for the light of life given to him (John 8:12). And I see that it is by this help that he has escaped the snares of death. Then they all wept again, crying out, Oh, woe be to the day!

On the next night Christiana had a dream. And, behold! She saw a broad parchment opened before her, in which were recorded all of her ways. And she thought that the crimes lay very black upon her. Then she cried out aloud in her sleep, *"Lord, have mercy on me, a sinner"* (Luke 18:13). And the little children heard her.

After this, she thought she saw two very repulsive creatures standing by her bed. And they were saying, What shall we do with this woman? For she is crying out for mercy, waking or sleeping. If she wished to go on as she had begun, then we will lose her as we have lost her husband. Therefore we must in one way or another try to take her off from the thoughts of what shall be hereafter. Otherwise, all the world could not keep her from becoming a pilgrim.

Then she awoke in a great sweat, and there was a trembling on her. But after a while she again fell asleep. And then she thought she saw her husband Christian in a place of bliss among many immortals, with a harp in his hand, standing and playing on it before One sitting on a throne, with a rainbow around His head. She also saw him as he bowed his head with his face to the paved work that was under the Prince's feet, saying, I heartily thank my Lord and King for bringing me into this place. Then a company of those that stood around shouted, and they harped with their harps. But no one living could tell what they said, only Christian and his companions.

The next morning, when she was up and had prayed to God, she was talking with her children when one knocked hard at the door. She spoke, saying, If you come in God's name, come in. So he said, Amen! And he opened the door and greeted her with, Peace be to this house. And when he had done this, he said, Christiana, do you know where I have come from? Then she blushed and trembled. And her heart began to become warm with desires to know where he came from and what his errand to her was. So he said to her, My name is Secret. I live with those that are on high. It is said where I dwell that you have a desire to go there. Also there is a report that you are aware of the evil you have formerly done to your husband, in that you hardened your heart against his way, and that you kept these babes in their ignorance. Christiana, the Merciful One has sent me to tell you that He is a God ready to forgive, and that He takes delight in multiplying the pardon of offenses. He also wants you to know that He invites you to come into His presence, to His table, and that He will feed you with the fat of His house and with the heritage of your father Jacob. There you will find Christian, who was your husband, with legions more as his companions, forever beholding that face that administers life to the beholders. And they will all be glad when they shall hear the sound of your feet step over your Father's threshold.

At this Christiana was greatly humbled within herself, and she bowed her head to the ground. Then this visitor went on, saying, Christiana, here is also a letter for you, which I have brought from your husband's King. So she took it and opened it, and it smelled as if it were the best perfume (S. of S. 1:3). And it was written in letters of gold. The contents of the letter were these: That the King would have her do as her husband Christian did, for that was the way to come to His city, and thus to dwell in His presence with joy forever. At this the good woman was quite overcome. So she cried out to her visitor, Sir, will you take me and my children with you, that we also may go and worship the King?

Then the visitor said, Christiana, the bitter is before the sweet. You must go through troubles, as did he that went before you, in order to enter this Celestial City. Therefore I advise you to do as your husband Christian did. Go to the Wicket-gate there across the plain. For that stands at the head of the way up which you must go. And I wish you all good speed. Also I advise that you put this letter in your bosom, that you read in it to yourself and to your children, until you have gotten it by root into your heart. For it is one of the songs that you must sing while you are in this house of your pilgrimage (Ps. 119:54). Also you must deliver it at the gate at the end of the way.

Now I saw in my dream that this old gentleman seemed to be greatly affected with his story as he told it. And he went on, saying:

Sag. So Christiana called her sons together and began to say to them, My sons, as you may see, I have lately been much exercised in my soul about the death of your father. It is not that I doubt at all of his happiness, for I am satisfied now that he is well. I have also been much affected with the thoughts of my own condition, and of yours, which I truly believe is by nature miserable. Also, my behavior toward your father in his distress is a great load on my conscience, for I hardened both my own heart and yours against him, refusing to go with him on pilgrimage. The thoughts of these things would now kill me outright, if it were not for the dream I had last night, and for the encouragement this stranger has given me this morning. Come, my children, let us pack up and go to the gate that leads to the Celestial Country, so that we may see your father and be with him and his companions in peace, according to the laws of that land.

Then her children burst out into tears of joy because the heart of their mother was so inclined. So their visitor bid them farewell. And they began to prepare to set out on their journey.

But while they were thus preparing to go, two of the women who were neighbors to Christiana came up to her house and knocked at the door. She spoke to them as to the visitor before, If you come in God's name, come in. The women were stunned at this, for they were not used to hearing this kind of language from Christiana. But they came in. And, behold, they found the good woman preparing to leave her house. So they began to say, Neighbor, please tell us what is the meaning of this?

Christiana answered, saying to the eldest of them, whose name was Mrs. Timorous,

Chr. I am preparing for a journey.

This Timorous was a daughter to the one that had met Christian on the hill Difficulty, who would have had him go back for fear of the lions.

Mrs. Timorous For what journey, I ask you?

Chr. Even to go after my good husband.

And at that, she fell to weeping.

Tim. I hope it is not so, good neighbor. Please do not cast yourself away in so unwomanly a way, for your children's sake.

Chr. No, but my children shall go with me. Not one of them is willing to stay behind.

Tim. I cannot but wonder in my heart what it is that brought you into this mind.

Chr. Oh, my neighbor, if you but knew as much as I do, I do not doubt but that you would also go with me.

Tim. Please tell me what new knowledge you have gotten, that you are so worked up in your mind as to cast off from your friends. What tempts you to go nobody knows where?

Chr. I have been deeply afflicted since my husband left me, and especially so since he went over the river. But what troubles me most is my beastly behavior toward him when he was under his distress. Besides, now I am as he was then, nothing will serve me but going on pilgrimage. I was dreaming last night, and I saw him. Oh, that my soul was with him! He is living in the presence of the King of that country. He sits and eats with Him at His table. He has become the companion of immortals, and a house has now been given him for him to live in, to which the best palace on earth, if compared, seems to me to be no more than a dunghill (2 Cor. 5:1-4). The King of that place has also sent for me, promising to receive me if I come to Him. His messenger was here just now, and he has brought me a letter which invites me to come. And she then plucked out her letter and read it to them. And she said to them, What will you now say to this?

Tim. Oh, the madness that has possessed you and your husband, that you should run yourselves into such difficulties! I am sure that you have heard what your husband encountered, even in a way at the very first step he took on his way, as our neighbor Obstinate can still testify, for he went along with him. Yes, and Pliable went too, until they, like wise men, were afraid to go any further. And beyond that, we also heard how he met with the lions, with Apollyon, with the Shadow of Death, and with many other things. Nor is the danger he fell into at Vanity Fair to be forgotten by you. For if he, though a man, was hard put to it, what can you do, being but a poor woman? Also consider that these four sweet babes are your children, your flesh and your bones. Why, even if you are so rash as to cast yourself away, yet you should stay at home for the sake of the fruit of your body.

But Christiana said to her,

Chr. Do not tempt me, my neighbor. I have now had a price put into my hand to get gain, and I would be a fool of the highest order if I should have no heart to strike in with the opportunity. And as for all the troubles that I am likely to encounter in the way, they are not only no discouragement to me, they also show that I am right. The bitter must come before the sweet, and that also will make the sweet the sweeter. Therefore, since you did not come to my house in God's name, as I said, please leave and do not bother me further.

Then Mrs. Timorous reviled her. And she said to her companion, neighbor Mercy, let us leave her in her own hands, since she scorns our counsel and company. But Mercy was at a standstill, not being able to readily comply with her neighbor. And this was for two reasons, (1) her bowels yearned over Christiana; so she said within herself, If my neighbor must go, then I will go a little way with her and help her; and, (2) her bowels yearned over her own soul, because of what Christiana had said, for it had taken hold of her mind. So she said within herself again, I still want to talk more with this Christiana. And if I find truth and life in what she shall say, I myself will go with her with all my heart. So Mercy began to reply in this way to her neighbor, Mrs. Timorous.

Mercy Neighbor, I did indeed come with you to see Christiana this morning. And since she is, as you see, taking her last farewell to this country, I think I will walk this sunshiny morning with her a little way, to help her on her way. But she did not tell her of the second reason, keeping it to herself.

Tim. Well, I see you have a mind to go and play the fool, too. But observe the time and be wise, for while we are out of danger, we are out; but when we are in, we are in.

So Mrs. Timorous returned to her house. And Christiana undertook her journey. But when Mrs. Timorous had gotten home to her house, she sent for some of her neighbors, even Mrs. Bat's-Eyes, Mrs. Inconsiderate, Mrs. Light-Mind, and Mrs. Know-Nothing. So, when they had come to her house, she fell to telling them the story of Christiana and her intended journey. And this is what she told:

Tim. Neighbors, not having much to do this morning, I went to visit Christiana. And when I came to the door I knocked, as you know is our custom. And she answered, If you come in God's name, come in. So I went in, thinking all was well. But when I came in, I found her preparing to leave the town, she and her children, too. So I asked her what was the meaning of that? And she told me briefly that she was now of a mind to go on pilgrimage, as her husband did. She also told me of a dream that she had, and how the King of the country where her husband was had sent an invitation to come there.

Then Mrs. Know-Nothing said:

Mrs. Know. And what? Do you think she will go?

Tim. Yes, she will go, whatever may come. And I think I know it by this, that when I argued that she should stay at home because of the troubles she was likely to meet with in the way, that was the one great argument with her to set her forward on her journey. For she told me in so many words, The bitter goes before the sweet; yea, and since it does so, it makes the sweet the sweeter.

Mrs. Bats'-Eyes Oh, this blind and foolish woman! Will she take no warning by her husband's afflictions? For my part, I see that if he were here again he would be contented to rest here in a whole skin and would never run so many hazards for nothing.

Mrs. Inconsiderate Away with such fantastic fools from the town. For my part, I say it is good riddance. If she should stay where she is and retain this mind in her, who could live quietly beside her? For she will either be gloomy and unneighborly, or she will talk of those things which no wise one can stand. So, for my part, I shall never be sorry for her departure. Let her go, and let someone better come instead. It was never a good world since these whimsical fools lived in it.

Mrs. Light-Mind Come, put this kind of talk away. Yesterday I was at Madam Wanton's, and we were as merry as the maids. For who do you think was there? There was Mrs. Love-the-Flesh and three or four more, with Mrs. Lechery, Mrs. Filth, and some others. So we had music and dancing there, and everything else which was suited for our pleasure. And, I dare say, my lady Wanton herself is a very admirable and well-bred gentlewoman, and Mr. Lechery is equally a pretty fellow.

By this time Christiana has gotten on her way, and Mercy went along with her. So as they went, her children being there also, Chistiana began to talk.

Chr. Mercy, I take this as an unexpected favor that you should set forth outdoors to accompany me a little in the way.

Mercy If I thought it would be to purpose to go with you, I would never go near the town any more.

Chr. Well, Mercy, then cast in your lot with me. I well know what will be the end of our pilgrimage. My husband is in a place he would not trade for all the gold in the Spanish mines. And you shall not be rejected, though you only go on my invitation. The King, who has sent for me and my children, is one that delights in mercy. Besides, if you desire it, I will hire you and you shall go along with me as my servant. Yet we will have all things in common between us.

But do go along with me.

Mer. But how shall I know that I will be received? If I had this hope from one that can tell, I would not hesitate, but I would go, being helped by Him that can help, though the way was very tedious.

Chr. Well, loving Mercy, I will tell you what you shall do. Go with me to the Wicket-gate and I will further inquire for you there. And If you do not meet with encouragement there, then I will be content for you to return to your place. I also will pay you for the kindness which you have shown to me and my children by accompanying us in our way, as you are doing.

Mer. Then I will go there and will take what follows. And may the Lord grant that my lot may fall there, even as the King of heaven shall have His heart on me.

Then Christiana was glad at heart, not only that she now had a companion, but also because she had prevailed with this poor girl to fall in love with her own salvation. So they went on together. Then Mercy began to weep.

Chr. Why do you weep so, my sister?

Mer. Alas! Who can but lament when they but rightly consider what a state and condition my poor relatives are in, those that still remain in our sinful town? And what makes my grief the more heavy is this, that they have no instructor, no one to tell them what is to come.

Chr. It is becoming to a pilgrim to have tender feelings. You feel for your friends as good Christian did for me when he left me. He mourned because I would not hear him or regard him. But his Lord and ours gathered up his tears and put them into His bottle. And now both you and I, and these sweet babes of mine, are reaping the fruit and benefit of them. I hope, Mercy, that these tears of yours will not be lost. For the Truth has said, *"They that sow in tears shall reap in joy"* and, *"he that goes forth and weeps, bearing precious seed, shall undoubtedly come again with rejoicing, bring his sheaves with him"* (Ps. 126:5,6).

Then Mercy said,

> Let the most Blessed be my guide
> If it be His blessed will,
> Unto his gate, into His fold,
> Up to his holy hill:
> And let Him never allow me
> To swerve or turn aside
> From His free grace and holy ways,
> Whatever shall me betide.
> And let him gather them of mine
> That I have left behind:
> Lord, make them pray they may be Thine,
> With all their heart and mind.

Sagacity But when Christiana came to the Slough of Despond, she began to be troubled. For she said that this was the place where her dear husband had nearly been smothered with mud. She also noted that in spite of the command of the King, that this place should be made good for pilgrims, yet it was worse than it formerly was.

So I asked if this was true.

Sag. Yes, it is too true. For there had been many who pretended to be the King's laborers, who said they were mending the King's highways, but who brought dirt and dung instead of stones. And so they have marred it, instead of mending it. So here Christiana and her boys were troubled. But Mercy said,

Mer. Come, let us venture. But let us be wary.

Then they looked carefully to their steps and tried to stagger over it. But Christiana nearly fell in, not once or twice. And they had no sooner gotten over it but they thought they heard words that said to them, *"Blessed is she that believes, for there shall be a fulfillent of what has been told her from the Lord"* (Luke 1:45).

Then they went on again. And Mercy said to Christiana,

Mer. If I had as good a ground to hope for a loving reception at the Wicket-gate as you have, I think that no Slough of Despond would discourage me.

Chr. Well, you know your sore, and I know mine. And, good friend, we shall all have enough evil before we come to our journey's end. But can you not imagine that the people who desire to attain such excellent glories as we desire, who are so envied for happiness as we are, will escape all the fears and snares, all the troubles and afflictions which they can possible assault us with, those that hate us?

And now Mr. Sagacity left me to dream out my dream by myself. Then I thought I saw Christiana, Mercy, and the boys, all of them go up to the gate. And when they came there, they began to debate between themselves about how they should manage to call at the gate, and what should be said to him that opened it to them. So it was concluded, since Christiana was the eldest, that she should knock for entrance, and that she should speak to him that opened. So Christiana began to knock. And, as her poor husband had, she knocked and knocked again. But instead of any answer, they all thought they heard a dog come barking at them, and a big dog, too. And this made the women and children afraid. Nor did they dare to knock any more for a while, for fear that the mastiff would fly upon them. Now, then, they were greatly tumbled up and down in their minds, not knowing what they should do. They dared not knock, for fear of the dog. They did not dare to go back, for fear that the keeper of that gate would see them as they went and for fear he would be offended with them. At last they thought of knocking again, and they knocked more vehemently than they did at first. Then the keeper of the gate said, Who is there? So the dog stopped barking, and then he opened to them. Then Christiana made a low bow and said,

Chr. Do not let our Lord be offended with His servants because we have knocked at His princely gate. Then the keeper said, Where do you come from, and what is it that you would have?

Chr. We have come from where Christian came, on the same errand as he; that is, to be, if it shall please you, admitted by this gate into the way that leads to the Celestial City. And in the next place, my lord, I answer that I am Christiana, once the wife of Christian, who now has gone above.

The keeper of the gate marveled at that, saying, What? Has she now become a pilgrim, when but a little while ago she abhorred that life? Then she bowed her head and said,

Chr. Yes, and so are these, my sweet children, also.

Then he took her by the hand and led her in, saying also, *"Allow the little children to come to me."* And with that he shut the gate. And having done this, he called to a trumpeter above over the gate, that he should entertain Christiana with shouting and the sound of trumpet, for joy. So he obeyed, sounding and filling the air with his melodious notes.

Now all this time poor Mercy was standing outside, trembling and crying for fear that she was rejected. But when Christiana had gotten admittance for herself and her boys, then she began to intercede for Mercy, saying,

Chr. My lord, I have a companion of mine who is standing outside, who had come here for the same reason as I have; one who is much dejected in her mind, for she thinks that she is coming without being sent for. But I was sent for by my husband's King.

Now Mercy began to be very impatient, each minute becoming as long as an hour to her. So she prevented Christiana from a fuller intercession on her behalf by knocking at the gate herself. And then she knocked so loud that she made Christiana start. Then the keeper of the gate said, Who is there? And Christiana said,

Chr. It is my friend.

So he opened the gate and looked out. But Mercy had fallen down in a faint, being afraid that no gate would be opened to her. Then he took her by the hand and said, Little girl, I command you to rise.

Mer. Oh, Sir, I am faint. There is scarcely any life left in me.

But he answered that one had once said this, *"When my soul fainted within me, I remembered the Lord, and my prayer came to You, into Your holy temple"* (Jonah 2:7). Do not fear, only stand on your feet and tell me where you are from.

Mer. I have come for that which I was never invited to have, in the way that my friend Christiana was. Her invitation was from the King, and my invitation was only from her. Therefore I fear that I am being presumptuous.

Good. Did she ask you to come with her to this place?

Mer. Yes, and as my Lord sees, I have come. And if there is any grace and forgiveness of my sins to spare, I beg that your poor servant may be a partaker of much forgiveness.

Then He took her by the hand again. And He led her gently in, saying, I pray for all those who believe on Me, by whatever means they come to Me. Then He said to those who stood by, Bring something to smell and give it to Mercy so that her faintness will stop. So they brought her a bundle of myrrh (S. of S. 1:13), and after a while she was revived.

And now Christiana and her boys were received by the Lord, as was Mercy, at the head of the way. And He spoke kindly to them. Then they said further to Him, We are sorry for our sins and beg our Lord to give His pardon, and to tell us what else we must do.

He said, I grant pardon by word and deed: by word, in the promise of forgiveness; by deed, in the way I obtained it. Take the first from my lips with a kiss, and the other as it shall be revealed (John 20:20).

Now I saw in my dream that He spoke many good words to them, by which they were very much gladdened. He also brought them up to the top of the gate and showed them by what deed they were saved. And with this He told them that they would have the sight of this again as they went along the way, to their comfort. So He left them a while in the summer parlor below, where they went to talk among themselves. And so Christiana began,

Chr. O Lord, how glad I am that we have gotten in here!

Mer. So you may well be, but I have all the more cause to leap for joy.

Chr. I thought at one time that all our labor had been lost, as I stood at the gate (because I had knocked and no one answered), especially when that ugly cur made such a heavy barking against us.

Mer. But my worst fear was when I saw that you had been taken into His favor, and that I was left behind. Then I thought that it which was written had been fulfilled, *"Two women shall be grinding together; the one shall be taken, and the other left"* (Matt. 24:41). I was hard put to keep from crying out, Undone! And I was afraid to knock any more. But when I looked up to what was written over the gate, I took courage. Also, I thought that I must either knock again or die. So I knocked, but I cannot tell you how. For my spirit now struggled between life and death.

Chr. You can't tell how you knocked? I am sure your knocks were so earnest that the very sound of them made me start. I thought that I had never heard such knocking in all my life. I thought you would come in by a violent hand, or would take the kingdom by storm (Matt. 11:12).

Merc. Alas! If you had been in my case, you would have done as I did. You saw that the door was shut on me, and that there was a most cruel dog around there. I say, who that was as fainthearted as I would not have knocked with all their might? But please tell me what my Lord said about my rudeness. Was He not angry with me?

Chr. When he heard your loud knocking, He smiled with a wonderful, innocent smile. I believe what you did pleased Him very much, for He showed no sign to the contrary. But I wonder in my heart why He keeps such a dog. If I had known that before, I would not have had the heart to venture myself in this way. But now that we are in, we are in; and I am glad with all my heart.

Mer. If you don't mind, the next time He comes down I will ask Him why He keeps such a filthy cur in His yard. I hope He will not take it amiss.

And the children said, Do so, and persuade Him to hang him, for we are afraid he will bite us when we leave here.

So at last He came down to them again. And Mercy fell to the ground on her face before Him, worshiping Him. And she said,

Mer. Let my Lord accept the sacrifice of praise which I now offer to Him with the calves of my lips.

So He said to her, Peace to to you. Stand up.

But she continued on her face, saying,

Mer. *"You are righteous, O Lord, when I plead with You. Yet let me talk with You of*

*Your judgments"* (Jer. 12:1,2). Why do you keep so cruel a dog in Your yard, the sight of which causes such women and children as we are ready to flee from Your gate in fear?

He answered and said, That dog has another owner. He is also kept up in another man's ground, but My pilgrims hear his barking. He belongs to the castle which you see there at a distance, but he can come up to the walls of this place. He has frightened many an honest pilgrim from worse to better, by the great voice of his barking. Indeed, he that owns him does not keep him out of any goodwill to Me or Mine, but with the intention of keeping the pilgrims from coming to Me, so that they may be afraid to come and knock at this gate for entrance. Sometimes, also, he has broken out and has worried some that I loved. But for now I take it all patiently. I also give my pilgrims help when they need it, so that they are not delivered to his power, to do with them what his doggish nature would lead him to do. But My purchased one, even if you had known ever so much beforehand, I do not think that you would have been afraid of a dog. The beggars that go from door to door will run the hazard of a bawling, barking and even a bitting dog rather than to lose a possible gift. Then shall a dog, a dog in another man's yard, a dog whose barking I turn to the profit of pilgrims, keep any one from coming to Me? I deliver them from the lions, *"my darling from the power of the dog"* (Ps. 22:20,21).

Mer. I confess my ignorance. I spoke of something I did not understand. I acknowledge that You do all things well.

Then Christiana began to talk of their journey, and to ask about the way. So He fed them and washed their feet, then set them in the way of His steps, as he had done with her husband before. So then I saw in my dream that they walked on their way, having very comfortable weather to go in. Then Christiana began to sing, saying,

> Blessed be the day that I began
> A pilgrim for to be;
> And blessed also be that man
> That thereto moved me.
> Tis true, 'twas long ere I began
> To seek to live forever;
> But now I run fast as I can:
> Tis better late than never.
> Our tears to joy, our fears to faith,
> Are turned, as we see;
> Thus our beginning (as one says)
> Shows what our end will be.

Now on the other side of the wall that fenced in the way which Christiana and her companions traveled was a garden. And that garden belonged to the one that had the barking dog mentioned before. And some of the fruit-trees that grew in that garden shot their branches over the wall. And they being mellow, those that found them gathered them up and ate them to their hurt. So Christiana's boys (as boys are apt to do), being pleased with the trees and with the fruit that hung on them, plucked the fruit and began to eat. Their mother rebuked them for doing so, but the boys still went on.

Chr. Well, my sons, you are transgressing, because that fruit is not ours.

But she did not know that the fruit belonged to the enemy. If she had, she would have been ready to die for fear. But that passed, and they went on their way. But when they had gone about two bowshots from the place that led them into the way, they saw two ugly ones coming down quickly to meet them. Then Christiana and Mercy covered themselves with their veils and kept on their journey, with the children also going before them. So at last they met together. Then those that came down to meet them came up to the women, as if they would embrace them. But Christiana said, Stand back! Or go peaceable, as you should. But these two, like deaf men, did not regard Christiana's words; instead they began to lay hands on them. At this, Christiana became very angry and struck at them with her feet. And Mercy, as well as she could, did what she could to drive them away. Christiana again said to them, Stand back and go, for we have no money to lose, being pilgrims, as you see. We live on the charity of our friends. Then one of the two men said, We are not assaulting you for money, but we have come to tell you that if you will but grant one small request of ours, then we will make women of you forever.

Now Christiana, imagining what they meant, answered again,

Chr. We will neither hear or have any regard, nor will we yield to what you shall ask. We are in a hurry and cannot stay. Our business is a business of life and death.

And, again, she and her companion made a fresh attempt to go past them. But they stopped them from going on their way. And they said, We do not intend to take your lives, but it is another thing we desire.

Chr. Yes, you would have us body and soul, for I know what it is that you have come for. But we will die on the spot rather than to allow ourselves to be brought into such snares as will hazard our well-being hereafter.

And with that, they both shrieked and cried out, Murder! Murder! And so they put themselves under those laws that are provided for the protection of women (Deut. 22:25-27). But the men still made their approach on them, desiring to prevail against them. So they cried out again.

Now since they were not far from the gate at which they had entered, their cry was heard there. So some from that house came out. And seeing that it was Christiana's voice, they hurried to her relief. By the time they got within sight of them, the women were in a very great scuffle, and the children were beside them, crying. Then he that came in to relieve them called out to the ruffians, What are you doing? Would you make my Lord's people transgress? He also attempted to take them, but they made their escape over the wall into the garden of the man who owned the great dog. So the dog became their protector. Then the Reliever came up to the women and asked them how they were. They answered him, We thank your King that we are pretty well. But we have been somewhat frightened. We also thank you that you came to our help, otherwise we would have been overcome.

Rel. I marveled very much when you were received at the gate above, knowing that you knew you were weak women, that you did not beg the Lord for a guard to conduct you. Then you might have avoided these troubles and dangers, for He would have granted you one.

Chr. Alas! We were so taken with our present blessing that the dangers to come were forgotten by us. Besides, who could have thought that these naughty ones could have lurked so near to the King's palace? It would truly have been well for us to have asked our Lord for one. But, since our Lord knew it would be for our profit, I wonder that He did not send one along with us.

Rel. It is not always necessary to grant things that are not asked for, lest by doing so they become of little esteem. But when the lack of a thing is felt, then the eyes of him that feels it begin to give a proper estimate to the lack and to the relieving of want, and so will thereafter use it. If my Lord had granted you a conductor, you would not either have bewailed your oversight in not asking for one, nor would you have had occasion to do so. So all things work for good and tend to make you more wary.

Chr. Shall we go back to my Lord again and confess our foolishness, then ask for one?

Rel. I will present Him with your confession of foolishness. You need not go back again, for in all places where you shall come you will not find any lack at all. For in every one of my Lord's lodgings, which He has prepared for the reception of His pilgrims, there is enough to furnish them against all attempts whatever. But, as I said, *"He will be inquired of by them, to do it for them"* (Ezek. 36:37). And it is a poor thing that is not worth asking for.

When he had said this, he went back to his place, and the pilgrims went on their way.

Mer. What an unexpected lack this is! I thought that we were past all danger and that we would never see sorrow any more.

Chr. Your innocency, my sister, may excuse you for the most part. But as for me, my fault is so much the greater, for I saw this danger before I came out of the doors. And yet I did not provide for it when provision might have been had. I am much to be blamed.

Mer. How did you know this before you left home? Please explain this riddle to me.

Chr. Why, before I set foot out of doors, one night I lay in my bed and dreamed about this. For I thought I saw two men, as like these as ever in the world could look. And they stood at the foot of my bed, plotting how they could prevent my salvation. It was when I was in my troubles, and I will tell you their very words; they said, What shall we do with this woman; For waking or sleeping, she cries out for forgiveness. If she is allowed to go on as she has begun, we shall lose her as we have lost her husband. This, you know, might have made me careful and to have provided when provision might have been had.

Mer. Well, as by this neglect we have an occasion given to us to behold our own imperfections, so our Lord has taken this occasion to make known to us the riches of His grace. For He, as we see, has followed us with unasked kindness and has delivered us from the hands of those who are stronger than we, out of His own good pleasure.

So now, when they had talked away a little more time, they drew near a house that stood in the way (which had been built for the relief of pilgrims, as you will find more fully related in the first part of these records of the Pilgrim's Progress). So they drew on towards the house, it being the house of the Interpreter. And when they had come to the door, they heard a loud talking in the house. Then they listened and heard, as they thought, Christiana mentioned by name. For you must know that even before she set out, talk of her and her children's going on pilgrimage preceded them. And this was more pleasing to them because they had heard that she was Christian's wife, that woman who was some time ago so unwilling to hear of going on pilgrimage. So, then, they stood still and heard the good people inside commending her, not knowing that they were at the door. At last Christiana knocked, as she had done at the gate before. And when she had knocked, a young girl came and opened the door. And she looked, and, behold, two women were there.

Girl With whom did you to desire to speak in this place?

Chr. We understand that this is a privileged place for those that have become pilgrims. And we are pilgrims. Therefore we ask that we might become partakers of that for which we have come at this time. For as you see, the day is very far gone, and we are unwilling to go any further tonight.

Girl Please tell me your name, so that I may tell it to my Lord inside.

Chr. My name is Christiana. I was the wife of that pilgrim that traveled this way some years ago. This woman is my companion and is going on pilgrimage too.

Then Innocent ran in (for that was her name) and said to those inside, Can you guess who is at the door? It is Christiana and her children, and her companion, all waiting to be received here! Then they leaped for joy and went to tell their master. So he came to the door. And looking at her, he said, Are you that Christiana whom the good man Christian left behind him when he undertook a pilgrim's life?

Chr. I am that woman, that was so hard-hearted as to slight my husband's troubles, the one that let him go on his journey alone. And these are his four children. But now I also have come, for I am convinced that no way is right but this.

Inter. Then that which is written of the man and his son has been fulfilled, *"Go, work today in my vineyard. And he said to his father, I will not. But afterwards he repented and went"* (Matt. 21:28,29).

Chr. So it is. Amen. God make it a true saying on me and grant that I may be found at the last in peace, without spot and blameless in Him.

Inter. But why are you standing this way at the door? Come in, daughter of Abraham. We were just now talking of you, for news had come to us before that you were to become a pilgrim. Come, children, come in! Come, young woman, come in! So he brought them all into the house.

So when they were inside, they were told to sit down and rest. And when they had done so, those that attended pilgrims in the house came into the room to see them. And one smiled, then another smiled; and they all smiled for joy that Christiana had become a pilgrim. They also looked at the boys, stroking their faces with their hands, to show their kind reception of them. They carried on lovingly with Mercy, too, and told them all they were welcome to their Master's house. After a while, because supper was not ready, the Interpreter took them into his Significant Rooms and showed them what Christian, Christiana's husband, had seen some time before. Here, then, they saw the man in the cage, the man and his dream, the man that cut his way through his enemies, and the picture of the biggest of all of them; together with the rest of those things that had been so profitable to Christian before.

This done, and after those things had been somewhat digested by Christiana and her company, the Interpreter took them apart again and brought them first into a room where there was a man that could look no way but downwards. And he had a muckrake in his hand. And one stood over his head with a celestial crown in his hand, offering the crown to him who had the muckrake. But the man neither looked up nor regarded him, but he raked straws, small sticks and dust to himself from off of the floor.

Chr. I persuade myself that I know somewhat the meaning of this. For this is a figure of a man of this world. Is it not so, good Sir?

Inter. You are right, and his muckrake reveals his carnal mind. And where you see him paying attention to his raking of straws and sticks and dust from off the floor, you see also that he would rather do this than to do what the One who calls to him would have him do, the One with the celestial crown in his hand. It is to show us that Heaven is only a fable to some, that things here are counted the only things substantial to them. Now, since it was shown that the man could look no way but downwards, it is to reveal to you that when earthly things have power on men's minds, they have their hearts quite carried away from God.

Chr. O deliver me from this muckrake!

Inter. That prayer has been around until it is almost rusty, *"Do not give me riches"* (Prov. 30:8) is hardly the prayer of one in ten thousand. Most desire straws and sticks and dust.

And at that Christiana and Mercy wept, saying, Alas! it is too true.

When the Interpreter had shown them this, he brought them into the very best room in the house (and a very big room it was, too). So he told them to look around and see if they could find anything profitable there. Then they looked around and around, for there was nothing to be seen but a very big spider on the wall; and they overlooked that.

Mer. Sir, I do not see anything.

But Christiana did not say anything.

Inter. Look again.

So she looked again, then said,

Mer. There is nothing here but an ugly spider hanging by her hands on the wall.

Inter. Is there only one spider in all this spacious room?

Then the tears sprang into Christiana's eyes, for she was a woman quick to apprehend. And she said,

Chr. Yes, Lord, there is more than one here; and they are spiders whose venom is far more destructive than that which is in her.

Then Interpreter looked pleasantly at her and said,

Inter. You have said the truth.

Then Mercy blushed, and the boys covered their faces. For all of them now began to understand the riddle.

Inter. *"The spider takes hold with her hands and is in king's palaces."* And why is this recorded, but to show you that however full of the venom of sin you may be, yet you may by the hand of faith lay hold on and dwell in the best room in the King's house above.

Chr. I thought of something like this, but I could not imagine all of it. I thought that we were like spiders, and that we looked like ugly creatures, however fine the rooms we occupy may be. But it did not come into my thoughts that we were to learn from this spider, that venomous and ill-favored creature, how to act out our faith. And yet I see that she had taken hold with her hands in the best room of the house. God made nothing in vain.

Then they all seemed to be glad. But the tears stood in their eyes, and they looked at one another, then bowed before the Interpreter. He brought them into another room where there was a hen and chickens. And he told them to watch them a while. So one of the chickens went to the trough to drink, and every time she drank she lifted up her head and her eyes toward heaven.

Inter. See what this little chick is doing? Learn from her to acknowledge where your mercies come from, by receiving them with looking up.

And he again told them to watch. So they paid attention, noticing that the hen walked toward her chickens in a fourfold method, (1) she had a common call, one that she had all the day long; (2), she had a special call, one that she only gave sometimes; (3), she had a brooding note; and, (4), she had an outcry (see Matt. 23:37).

Inter. Now compare this hen to your King, and these chickens to His obedient ones. For as she has her methods, so He has His methods in which He walks toward His people. By His common call, He gives nothing. By His special call, He always has something to give. He also has a brooding voice for those that are under His wing. And He has an outcry, to give the alarm when He sees the enemy coming. I choose, my darlings, to lead you into the room where such things are because you are women, and they are easy for you.

Chr. And, Sir, said Christiana, please let us see more.

So he brought them into the slaughterhouse, where a butcher was killing a sheep. And, behold, the sheep was quiet, taking her death patiently. Then the Interpreter said,

Inter. You must learn from this sheep to suffer and to put up with wrongs without murmurings or complaints. See how quietly she takes her death, how she without objecting allows her skin to be pulled over her ears. Your King calls you His sheep.

After this he led them into his garden, where there was a great variety of flowers. And he said,

Inter. Do you see all these?

Chr. Yes.

Inter. See, the flowers are different in stature, in quality, in color, and smell, and in virtue. And some are better than others. Also, wherever the gardener has set them, there they stay, not quarreling with one another.

Again, he brought them into his field, in which he had sown wheat and corn. But when they looked, the tops of all had been cut off and only the straw remained.

Inter. This ground was fertilized, and plowed, and sown. But what shall we do with the crop?

Chr. Burn some, then make muck of the rest.

Inter. You see, the thing you look for is fruit. And for lack of that, you condemn it to the fire, and to be trodden under foot of men. Beware that you do not condemn yourselves in this.

Then, as they were coming in from outside, they spied a little robin with a gread spider in his mouth.

Inter. Look here.

So they looked, and Mercy wondered. But Christiana said,

Chr. What a discredit it is such a pretty little bird as the robin-redbreast, since he is a bird that loves to maintain a kind of sociableness with men, more than most. I would have thought that he would live on crumbs of bread, or on some other harmless matter. I do not like him as well as I did.

Inter. This robin, is an emblem, very apt to set forth certain kinds of professors. For they are to our sight like this robin, pretty, with color and bearing. They also seem to have a very great love for those that are sincere in their profession. And, above all others, they seem to desire to associate with them and to be in their company, as if they could live on the good man's crumbs. They also pretend that it is the reason they frequent the house of the godly and the appointments of the Lord. But when they are by themselves, like the robin they can catch and gobble up spiders; they can change their diet, drink iniquity, and swallow down sin like water.

So when they had come again into the house, because supper was not yet ready, Christiana again asked the Interpreter to either show or tell some other things that would be profitable.

Inter. The fatter the sow is, the more she loves the mire. The fatter the ox is, the more merrily he goes to the slaughter. And the more healthy the lustful man is, the more prone he is to do evil. There is a desire in a woman to be neat and fine; and it is a beautiful thing to be adorned with that which is of great price in God's sight.

It is easier to watch a night or two than to sit up a whole year at a time; so it is easier for one to begin to profess well than to hold out as he should to the end.

Every shipmaster, when in a storm, will willingly cast overboard anything that is of the smallest value in the vessel; but who will throw the best out first? No one but he that does not fear God.

One leak will sink a ship, and one sin will destroy a sinner.

He that forgets his friend is ungrateful to him; but he that forgets his Savior is unmerciful to himself.

He that lives in sin and still looks for happiness hereafter is like one that sows cockle and thinks that he will fill his barn with wheat or barley.

If a man desires to live well, let him clutch his last day to himself and always make it his company-keeper.

Whispering and change of thoughts prove that sin is in the world.

If the world, which God sets light by, is counted to be a thing of worth with men, then what is Heaven, which is commended by God?

If we are so unwilling to let go of that life which is so attended by troubles, what then is the life above?

Everybody will cry up the goodness of men; but who is there that is affected with the goodness of God as he ought to be?

We seldom sit down to the table without eating, then leaving; so there is in Jesus Christ more merit and righteousness than the whole world has need of.

When the Interpreter had finished, he took them out into his garden again. And he brought them to a tree which had rotted inside and was hollow. Yet it grew and had leaves.

Mer. What does this mean?

Inter. This tree, which is beautiful on the outside and rotten on the inside, is like many that are in the garden of God. With their mouths they speak highly of God, but in deed they will do nothing for Him. Their leaves are fair, but their heart is good for nothing, except to be tinder for the devil's tinder-box.

Now supper was ready, the table was spread, and all things were set on the board. So they sat down and ate, after one had given thanks. And the Interpreter usually entertained those that stayed with him, furnishing music at the meals. So the minstrels played. Also, there was one that sang, having a very fine voice indeed. His song was this,

> The Lord is my only support,
> And He that feeds me:
> How, then, can I lack anything
> Of which I stand in need?

When the song and music had ended, the Interpreter asked Christiana what it was that at first moved her to take up a pilgrim's life.

Chr. First, it was the loss of my husband that came into my mind, at which I was heartily grieved. But all that was but natural affection. Then the troubles and pilgrimage of my husband came into my mind, and also how beastly I had acted toward him because of that. So guilt took hold of my mind, and it would have drawn me into the pond if I had not opportunely dreamed of the well-being of my husband. Then a letter was sent by the King of that country where my husband dwells, that I should come to Him. The dream and the letter together so worked on my mind that they forced me into this way.

Inter. But did you not meet with any opposition before you set out?

Chr. Yes, a neighbor of mine, one Mrs. Timorous (who was kin to him that would have persuaded my husband to go back, for fear of the lions) tried to fool me, saying that my intended adventure was a desperate one. She also urged what she could to dishearten me from it; the hardships and troubles that my husband met with in the way, etc. But I got over this pretty well. But a dream that I had, of two ill-looking ones that I thought were plotting to make me miscarry in my journey, troubled me much. Yes, it still runs in my mind and makes me afraid of everyone that I meet, lest they should meet me to do mischief to me and to turn me out of my way. Yes, I may tell my Lord, though I would not want everyone to know it, that between this and the gate by which we entered the way, we were both so violently assaulted that we were caused to cry out, Murder! And the two that made this assault on us were like the two that I saw in my dream.

Inter. Your beginning is good, your latter end shall greatly increase.

Then turning to Mercy, he asked her what moved her to come here. Then Mercy blushed and trembled, and for a while she said nothing.

Inter. Do not be afraid. Only believe, and speak your mind.

Mer. Truly, Sir, my lack of experience is what makes me like to be silent. And it is that also which fills me with fears of coming short at last. I cannot tell of visions and dreams, as my friend Christiana can. Nor do I know what it is to mourn because I have refused the counsel of those who were good relatives.

Inter. My dear, what then was it which prevailed with you to do as you have done?

Mer. Why, when our friend here was packing to leave our town, I and another accidentally went to see her. So we knocked at the door and went in. When we were inside and had seen what she was doing, we asked her what it meant. She said she was sent for to go to her husband. And then she told us how she had seen him in a dream, living in a curious place with immortals, wearing a crown, playing on a harp, eating and drinking at his King's table, and singing praises to Him for bringing him there, etc. Now while she was telling these things to us, my heart burned within me. And I said in my heart, If this is true, I will leave my father and my mother, and the land of my nativity, and I will go along with Christiana, if I may. So I asked her further of the truth of these things, and if she would let me go with her. For I now saw that it was impossible to live in our town any longer without danger of being ruined. Still I came away with a heavy heart, not that I was unwilling to leave, but because so many of my relatives were left behind. And I have come with all the desire of my heart, and I will go with Christiana, if I may, to her husband and to his King.

Inter. Your setting out is good, for you have given credit to the truth. You are a Ruth, who for the love she bore to Naomi, and to the Lord her God, was willing to leave father and mother, and the land of her nativity, to come out and go with a people that she had not known before this. *"The Lord reward your work, and may a full reward be given to you by the Lord God of Israel, under whose wings you have come to trust"* (Ruth 2:11,12).

Now supper was over and preparation was being made for bed. The women were placed by themselves, and the boys by themselves. But when Mercy had gotten in bed, she could not sleep for joy. For now her doubts that she would miss Heaven had been moved further from her than ever before. So she lay there blessing and praising God, who had such favor for her.

In the morning they arose with the sun and prepared themselves for their departure. But the Interpreter wanted them to stay for a while, saying that they must go from there in good order. Then he told the girl that first opened to them, Take them and bring them into the garden for a bath. And wash them there and make them clean from the soil which they have gathered by traveling. Then Innocent took them and led them into the garden. And she brought them their bath. So she told them that they must wash there and be clean, for it was her Master's wish that all the women who came to that house should do so before they went on pilgrimage. So they went in and washed; yes, they and the boys and all. And they came out of that bath not only sweet and clean, but also much enlivened and strengthened in their joints. So when they came in, they looked a great deal more beautiful than when they went out to be washed.

When they had returned from the garden and bathing, the Interpreter took them and looked at them. And he called them fairer than the moon Then he called for the seal with which those that had been bathed should be sealed, so that they might be known in the places where they yet had to go. And this seal was the contents and sum of the passover which the children of Israel ate when they came out of the land of Egypt (Exod. 13:8-10). And the mark was set between their eyes. This seal greatly added to their beauty, for it was an ornament to their faces. It also added to their gravity, and it made their faces more like those of angels.

Then the Interpreter again told the girl that waited on these women to go into the vestry, and to bring out garments for these people. So she went and brought out white clothing, laying it down before him. So he commanded them to put it on, it being fine linen, white and clean. And when the women were adorned in this way, they seemed to be a terror to one another. For they could not see the glory in themselves which they could see in the other. So, then, they began to think the other to be better than themselves. For, one said, you are more beautiful than I am. And another, You are more lovely than I am. The children also were amazed to see what fashion they had been brought into.

The Interpreter then called for a man of his, one Great-heart. And he told him to take a sword and helmet and shield, and to take these daughters of his and conduct them to the house called Beautiful, the place where they were to rest next. So he took his weapons and went before them, with the Interpreter's Godspeed following them. And those that belonged to the family sent them away with many a good wish. So they went on their way and sang:

> This place has been our second stage:
> Here we have heard and seen
> Those good things that from age to age
> To others hidden have been.
> The dunghill-raker, spider, hen,
> The chicken too, to me
> Have taught a lesson: let me, then,
> Conformed to it be.
> The butcher, garden, and the field,
> The robin and his bait,
> Also the rotten tree does yield
> Me argument of weight;
> To move me to watch and to pray,
> To strive to be sincere,
> To take my cross up day by day,
> And serve the Lord with fear.

Now I saw in my dream that these went on, with Great-heart before them. So they came to the place where Christian's burden had fallen off his back and had tumbled into a grave. Then they paused here, and they also blessed God here.

Chr. It now comes to my mind what was said to us at the gate, that we should have pardon by word and deed; by word, that is by promise; by deed, that is in the way that it was obtained. I know something of what the promise is, but what is it to have pardon by deed, or in the way that it was obtained? I suppose you know, Mr. Great-heart. Therefore, if you please, let me hear you discourse of it.

Great. Pardon by the deed done is pardon obtained by someone for another person that has need of that pardon. It is not by the person pardoned, but it is in the way another has obtained it. To speak of the question at large, the pardon that you and Mercy and these boys have attained was obtained for you by Another. That is, it was obtained by Him that let you in at the gate. And He has obtained it in this double way: He has performed righteousness to cover you, and He has spilled His blood to cleanse you.

Chr. But if He gives up His righteousness for us, what will He have for Himself?

Great. He has more righteousness than you have any need of, or than He needs Himself.

Chr. Please explain that to us.

Great. With all my heart, but first I must say that He of whom we are now about to speak is One that has no match. He has two natures in one person, plain to be distinguished, impossible to be divided. There is a righteousness which belongs to each of these natures, and each righteousness is essential to that nature. So that one may as easily cause the nature to become extinct as to separate its justice or righteousness from it. So we are not made partakers of these righteousnesses in such a way that they, or any of them, should be put upon us, that we might be made just and to live by them. And this is not the righteousness of the Godhead, as distinguished from the manhood; nor is it the righteousness of the manhood, as distinguished from the Godhead. But it is a righteousness which stands in the union of both natures, and it may be properly called the righteousness that is essential to His being prepared by God to have the capacity of the mediatory office which He was entrusted with. If He parts with His first righteousness, He parts with His Godhead.

But if He parts with His second righteousness, He parts with the purity of his manhood. If He parts with His third, then He parts with that perfection which capacitates him for the office of mediation.

Therefore He must have another righteousness which consists in performance, or obedience to a revealed will. And that is what He puts on sinners, and that is it by which their sins are covered. Therefore He says, *"As by one man's disobedience many were made sinners, so by the obedience of One shall many be made righteous"* (Rom. 5:19).

Chr. But are the other righteousnesses of no use to us?

Great. Yes. For even though they are essential to His natures and office, and even though they cannot be communicated to another, yet it is by virtue of them that the righteousness which justifies is efficacious for that purpose. The righteousness of His Godhead gives virtue to His obedience. The righteousness of His manhood gives capability to His obedience to justify. And the righteousness that consists in the union of these two natures to His office gives authority to that righteousness to do the work for which it was ordained.

So, then, here is a righteousness that Christ, as God, has no need of. For He is God without it. Here is a righteousness that Christ, as man, has no need of to make Him a man, for He is perfect man without it. Again, here is a righteousness that Christ, as God-man, has no need of, for He is perfectly so without it. Here, then, is a righteousness that Christ, as God, and as God-man, has no need of, with reference to Himself — therefore He can spare it. It is a justifying righteousness that He does not lack Himself, therefore He gives it away. So it is called *"the gift of righteousness."* Since Christ Jesus the Lord has made Himself under the law, this righteousness must be given away. For the law not only binds him that is under it to do justly, but to also be charitable. So he that owns two coats must, or ought by the law, to give one to him that has none. Now our Lord indeed has two coats, one for Himself and one to spare. So He freely bestows one on those that have none. And so, Christiana and Mercy, and the rest of you that are here, your pardon comes by deed, or by the work of another Man. Your Lord Jesus Christ is He that worked and has given away what He worked for, to the next poor beggar He meets.

But, again, in order to pardon by deed, there must be something paid to God as a price, as well as something prepared to cover us with. Sin has delivered us up to the just curse of a righteous law; now we must be justified by way of redemption from this curse, a price being paid for the harms we have done. And this is by the blood of your Lord, who came and stood in your place and stead and died your death for your transgressions. So He has ransomed you from your transgressions by blood and has covered your polluted and deformed souls with righteousness (Rom. 8:34; Gal. 3:13). For His sake, God passes by you and will not hurt you when He comes to judge the world.

Chr. This is great. Now I see that there was something to be learned by our being pardoned by word and deed. Good Mercy, let us labor to keep this in mind. And, my children, you remember this also. But, Sir, was this not that which made my good Christian's burden fall from his shoulders, that which made him give three leaps for joy?

Great. Yes. It was the belief of this that cut those strings, that could not be cut by any other means. And it was to give him a proof of the virtue of this that he was allowed to carry his burden to the cross.

Chr. I thought so. For though my heart was lightsome and joyous before, yet it is ten times lighter and more joyous now. And I am persuaded by what I have felt, though I have felt it but little yet, that if the most burdened man in the world was here, and if he saw and believed as I now do, it would make his heart more merry and exultant.

Great. There is not only comfort, and the ease from a burden, bought to us by the sight and consideration of these, but there is an endeared affection begotten in us by it. For if one will but once think that pardon comes not only by promise, but by deed, how can he fail to be affected with the way and means of his redemption, as well as with the One that has worked it out for him?

Chr. True. I think that it makes my heart bleed to think that He should bleed for me. Oh, my loving One! O, my blessed One! You deserve to have me; You have bought me; You deserve to have all of me! You have paid for me ten thousand times more than I am worth! It is no wonder that this made the tears stand in my husband's eyes, that it made him step forward so nimbly. I am persuaded that he wished me to be with him, but, vile wretch that I was, I let him come all alone. Oh, Mercy, if only your father and mother were here, and Mrs. Timorous, too! I even wish now with all my heart that Madam Wanton were here too. Surely, surely, their hearts would be affected. Nor could the fear of the one, nor the powerful lusts of the other prevail with them to ever go home again; they would not refuse to become good pilgrims.

Great. You speak now in the warmth of your affections. Do you think it will always be so with you? Besides, this is not communicated to everyone, nor to everyone that saw your Jesus bleed. There were those that stood by, that saw the blood run from His heart to the ground, and yet they were so far from this feeling of yours that they laughed at Him, instead of lamenting. And instead of becoming His disciples, they hardened their hearts against Him. So that all you have, my daughters, you have by peculiar impression made by a divine contemplating on what I have spoken to you. Remember that you were told that the hen by her common call gives no meat to her chickens. Therefore, you have this by special grace.

Now I saw in my dream that they went on until they had come to the place that Simple, Sloth and Presumption had slept in, when Christian went by on his pilgrimage. And, behold, they were hung up in irons a little way off to the other side!

Mer. Who are these three men, and for what are they hung up?

Great. These three men were men of bad qualities. They had no mind to be pilgrims themselves, and they hindered whomever they could. They were sloth and folly themselves, and they persuaded whomever they could to be so too. And with it all, they taught them to presume that they would do well at last. They were asleep when Christian went by. And now when you go by, they are hanged.

Mer. But could they persuade any to be of their opinion?

Great. Yes, they turned several out of the way. There was Slow-pace, who was persuaded to do as they did. They also prevailed with one Short-wind, with one No-heart, with one Linger-after-lust, and with one Sleepyhead, and with a young woman whose name was Dull, to turn out of the way and become as they were. Besides, they brought up an ill report of your Lord, persuading others that He was a hard taskmaster. They also brought up an evil report of the good land, saying it was not half as good as some pretended it was. They also began to vilify His servants, and to count the best of them as meddlesome and troublesome busybodies. Further, they would call the bread of God husks, the comforts of His children were but fancies, and the travail and labor of pilgrims were things to no purpose.

Chr. But if they were such, I ought not to ever mourn for them. They have only gotten what they deserve. And I think that it is well that they hang so near the highway, so that others may see and take warning. But would it not have been good for their crimes to be engraved in some plate of iron or brass and left here where they did their mischiefs, for a caution to other bad men?

Great. So it is, as you may well see, if you will but go a little toward the wall.

Mer. No, no. Let them hang, and let their names rot, and let their crimes live forever against them. I think it is a great favor that they were hanged before we came here. Who knows what they might have done to such poor women as we are?

Then she turned it into a song, saying,

> Now then you three hang there, and be a sign
> To all that shall against the truth combine.
> And let him that comes after fear this end,
> If to pilgrims he is not a friend.
> And you, my soul, of all such men beware,
> That to holiness opposers are.

So they went on, until they had come to the foot of the hill Difficulty. Here again the good Mr. Great-heart took an occasion to tell them what happened there when Christian went by. So he first brought them to the spring.

Great. Lo, this is the spring that Christian drank from before he went up this hill. And then it was clear and good, but now it is dirty with the feet of some that do not desire for pilgrims to quench their thirst there (Ezek. 34:18).

Mer. And why are they so envious?

Great. It will do, if you take it up and put it into a vessel that is sweet and good. For then the dirt will sink to the bottom, and the water will then come out by itself more clear.

This, then, Christiana and her companions were compelled to do. They took it up and put it into an earthen pot, letting it stand until the dirt had gone to the bottom. And then they drank of it.

Next he showed them the two by-ways that were at the foot of the hill, where Formality and Hypocrisy lost themselves.

Great. These are dangerous paths. Two were cast away here when Christian came by. And although, as you see, these ways are now stopped up with chains, posts and a ditch, yet there are those that will choose to adventure here, rather than to take the pains to go up this hill.

Chr. *"The way of transgressors is hard"* (Prov. 13:15). It is a wonder that they can get into those ways without breaking their necks.

Great. They will try it. Yes, if at any time any of the King's servants happens to see them and calls out to them to tell them they are in the wrong way, thus telling them to beware of the danger, then they railingly reply, saying, *"As for the word that you have spoken to us in the name of the King, we will not listen to you; but we will certainly do whatever goes out of our own mouth"* (Jer. 44:16,17). But if you will look further, you shall see that these ways are made to give warning enough, not only by these posts and the ditch and chains, but also by being hedged up. Yet they will still choose to go there.

Chr. They are idle. They do not love to take pains. The up-hill way is unpleasant to them.. So it is fulfilled to them as it is written, *"The way of the lazy man is a hedge of thorns"* (Prov. 15:19). Yes, they will rather choose to walk on a snare than to go up this hill, and the rest of this way to the City.

Then they went forward and began to go up the hill. But before they got to the top, Christiana began to pant. And she said,

Chr. I dare say this is a breathing hill. It is no wonder that those who love their ease more than their souls choose a smoother way for themselves.

Mer. I must sit down.

Also, the smallest of the children began to cry.

Great. Come, come, do not sit down here, for just a little above is the King's arbor.

Then he took the little boy by the hand and led him up to it.

When they had come to the arbor, they were very willing to sit down, for they were all in a great heat.

Mer. How sweet it is for those who labor to rest (Matt. 11:28). And how good the Prince of pilgrims is to provide such resting-places for them! I have heard much of this arbor, but I never saw it before. But let us beware of sleeping, for I have heard that it cost poor Christian much.

Great. Come, my pretty boys, how are you doing? What do you think now of going on pilgrimage?

The smallest boy said, I was almost beaten out of heart, but I thank you for lending me a hand when I needed it. And I remember now what my mother has told me, that the way to Heaven is like a ladder, and the way to Hell is like going down a hill. But I would rather go up the ladder to life than to go down the hill to death.

Mer. But the proverb says, 'to go down the hill is easy.'

James (for that was his name), The day is come when, in my opinion, going down the hill will be the hardest of all.

Great. You are a good boy, you have given her a right answer.

Then Mercy smiled, but the boy blushed.

Chr. Come, will you eat a bit and sweeten your mouths while you sit and rest your legs here? For I have here a piece of pomegranate which Mr. Interpreter put into my hand just as I came out of his door. He also gave me a piece of a honeycomb and a little bottle of spirits.

Mer. I thought he gave you something, because he called you aside.

Chr. Yes, so he did. But it shall still be as I said it would when we first came from home. You shall be a sharer in all the good that I have, because you so willingly became my companion.

Then she gave some to them, and they ate, both Mercy and the boys.

Chr. Sir, will you do as we are?

Great. You are going on pilgrimage and I will soon return. What you have may do you much good. I eat the same at home every day.

Now, when they had eaten and had drunk, and when they had chatted a little longer, their guide said,

Great. The day is wearing away. If you think it good, let us get ready to go.

So they got up to go, and the little boys went before them. But Christiana forgot to take her bottle of spirits with her, so she sent the boy back to get it.

Mer. I think that this is a losing place. Christian lost his roll here, and Christiana has now left her bottle behind here. Sir, what is the cause of this?

Inter. The cause is sleepiness or forgetfulness. Some sleep when they ought to keep awake, and some forget when they should remember. And this is the reason why it is often true that some pilgrims come off the losers of some things at resting-places. Pilgrims should watch and remember what they have already received under their greatest enjoyments. For failing to do so, oftentimes their rejoicing ends in tears, and their sunshine is turned into a cloud. The story of Christian at this place is a witness to this.

98

When they had come to the place where Mistrust and Timorous met Christian to persuade him to go back for fear of the lions, they saw as it were a stage; and before it, toward the road, there was a broad plate with a copy of some verses written on them. Then underneath the reason that the stage was raised up in that place was told. The verses were,

Let him that sees this stage take heed

To his heart and tongue;

Lest, if he do not, here he speed

As some have long ago.

The words underneath the verses were these, This stage was built to punish those who through timorousness or mistrust shall be afraid to go further on pilgrimage. On this stage both Mistrust and Timorous were burned through the tongue with a hot iron for trying to hinder Christian on his journey.

Mer. This is much like that saying of the Beloved, *"What shall be given to you, or what shall be done to you, O false tongue? Sharp arrows of the mighty, with coals of juniper"* (Ps. 120:3,4).

So they traveled on until they came within sight of the lions. Now Mr. Great-heart was a strong man, so he was not afraid of a lion. But even so, when they had come to the place where the lions were, the boys who had gone in front were now glad to cringe behind. For they were afraid of the lions. So they stepped back and went behind.

Great. What now, my boys? Do you love to go before when there is no danger approaching, but love to come behind as soon as the lions appear?

Now as they went on, Mr. Great-heart drew his sword, intending to make a way for the pilgrims in spite of the lions. Then one appeared, who seemed to take it upon himself to back the lions. And he asked the pilgrims' guide, What is the cause of your coming here? And the name of that man was Grim, or Bloodyman, because he had slain the pilgrims. And he was of the race of the giants.

Great. These women and children are going on pilgrimage. And this is the way they must go; and they shall go in spite of you and the lions.

Grim This is not their way, nor shall they go in here. I have come out to stop them, and I will back the lions to that end.

Now to tell the truth, because of the fierceness of the lions and because of the grim behavior of him that backed them, this way had lately lain much unoccupied – it was almost grown over with grass.

Chr. Though the highways have been unoccupied before now, and though the travelers have been forced in times past to walk through by-paths, it must not be so now for I have risen, *"I arose a mother in Israel"* (Judges 5:6,7).

Then he swore by the lions that it would continue to be unoccupied. Therefore, he commanded them to turn aside, for they would not be allowed to pass there. But Mr. Great-heart then made his approach to Grim, and he laid so heavily on him with his sword that he was forced to retreat. Then Grim said, Will you kill me on my own ground?

Great. It is the King's highway that we are in, and it is in this way that you have placed the lions. But these women and children, though weak, shall hold on their way in spite of your lions. And with that he again gave him a mighty blow and brought him to his knees. Also with this blow, he broke his helmet. And with the next blow, he cut off an arm. Then the giant roared so hideously that his voice frightened the women. And yet they were glad to see him lie sprawling on the ground. Now the lions were chained, and so they could not do anything by themselves. So when old Grim, who had intended to back them, was dead, Mr. Great-heart said to the pilgrims,

Great. Come now and follow me, then no harm will come to you from the lions.

So they went on, but the women trembled as they passed by them. And the boys looked as if they would die. But they all got by without further hurt.

Now when they came within sight of the Porter's lodge, they soon came up to it. But they hurried more to go there after this, because it is dangerous traveling there at night.

So when they had come to the gate, the guide knocked. And the Porter cried out, Who is there? But as soon as the guide had said, It is I, he knew his voice and came down. For the guide had often been there before as a conductor of pilgrims. When he had come down, he opened the gate. And seeing the guide standing just in front of it (for he did not see the women, they being behind him), he said to him,

Port. What now, Mr. Great-heart? What is your business here so late at night?

Great. I have brought some pilgrims here, where by their Lord's commandment they are to lodge. I would have been here some time ago, but I was opposed by the giant that used to back the lions. But after a long and tedious combat with him, I have cut him off and have brought the pilgrims here in safety.

Port. Will you not go in and stay until morning?

Great. No, I will return to my Lord tonight.

Chr. Oh, Sir, I do not know how to be willing for you to leave us in our pilgrimage. You have been so faithful and so loving to us, you have fought so stoutly for us, you have been so hearty in counseling us, that I shall never forget your favor toward us.

Mer. Oh that we might have your company to the journey's end! How can such poor women as we hold out in a way so full of troubles as this way is, without a friend and defender?

James Please, Sir, be persuaded to go with us and help us, because we are so weak, and the way is so dangerous.

Great. I am at my Lord's command. If He will assign me to be your guide all the way through, I will willingly wait on you. But you failed here first, for when He told me to come this far with you, then you should have begged of Him that He should send me all the way through with you. And he would have granted your request. However, for now I must withdraw. And so, good Christiana, Mercy, and my brave children, adieu.

Then the Porter, Mr. Watchful, asked Christiana of her country and of her kindred.

Chr. I came from the city of Destruction. I am a widow, and my husband is dead. His name was Christian, the pilgrim.

Port. Well! Was he your husband?

Chr. Yes, and these are his children. And this is one of my townswomen.

Then the Porter rang his bell, as he did at such times. And one of the girls came to the door, whose name was Humble-mind. And the Porter said to her, Go tell it inside that Christiana, the wife of Christian, and her children have come here on pilgrimage. She therefore went in and told it. But, oh, what noise of gladness was there inside when the girl had but dropped it out of her mouth! So they came with haste to the Porter, for Christiana still stood at the door. Then some of the most grave ones said to her, Come in, Christiana. Come in, O wife of that good man. Come in, O blessed woman; and all those with you, come in. So they went in, and her children and companions followed her. Now when they had entered, they were brought into a large room, where they were told to sit down. So they sat down. And the chief ones of the house were called to come and see and to welcome the guests. Then they came in, and when they had understood who they were, they greeted each other with a kiss, saying, Welcome, vessels of the grace of God; welcome to us your friends.

Now because it was somewhat late, and because the pilgrims were weary from their journey (and also faint because of the sight of the fight and of the terrible lions), they asked that they might prepare to rest as soon as possible. But those of the family said, No, but refresh yourselves first with a bit of meat. For they had prepared a lamb for them, with the usual sauce (Exod. 12:3; John 1:29). For the Porter had heard before that they were coming, and he had told it to those inside. So when they had eaten, and had ended their prayer with a psalm, they asked that they might go to rest.

Chr. But if we may be so bold as to choose, let us be in that room which was my husband's when he was here. So they brought them there, and they all lay in that room. When they were at rest, Christiana and Mercy entered into a discourse about things that were convenient.

Chr. Little did I think once, when my husband went on pilgrimage, that I would ever be following him.

Mer. And you as little thought of lying in his bed, and in his room to rest, as you do now.

Chr. And much less did I ever think of seeing his face with comfort, and of worshiping the Lord the King with him. Yet now I believe that I shall.

Mer. Listen! Do you not hear a noise?

Chr. Yes, I believe it is a sound of music for joy that we are here.

Mer. Wonderful! Music in the house, music in the heart, and music also in Heaven for joy that we are here!

Then they talked awhile before they went off to sleep. And when they had awakened in the morning, Christiana said to Mercy, What was it that caused you to laugh in your sleep last night. I suppose you were in a dream.

Mer. So I was, and a sweet dream it was. But are you sure I laughed?

Chr. Yes, you laughed heartily. But please tell me your dream, Mercy.

Mer. I was dreaming that I sat all alone in a solitary place and was bemoaning the hardness of my heart. But before I had sat there long, many gathered around to look at me and to hear what it was I had to say. So they listened as I went on bemoaning the hardness of my heart. At this, some of them laughed at me, some called me a fool, and some began to push me around. As that happened, I looked up and saw one coming with wings toward me. And he came directly to me and said, Mercy, what is wrong with you? And when he had heard me make my complaint, he said, Peace be to you. He also wiped my eyes with his handkerchief and clothed me in silver and gold. He put a chain around my neck, and earrings in my ears, and a beautiful crown on my head (Ezek. 16:8-13).

Then he took me by the hand and said, Mercy, follow me. So he went up, and I followed until we came to a golden gate. Then he knocked. And when those within had opened, the man went in. And I followed him up to a throne on which One sat. And he said to me, Welcome, daughter. The place looked bright and twinkling, like the stars, or rather like the sun. And I thought that I saw your husband there. So I awoke from my dream. But did I laugh?

Chr. Laugh? Yes, and well you might, to see yourself so well. For you must believe me when I tell you it was a good dream; and that, as you have begun to find the first part true, so you shall find the second at last. *"God speaks once, yes, twice, yet man does not see it; in a dream, in a vision of the night, when deep sleep falls on men, in slumbering on the bed"* (Job 33:14,16). When we are in bed, we do not need to lie awake to talk with God. He can visit us while we sleep and cause us then to hear His voice. Our heart oftentimes awakes when we sleep. And God can speak to our heart either by words, by proverbs, by signs and similitudes, as well as if one were awake.

Merc. Well, I am glad of my dream, for I hope before long to see it fulfilled, so as to make me laugh again.

Chr. I think it is now high time for us to rise and to find out what we must do.

Mer. Please, if they invite us to stay awhile, let us willingly accept their invitation. I am very willing to stay awhile here in order to grow better acquainted with these girls. I believe Prudence, Piety and Charity have very becoming and serious countenances.

Chr. We shall see what they will do.

So when they were up and ready, they came down. And they asked one another of their rest, if they were comfortable or not.

Mer. It was very good, one of the best night's lodgings that I ever had in my life.

Then Prudence, and Piety asked if they could be persuaded to stay here awhile, offering all that the house could afford. And Charity added that they would be glad if they would. So they consented and stayed there a month or more, becoming very profitable to one another. And because Prudence wanted to see how Christiana had brought up her children, she asked permission to catechise them. So she freely gave her consent. Then Prudence began with the youngest, James.

Prud. Come, James, can you tell me who made you?

James. God the Father, God the Son and God the Holy Spirit.

Prud. Good boy. And can you tell me who saved you?

James God the Father, God the Son and God the Holy Spirit.

Prud. Good boy still. But how does God the Father save you?

James By His grace.

Prud. How does God the Son save you?

James By His righteousness, by His death, by His blood, and by His life.

Prud. And how does God the Holy Spirit save you?

James By His illumination, by His renovation, and by His preservation.

Prud. Christiana, you are to be commended for bringing up your children this way. I suppose I need not ask the rest of them these questions, since the youngest of them can answer them so well. But I will now apply myself to the next youngest.

Come, Joseph, will you let me catechise you?

Joseph With all my heart.

Prud. What is man?

Jos. A reasonable creature, made to be so by God, as my brother said.

Prud. What is supposed by this word, saved?

Jos. That man by sin has brought himself into a state of captivity and misery.

Prud. What is supposed by his being saved by the Trinity?

JOos. That sin is so great and mighty a tyrant that none can pull us out of its clutches but God; and that God is so good and loving to man as to truly pull him out of this miserable state.

Prud. What is God's design in saving poor men?

Jos. The glorifying of His name, of His grace, of His justice, etc., and the everlasting happiness of His creature.

Prud. Who are the ones that must be saved?

Jos. Those that accept His salvation.

Prud. Good boy, Joseph. Your mother has taught you well, and you have listened to what she has said to you.

Samuel (who was next to the Oldest), Come, are you willing for me to catechise you?

Samuel. Yes, indeed, if you please.

Prud. What is Heaven?

Sam. A place and state that is most blessed, because God dwells there.

Prud. What is hell?

Sam. A place and state that is most woeful, because it is the dwelling-place of sin, the devil and death.

Prud. Why do you desire to go to Heaven?

Sam. So that I may see Christ and love Him everlastingly, and so that I may have that fullness of the Holy Spirit in me which I can in no way enjoy here.

Prud. A very good boy, and one that has learned well.

Matthew (who was the oldest boy), Come, may I also catechise you?

Matthew Yes, I am very willing.

Prud. Then I ask if there was ever anything that had a being antecedent to, or before God?

Matt. No, for God is eternal. Nor is there anything, excepting Himself, that had a being until the beginning of the first day, *"For in six days the Lord made the heavens and the earth, the sea, and all that is in them"* (Exod. 20:11).

Prud. What do you think of the Bible?

Matt. It is the holy word of God.

Prud. Is there nothing written in it but what you understand?

Matt. I think that God is wiser than I am. I also pray that He will be pleased to let me know all that is in the Bible which He knows will be for my good.

Prud. How do you believe as to the resurrection of the dead?

Matt. I believe that they shall rise, the same that was buried: the same in nature, though not in corruption. And I believe this for two reasons: First, because God has promised it; secondly, because He is able to perform it.

Prud. You boys must still listen to your mother, for she can teach you more. You must also diligently listen to whatever good talk you shall hear from others, for it is for your sakes that they speak good things. Also carefully observe what the heavens and the earth teach you. But especially be much in the meditation of that book which was the cause of your father's becoming a pilgrim. For my part, my children, I will teach you what I can while you are here. And I shall be glad if you will ask me questions that tend to godly edification.

Now when the pilgrims had been at this place a week, Mercy had a visitor who pretended some good will toward her, and his name was Mr. Brisk. He was a man of some breeding, one that pretended to religion, but a man who stuck very close to the world. So he came once or twice to Mercy and offered love to her. Now Mercy was of a beautiful face, and so she was all the more alluring. Also her mind was always busy in doing something. For when she had nothing to do for herself, she would be making hose and garments for others, and she would give them to those who had need. And Mr. Brisk, not knowing where or how she disposed of what she made, seemed to be greatly taken, for he never found her idle. And he said to himself, I believe she will be a good housewife.

Mercy then revealed the matter to the girls that were in the house, asking them concerning him, for they knew him better than she did. So they told her that he was a very busy young man, and one that pretended to religion. But he was, they feared, a stranger to the power of that which was good.

Mer. Then I will look no more at him, for I do not want ever to have a clog to my soul.

Prudence then replied that there was no great need to discourage him, for if she but continued to do as she had begun, to do things for the poor, then he would quickly find his courage cooled.

So the next time he came, he found her at her old work, making things for the poor. Then he said,

Mr. B. What! Always at it.

Mer. Yes, either for myself or for others.

Mr. B. And what can you earn a day?

Mer. I do these things so *"that I may be rich in good works, laying a foundation for the time to come"* so that I may lay hold on everlasting life (1 Tim. 6:18,19)

Mr. B. Please tell me what you do with them.

Mer. I clothe the naked.

With that, his countenance fell. So he did not come back to her again. And when he was asked the reason why, he said that Mercy was a pretty girl, but that she was troubled with ill conditions.

When he had left her, Prudence said,

Prud. Did I not tell you that Mr. Brisk would soon leave you? Yea, he will raise up an ill report of you. For in spite of his pretence to religion, and his seeming love to Mercy, yet Mercy and he are of such different tempers that I believe they will never come together.

Mer. I could have had husbands before now, though I never spoke of it to any. But they were the kind that did not like my conditions, though none of them ever found fault with my person. So they and I could not agree.

Prud. In our days, mercy is little appreciated, no more than as to its name. The practice of it, as you set forth in your conditions, cannot be tolerated by many.

Mer. Well, if no one will have me, I will die an old maid, or my conditions will have to be a husband to me. For I cannot change my nature. And I am determined never to admit one that differs from me in this, as long as I live. I had a sister named Bountiful, who married one of these ungodly ones. But he and she could never agree. And because my sister was resolved to do as she had begun, that is, to show kindness to the poor, therefore her husband first cried her down at the cross, and then he turned her out of his doors.

Prud. And yet he was a professor. I warrned you!

Mer. Yes, he was one of that kind, the kind that the world is full of. But I am not for any of them.

Then Matthew, the oldest son of Christiana, fell sick. And his sickeness was very severe, he being very much pained in his bowels. And it at times pulled, it seemed, both ends together. And there lived not far from there one Mr. Skill, an ancient and well-approved physician. So Christiana asked, and they sent for him. And he came. When he had entered the room and had observed the boy a little while, he concluded that he was sick of the gripes. And he asked Christiana what Matthew had been eating lately.

Chr. Nothing but what is wholesome.

Mr. S. This boy has been tampering with something that lies in his maw undigested, something that will not go away without help. And I tell you that he must be purged, or else he will die.

Sam. Mother, what was that which my brother gathered and ate soon after we had come from the gate that is at the head of the way? You know that there was an orchard on the left, on the other side of the wall, and some of the trees hung over the wall. And my brother plucked some and ate.

Chr. True, my child. He did take and he did eat of them. And I scolded him for being such a naughty boy, yet he had to eat of it.

Mr. S. I knew that he had eaten something that was not wholesome food. And that food, that fruit which he ate, is the most hurtful of all. It is the fruit from Beelzebub's orchard. I marvel that no one warned you of it. Many have died of it.

Then Christiana began to cry, and she said,

Chr. O you naughty boy! O what a careless mother I am! What shall I do for my son?

Mr. S. Come, do not be too much dejected. The boy may get well again, but he must be purged so that he vomits.

Chr. Please, sir, try the utmost of your skill with him, whatever it costs.

So he made up a purge for him, but it was too weak. It was said that it was made of the blood of a goat, the ashes of a heifer, and with some of the juice of hyssop (Heb. 9:19; 10:1-4). When Mr. Skill had seen that the purge was too weak, he made one more suited to his purpose. It was made *ex carne et sanguine Christi* (John 6:54-57). You know that physicians give strange medicines to their patients. And it was made into pills, with a promise or two, and a proportionable quantity of salt (Mark 9:49). And he was to take them three at a time, fasting, in half a quarter of a pint of the tears of repentance. But when this preparation was made and brought to the boy, he did not want to take it, even though he was torn with the gripes to the point of being pulled to pieces.

Mr. S. Come, come, you must take it.xxx

Matt. It goes against my stomach.

Chr. I must have you take it (Zech. 12:10).

Matt. I will vomit it up again.

Chr. Please, sir, how does it taste?

Mr. S. It has no ill taste.

Then Christiana touched one of the pills with her tongue.

Chr. O. Matthew, this potion is sweeter than honey. If you love your mother, if you love your brothers, if you love Mercy, if your love your life, then take it.

So after a short prayer for God's blessing on it, he took it. And it worked well for him, causing him to be purged. Then he was caused to sleep and to rest quietly. It put him into a hot, breathing sleep, and it completely rid him of his gripes. So in a little time he got up and walked about with a staff. And he would go from room to room, talking with Purdence, Piety and Charity about his distemper, and about how he was healed.

So when the boy had been healed, Christiana asked Mr. Skill,

Chr. Sir, what can I pay you for you pains and care for my son?

Mr. S. You must pay the Master of the College of Physicians, according to rules made and provided for such a case (Heb. 13:15).

Chr. But, sir, what else is this pill good for?

Mr. S. It is a universal pill. It is good against all the diseases that pilgrims are susceptible to. And when it is well prepared, it will keep good health perpetually.

Chr. Please, sir, make me up twelve boxes of them. For if I can get these, I will never take any other medicine.

Mr. S. These pills are good to prevent diseases, as well as to cure when one is sick. Yes, I dare say it and stand to it, that if a man will only use this medicine as he should, it will make him live forever (John 6:51). But, good Christiana, you must not give these pills any other way than the way I prescribed. For if you do, they will do no good.

So he gave medicine to Christiana for herself, and for her boys, and for Mercy. And he told Matthew to be careful about eating any more green plums. Then he kissed them and went away.

As was mentioned before, Prudence told the boys that if they at any time desired to ask her some questions, for their profit, she would be glad to answer them. Then Matthew, who had been sick, asked her, Why are most medicines so bitter to our taste?

Prud. To show how unwelcome the word of God and its effects are to a carnal heart.

Matt. If medicine is to do good, why does it purge and cause us to vomit?

Prud. To show that the word, when it works effectually, cleans the heart and mind. For what the one does for the body, the other does for the soul.

Matt. What should we learn from watching the flames go upwards, and by seeing the beams and sweet influences of the sun strike downwards?

Prud. The going up of flames teaches us to ascend to Heaven by fervent and hot desires. And by the sun's sending its heat, beams and sweet influences downwards, we are taught that the Savior of the world, though high, reaches down with His grace and love to us below.

Matt. Where do the clouds get their water?

Prud. Out of the sea.

Matt. What may we learn from that?

Prud. That ministers should get their doctrine from God.

Matt. Why do clouds empty themselves on earth?

Prud. To show that ministers should give out what they know of God to the world.

Matt. Why is the rainbow caused by the sun?

Prud. To show that the covenant of God's grace is confirmed to us in Christ.

Matt. Why do the springs come from the sea to us through the earth?

Prud. To show that the grace of God comes to us through the body of Christ.

Matt. Why do some of the springs rise out of the tops of high hills?

Prud. To show that the Spirit of grace shall spring up in some that are great and mighty, as well as in many that are poor and lowly.

Matt. Why does the fire fasten on the candlewick?

Prud. To show that unless grace kindles on the heart, there will be no true light of life in us.

Matt. Why are the wick and tallow spent to maintain the light of the candle?

Prud. To show that body and soul should be at the service of and spend themselves to maintain in good condition that grace of God that is in us.

Matt. Why does the pelican pierce her own breast with her bill?

Prud. To nourish her young ones with her blood. And this shows that Christ the Blessed so loved His young, His people, as to save them from death by His blood.

Matt. What may one learn by hearing the cock crow?

Prud. One may learn to remember Peter's sin and Peter's repentance. The cock's crowing also shows that the day is coming on; then let the crowing of the cock remind you of that last and terrible day of judgment.

Now about this time their month ended. So they made it known to those of the house that it was the right time for them to get up and go. Then Joseph said to his mother,

Jos. It is proper for you not to forget to send to the house of Mr. Interpreter, to ask him to grant that Mr. Great-heart should be sent to us, that he may be our conductor for the rest of the way.

Chr. Good boy! I almost forgot.

So she drew up a petition and asked Mr. Watchful, the porter, to send it by some worthy man to her good friend, Mr. Interpreter. And when it had come, Mr. Interpreter read the contents of the petition. And he said to the messenger, Go tell them that I will send him.

When the family at the house saw that Christiana and her company were of a mind to go forward, they called the house together to give thanks to their King for sending them such profitable guests as these. This done, they said to Christiana, And shall we not show you something, as it is our custom to do to pilgrims, on which you may meditate when you are on the way? So they took Christiana, her children, and Mercy into the closet. And they showed them one of the apples that Eve ate, and that she also had given to her husband (for the eating of which they were both turned out of Paradise). And they asked her what she thought it was.

Chr. It is food or poison, I do not know which.

So they opened the matter to her, and she held up her hands and wondered (Gen. 3:1-6; Rom. 7:24). Then they brought her to a place and showed her Jacob's ladder. Now at that time there were some angels ascending on it. So Christiana looked and looked, to see the angels go up. So did the rest of the company (Gen. 28:12). Then they were going into another place, to show them something else. But James said to his mother,

James Please ask them to stay here a little longer, for this is an interesting sight.

So they turned back again and stood feeding their eyes on a beautiful scene. Then they brought them into a place where a golden anchor hung. And they told Christiana to take it down. For, they said, you shall have it with you, for it is of absolute necessity that you should, so that you may lay hold of that within the veil and stand steadfast in case you should meet with turbulent weather. And they were glad to have it (Joel 3:16; Heb. 6:19). Then they took them and brought them to the mountain on which Abraham our father offered up Isaac his son. And they showed them the altar, the wood, the fire, and the knife; for they remain to be seen to this very day. When they had seen it, they held up their hands and blessed themselves, saying, Oh, what a man for love to his Master, and for denial of himself, was Abraham!

After they had shown them all these things, Prudence took them into a dining room where a pair of excellent virginals stood. And she played on them, turning what she had shown them into this excellent song:

> Eve's apple we have shown you;
> Of that be you aware;
> You have seen Jacob's ladder, too,
> Upon which angels are.
> An anchor you received have;
> But let not these suffice,
> Until with Abraham you have gave
> Your best a sacrifice.

Now about this time one knocked at the door. And when the porter had opened it, behold, Mr. Great-heart was there. And when he had come in, what joy there was! For it once again came freshly to mind how but a little while ago he had slain old Grim Bloody-man, the giant, and had delivered them from the lions.

Then Mr. Great-heart said to Christiana and to Mercy,

Great.My Lord has sent a bottle of wine to each of you, and also some parched corn, together with a couple of pomegranates. He has also sent the boys some figs and raisins, to refresh you in your way.

Then they prepared to journey. And Prudence and Piety went along with them. When they came to the gate, Christiana asked the porter if anyone had gone by lately. He said, No, only one some time ago, who also told me that there had been a great robbery committed on the King's highway lately.

But, he said, the thieves have been caught, and shortly they will be tried for their lives. Then Christiana and Mercy were afraid. But Matthew said,

Matt. Mother, there is nothing to fear as long as Mr. Great-heart is to go with us and be our conductor.

Chr. Mr. Porter, I am much obliged to you for all the kindnesses you have shown me since I came here; and also for your lovingkindness to my children. I do not know how to gratify your kindness; so, please, as a token of my respect to you, will you not accept this small mite?

So she put a golden angel in his hand. And he made a low bow and said,

Port. Let your garments always be white, and let your head lack no ointment. Let Mercy live and not die, and let her works be many. And as for the boys, flee from your youthful lusts and follow after godliness with those that are grave and wise. In this way you shall put gladness into your mother's heart, and you shall obtain praise from all that are sober-minded.

So they thanked the porter and left. Now I saw in my dream that they went forward until they had come to the brow of the hill. And there Piety, quickly remembering, cried out,

Piety Alas! I have forgotten what I intended to give to Christiana and her companions. I will go back and get it.

So she ran and got it. While she was gone, Christiana thought she heard a most curious melody in a little grove a little way off on the right hand. And the words went like this:

> Through all my life Your favor is
> So frankly shown to me,
> That in Your house forevermore
> My dwelling-place shall be.

And listening still, she thought she heard another answer:

> For why? The Lord our God is good;
> His mercy is forever sure;
> His truth at all times firmly stood,
> And shall from age to age endure.

So Christiana asked Prudence who it was that was making those curious notes.

Prud. They are our country birds. They sing these notes but seldom, except it be at the springtime, when the flowers appear, and the sun shines warm. Then you may hear them all day long. I often go out to hear them. We also oftentimes keep them tame in our house. They are very fine company for us when we are melancholy. Also they make the woods, and groves, and solitary places very desirable places to be in (S. of S. 2:11,12).

By this time Piety had come again. And she said to Christiana,

Piety Look here, I have brought you a drawing of all those things which you have seen at our house, on which you may look when you find yourself forgetful. Then you can call those things again to your memory, for your edification and comfort.

Now they began to go down the hill into the Valley of Humiliation. It was a steep hill and the way was slippery. But they were very careful, so they got down pretty well. When they were down in the valley, Piety said to Christiana,

Piety This is the place where Christian your husband met with the foul fiend Apollyon. And this is where they had that dreadful fight. I know that you must have heard of it. But be brave, for as long as you have Mr. Great-heart here to be your guide and conductor, we hope you will fare better.

So when these two had committed the pilgrims to the conduct of their guide, he went forward, and they followed after him. Then Mr. Great-heart said,

Great. We do not need to be afraid of this valley, for there is nothing here to hurt us, unless we bring it on ourselves. It is true that Christian met Apollyon here, with whom he had a severe battle. But that contest was the fruit of his slips as he came down the hill.

For they that slip there must look for battles here. And that is why the valley has gotten such a hard name. For when they hear that some frightful thing has happened to such a person in such a place, the common people are of the opinion that the place is haunted with some foul fiend or evil spirit. But, alas, it is because of their own doing that such things happen to them there.

This Valley of Humiliation is in itself as fruitful a place as any that the crow flies over. And I am persuaded that if we could hit upon it, we might find something somewhere around here that would tell us why Christian was so fiercely assaulted in this place.

Then James said to his mother,

James Look! Yonder stands a pillar, and it looks as if something is written on it. Let us go and see what it is.

So they went and found written on it, 'Let Christian's slips before he came here, and the battles that he encountered in this place, be a warning to those that come afterwards.'

Great. Look, did I not tell you that there was something around here that would give some reason why Christian was so fiercely assaulted in this place. It is no disparagement to Christian, any more than it is to others who did not happen to have this as their lot. For it is easier going up this hill than it is to go down it. And that is something that can be said of but very few hills in all these parts of the world. But we will leave the good man, for he is at rest. He also had a brave victory over his enemy. Let Him that dwells above grant that we fare no worse than Christian, when we have been tried.

But we will come again to this Valley of Humiliation. It is the best and most fruitful piece of ground in all this country. It is fat ground. And as you see, it consists much in meadows. And if a man was to come here in the summertime, as we do now, if he did not know anything of it before, and if he also delighted himself in the sight of his eyes, he might see that which would be delightful to him. See how green this valley is, and how beautiful the lilies are (S. of S. 2:1). I have known many laboring men that have gotten good estates in this Valley of Humiliation (for *"God resists the proud, but gives grace to the humble"* —James 4:6; 1 Pet. 5:5). For indeed it is a very fruitful soil, bringing forth by handfuls. Some have also wished that the next way to their Father's house were here, that they might be troubled no more with either hills or mountains to go over. But the way is the way — and there is an end.

Now, as they were going along talking, they saw a boy feeding his father's sheep. The boy was in shoddy clothing, but he had a fresh and well-favored look. And he was sitting by himself and singing.

Great. Listen to what the shepherd boy says. So they listened, and heard,

> He that is down needs fear no fall;
> He that is low, no pride:
> He that is humble, ever shall
> Have God to be his guide.
> I am content with what I have,
> Little be it or much;
> And, Lord, contentment still I crave,
> Because You save such.
> Fulness to such a burden is,
> That go on pilgrimage;
> Here little, and hereafter bliss,
> Is best from age to age (Heb. 13:5).

Great. Do you hear him? I dare say this boy lives a merrier life, and wears more of that herb called heart's-ease in his bosom, than he that is clad in silk and velvet. But we will proceed in our discourse.

In this valley our Lord formerly had His country-house. He loved very much to be here. He also loved to walk these meadows, for he found the air to be pleasant. Besides, here a man shall be free from the noise, and from the hurryings of this life. All states are full of noise and confusion − only the Valley of Humiliation is truly an empty and solitary place. This is a valley that nobody walks in, except those that love a pilgrim's life. And though Christian had the misfortune of meeting Apollyon here, and of entering into a brisk battle with him, yet I must tell you that in former times men have met with angels here. Pearls have been found here, and the words of life have been found here (Hos. 12:4,5).

Did I say that our Lord had His country-house here in former days, and that He loved to walk here? I will add that He has left to the people who love and travel these grounds a yearly revenue, which is to be faithfully paid to them at a certain time for their maintenance by the way, and for their further encouragement to go on in their pilgrimage.

Samuel **Mr.** Greatheart, I understand that it was in this valley that my father and Apollyon battled. But where was the fight? I see that the valley is very large.

Great. Your father had the battle with Apollyon at a place yonder before us, in a narrow passage, just beyond Forgetful Green. And, indeed, that place is the most dangerous place in this region. For if pilgrims at any time meet with any shock, it is when they forget the favors that they have received, and they forget how unworthy they are of them. This is the place, too, where others have been hard pressed. But more of the place when we have come to it. For I am sure that there remains some sign of the battle or some monument to testify that such a battle was fought there at the place, even until today.

Mer. I think that I am as well in this valley as I have been anywhere else in all our journey. The place suits my spirit. I love to be in such places, where there is no rattling of coaches, no rumbling of wheels. I believe that one may here without molestation meditate on what one is, where we came from, what we have done, and to what the King has called us. Here one may think with a breaking heart; one may melt in his spirit until one's eyes become *"as the fish-pools of Heshbon."* Those who go through this *"valley of Baca make it a well."* God sends down the rain from Heaven on those that are here and fills up their pools. This valley is that from which the King will give to His their vineyards (Song of S. 7:4; Ps. 84:5-7; Hos. 2:15). And those who go through it shall sing as Christian did, even though he met Apollyon here.

Great. It is true. I have gone through this valley many a time, and I never was better than when I was here. I have also conducted several pilgrims and they have confessed the same: *"To this one I will look, even to him that is poor and of a contrite spirit, he that trembles at My word"* says the King.

Now they had come to the place where the aforementioned battle had been fought.

Great. This is the place. Christian stood on this ground, and up there is where Apollyon came against him. And, look! Did I not tell you? Here is some of your husband's blood on these stones to this day! Also, you can see here there are some of the shivers of Apollyon's broken darts to be seen. And see how they beat the ground with their feet as they fought, in order to make good their places against each other. And you can also see how they split the very stones in pieces with their blows. Truly Christian played the man here, showing himself to be strong. Hercules himself could have done no better if he had been here. When Apollyon had been beaten, he made his retreat to the next valley, which is called the Valley of the Shadow of Death, to which we will be coming soon.

Look, yonder stands a monument, also, on which is engraven this battle, and Christian's victory, to his fame throughout the ages.

Because it stood just on the wayside before them, they stepped up to it and read the writing, which was this, word-for-word;

> Hard by here was a battle fought,
> Most strange, and yet most true;
> Christian and Apollyon sought
> Each other to subdue.
> The man so bravely played the man,

He made the fiend to fly;
Of which a monument I stand,
The same to testify.

When they had passed by this place, they came on the borders of the Shadow of Death. And this valley was longer than the other, a place that was also most strangely haunted with evil things, as many are able to testify. But these women and children went more easily through it, because they had daylight, and because Mr. Great-heart was their guide. When they had entered the valley, they thought they heard a groaning, as of dying men – a very great groaning. They also thought they heard words of lamentation, spoken as if some were in extreme torment. These things made the boys shake, and the women looked pale and gloomy. But their guide encouraged them to be comforted.

So they went on a little further. And they thought they felt the ground begin to shake under them, as if some hollow place was there. They also heard a kind of hissing, as of serpents, but nothing as yet appeared. Then the boys asked if they were never to get to the end of this doleful place. But Mr. Great-heart also told them to be courageous and to look well to their feet, lest they might happen to fall into some snare. But James now began to be sick, no doubt it was from fear. So his mother gave him some of that glass of spirits that had been given her at the house of Mr. Interpreter, and three of the pills that Mr. Skill had prepared. And the boy began to revive.

So they went on until they came nearly to the middle of the valley. And then Christiana said that she saw something further down the road, a thing the shape of which she had never seen.

Jos. Mother, what is it?

Chr. It is an ugly thing, child, an ugly thing.

Jos. But mother, what is it like?

Chr. I cannot tell what it is like. And now it is only a little way off. It is coming near.

Great. Well, let those that are most afraid keep close to me. So the fiend came on. And Mr. Great-heart stepped forward to meet it. But when it had come up to him, it vanished out of their sight. Then they remembered what had been said some time ago, *"Resist the devil, and he will flee from you"* (James 4:7).

So they went on, now being a little refreshed. But they had not gone far before Mercy looked behind her and saw what she thought was a lion. And it came padding quickly after her. And it had a hollow voice roaring. And at every roar it gave, the whole valley echoed. And all their hearts ached, except the heart of their guide. So it came up. And Mr. Great-heart went behind them, putting the pilgrims all in front of him. The lion also came on quickly, and Mr. Great-heart prepared to do battle with him. But when he saw that he was going to meet a determined resistance, the lion drew back and came no further (1 Pet. 5:9).

Then they went on again, with their guide going before them, until they came to a place where a pit had been dug across the whole breadth of the way. And before they could get ready to go over it, a great mist and a darkness fell on them, so that they could not see. Then the pilgrims cried out, Alas! What shall we do now? But Mr. Great-heart answered, Do not fear, stand still and see what an end will be put to this also. So they stayed there, because their path was blocked. And then they thought they heard what appeared to be the noise and rushing of enemies. And they could now more easily see the fire and the smoke of the pit. Then Christiana said to Mercy,

Chr. Now I see what my poor husband went through. I have heard much of this place, but I was never here before now. Poor man! He went through here all alone in the night. He was covered by darkness almost completely through the way. Also these fiends were busy around him, as if they would have torn him to pieces. Many have spoken of it, but no one can tell what the Valley of the Shadow of Death can mean until they come into it themselves: *"The heart knows its own bitterness; and a stranger does not meddle with its joy."* It is a fearful thing to be here.

Great. This is like doing business in great waters, or like going down into the deep. This is like being in the heart of the sea, and like going down to the bottoms of the mountains. Now it seems as if the earth with its bars were around us forever; *"But let those that walk in darkness, and have no light, trust in the name of the Lord, and rest on his God"* (Isa. 50:10). As for me, as I have told you already, I have often gone through this valley. And I have been much more tried than I am now. And yet you see that I am alive. I would not boast, because I am not my own deliverer. But I trust that we shall have a good deliverance. Come, let us pray for light, to Him who can lighten our darkness, to Him who can not only rebuke these, but all the satans in hell.

So they cried out and prayed. And God sent light and deliverance. For now there was no hindrance in their way, nothing was there where the pit had filled their way and stopped them. Yet they were not yet through the valley. So they traveled on. And, behold, great stinks and loathsome smells came to them, to their great annoyance. Then Mercy said to Christiana,

Mer. It is not so pleasant here, as it was at the gate, or at Mr. Interperter's, or at the house where we last were.

But one of the boys said that it was not so bad going through here as it would be to have to stay here forever; and, that the reason why they must go through here on the way to the house prepared for them was no doubt this, that it would make their new home the sweeter to them.

Great. Well said, Samuel. You have spoken like a man.

Sam. If I ever get out of here again, I think I shall prize light and the good way better than I ever did in my whole life.

Great. We shall be out soon.

So they went on. And Joseph said,

Jos. Can we not see the end of this valley yet?

Great. Look to your feet, for we shall soon be among the snares.

So they looked to their feet, and went on. But they were much troubled with the snares. And when they were among the snares, they saw a man thrown into the ditch on the left hand, with all his flesh torn.

Great. This is one Heedless, who was going this way. He has been lying there a long time. There was one Take-heed with him when he was taken and slain, but he escaped their hands. You cannot imagine how many are killed around here. And yet men are so foolishly bold as to set out lightly on pilgrimage, and to come here without a guide. Poor Christian, it was a wonder that he escaped here! But he was loved by His God, and he also had a good heart of his own, otherwise he could never have done it.

Now they drew near the end of this way. And there where Christian had seen the cave when he went by, out of there came Maul, a giant. This Maul was used to spoiling young pilgrims with sophistry. And he called Mr. Great-heart by name, saying,

Maul How many times have you been forbidden to do these things?

Great. What things?

Maul What things! You know what things. But I will put an end to your trade.

Great. But before we fall to it, let us understand why it is that we must fight.

Now the women and children stood there trembling, for they did not know what to do.

Maul You rob the country, you rob it with the worst of thefts.

Great. You are talking in generalities. Come down to particulars, man.

Maul. You practice the craft of a kidnapper. You gather up women and children and carry them into a strange country, to the weakening of my master's kingdom.

Great. I am a servant of the God of Heaven. My business is to persuade sinners to repent. I am commanded to do my best to turn men, women and children *"from darkness to light, and from the power of Satan to God;"* and if this is indeed the ground of your quarrel, then let us fall to it as soon as you like.

Then the giant came up. And Mr. Great-heart went to meet him. And as he went, he drew his sword. But the giant had a club. So with no more waiting, they fell to it. And with the first blow, the giant struck Mr. Great-heart, knocking him down on one knee. At that, the women and children cried out. But Mr. Great-heart recovered himself and laid about him in a flurry of heavy blows, giving the giant a wound in his arm. So they fought for an hour to such a height of heat that the breath came out of the giant's nostrils, like the heat from a boiling cauldron.

Then they sat down to rest. But Mr. Great-heart fell down to pray. And the women and children did nothing but sigh and cry all the time the battle lasted. When they had rested and had taken breath, they both fell to fighting again. And with a blow, Mr. Great-heart brought the giant down to the ground. And the giant cried out, No, let me recover. So Mr. Great-heart let him get up, to be fair. And they went at it again, and the giant missed but a little of breaking Mr. Great-heart's skull with his club. Then Mr. Great-heart ran to him in the full heat of his spirit, and he pierced him through under the fifth rib. Then the giant began to faint, and he could no longer hold up his club. Then Mr. Great-heart gave him a second blow, striking the head of the giant from his shoulders. Then the women and children rejoiced, and Mr. Great-heart also praised God for the deliverance He had worked.

When this was over, they erected a pillar, fastening the giant's head on it. And they wrote under it, in letters that those who passed by might read:

> He that did wear this head was one
> That pilgrims did misuse;
> He stopped their way, he spared none,
> But did them all abuse:
> Until that I, Great-heart, arose,
> The Pilgrims' guide to be:
> Until that I did him oppose,
> That was their enemy.

Now I saw that they went on to the ascent that was a little way off, cast up to be a prospect for pilgrims. It was the place from which Christian had the first sight of his brother Faithful. So they sat down here and rested. They also ate and drank and made merry here, because they had gotten deliverance from so dangerous an enemy here. As they sat and ate, Christiana asked the guide if he had not been hurt in the battle.

Great. No, except a little of my flesh. But that also will be so far from being a detriment to me, that is now a proof of my love to my Master and to you. And, by grace, it shall be a means to increase my reward at last.

Chr. But were you not afraid, good sir, when you saw him come at you with his club?

Great. It is my duty to mistrust my own ability, so that I might have reliance on Him that is stronger than all (2 Cor. 4).

Chr. But what did you think when he brought you down to the ground with the first blow?

Great. Why, I thought that my Master was so treated, yet He was the one who conquered at last.

Matt. When you all have thought what you please, I think that God has been wonderfully good to us, both in bringing us out of this valley, and in delivering us out of the hands of this enemy. As for me, I see no reason why we should distrust our God any more, since He has now, and in such a place as this is, given us such testimony of His love.

Then they got up and went forward. And a little before them was an oak. And when they came to it, they found an old pilgrim fast asleep under it. They knew that he was a pilgrim by his clothes, and his staff, and his girdle.

So Mr. Great-heart awakened him. And as he lifted up his eyes, the old gentleman cried out, What's the matter? Who are you? And what is your business here?

Great. Come, man, do not be so hot. There is no one here but friends.

But the old man got up and stood his guard, demanding to know of them who they were.

Great. My name is Great-heart. I am the guide of these pilgrims that are going to the Celestial Country.

Honest I beg mercy from you. I was afraid that you were of the company of those that some time ago robbed Little-faith. But now that I look more closely, I see that you are people of more honesty.

Great. Why, what would or what could you have done? How could you have helped yourself if we had indeed been of that company?

Honest Done? Why I would have fought as long as I had breath in me. And if I had done so, I am sure you could never have given me the worst of it. For a Christian can never be overcome, unless he yields himself.

Great. Well said, father Honest, for by this I know that you are a cock of the right kind, for you have said the truth.

Hon. And it is also by this that I know that you know what true pilgrimage is. For all others think that we are the easiest to overcome of any.

Great. Well, now that we have so happily met, please let me ask your name, and the name of the place you came from.

Hon. I cannot tell my name. But I came from the town of Stupidity, which lies about four degrees beyond the city of Destruction.

Great. Oh, are you that countryman? Then I think I have half a guess of you. Your name is Old Honesty, is it not?

Then the old gentleman blushed, saying,

Hon. Not Honesty in the abstract, but Honest is my name. And I hope that my nature will agree with what I am called. But, sir, how could you guess that I am such a man, since I came from such a place?

Great. I had heard of you before, from my Master. For He knows all things that are done on the earth. But I have often wondered that any should come from your place, for your town is worse than the city of Destruction itself.

Hon. Yes, we lie more off from the sun, and so we are more cold and senseless. But was there ever a man such a mountain of ice that the Sun of Righteouness might not thaw his frozen heart by arising on him? And so it has been with me.

Great. I believe it, father Honest, I believe it. For I know the thing is true.

Then the old gentleman saluted all the pilgrims with a holy kiss of charity. And he asked each of them their names and how they had fared since they had set out on their pilgrimage.

Chr. I suppose you have heard of my name, for good Christian was my husband, and these four are his children.

You wouldn't dream how the old gentleman was affected when she told him who she was! He skipped, he smiled, he blessed them with a thousand good wishes, saying,

Hon. I have heard much of your husband, and of his travels and wars, which he underwent in his days. Let is be spoken to your comfort, the name of your husband rings all over these parts of the world; his faith, his courage, his endurance, and his sincerity under all, have made his name famous.

Then he turned to the boys and asked of them their names, which they told him. And then he said to them,

Hon. Matthew, you be like Matthew the publican, not in vice, but in virtue. Samuel, you be like Samuel the prophet, a man of faith and prayer. Joseph, you be like Joseph in Potiphar's house, chaste, and one that flees from temptation. And James, you be like James the Just, and like James the brother of our Lord (Matt. 10:3; Ps. 99:6; Gen. 39; Acts 1:13,14; James 1:1).

Then they told him of Mercy, and how she had left her town and her kindred to come along with Christiana and her sons. At that the old man said,

Hon. Mercy is your name, by mercy you shall be sustained and carried through all those difficulties that shall assault you in your way, until you shall come there where you shall look the Fountain of Mercy in the face with comfort. All this time Mr. Great-heart was well-pleased, and he smiled on his companions.

Now as they walked along together, the guide asked the old gentleman if he knew one Mr. Fearing, who had come on pilgrimage out of his community.

Hon. Yes, very well. He was a man that had the root of the matter in him. But he was one of the most troublesome pilgrims that I ever met with in all my days.

Great. I see that you know him. For you have given a very right description of him.

Hon. Knew him? I was a great companion of his. I was with him almost to the end. When he first began to think upon what would come on us hereafter, I was with him.

Great. I was his guide from my Master's house to the gates of the Celestial City.

Hon. Then you knew him to be a troublesome one.

Great. I did so. But I could very well bear it. For men of my calling are oftentimes entrusted with the conduct of such as he was.

Hon. Why, then, please let us hear a little of him, and how he managed himself under your guidance.

Great. Why, he was always afraid that he would come short of where he desired to go. Everything frightened him, anything anyone said, if it had but the least appearance of opposition in it. I heard that he lay roaring at the Slough of Despond for over a month. And though he saw several go over before him, and many who offered to lend their hands, he dared not venture. Nor would he go back again, saying that he would die if he did not come to the Celestial City. And yet he was dejected at every difficulty, stumbling at every straw that anyone cast in his way. Well, after he had lain at the Slough of Despond a great while, as I told you, one sunshiny morning, I don't know how, he tried and got over it. But when he was over it, he could scarcely believe it. I think he had a Slough of Despond in his mind, a slough that he carried everywhere with him. Otherwise he could never have been as he was.

So he came up to the gate (you know what I mean), the one that stands at the head of this way. And there he also stood a great while before he would try to knock. When the gate was opened, he would give back and give place to others, saying that he was not worthy. For even though he got to the gate before some others, yet many of them went in before he did. There the poor man would stand shaking and shrinking. I dare say it would have melted one's heart to have seen him. Nor would he go back again. At last he took the hammer that hung on the gate in his hand, and he gave a small rap or two. Then one opened to him, but he shrunk back as before. He that opened stepped out after him and said, O trembling one, what do you want? At that, he fell to the ground. He who spoke to him wondered to see him so faint, so he said to him, Peace be to you. Up, for I have set the door open to you. Come in, for you are blessed. With that he got up and went in, trembling. And when he was in, he was ashamed to show his face. Well, after he had been entertained there a while, and you know how it is there, he was told to go on his way, and he was told the way that he should take.

So he went on until he came to our house. But he behaved himself at my Master the Interpreter's door as he had behaved at the gate. He lay there in the cold a good while before he would try to call out. But he would not go back. And the nights were long and cold then. Still, he had a note of necessity in his bosom to my Master to receive him, and to grant to him the comfort of His house; and He was also to allow him a strong and valiant conductor (because he himself was such a chicken-hearted man). And yet, for all that, he was afraid to call at the door. So he lay around there until he was almost starved. Poor man, so great was his dejection that he was afraid to try to go in, though he saw several others knock and get in. At last, I think, I looked out of the window. And seeing a man going up and down by the door, I went out to him and asked him who he was. But, poor man, the tears stood in his eyes. So I saw what it was he wanted. Therefore I went in and told it in the house, and we revealed the thing to our Lord. So He sent me out again to beg him to come in. But I dare say that I had hard work to do it. At last he came in. And I will say this for my Lord, He was wonderfully loving toward him. There were but a few good bits at the table, but some of it was laid on his plate. Then he presented the note. And my Lord looked at it, then said that his desire would be granted. So when he had been there a good while, he seemed to get some heart and to be a little more comfortable. For as you know, my Master is one of very tender affections, especially toward those that are afraid. So He conducted Himself toward him in the way that might tend most to his encouragement. Well, when he had had a sight of the things of the place, and was ready to take his journey to go to the city, my Lord gave him a bottle of spirits and some comfortable things to eat (as He had done to Christian before). So we set forward, and I went in front of him. But the man was of very few words, only he would sigh aloud.

When we had come to where the three fellows were hung, he said that he doubted not that this would be his end also. Only he seemed glad when he saw the Cross and the Sepulchre. I confess he wanted to stay there to look a little, and he seemed to be a little cheery a while afterward. When he came to the hill Difficulty, he was not afraid of that, nor did he have much fear of the lions. For you must know that his trouble was not about such things as these. His fear was about his acceptance at last.

I got him in at the house Beautiful, I think before he was willing. Also, when he was in there, I made him acquainted with the girls of the place. But he was ashamed to make himself available in company. He desired to be alone much. Yet he loved good talk, and often he would get behind the screen to hear it. He also loved very much to see ancient things, and to be pondering them in his mind. He told me afterward that he loved to be in those two houses, that is, those at the Gate and at the Interpreter's, but he dared not be so bold as to ask.

When we left the house Beautiful and went down the hill into the Valley of Humiliation, he went down as well as I ever saw a man in my life. For he did not care how lowly he was, just so he might be happy at last. Yes, I think there was a kind of sympathy between that valley and him. For I never saw him better in all his pilgrimage than he was in that valley. He would lie down there, embrace the ground and kiss the flowers that grew in the valley (Lam. 3:27,29). He now would get up every morning at the break of day, exploring and walking to and fro in the valley.

But when he had come to the entrance of the Valley of the Shadow of Death, I thought that I had lost my man. It was not that he had any inclination to go back, for he always abhorred that. But he was ready to die from fear. He would cry out, Oh, the hobgoblins will get me, the hobgoblins will get me! And I could not beat him out of it. He made such a noise and an outcry that if they had heard him, they would have been encouraged to come and fall on us. But I noticed this, that strangely this valley was as quiet when we went through it as I ever knew it to be, before or afterward. I suppose those enemies here now had a special check from our Lord, a command not to meddle with Mr. Fearing until he had passed through it.

It would be too tedious to tell you all of it. We will then only mention a passage or two more. When he had come to Vanity Fair, I thought he would have fought with all the men in the fair. I feared we would both have our heads knocked in there, he was so hot against their foolish notions. On the Enchanted Ground, he was very wakeful. But when he had come to the river where there is no bridge, there again he was in a sad state. He mourned that now he would be drowned forever, thus never seeing that Face with comfort, that which he had come so many miles to behold. And here I also noticed something very remarkable: the water of that river was lower than at any time I ever saw it in my life. So he went over at last, wet not much above his shoes. And when he was going up to the gate, I began to take leave of him and to wish him a good reception there. And he said, I shall, I shall! Then we parted and I saw him no more.

Hon. Then it seems he was well at last?

Yes, yes, I never had any doubt about him. He was a man of choice spirit, only he was always kept very low. And that made his life so burdensome to himself, and so troublesome to others (Ps. 88). More than many, he was tender of sin. He was so afraid of doing injury to others that he often would deny himself of that which was lawful, because he did not want to offend any (Rom. 14:21; 1 Cor. 8:13).

Hon. But what is the reason that such a good man should be so much in the dark all his days?

Great. There are two sorts of reasons for it. One is this, that the wise God will have it so: some must pipe, and some must weep. (see Matt. 11:16,17). Now Mr. Fearing was one that played on the bass. He and his fellows sound the sackbut, whose notes are more doleful than the notes of other music (though, indeed, some say the bass is the ground of all music; and, for my part, I do not care at all for that profession that does not begin in heaviness of mind). The first string that the musician usually touches is the bass, when he intends to put it all in tune. God also plays on this string first, when He sets the soul in tune for Himself. Only there was the imperfection of Mr. Fearing, that he could not play any other music except this, till towards his latter end.

I am bold to talk in this way, metaphorically, for the ripening of the wits of the young, and because in the book of Revelation the saved are compared to a company of musicians, that play on their trumpets and harps, and sing their songs before the throne (Rev. 7; 14:2,3).

Hon. He was a very zealous man, as one may see by that history which you have given of him. Difficulties, lions, or Vanity Fair, he never feared at all. It was only sin, death, and hell, that were a terror to him, because he had some doubts about his interest in that celestial country.

Great. You are right. Those were the things that troubled him. And as you have well observed, they arose from the weakness of his mind in those areas, not from weakness of spirit as to the practical part of a pilgrim's life. I dare believe that he could have bitten a firebrand (as the proverb goes), if it had stood in his way. But the things with which he was oppressed, no man could ever shake off with ease.

Chr. This story of Mr. Fearing has done me good. I thought no one had been like me. But I see there is some resemblance between this good man and me. Only we differed in two things. His troubles were so great that they broke out, but I kept mine within. His also lay so hard on him that they made him so that he could not knock at the houses provided for help, but my trouble was always such that made me knock the louder.

Mer. If I might also speak my heart, I must say that something of him has also dwelt in me. For I have always been more afraid of the lake, and the loss of a place in Paradise, than I have been of the loss of other things. Oh, I have thought, may I have the happiness to have a habitation there! It is enough, even though I must part with all the world to win it.

Matt. Fear was one thing that made me think that I was far from having that within me that accompanies salvation (Heb. 6:9). But if it was so with such a good man as he was, why may it not also go well with me?

James No fears, no grace! Though there is not always grace where there is the fear of hell, yet there is surely no grace where there is no fear of God.

Great. Well said, James. You have hit the mark. For the fear of God is the beginning of wisdom (Prov. 1:7). And surely they that lack the beginning will have neither a middle nor an end. But we will conclude our discourse of Mr. Fearing after we have sent after him this farewell:

> Well, Master Fearing, you did fear
> Your God, and were afraid
> Of doing anything, while here,
> That would have you betrayed.
> And did you fear the lake and pit?
> Would others do so too!
> For, as for those that lack your wit,
> They do themselves undo.

I saw that they now went on in their talk. For after Mr. Great-heart had made an end with Mr. Fearing, Mr. Honest began to tell them of another whose name was Mr. Self-will.

Hon. He pretended to be a pilgrim, but I persuade myself that he never came in at the gate that stands at the head of the way.

Great. Did you ever talk with him about it?

Hon. Yes, more than once or twice. But he would always be like himself, self-willed. He did not care for man, nor argument, nor even example. Whatever his mind prompted him to do, that he would do. And he could not be gotten to do anything else.

Great. Please tell what principles he held. For I suppose you can tell us.

Hon. He held that a man could follow the vices as well as the virtues of the pilgrims. And he argued that if he did both, he would certainly be saved.

Great. How? If he had said that it is possible for the best to be guilty of the vices, as well as to partake of the virtues of pilgrims, he could not have been blamed much. For indeed none of us is ever absolutely exempted from any vice, it is only on condition that we watch and strive. But I see that this is not the thing you mean. For if I understand you right, your meaning is that he was of the opinion that it was allowable.

Hon. Yes, yes, that is what I mean, and it was so that he believed and practiced.

Great. But what grounds did he have for saying so?

Hon. Why, he said that he had the Scripture as his warrant.

Great. Please, Mr. Honest, give us a few particulars.

Hon. So I will. He said that adultery had been practiced by David, God's beloved, therefore he could do it. He said that to have more than one woman was no more than what Solomon practiced, and therefore he could do it. He said that Sarah, and the godly midwives, lied, and so had Rahab the saint, and therefore he could do it. He said that the disciples went at the command of their Master and took away the owner's ass, and therefore he could do so too. He said that Jacob got his inheritance from his father by guile and dissimulation, and therefore he could do so too.

Great. Exalted sin, indeed! And are you sure he was of this opinion?

Hon. I have heard him plead for it, bring Scripture for it, bring arguments for it, etc.

Great. If I had anything to say about it, this is an opinion that is not fit to be in the world.

Hon. You must understand me rightly. He did not say that any man could do this, but that those who had the virtues of those who did such things might also do the same.

Great. But what is more false than such a conclusion? For this is as much as to say that because good men have sinned from infirmity before, therefore he had permission to do it from a presumptuous mind. If a child were to fall because of the blast of the wind, or because it stumbled on a stone and fell into the mire, therefore he argues he can willfully lie down and wallow in the mire like a boar. Who could have thought that anyone could so far have been blinded by the power of lust! But that which is written must be true, they *"stumble at the word, being disobedient, to which they also were appointed"* (1 Pet. 2:8). His supposing that such may have the godly men's virtues, those who addict themselves to their vices, is also a delusion as strong as the other. It is as if a dog should say, I have, or may have, the qualities of a child because I lick up its stinking excrements. To eat up the sin of God's people (Hosea 4:8) is not a sign of one that is possessed with their virtues. Nor can I believe that one that is of this opinion can at present have faith or love in him. But I know you have made some strong objections against him. Please, what can he say for himself?

Hon. Why, he says that to do this by way of opinion seems to be far more honest than to do it and at the same time hold to the contrary opinion.

Great. A very wicked answer! For though to let loose the bridle to lusts is bad, when we at the same time hold opinions against such things; yet to sin and plead for a toleration to do so is worse. The one accidentally causes those who watch to stumble over him, but the other deliberately leads them into the snare.

Hon. There are many of this man's mind, yet do not have this man's mouth. And that makes going on pilgrimage of such little esteem.

Great. You have said the truth, and it is to be lamented. But he who fears the King of

Paradise will come out from all of them.

Chr. There are strange opinions in the world. I know one that said that it was time enough to repent when we come to die.

Great. Such people are not very bright; if they were given a week to run twenty miles in life, they would have you believe they would defer it until the last hour of the week.

Hon. You are right. And yet most of those who count themselves to be pilgrims do indeed act this way. As you see, I am an old man and I have been a traveler in this road for many a day. And I have noticed many things. I have seen some that have set out as if they would fight all the world before them, who yet have in a few days died like those in the wilderness, never getting sight of the promised land. I have seen some that have promised nothing at first, setting out to be pilgrims, those that one would think could not survive for a day, but they have proved to be good pilgrims. I have seen some who have run forward hastily, that have again in a little while run just as fast back again. I have seen some who have spoken very well of a pilgrim's life at first, but afterwards they have spoken just as much against it. I have heard some when they first set out for Paradise say positively that there is such a place, but when they have almost been there, they have come back again saying there is no such place. I have heard some boast what they would do in case they should be opposed, but when they have only a false alarm, they have left the faith, the pilgrim's way, and all.

Now as they were there on their way, one came running up to meet them. And he said, Gentlemen, and you of the weaker sort, if you love life, look out for yourselves, for the robbers are there in front of you.

Great. They are the three who set upon Little-Faith before. Well, we are ready for them.

So they went on their way, watching at every turn where they expected to meet the villains. But whether they had heard of Mr. Great-heart, or whether they had some other game, they did not come up to the pilgrims. Christiana then wished for an inn that she and her children might refresh themselves.

Hon. There is one a little before us, where Gaius, a very honorable disciple, lives (Rom. 16:23). So they all decided to turn in there, much more so since the old gentleman had given him such a good report. When they came to the door, they went in without knocking (for folks do not usually knock at the door of an inn). Then they called for the master of the house, and he came to them. So they asked if they might stay there that night.

Gaius Yes, gentlemen, if you are true men. For my house is for no one but pilgrims.

Then Christiana, Mercy and the boys were glad, because the innkeeper was a lover of pilgrims. So they called for rooms, and he showed them one for Christiana, and one for her children, and one for Mercy, and another for Mr. Great-heart and the old gentleman.

Great. Good Gaius, what do you have for supper? For these pilgrims have come far today and are very weary.

Gaius It is late, so we cannot very well go out to look for food. But such as we have, you are welcome to share, if that will content you.

Great. We will be content with what you have in the house, for I have tried you before. You are never destitute of that which is convenient.

Then he went down and told the cook, whose name was Taste-that-which-is-good, to get supper ready for the pilgrims. This done, he came up again and said,

Gaius. Come, my good friends, you are welcome to me. And I am glad that I have a house to entertain you in. And while supper is getting ready, if you please, let us entertain one another with some good discourse.

Then they all said they were glad to do so.

Gaius Whose wife is this aged matron? And whose daughter is this young girl?

Great. This woman is the wife of one Christian, a pilgrim of former times. And these are his four children. The girl is one of her acquaintances, one that she has persuaded to come with her on pilgrimage. The boys all take after their father, coveting to tread in his steps. Yea, if they but see any place where the old pilgrim has lain, or any print of his foot, it brings joy into their hearts, and they covet to lie or tread in the same place.

Gaius Is this Christian's wife? And are these Christian's children? I knew your husband's father, yea, also his father's father. Many of this stock have been good, their ancestors first lived at Antioch (Acts 11:26). Christian's progenitors (I suppose you have heard your husband talk of them) were very worthy men. Above any that I know, they have shown themselves to be men of great virtue and courage, for the Lord of the pilgrims, His ways, and those that loved Him. I have heard of many of your husband's relatives that have stood all trials for the sake of the truth. Stephen, one of the first of the family from which your husband sprang, was knocked in the head with stones (Acts 7:59,60). James, another of this generation, was slain with the edge of the sword (Acts 12:2). To say nothing of Paul and Peter, men of old who came from the family from which your husband came, and Ignatius, who was cast to the lions; Romanus, whose flesh was cut from his bones in pieces; and Polycarp, who played the man in the fire. There was the one who was hung up in a basket in the sun for the wasps to eat; and he whom they put into a sack and threw into the sea to be drowned. It would be utterly impossible to count up all of that family that have suffered injuries and death for the love of a pilgrim's life. Nor can I be anything but glad that your husband has left behind him four such boys as these. I hope they will bear up their father's name, tread in their father's steps, and come to their father's end.

Great. Indeed, sir, they are likely lads, they seem to choose their father's ways heartily.

Gaius That is what I said. So, then, Christian's family is likely to spread still further abroad on the face of the ground, and to be numerous on the face of the earth. So let Christiana search out some girls for her sons, to whom they may be betrothed, so that the name of their father, and the house of his progenitors, may never be forgotten in the world.

Hon. It would be a pity for his family to fall and be extinct.

Gaius It cannot fall, but it may be diminished. But let Christiana take my advice, for that is the way to uphold it. Also, Christiana, I am glad to see you and your friend Mercy together here, a lovely couple. And if I may advise, take Mercy as a near relation to you. If she desires, let her be given to your oldest son, Matthew. It is the way to preserve a posterity on the earth.

So this match was concluded, and in process of time they were married. But more of that hereafter.

Gaius Now I will speak on behalf of women, to take away their reproach. For as death and the curse came into the world by a woman, so also life and health came. God sent forth His Son, made of a woman (Gen. 3; Gal. 4:4). And to show how much those that came afterward hated the act of their mother, in the Old Testament this sex coveted children, if perhaps this or that woman might be the mother of the Savior of the world. And, again, when the Savior had come, women rejoiced in Him, before both men and angels (Luke 2). I do not read that any man ever gave to Christ as much as one penny, but the women followed Him and ministered to Him from their substance. It was a woman that washed His feet in tears, and it was a woman that anointed His body for burial. They were women that wept when He was going to the cross, and women followed Him from the cross. And women sat by His sepulcre when He was buried. The first with Him on His resurrection-morn were women. And women first brought the news to His disciples that He had risen from the dead (Luke 7:37-50; 8:2,3; 23:27; 24:22,23; John 2:3; 11:2; Matt. 27:55-61). So women are highly favored, proving by these things that they are sharers with us in the grace of life.

Now the cook sent up to say that supper was almost ready, sending one to lay the cloth, with the plates, and to set the salt and bread in order.

Matt. The sight of this cloth, and of this forerunner of the supper, gives me a greater appetite for my food than I had before.

Gaius So let all ministering doctrines to you in this life give you a greater desire to sit at the supper of the great King in His kingdom. For all preaching, books, and ordinances here, are but the laying of the plate, the setting of salt on the board, when compared with the feast that our Lord will make for us when we come to His house.

So supper came up. And first there was a heave-shoulder and a wave-breast set on the table before them; to show that they must begin their meal with prayer and praise to God (Lev. 7:32-34; 10:14,15; Ps. 25:1; Heb. 13:15). David lifted up the heave-shoulder with his heart to God. And with the wave-breast, where his heart lay, he used to lean on his harp when he played. These two dishes were very fresh and good, and they all ate heartily of it.

Next they brought up a bottle of wine, as red as blood.

Gaius Drink freely, for this is the true juice of the vine, that makes glad the heart of man (Ps. 104:15). So they drank and were merry (Deut. 32:14; Judg. 9:13; John 15:5).

Next came a dish of milk with crumbs.

Gaius Let the boys have that, so that they may grow by it (1 Pet. 2:1,2).

Then they brought up in course a dish of butter and honey.

Gaius Eat freely of this, for this is good to cheer up and strengthen your judgments and understandings. This was our Lord's dish when He was a child, *"Butter and honey shall He eat, so that He may know how to refuse the evil and to choose the good"* (Isa. 7:15).

Then they brought up a dish of apples. And they were very good-tasting fruit.

Matt. May we eat apples, since they were such as was used by the serpent in beguiling our first mother?

Gaius Yes, for

> Apples were they with which we were beguiled,
> Yet sin, not apples, has our souls defiled:
> Apples forbid, if eaten, corrupt the blood;
> To eat such, when commanded, does us good;
> Drink of His flagons, then, O church, His dove,
> And eat of His apples, who are sick of love.

Matt. I raised this doubt because a while back I was sick from the eating of fruit.

Gaius Forbidden fruit will make you sick, but not the fruit that our Lord tolerated.

While they were talking in this way, they were presented with another dish, a dish of nuts (S. of S. 6:11). Then some at the table said that nuts spoil tender teeth, especially the teeth of children.

Gaius Yes, for,

> Hard texts are nuts (I will not call them cheaters),
> Whose shells keep their kernels from the eaters;
> Open then the shells, and you shall have the meat;
> They here are brought for you to crack and to eat.

Then they were very merry, and they sat at the table for a long time, talking of many things. Then the old gentleman said,

Hon. My good landlord, while we are cracking your nuts, if you please, please open this riddle for me:

> There was a man, though some called him mad,
> The more he threw away, the more he had.

Then they all paid close attention, wondering what good Gaius would say. So he sat still a while, then he replied:

> He who thus bestows his goods on the poor,
> Shall have as much again, and ten times the more.

Jos. Sir, I dare say that I did not think you could find out the riddle.

Gaius Oh, I have been trained up in this way a great while. Nothing teaches like experience. I have learned from my Lord to be kind, and I have found by experience that

I have gained by it. There are those that scatter and yet they increase. And there are those that withhold more than is right, but it tends to poverty. There are those that make themselves rich, yet they have nothing. And there are those that make themselves poor, yet they have very great riches (Prov. 11:24; 13:7).

Then Samuel whispered to Christiana, his mother, saying,

Sam. Mother, this is a very good man's house. Let us stay here a good while, and let my brother Matthew be married here to Mercy before we go any further. And the host overheard him, and said,

Gaius With a very good will, my son.

So they stayed there more than a month. And Mercy was given to Matthew for his wife. While they stayed here, Mercy, as was her custom, was making coats and clothing to give to the poor, by which she brought a very good report on the pilgrims.

But to return again to our story, after supper the boys desired a bed, for they were weary from traveling. So Gaius called some to show them to their room. But Mercy said, I will take them there. So she took them, and they slept well. But the others sat up all night, for Gaius and they were such suitable company that they could not bear to part. Then after much talk of their Lord, themselves, and their journey, he that put forth the riddle, old Mr. Honest, began to nod.

Great. What, Sir? You are beginning to be drowsy. Come, rub up now, for here is a riddle for you.

Hon. Let us hear it.

Then Mr. Great-heart put forth this:

> He that would kill must first be overcome:
> Who would live abroad must first die at home.

Hon. Ha! It is a hard one; hard to expound, and harder to practice. But come, landlord, I will if you please leave my part to you. You expound it, and I will hear what you say.

Gaius No, it was put to you, and it is expected that you should answer it.

Then the old gentleman answered:

> He first by grace must conquered be,
> That sin would mortify;
> Who, that he lives, would convince me,
> To himself must die.

Gaius It is right. Good doctrine and experience teach this. For, first, until grace displays itself and overcomes the soul with its glory, it is altogether without heart to oppose sin. Besides, if sin is Satan's cords, by which the soul lies bound, how can it make resistance before it is loosened from that infirmity? Secondly, no one that knows either reason or grace will believe that such a man can be a living monument of grace when he is at the same time a slave to his own corruptions. And now it comes into my mind, I will tell you a story worth hearing. There were two men that went on pilgrimage; the one began when he was young, the other when he was old. The young man had strong corruptions to grapple with; the old man's were weak with the decays of nature. The young man was as even in his steps as was the old man, and he was in every way as light as he. Who now, or which of them, had their graces shining the clearest, since both seemed to be alike?

Hon. No doubt it was the young man's. For that which drives ahead against the greater opposition is that which gives the best demonstration that it is the strongest. This is especially so when it also holds pace with that which does not meet with half as much opposition, which old age surely does not. Besides, I have observed that old men have blessed themselves with this mistake; namely, taking the decays of nature for a gracious conquest over corruptions. And so they are apt to deceive themselves. Indeed, old men who are gracious are best able to give advice to those that are young, because they have seen most of the emptiness of things. But still, for an old man and a young man to set out together, the young one has the advantage of the fairest discovery of a work of grace within him, though the old man's corruptions are naturally the weakest.

So they sat talking until daybreak. And when the family was up, Christiana told her son James that he should read a chapter. So he read the fifty-third chapter of Isaiah.

Hon. Why is it said that the Savior is said to be *"as a root out of dry ground"*? And why is it said that *"He had no form or comeliness in Him"*?

Great. First, I would answer that it was because the church of the Jews, from which Christ came, had then lost almost all the sap and spirit of religion. To the second, I say that the words are spoken in the person of unbelievers, who, because they lack the eye that can see into our Prince's heart, therefore they judge Him by the seeming lack of beauty on His outside. They are like those that do not know that precious stones are covered with an ugly crust; and when they have found one, because they do not know what they have found, they throw it away again, as men do a common stone.

Gaius Now that you are here, since I know that Mr. Great-heart is good with his weapons, after we have refreshed ourselves, let us walk into the fields and see if we can do any good. About a mile from here there is one Slay-good, a giant who much annoys the King's highway in these parts. I know about where his haunt is. He is a master of a number of thieves, and it would be well if we could clear this country of him.

So they consented and went. Mr. Great-heart had his sword, helmet and shield. And the rest had spears and staves. And when they came to the place where he was, they found him with one Feeble-mind in his hand, whom his servants had brought to him, having caught him in the way. Now the giant was rifling him, purposing after that to pick his bones. For he was by nature a flesh-eater. Well, as soon as he saw Mr. Great-heart and his friends at the mouth of his cave, with their weapons, he demanded what they wanted.

Great. We want you. For we have come to revenge the quarrels of the many that you have slain of the pilgrims, when you have dragged them out of the King's highway. So come out of your cave. So he armed himself and came out. And they began to fight, fighting for over an hour. Then they stopped to get their wind. And the giant said, Why are you here on my ground?

Great. To revenge the blood of pilgrims, as I told you before.

So they went at it again. And the giant made Mr. Great-heart retreat. But he came up again, and from the greatness of his heart he let fly with such strength at the giant's head and sides that he made him drop his weapon. So he smote him and killed him. And he cut off his head and brought it away to the inn. He also took Feeble-mind the pilgrim and brought him with him to his lodgings. When they had arrived home, they showed his head to the family. And they set it up, as they had done others before, as a terror to those that would in the future attempt to do as he did. Then they asked Mr. Feeble-mind how he had fallen into the giant's hands.

Feeble. I am a sickly man, as you see. And because death usually knocks at my door once a day, I thought that I would never be well at home. So I gave myself to a pilgrim's life, and I have traveled here from the town of Uncertain, where my father and I were born. I am a man without strength of body, or even of mind. But I would if I could spend my life in the pilgrim's way, though I can only crawl in it. When I came to the gate that is at the head of the way, the Lord of that place entertained me freely. He did not object to my weakly looks nor to my feeble mind. But He gave me the things that were necessary for my journey, and He commanded me to hope to the end. When I came to the house of the Interpreter, I received much kindness there. And because the hill of Difficulty was judged to be too hard for me, I was carried up that by one of His servants. Indeed, I have found much relief from pilgrims, though no one was willing to go so slow as I am forced to go. Yet still, as they came on, they encouraged me to be of good cheer, saying that it was the will of their Lord that comfort should be given to the feeble-minded (1 Thess. 5:14). And so they went on in their own pace.

When I had come to Assault-lane, this giant met me and told me to prepare to fight. But, alas! Feeble one that I was, I had more need of a cordial. So he came up and took me. I thought that he would not kill me. And when he got me into his den, since I did not go with him willingly, I believed that I would come out alive again. For I have heard that no pilgrim that is taken captive by violent hands, if he keeps heart-whole towards his Master, is allowed by the laws of providence to die in the hand of the enemy. I believed I would be robbed, and to be sure I am robbed. But as you see, I have escaped with my life, for which I thank my King as the author, and you as the means. I look for other troubles, too, but I have resolved to run when I can, to go when I cannot run, and to creep when I cannot go. As to the main thing, I thank Him that loves me, and I am fixed. My way is before me, my mind is beyond the river that has no bridge, even though as you see I am but of a feeble mind.

Hon. Did you not some time ago become acquainted with one Mr. Fearing, a pilgrim?

Feeble Acquainted with him? Yes, he came from the town of Stupidity, which lies four degrees north of the city of Destruction, and that far off from where I was born. Yet we were well acquainted, for indeed he was my uncle, my father's brother. He and I have been much of the same temper. He was a little shorter than I, but still we were much of the same complexion.

Hon. I see that you knew him. And I believe that you also were related to one another. For you have his pale look, a cast like his in your eye, and your speech is much alike.

Feeble. Most who have known us both have said so. And, besides, what I have read of him, I have for the most part found in myself.

Gaius Come, sir, be of good cheer. You are welcome to me and to my house. Whatever you desire, call for it freely. And what you desire for my servants to do for you, they will do it with a ready mind.

Feeble. This is an unexpected favor, like the sun shining out of a very dark cloud. Did giant Slay-good intend for me to have this favor when he stopped me and resolved to let me go no further? Did he intend, that after he had rifled my pockets, I should go to my host Gaius? Yet it is so.

Now as Mr. Feeble-mind and Gaius were talking this way, one came running and called at the door, saying that there was a Mr. Not-right, a pilgrim, struck dead about a mile and a half from there, with a thunderbolt.

Feeble. Alas! Is he dead? He overtook me some days before I came as far as this, and he desired to keep company with me. He also was with me when Slay-good the giant caught me, but he was nimble and able to escape. But it seems that he escaped to die, while I was caught to live,

> One would think that whatever seeks to slay outright,
> Oftentimes delivers from the saddest plight.
> That very Providence whose face is death,
> Oftentimes to the lowly life will bequeath:
> I was taken; he did escape and flee;
> Hands crossed gave death to him, and life to me.

Now about this time Matthew and Mercy were married. And also Gaius gave his daughter Phebe to James, Matthew's brother, for his wife. After this, they stayed another ten days at Gaius' house, spending their time and the seasons as pilgrims usually do.

When they were ready to depart, Gaius made a feast for them. And they ate and drank and were merry. And the hour came when they must leave. So Mr. Great-heart called for a reckoning. But Gaius told him that it was not the custom of pilgrims to pay for their entertainment at his house. He boarded them by the year, but he looked for his pay from the good Samaritan who had promised him that when he returned he would faithfully pay all charges he had incurred for them.

Great. Beloved, whatever you do for the brethren and the strangers, you do it in faith; which acts have borne witness of your charity before the church. Whoever you may yet bring forward on their journey, those of a godly sort, you will do well, (3 John 5,6).

Then Gaius took his leave of them all, and of his children, and particularly of Mr. Feeble-mind. He also gave him something to drink by the way. Now when they were going out the door, Mr. Feeble-mind made as if he intended to linger. But when Mr. Great-heart noticed it, he said, Come, Mr. Feeble-mind, please go along with us. I will be your conductor, and you shall fare as the rest.

Feeble. Alas! I am not a suitable companion. You are all robust and strong, but as you see, I am weak. Therefore, I choose rather to come on behind, lest because of my many infirmities I should be both a burden to myself and to you.

As I said, I am a man of weak and feeble mind, and I shall be offended and made weak at that which others can bear. I will not like any laughing; I will not like any bright clothing; I will not like any unprofitable questions. So I am such a weak man that I am apt to be offended with that which others have a liberty to do. I do not yet know all the truth. I am a very ignorant Christian man. Sometimes, when I hear some rejoice in the Lord, it troubles me because I cannot do so too. It is with me as it is with a weak man among the strong; or as it is with a sick man among the healthy; or as a lamp despised: *"He that is ready to slip with his feet is like a lamp despised in the thought of him that is at ease"* (Job 12:5). So I do not know what to do.

Great. But, brother, I have it in my commission that I should comfort the feeble-minded, and support the weak. You must go along with us. We will wait for you. We will lend you our help. We will deny ourselves some things, both in opinion and in practice, for your sake. We will not enter into doubtful disputations before you. We will be made all things to you, rather than you should be left behind (Rom. 14; 1 Cor. 7).

Now all this while they were at Gaius' door. And, behold, as they were in the heat of their discussion, Mr. Ready-to-halt came by, with his crutches in his hand. And he also was going on pilgrimage (Ps. 38:17).

Feeble. Man, how did you get here? I was just now complaining that I did not have a suitable companion, but you are according to my wish. Welcome, welcome, good Mr. Ready-to-halt. I hope you and I may be some help to each other.

Ready. I shall be glad of your company. And, good Mr. Feeble-mind, rather than part from you now that we have so happily met, I will lend you one of my crutches.

Feeble. No, though I thank you for your good will, I am not inclined to limp before I am lame. But when the occasion arises, I think it may help me against a dog.

Ready. If either my cruthes or I can do you a favor, we are both at your command, good Mr. Feeble-mind.

So, then, they went on. Mr. Great-heart and Mr. Honest went on before, Christiana and her children next, then Mr. Feeble-mind, and Mr. Ready-to-halt came behind, with his crutches.

Hon. Please, sir, now that we are on the road, tell us some profitable things of some that have gone on pilgrimage before us.

Great. Gladly. I suppose you have heard how Christian met with Apollyon in the Valley of Humiliation, and also what hard work he had of it to go through the Valley of the Shadow of Death. Also I think you cannot but have heard how Faithful was tried by Madam Wanton, with Adam the First, with one Discontent, and with Shame, four deceitful villains such as a man meets with on the road?

Hon. Yes, I have heard of all this. But indeed, good Faithful was tested most of all by Shame. He was a tireless one.

Great. Yes, for as the pilgrim well said, he of all men had the wrong name.

Hon. But please, sir, where was it that Christian and Faithful met Talkative? He also was a notable one.

Great. He was a confident fool. Yet many follow his ways.

Hon. He nearly fooled Faithful. - re do

Great. Yes, but Christian put him into a way that would quickly find him out.

So they went on until they came to the place where Evangelist met with Christian and Faithful, where he prophesied to them what would happen to them at Vanity Fair.

Great. It is around here that Christian and Faithful met Evangelist, who prophesied to them what troubles they would meet with at Vanity Fair.

Hon. Is that so? I dare say it was a hard chapter when he read that to them.

Great. It was so. But he gave them encouragement along with it. But why do we talk of them. They were a couple of lion-like men. They had set their faces like flint. Do you remember how undaunted they were when they stood before the judge?

Hon. Well, Faithful bravely suffered.

Great. So he did, and as brave things as could be. For Hopeful and some others were converted by his death.

Hon. Well, but please go on. For you are well acquainted with things.

Great. Above all that Christian encountered after he had passed through Vanity Fair, one By-ends was the arch one.

Hon. By-ends? What was he?

Great. A very shrewd fellow, a downright hypocrite; one that would be religious whichever way the world went. But he tried to be so cunning that he would be sure neither to lose nor suffer for it. He had his mode of religion for each fresh occasion, and his wife was as good at it as he. He would turn from opinion to opinion. Yes, and he would plead for doing so, too. But, so far as I could learn, he came to an ill end with his by-ends. Nor did I ever hear that any of his children was ever of any esteem with any that truly feared God.

Now by this time they had come within sight of the town of Vanity, where Vanity Fair is kept. So, when they saw that they were so near the town, they consulted with one another how they should pass through the town. And some said one thing, and some another. At last, Mr. Great-heart said,

Great. As you know, I have often conducted pilgrims through this town. Now I am acquainted with one Mr. Mnason, of Cyprus, an old disciple, at whose house we may lodge (Acts 21:16). If you agree, we will turn in there.

Hon. I agree.

And Christiana, Mr. Feeble-mind and all of them agreed. But it was eventide before they got to the outside of the town. But Mr. Great-heart knew the way to the old man's house. So there they came. And he called at the door, and the old man inside knew his voice as soon as he heard it. So he opened, and they all came in.

Mnason How far have you come today?

And they told him they came from the house of Gaius.

Mna. You have come a good way. You must be weary. Sit down.

So they sat down.

Great. Come, what cheer, good sirs? I know that you are welcome to my friend.

Mna. I do bid you welcome. And whatever you want, do but say it and we will do what we can to get it for you.

Hon. Our great lack for a while was for harbor and good company, and now I hope we have both.

Mna. For harbor, you see what it is. But for good company, we shall see what appears when we try it.

Great. Well, will you take the pilgrims up to their rooms?

Mna. I will.

So he showed them to their respective places. And he also showed them a very pretty dining-room, where they might be and eat together until the time came for them to go to rest. And when they were seated in their places, and had become a little cheery after their journey, Mr. Honest asked his landlord if there were very many good people in the town.

Mna. We have a few. But they are indeed only a few when compared with those on the other side.

Hon. But how shall we see some of them? For the sight of good men that are going on pilgrimage is like the appearing of the moon and stars to those who are sailing the seas.

Then Mr. Mnason stamped his foot. And his daughter Grace came in. So he told her,

Mna. Grace, go tell my friends, Mr. Contrite, Mr. Holy-man, Mr. Love-saints, Mr. Dare-not-lie, and Mr. Penitent, that I have a friend or two at my house who desire to see them this evening.

So Grace went to call them. And they came. And after greetings, they sat down together at the table. Then Mr. Mnason said,

Mna. As you see, I have a company of strangers who have come to my house. They are pilgrims who have come from a distance and are going to Mount Zion. But who do you think this one is (pointing his finger at Christiana)? It is Christiana, the wife of Christian, the famous pilgrim, who with his brother Faithful was so shamefully handled in our town.

At that they stood amazed, saying, We never thought to see Christiana when Grace came to call us. Why, this is a comfortable surprise. They then asked her of her welfare, and if these young men were her husband's sons. And when she had told them that they were, they said, The King, whom you love and serve, make you as your father and bring you where he is in peace.

Then Mr. Honest asked Mr. Contrite, and the rest, in what posture their town was in at present.

Contr. You may be sure we are full of hurry at fair-time. It is hard to keep our hearts and spirits in good order when we are in such a busy condition. He that lives in such a place as this is, and that has to ao with such as we have, has need of an item to caution him to be careful every moment of the day.

Hon. But how are your neighbors now for quietness?

Contr. They are much more moderate now than formerly. You know how Christian and Faithful were abused in our town. But lately, I say, they have been far more moderate. I think the blood of Faithful lies with a load on them until now. For since they burned him, they have been ashamed to burn any more. In those days we were afraid to walk the streets, but now we can show our heads. Then the name of a professor was odious, but now, especially in some parts of our town (for you know that our town is large), religion is counted honorable. But please tell us how it has fared with you on your pilgrimage? How has the country treated you?

Hon. It is with us as it is with wayfaring men. Sometimes our way is clean, sometimes it is foul. Sometimes it is uphill, sometimes it is downhill. We are seldom assured. The wind is not always at our backs, nor is everyone a friend that we meet with in the way. We have met with some notable rubs already, and what are still to come we do not know. But for the most part we find it true that was said of old, A good man must suffer trouble.

Contr. You talk of rubs. What rubs have you had?

Hon. Ask Mr. Great-heart, our guide, for he can give the best account of that.

Great. We have been assaulted three or four times already. First, Christiana and her children were attacked by two ruffians, so that they feared they would lose their lives. Then we were attacked by Giant Bloody-man, Giant Maul, and Giant Slay-good. The truth is, we attacked the last one, instead of being set upon by him. And so it was. After we had been for some time at the house of Gaius, my host, and the host of the whole church, we were of a mind one time to take our weapons with us and to go see if we could find any of those who are enemies to pilgrims. For we heard that there was a notable one around there. And Gaius knew his haunt better than I, because he lived around there. So we looked and looked, until at last we saw the mouth of his cave. Then we were glad, and we plucked up our spirits. So we approached his den. And, lo, when we came there, he had dragged by sheer force one poor Mr. Feeble-mind into his net, and he was about to bring him to an end. But when he saw us, supposing, as we thought, that he had another prey, he left the poor man in his hole and came out. So we fell to it full force. And he laid lustily about him. But in the end, he was brought down to the ground, and his head was cut off and set up by the wayside as a terror to those that would practice such ungodliness. I tell you the truth, here is the man himself to affirm it, this is the one who was as a lamb taken out of the mouth of the lion.

Feeble. It is true, to my cost and comfort. It is to my cost for he threatened to pick my bones every moment. It is to my comfort that I saw Mr. Great-heart and his friends come with their weapons, so near for my deliverance.

Holy-man There are two things that pilgrims should possess: courage, and an unspotted life. If they do not have courage, they can never hold on their way. And if their lives are loose, they will make the very name pilgrim to stink.

Love-saints. I hope this caution is not needed among you, but truly there are many who go on the road who would rather declare themselves strangers to pilgrimage, than strangers and pilgrims on the earth.

Dare-not-lie It is true. They neither have the pilgrim's weed nor the pilgrim's courage. They do not go uprightly, but crookedly with their feet – one shoe goes inward, another outward; and their hose is out behind – here is a rag, there is a tear, to the disparagement of the Lord.

Penitent They ought to be troubled for these things. Nor are pilgrims likely to have that grace put upon them and their pilgrim's progress as they desire, until the way is cleared of such spots and blemishes.

So they sat talking and spending the time until supper was set on the table, to which they went and refreshed their weary bodies. Then they went to rest.

Now they were at the house of this Mr. Mnason a great while, in the Fair. And he in time gave his daughter Grace to Samuel, Christiana's son, for a wife. And he gave his daughter Martha to Joseph. And the time they lay there was long, for it was not now as it was in former times. So the pilgrims grew acquainted with many of the good people of the town, and they served them as well as they could. As was her way, Mercy labored for the poor, so that their bellies and their backs blessed her. And she was an ornament to her profession there. And to say the truth for Grace, Phebe and Martha, they were all of a very good nature and did much good in their places. They were also all of them very fruitful, so that Christian's name, as was said before, was likely to live in the world.

While they remained here, a monster came out of the woods and killed many of the people of the town. It would also carry away their children and teach them to suckle its whelps. And no man in the town dared to so much as face this monster. But all of them fled when they heard the noise of his coming. And this monster was like no other beast on earth. Its body was like a dragon, and it had seven heads and ten horns (Rev. 12:3). It made great havoc among the children, and yet it was governed by a woman. This monster declared the conditions under which men could operate, and those men who loved their lives more than their souls accepted those conditions. So they submitted to him.

Then Mr. Great-heart, Mr. Contrite, Mr. Holy-man, Mr. Dare-not-lie, and Mr. Penitent, went forth to meet him with their weapons. And at first the monster continued unchecked, looking on these enemies with great disdain. But they beat upon him, being sturdy men at arms, so that they made him retreat. Then they came home to Mr. Mnason's house again.

This monster had his certain times when he came out to make his attempts on the children of the people of the town. At these times these valiant men would watch him, and they would continually assault him; so much so that in the process of time he not only became wounded, but lame. Also he had not made the same havoc among the children of the town that he formerly had done. And some truly believe that this beast will die of his wounds.

This, then, made Mr. Great-heart and his fellows of great fame in this town., so that many of the people desired to taste of their things, yet they had a reverent esteem and respect for them. On account of this, then, these pilgrims did not meet much harm here. True, there were some of the baser sort that could see no more than a mole, nor could they understand any more than a beast. These had no reverence for these men, nor did they take notice of their valor and adventures.

Well, the time came when the pilgrims must go on their way. So they prepared for their journey. They sent for their friends; they conferred with them. And they had some time set apart so that they could commit each other to the protection of their King. Again they brought them such things as they had, that were fit for the weak and the strong, for the women and the men, and so they loaded them with those things that were necessary (Acts 28:10). Then they set forward on their way. And their friends accompanied them as far as was convenient. Then they again committed each other to the protection of their King and parted.

Those that were of the pilgrims' company went on, and Mr. Great-heart went before them. The women and children being weaker, they were forced to go as they could bear it. By this means Mr. Ready-to-halt and Mr. Feeble-mind had more to sympathize with their condition. When they had left the town, and when their friends had said farewell, they quickly came to the place where Faithful had been put to death. So they stopped there and thanked Him that had enabled him to bear his cross, and this the more because they now found that they had a benefit by such a manly suffering as his was.

Then they went on a good way further, talking of Christian and Faithful, and how Hopeful joined himself to Christian after Faithful was dead. Now they had come to the hill Lucre, where the silver mine was, the one that took Demas off from his pilgrimage; and some think that it was here that By-ends fell and perished. So they stopped to consider that. But when they had come to the old monument that stood over across from the hill Lucre, that is to the pillar of salt which stood within view of Sodom and its stinking lake, they marveled (as Christian did before) that men of that knowledge and ripeness of wit, as they were, should be so blinded as to turn aside here. Only they considered again that nature is not affected with the harms that others have met with, especially if that thing on which they look has an attracting virtue on the foolish eye.

I did not see where they went until they came to the river that was on this side of the Delectable Mountains; to the river where the fine trees grow on both sides, and whose leaves, if taken inwardly, are good against satiety (Ps. 23); where the meadows are green all the year long; and where they might lie down safely. By this riverside, in the meadows, there were cotes and folds for sheep, a house built for the nourishing and bringing up of those lambs, the babes of those women that go on pilgrimage. Also there was here one that was entrusted with them, who could have compassion. He was one who could gather these lambs with his arm, and carry them in his bosom, and that could gently lead those that are with young (Heb. 5:2; Isa. 63).

Now to the care of this man, Christiana admonished her four daughters to commit their little ones, that by these waters they might be housed, harbored, succoured, and nourished, and that none of them might be lacking in time to come. This man will bring them back again if any of them go astray or become lost. He will also bind them up when they are broken, and will strengthen those that are sick (Jer. 23:4; Ezek. 34:11-16). Here they will never lack food, drink and clothing. Here they will be kept from thieves and robbers. For this man will die before one of those committed to his trust shall be lost. Besides, here they will surely have good nurture and admonition, and they shall be taught to walk in right paths — and that, you know, is a favor of no small account. Also here, as you see, are delicate waters, pleasant meadows, dainty flowers, variety of trees, and those the kind that bear wholesome fruit. This fruit was not like that which Matthew ate, that which fell over the wall out of Beelzebub's garden, but it was fruit that procures health where there is none, that continues and increases it where it is.

So they were content to commit their little ones to him. And they were encouraged to do so because all this was to be at the charge of the King, and so it was a hospital to young children and orphans.

Now they went on. And when they had come to By-path meadow, to the stile over which Christian and his companion Hopeful went, when they were taken by Giant Despair and were put into Doubting-castle, they sat down and consulted what was best to be done. Now they were so strong, and they had such a man as Mr. Great-heart for their conductor, would it not be best to make an attempt to demolish the giant and his castle, and if there were any pilgrims in it, thus to set them free? One said one thing, and another said the contrary. One questioned whether it was lawful to go on unconsecrated ground. Another said they might do so provided their end was good. Then Mr.

Great-heart spoke,

Great. Though that last assertion cannot be universally true, yet I have a commandment to resist sin, to overcome evil, to fight the good fight of faith. And with whom should I fight this good fight, if not with Giant Despair? Therefore I will attempt to take away his life and to demolish his castle. Who will go with me?

Then old Honest said that he would. And Christiana's four sons said that they would go too, for they were young and strong (1 John 2:13,14). So they left the women in the road, and with them Mr. Feeble-mind and Mr. Ready-to-halt with his crutches, to be their guard, until they came back. For in that place, the Giant Despair living so near, they being still in the road, a little child could lead them (Isa. 11:6).

So Mr. Great-heart, Mr. Honest, and the four young men started toward Doubting-castle to look for Giant Despair. When they came to the castle gate, they knocked for entrance with an unusually loud noise. At that the old giant came to the gate, and his wife Diffidence followed. Then he said, Who and what is he that is so hardy as to molest the Giant Despair in this way? Mr. Great-heart replied,

Great. It is I, Great-heart, one of the King of the Celestial Country's conductors of pilgrims to their place. And I demand that you open your gates for me to enter. Prepare yourself to fight, for I have come to take away your head, and to demolish Doubting-castle.

Now Giant Despair thought no man could overcome him, because he was a giant. And he also thought that since he had before made a conquest of angels, one Great-heart ought not to make him afraid. So he armored himself and went out. He had a cap of steel on his head, a breastplate of fire was girded on him, and he came out in iron shoes, with a great club in his hand. Then these six men ran up to him and attacked him, both in front and behind. And when the giantess Diffidence came up to help him, old Mr. Honest cut her down at one blow. Then they fought for their lives, and Giant Despair was brought down to the ground. But he died hard, struggling, and seemed to have, as they say, the nine lives of a cat. But Mr. Great-heart was his death, for he did not leave him until he had severed his head from his shoulders. Then they fell to demolishing Doubting-castle. And as you might know, that was easy since Giant Despair was dead. They were seven days in destroying it. And in it they found one Mr. Despondency, almost starved to death; also Much-afraid, his daughter. They saved these two alive.

But it would have made you wonder if you could have seen the dead bodies that lay here and there in the castleyard, and how full the dungeon was with dead men's bones.

When Mr. Great-heart and his companions had finished this exploit, they took Mr. Despondency, and his daughter Much-afraid, into their protection. For they were honest people, though they were prisoners in Doubting-castle to that tyrant Giant Despair. So they took with them the head of the giant (having buried his body under a heap of stones), and came down to the road and to their companions. And they showed them what they had done. Now when Mr. Feeble-mind and Mr. Ready-to-halt saw that it was truly the head of Giant Despair, they were very joyful and merry.

Now as the need arose, Christiana could play on the viol, and her daughter Mercy could play the lute. So since they were so disposed to be merry, she played them a song. And Ready-to-halt wanted to dance. So he took Despondency's daughter, Much-afraid, by the hand and they went dancing in the road. True, he could not dance without one crutch in his hand, but I promise you that he footed it well. And the girl was to be commended, too, for she answered the music very well. As for Mr. Despondency, the music was not so much for him. He was for eating, rather than dancing, for he was almost starved. So Christiana gave him some of her bottle of spirits for present relief, and then she prepared him something to eat. And in a little time the old gentleman came to himself and began to be greatly revived.

Now I saw in my dream, when all these things were finished, Mr. Great-heart took the head of the Giant Despair and set it on a pole by the wayside, right over across from the pillar that Christian erected to warn pilgrims that came after him, that they should be careful not to enter his grounds. Then he wrote under it, on a marble stone, these verses:

> This the head of him, whose name only
> In former times did pilgrims terrify.
> His castle is down, and Diffidence his wife
> Brave Mr. Great-heart has bereft of life.
> Despondency, his daughter Much-afraid,
> Great-heart for them also the man has played.
> Whoe-er doubts of it, if he'll but cast his eye
> Up here, he may his scruples satisfy.
> This head also, when doubting cripples dance,
> Does show from fears they have deliverance.

When these men had so bravely revealed themselves against Doubting-castle, and had slain Giant Despair, they went forward. And they traveled until they came to the Delectable Mountains, where Christian and Hopeful refreshed themselves with the varieties of the place. They also acquainted themselves with the shepherds there, who welcomed them, as they had Christian before, to the Delectable Mountains. Now the shepherds having seen such a great train following Mr. Great-heart (for they were acquainted with him), they said to him, Sir, you have quite a good company here. Please tell us where you found all these.

Mr. Great-heart replied,

> First, here is Christiana and her train,
> Her sons, and her sons' wives, who, like the wain,
> Keep by the pole, and do by compass steer
> From sin to grace, else they had not been here.
> Next, here's old Honest come on pilgrimage,
> Ready-to-halt too, who, I dare engage,
> True-hearted is, and so is Feeble-mind,
> Who willing was not to be left behind;
> Despondency, good man, is coming after,
> And so also is Much-afraid, his daughter.
> May we have entertainment here, or must
> We further go? Let's know on what to trust.

Then the shepherds said, This is a comfortable company. You are welcome to us, for we have provision for the feeble, as well as for the strong. Our King has an eye to what is done to the least of these (Matt. 25:40), therefore infirmity must not stop us from entertaining them. So they brought them to the palace door, and then they said to them, Come in, Mr. Feeble-mind; come in, Mr. Ready-to-halt; come in, Mr. Despondency, and Mrs. Much-afraid his daughter. We call these in by name, Mr. Great-heart, because they are most inclined to draw back. But as for you and the rest that are strong, we leave you to your desired liberty.

Great. Today I see that grace shines in your faces and that you are my Lord's shepherds indeed. For you have not pushed those diseased either with side or shoulder, but you have rather strewed their way into the palace with flowers, as you should (Ezek. 34:21).

So the feeble and the weak went in, and Mr. Great-heart and the rest followed. When they were seated, the shepherds said to those of the weaker sort, What is it that you desire? For all things must be managed here for the support of the weak, as well as for warning the unruly. So they made a feast of things easy to digest for them, things that were pleasant to the palate, yet nourishing. And when they had received them, they went to their rest, each one respectively to his proper place.

When morning had come, because the mountains were high and the day clear, and because it was the custom of the shepherds to show the pilgrims some rarities before they left, therefore when they had gotten ready and had refreshed themselves, the shepherds took them out into the fields and showed them first what they had shown Christian before. Then they took them to some new places. The first was Mount Marvel, where they looked and saw a man at a distance, one that tumbled the hills about with words. Then they asked the shepherds what that meant. So they told them that the man was the ;on of one Mr. Great-grace, of whom you read in the first part of the Pilgrim's Progress. And he is there to teach pilgrims how to believe down, or to tumble out of their ways what difficulties they may meet with, by faith (Mark 11:23,24). Then Mr. Great-heart said,

Great. I know him. He is a man among many.

Then they took them to another place, called Mount Innocence. And they saw a man there clothed all in white, and two men, Prejudice and Ill-will, were continually throwing dirt on him. Now, behold, whatever dirt they threw upon him, would in a little time fall off again. And his garment would look as clear as if no dirt had been thrown on it. Then the pilgrims said, What does this mean? The shepherds answered, This man is named Godly-man, and this garment is to show the innocency of his life. Now those that throw dirt at him are such as hate his well-doing. But as you see, the dirt will not stick on his clothes. So it shall be with him that lives innocently in the world. Whoever they are that would make such men dirty, they labor all in vain. For God, when a little time has passed, will cause their innocence to break forth as the light, and their righteousness as the noonday.

Then they took them to Mount Charity, where they showed them a man that had a bundle of cloth lying before him, out of which he cut coats and garments for the poor that stood about him. Yet his bundle or roll of cloth was never the less. Then they said, What does this mean? The shepherds said, This is to show you that he who has a heart to give of his labor to the poor shall never lack anything. He that waters shall be watered himself. And the cake that the widow gave to the prophet, did it ever cause her to have less in her barrel?

They took them also to the place where they saw one Fool and one Want-wit washing an Ethiopian, intending to make him white. But the more they washed him, the blacker he became. Then they asked the shepherds what that meant. So they told them, This is the way it is with the vile person. Whatever means is used to get such a one a good name will in the end but tend to make him more abominable. So it was with the Pharisees, and so it shall be with all hypocrites.

Then Mercy, the wife of Matthew, said to Christiana, her mother,

Mer. Mother, if I may, I would like to see the hole in the hill, that which is commonly called the By-way to hell.

So her mother told the shepherds. Then they went to the door. It was in the side of a hill. And they opened it and told Mercy to listen for a while. So she listened, and then she heard one saying, Cursed be my father for holding my feet back from the way of peace and life. Another said, Oh, that I had been torn in pieces before I lost my soul in order to save my life! And another said, If I were to live again, how I would deny myself rather than to come to this place! Then there was a groaning and quaking of the very earth under the feet of this young woman, for she feared and looked white, and she came away trembling, saying,

Mer. Blessed is he and she that is delivered from this place!

Now when the shepherds had shown them all these things, they they took them back to the palace and entertained them with what the house could afford. But being a young, breeding woman, Mercy longed for something that she saw there. But she was ashamed to ask. Her mother-in-law then asked her what was wrong with her, for she did not look well. Then Mercy said,

Mer. There is a mirror hanging in the dining-room, and I cannot take my mind off of it. Therefore, if I cannot have it, I think that I shall miscarry. Then her mother said, I will mention your desires to the shepherds, and they will not deny it to you. But she said, I am ashamed that these men should know that I have longed for it. But she said, my daughter, it is no shame, but it is a virtue to long for such a thing as that. So Mercy said,

Mer. Then, mother, if you please, ask the shepherds if they are willing to sell it.

Now the mirror was one of a thousand. It would present a man, one way, with his own feathers exactly; but turn it another way and it would show one the very face and similitude of the Prince of Pilgrims Himself. Yes, I have talked with those who know, and they have said that they have seen the very crown of thorns on His head, by looking into that mirror. They have also seen the holes in His hands, His feet and His side. Yes, such an excellency is there in this mirror that it will show Him to one if they have a mind to see Him, whether living or dead; whether in Heaven, or in earth; whether in a state of humiliation, or in His exaltation, whether coming to suffer, or coming to reign (James 1:23-25; 1 Cor. 13:12; 2 Cor. 3:18).

Then Christiana went to the shepherds apart, whose names were Knowledge, Experience, Watchful and Sincere. And she said to them, One of my daughters, a breeding woman, longs for something she has seen in this house. And she thinks that she shall miscarry if she should be denied it by you.

Experience Call her, call her. She shall surely have what we can give her.

So they called her and said to her, Mercy, what is the thing that you desire? Then she blushed and said,

Mer. It is the great mirror that hangs up in the dining-room. So Sincere ran and brought it. And with a joyful consent, it was given to her. Then she bowed her head and gave thanks, saying,

Mer. By this I know that I have obtained favor in your eyes.

They also gave to the other young women the things that they desired, and to their husbands great commendations (because they had joined Mr. Great-heart in the slaying of Giant Despair, and the demolishing of Doubting-castle). And the shepherds put a necklace around the neck of Christiana, and so they also did around the necks of the four daughters. Also they put earrings in their ears, and jewels on their foreheads.

When they were of a mind to leave here, they let them go in peace. but they did not give to them those certain cautions which before were given to Christian and his companion. The reason was because these had Great-heart as their guide, who was one that was well acquainted with things. And so he could give them cautions more seasonably, that is even when the danger was near. Also, what cautions Christian and his companion had received from the shepherds, they had lost by the time they needed to put them into practice. Therefore, here was the advantage that this company had over the other.

From there they went on singing, and they sang,

> Behold, how fitly are the stages set
> For their relief that pilgrims are become,
> And how they us receive without one let,
> That make the other life our mark and home!
> What novelties they have to us they give,
> That we, though pilgrims, joyful lives may live;
> They do upon us, too, such things bestow,
> That show we pilgrims are wherever we go.

When they had left the shepherds, they quickly came to the place where Christian met one Turn-away, who lived in the town of Apostasy. So their guide, Mr. Great-heart, reminded them of him, saying,

Great. This is the place where Christian met one Turn-away, who carried with him the character of his rebellion on his back. And I have to say this concerning this man, he would not listen to any counsel. When he once began to fall, persuasion could not stop him. When he came to the place where the cross and sepulchre were, he met with one that told him to look there. But he gnashed his teeth and stamped his foot and said that he was resolved to go back to his own town. Before he came to the gate, he met Evangelist, who offered to lay hands on him and to turn him into the way again. But this Turn-away resisted him, and having done much despite to him, he got away over the wall. And so he escaped out of his hand.

Then they went on. And at the place where Little-faith formerly was robbed, a man stood with his sword drawn, and his face was covered all over with blood. Then Mr. Great-heart said,

Great. Who are you?

The man answered, I am one whose name is Valiant-for-truth. I am a pilgrim and I am going to the Celestial City. Now as I was in my way, three men attacked me and offered me these three things: (1) That I should become one of them; (2) that I should go back where I came from; or, (3) that I should die here (Prov. 1:10-19). To the first I answered that I had been a true man for a long time, and therefore it could not be expected that I would now cast in my lot with thieves. Then they demanded what I would say to the second. So I told them that I had not found any comfort there at the place where I came from, else I would not have left it at all. But I had found it altogether unsuitable for me, and very unprofitable to me, so I left it for this way. Then they asked me what I said to the third. And I told them that my life cost far more dear than that I should lightly give it away. Besides, I said, you have no right to put things to my choice in this way. Therefore, it will be to your peril if you meddle with me. Then these three, who were Wild-head, Inconsiderate, and Pragmatic, drew on me. And I also drew on them. So we fell to it, one against three, for about three hours. They have left some of the marks of their valor on me, as you see, and they have also carried away with them some of my marks on them. They have just now left. I suppose they might have heard your horse dash (as the saying is), so they took to flight.

Great. But those were great odds, three against one.

Valiant It is true, but little or more are nothing to him that has the truth on his side. One said, *"though a host should camp against me, my heart shall not fear; though war should rise against me, in this I will be confident," etc.* Besides, I have read in some records that one man fought an army. And how many did Samson slay with the jawbone of an ass?

Great. Why did you not cry out so that some might have come to your rescue?

Valiaant So I did, I cried to my King, who I knew would hear me and would give me invisible help. And that was sufficient for me.

Great. You have behaved yourself worthily. Let me see your sword.

So he showed it to him. And when he had taken it in his hand and had looked at it for a while, he said,

Great. Ha! It is a right Jerusalem blade!

Valiant It is so. Let a man have one of these blades, with a hand to wield it and skill to use it, and he may venture upon an angel with it. He need not fear to hold it, if he can but tell how to lay it on. Its edge will never blunt. It will cut flesh and bones, and soul and spirit, and all.

Great. But you fought a great while. I wonder that you were not weary.

Valiant I fought until my sword melted into my hand, til they were joined together; it was as if a sword grew out of my arm. And when the blood ran through my fingers, then I fought with the most courage.

Great. You have done well. You have resisted to blood, striving against sin. You shall stay with us, come in and go out with us, for we are your companions. Then they took him and washed his wounds. And they gave him of what they had, to refresh him. And so they went on together. And as they traveled, because Mr. Great-heart was delighted with him (for he loved one greatly that he found to be a man of his hands), and because there were in the company those that were feeble and weak, therefore he asked him about many things, as, first, what countryman he was.

Valiant I am from Dark-land. For there I was born, and there my father and mother are still.

Great. Dark-land? Does that not lie on the same coast with the city of Destruction?

Valiant Yes, it does. Now that which caused me to come on pilgrimage was this: We had one Mr. Tell-true come into our country. And he told about what Christian had done, he who had left the city of Destruction — how he had forsaken his wife and children and had taken up a pilgrim's life. It was also confidently reported that he had killed a serpent that came out to resist him in his journey, and how he had gotten through to where he intended. It was also told what welcome he had at all his Lord's lodgings, especially when he came to the gates of the Celestial City. For the man said that he was received with the sound of trumpets, by a company of shining ones. He also told how all the bells in the city rang for joy at his reception, and what golden garments he was clothed in, with many other things that I now shall not relate. In a word, that man so told the story of Christian and his travels that my heart fell into a burning haste to follow him. Nor could my father and mother stop me. So I left them and have come this far on my way.

Great. You came in at the gate, did you not?

Valiant Yes, yes, for the same man also told us that all would be nothing if we did not begin to enter this way at the gate.

Great. Christiana, take note that the pilgrimage of your husband has its fruits, his story is spread abroad far and near.

Valiant Why, is this Christian's wife?

Great. Yes, it is. And also these are his four sons.

Valiant. What, and going on pilgrimage too?

Great. Yes, truly, they are following after him.

Valiant It makes me glad at heart. Good man, how joyful will he be when he shall see the ones who would not go on pilgrimage with him, yet to enter after him in at the gates into the Celestial City!

Great. Without doubt it will be a comfort to him. For next to the joy of seeing himself there, it will be a joy to meet his wife and children there.

Valiant But now that you mention that, please let me have your opinion about it. Some ask if we will know one another when we are there.

Great. Do you think they shall know themselves then, or that they shall rejoice to see themselves in bliss? And if they think they shall know and do this, why not know others and rejoice in their welfare also? Again, since relatives are our second self, though that state will be dissolved there, yet why may it not be rationally concluded that we shall be more glad to see them there than to see that they are missing?

Valiant Well, I see where you are as to this. Have you any more things to ask me about my beginning to come on pilgrimage?

Great. Yes, were your father and mother willing that you should become a pilgrim?

Valiant Oh, no! They used every means imaginable to persuade me to stay at home.

Great. Why, what could they say against it?

Valiant They said it was an idle life, and that if I myself were not inclined to sloth and laziness I would never countenance a pilgrim's condition.

Great. And what else did they say?

Valiant Why, they told me that it was a dangerous way. Yes, they said it was the most dangerous way in the world, that on which the pilgrims go.

Great. Did they show you in what way the way is dangerous?

Valiant Yes, and that in many particulars.

Great. Name some of them.

Valiant They told me of the Slough of Despond, where Christian was nearly smothered. They told me that there were archers standing ready in Beelzebub-castle to shoot those who knocked at the Wicket-gate for entrance. They told me also of the wood and dark mountains, of the hill Difficulty, of the lions, and also of the three giants, Bloody-man, Maul and Slay-good. They also said that there was a foul fiend haunting the Valley of Humiliation, and that Christian almost lost his life to him. Besides, they said, you must go over the Valley of the Shadow of Death, where the hobgoblins are, where the light is darkness, where the way is full of snares, pits, traps and gins. They gold me of Giant Despair, too, of Doubting-castle, and of the ruin that the pilgrims met with there. Further, they said that I must go over the Enchanted Ground, which was dangerous. And after all this, I would find a river over which there was no bridge. And that that river lay between me and the Celestial Country.

Great. And was this all?

Valiant No. They also told me that this way was full of deceivers, and of persons that lay in wait there to turn good men out of the path.

Great. But how did they make that out?

Valiant They told me that Mr. Worldly-wiseman lay there to deceive. Also, they said, Formality and Hypocrisy were continually on the road. They also siad that By-ends, Talkative or Demas would come to gather me up; that Flatterer would catch me in his net; or that with green-headed Ignorance, I would presume to go on to the gate, from which he was sent back to the hole that was in the side of the hill, and made to go the by-way to hell.

Great. This was enough to discourage you, but did they stop there?

Valiant No. wait. They told me also of many that had tried that way in times past, and who had gone a great way in it to see if they could find something of the glory there that so many had talked about from time to time. And they told of how they had come back again and called themselves fools for setting a foot out of doors into that path, to the satisfaction of all the country. And they named several who had done this, such as Obstinate and Pliable, Mistrust and Timorous, Turn-away and old Atheist, with many more.

They said that some of them had gone far to see what they could find, but that not one of them had found so much advantage from going as would add up to the weight of a feather.

Great. Did they say anything more to discourage you?

Valiant Yes. They told me of one Mr. Fearing, who was a pilgrim, and how he found his way so lonely that he never had a comfortable hour in the way. And they said that Mr. Despondency had nearly starved in it. Yes, and also (which I had almost forgotten) that Christian himself, about whom there had been so much told, after all his ventures for a celestial crown, was certainly drowned in the Black River, and never went a foot further, however it was smothered up.

Great. And did none of these things discourage you?

Valiant No, they only seemed to be so many nothings to me.

Great How did that happen?

Valiant Why, I still believed what Mr. Tell-true had said, and that carried me beyond all of them.

Great. Then this was your victory, even your faith (1 John 54).

Valiant Yes, it was. I believed, therefore I came out and got into the way. I fought all that set themselves against me, and by believing I have come to this place

> Who would true valor see,
> Let him come hither
> One here will constant be,
> Come wind, come weather.
> There's no discouragement
> Shall make him once relent
> His first avowed intent
> To be a pilgrim.
> Whoever besets him round
> With dismal stories,
> Do but themselves confound
> His strength the more is.
> No lion can him fright,

He'll with a giant fight,
But he will have a right
To be a pilgrim.
Hobgoblin, nor foul fiend,
Can daunt his spirit
He knows he at the end
Shall life inherit
Then fancies fly away,
He'll not fear what men say
He'll labor night and day
To be a pilgrim.

By this time they had gotten to the Enchanted Ground, where the air naturally tended to make one drowsy. And that place was all grown over with briers and thorns, excepting here and there, where an enchanted arbor was, on which if a man sits, or in which if a man sleeps, it is doubtful (some say) whether he shall ever rise or wake again in this world. Therefore they went through this forest together, with Mr. Great-heart in front, he being the guide, and Mr. Valiant-for-truth coming behind, being the rear-guard — for fear that some fiend, or dragon, or giant, or thief should happen to fall upon them from the rear and so do them mischief. They went on here, each one with his sword drawn in his hand, for they knew that it was a dangerous place. Also they cheered one another up as well as they could. Mr. Great-heart commanded that Feeble-mind should come up after him, and Mr. Despondency was under the eye of Mr. Valiant.

Now they had not gone far when a great mist and darkness fell upon all of them. For a great while, they could hardly see one another. So for some time they were forced to feel for one another by words, for they did not walk by sight. And as you may think, it was heavy going for the best of them but how much worse it was for the women and children, who were both tender of heart and tender of foot. Yet as it happened, through the encouraging words of him that led in front, and of him who brought them up behind, they managed to move along pretty well.

Also the way here was very wearisome, through dirt and mire. Nor was there on all of this ground so much as one inn or eating-place where the feeble ones could refresh themselves. So they were grunting, and puffing, and sighing, while one tumbled over a bush, another stuck fast in the dirt. And some of the children lost their shoes in the mire. One would cry out, I am down and another, Ho, where are you? And a third would call out, The bushes have gotten such a fast hold on me that I do not believe I can get away from them!

Then they came to an arbor which was warm, promising much refreshment to the pilgrims. For it was finely worked overhead, beautified with greens, furnished with benches and settles. It also had a soft couch in it, on which the weary might lie. As you might think, this was very tempting, all things considered. For the pilgrims had already begun to be frustrated by the badness of the way. But there was not one of them that had made so much as a motion to stop there. But, for all that I could see, they continually paid close attention to the advice of their guide. And he so faithfully told them of the dangers, and of the nature of the dangers when they were there, that usually when they were nearest to danger they plucked up their spirits the most, heartening one another to deny the flesh. This arbor was called the Slothful's Friend, being placed on purpose to allure, if it were possible, some of the pilgrims there to take up their rest when weary.

I saw then in my dream that they went on in this deserted ground until they came to a place at which a man is apt to lose his way. Now when it was light, their guide could tell well enough how to miss those ways that led wrong, but in the dark he could not tell. But he had in his pocket a map of all ways leading to or from the Celestial City. So he struck a light (for he never left without his tinder-box) and took a look at his map, which told him to be careful to turn to the right hand in that place. And if he had not been careful to look at his map here, they all probably would have been smothered in the mud. For just a little in front of them, even at the end of the clearest way, too, was a pit, no one knows how deep, full of nothing but mud. It was put there on purpose to destroy the pilgrims.

Then I thought to myself, Whoever goes on pilgrimage must have one of these maps with him, that he may look when he cannot tell which way he must take.

Then they went on in this Enchanted Ground until they came to another arbor, and it was built by the highway-side. And in that arbor lay two men, whose names were Heedless and Too-bold. These two went this far on pilgrimage. But being wearied with their journey here, they sat down to rest themselves, and so fell fast asleep. When the pilgrims saw them, they stood still and shook their heads, for they knew that the sleepers were in a pitiful case. Then they consulted as to what to do, whether to go on and leave them in their sleep, or to step up to them and try to awaken them. So they decided to go to them and awaken them, that is, if they could. But they decided to be cautious that they might not sit down themselves, nor embrace the offered benefit of that arbor.

So they went in and spoke to the men, calling each by his name (for it seems the guide knew them). But there was no voice nor answer. Then the guide shook them, doing what he could to disturb them. Then one of them said, I will pay you when I get my money. At this, the guide shook his head. Then the other said, I will fight as long as I can hold my sword in my hand. At that, one of the boys laughed.

Then Christiana asked what the meaning of this was.

Great. They are talking in their sleep. If you strike them, beat them, or whatever else you may do, they will answer you in this way. Or as one of them said in days past, when the waves of the sea were beating on him, and he was sleeping like one on the mast of a ship, *"When I awake, I will seek it again"* (Prov. 23:34,35). You know that when men talk in their sleep they will say anything, but their words are not governed either by faith or reason. There is an incoherency in their words now, as there was before between their going on pilgrimage and sitting down here. This, then, is the mischief of it. When heedless ones go on pilgrimage, it is twenty to one they end up this way. For this Enchanted Ground is one of the last refuges that the enemy to pilgrims has. So it is, as you see, placed almost at the end of the way, and so it stands against us with the more advantage. For the enemy thinks, When will these fools be so desirous of sitting down as when they are weary? And when are they so likely to be weary as when they are almost at their journey's end? So it is, I say, that the Enchanted Ground is placed so near to the land Beulah, and so near the end of their race. Therefore, let pilgrims look carefully to themselves less it happen to them as it has to these who have fallen asleep – and no one can awaken them.

Then the pilgrims desired with trembling to go forward. Only they prayed their guide to strike a light so that they might go the rest of their way by the help of the light of a lantern. So he struck a light and they traveled by the help of that through the rest of the way, though the darkness was very great (2 Peter 1:19). But the children began to be very weary, and they cried out to Him who loves pilgrims, that He should make their way more comfortable. So before they had gone much further, a wind arose that drove away the fog, and the air became much more clear. Still they were not off of the Enchanted Ground, only now they could see one another better and also the way in which they should walk.

Now when they were almost at the end of this ground, they heard a solemn noise a little in front of them, as of one that was much concerned. So they went on and looked before them. And, behold, they saw what they thought to be a man on his knees, with his hands and eyes lifted up, speaking earnestly to One that was above. They drew near, but they could not tell what he said. So they went quietly until he had finished. When he had finished, he got up and began to run toward the Celestial City. Then Mr. Great-heart called after him, saying,

Great. Ho, friend! Let us have your company if you are going, as I suppose you are, to the Celestial City.

So he stopped. And they came up to him. But as soon as Mr. Honest saw him, he said,

Hon. I know this man.

Valiant Please tell us who he is.

Hon. It is one that comes from the area where I lived. His name is Standfast, and he is certainly a very fine pilgrim.

So they came up to one another. And soon Standfast said to old Honest,

Stand. Ho, father Honest, is that you?

Hon. Yes, it is me, as sure as it is you there.

Stand. I am very glad that I have found you on this road.

Hon. And I am as glad that I espied you on your knees.

Stand. Did you see me?

Hon. Yes, I did, and with my heart I was glad at the sight.

Stand. Why, what did you think?

Hon. Think? What could I think? I thought we had an honest man on the road and that we should therefore have his company by and by.

Stand. If you thought nothing amiss, how happy I am! But if I am not as I should be, then it is I alone who must bear it.

Hon. That is true, but your fear further confirms to me that things are right between the Prince of Pilgrims and your soul. For He has said, *"Blessed is the man that fears always."*

Valiant Well, brother, Please tell us what it was that caused you to be on your knees just now. Was it because some special mercy had laid obligations on you? Or what?

Stand. Why, as you see, we are on the Enchanted Ground. And as I was coming along, I was musing within myself of what a dangerous nature the road in this place was, and how many there were who had come even this far on pilgrimage only to be stopped and destroyed here. I also thought of the manner of the death with which this place destroys men. Those that die here do not die of a violent distemper. The death which they die is not grievous to them. For he that goes away in his sleep begins that journey with desire and pleasure. Yea, such ones acquiesce in the will of that disease.

Hon. Did you see the two men asleep in the arbor?

Stand. Yes, yes. I saw Heedless and Too-bold there. And for all I know, they may lie there until they rot (Prov. 10:7). But let me go on with my tale. As I was thus musing, there was one in very pleasing attire, but old, who presented herself to me and offered me three things; that is, her body, her purse, and her bed. Now the truth is, I was both weary and sleepy. I am also as poor as an owlet, and the witch perhaps knew that. Well, I repulsed her again and again, but she passed by my rejection and smiled. Then I began to be angry. But she paid no attention to that at all. Then she made offers again, saying that if I would be ruled by her, then she would make me very great and very happy. For, she said, I am the mistress of the world, and men are made happy by me. Then I asked her name, and she told me it was Madam Bubble. This drove me further from her. But she still followed me with enticements. Then, as you saw, I took to my knees, and with my hands lifted up, I cried out and prayed to Him who said that He would help me. And just as you came up, the woman fled away. Then I continued, to give thanks for this great deliverance. For I truly believe she intended no good to me, but rather that she sought to make me stop in my journey.

Hon. Without doubt her designs were evil. But, wait, now that you talk of her, I think I either have seen her or have read some story about her.

Stand. Perhaps you have done both.

Hon. Madam Bubble? Is she not a tall, attractive woman, somewhat of a swarthy complexion?

Stand. Right! You have hit it, she is just such a one.

Hon. Does she not speak very smoothly, and does she not give you a smile at the end of every sentence?

Stand. You are right on it again, for these are her very actions.

Hon. Does she not wear a great purse on her side, and is her hand not often on it, fingering her money as if that were her heart's delight?

Stand. It is just so. If she was still standing here, you could not have more fully described her to me, nor set forth her features.

Hon. Then he that drew her picture was a good painter, for what he wrote of her is true.

Great. This woman is a witch, and it is because of her sorceries that this ground is enchanted. Whoever lays his head down in her lap may as well lay it down on that block over which the axe hangs. And whoever lays their eyes on her beauty will be counted as the enemy of God (James 4:4; 1 John 2:14,15). This is the one that maintains the enemies of the pilgrims in all their splendor. Yes, this the one that has bought off many a man from a pilgrim's life. She is a great gossiper. And she is always, both she and her daughters, at the heels of one pilgrim or another, now commending, and then preferring the excellences of this life. She is a bold and impudent slut. She will talk with any man. She always laughs poor pilgrims to scorn, but she highly commends the rich. If there is one who is cunning enough to heap up money in a place, she will speak well of him from house to house. She loves banqueting and feasting. She is always at one full table or another. She has set herself out as a goddess in some places, and so some worship her. She has her time, and open places of cheating. And she will avow that no one can show a good which compares to hers. She promises to dwell with children's children, if they will but love her and make much of her. She will cast gold out of her purse like dust in some places and to some persons. She loves to be sought after, spoken well of, and to lie in the bosoms of men. She is never weary of commending her commodities, and she loves them most that think best of her. She will promise crowns and kingdoms to some, if they will but take her advice. Yet she has brought many to the bridle, and ten thousand times more to hell.

Stand. Oh! What a mercy it is that I resisted her. For where might she have drawn me!

Great. Where? No one but God knows where. But to be sure, she would have drawn you into many foolish and hurtful lusts, which drown men in destruction and perdition (1 Tim. 6:9). It was she that set Absalom against his father, and Jeroboam against his master. It was she that persuaded Judas to sell his Lord, who prevailed with Demas to forsake the godly pilgrim's life. No one can tell all the mischief that she has done. She makes rulers and subjects to disagree, as well as parents and children, neighbor and neighbor, a man and his wife, a man and himself, the flesh and the Spirit. So, good Mr. Standfast, be as your name is, and when you have done all, stand.

All this discourse brought joy and trembling to the pilgrims. But finally they broke out and sang:

> What danger the pilgrim is in!
> How many are his foes!
> How many ways there are to sin,
> No living mortal knows.
> Some in the ditch are spoiled, yea, can
> Lie tumbling in the mire
> Some, though they shun the frying-pan,
> Do leap into the fire.

After this I watched until they had come into the land of Beulah, where the sun shines day and night. Here, because they were weary, they took a while to rest themselves. And because this country was for pilgrims, and because the orchards and vineyards here belonged to the King of the Celestial Country, they were free to take any of His things. But they were refreshed quickly, though the bells rang and the trumpets were continuously sounding out melodiously so that they could not sleep, yet they received as much refreshing as if they had slept their sleep ever so soundly. Also here there was much joyful noise as the people exclaimed, More pilgrims have come to town! And another would answer, And so many went over the water and were admitted at the golden gates today!

Again, others would cry, A legion of shining ones have just come to town, so that we know now there are more pilgrims on the road for they have come here to wait for them, and to comfort them after all their sorrow!

So the pilgrims got up and walked to and fro. And their ears were now filled with heavenly noises, and their eyes delighted with celestial visions! In this land they heard nothing, saw nothing, felt nothing, smelled nothing, tasted nothing that was offensive to their stomach or to their mind. Only when they tasted of the water of the river over which they were to go, they thought that it tasted a little bitter to the palate. But when it was down, it proved to be sweeter.

There was a record kept of the names of those that had been pilgrims in the past, and there was a history of all the famous acts that they had done in this place. It also was much discussed here how the river had flowed to some, and what ebbings it has had while others have gone over. It has been in a way dry for some, while it has overflowed its banks for others.

In this place the children of the town would go into the King's gardens and gather bouquets for the pilgrims, bringing them to them with much affection. Camphire, with spikenard and saffron, calamus and cinnamon, with all the trees of frankincense, myrrh and aloes, and all the chief spices also grew here. The pilgrims rooms were perfumed with these while they stayed here. And their bodies were anointed with these, to prepare them to go over the river when the time appointed had come.

Now while they lay here and waited for the good hour, there was a report in the town that there was a Post coming from the Celestial City, who carried matter of great importance to one Christiana, the wife of Christian the pilgrim. So they made inquiry as to her, and the house was found where she was. So the Post presented her with a letter, the contents of which were Hail, good woman! I bring you news that the Master is calling for you, and He expects you to stand in His presence, in the clothes of immortality, within ten days. When he had read this letter to her, he gave her with it a sure token that he was a true messenger and that he had come to tell her to make haste to depart. The token was this, an arrow with a point sharpened by love to let it easily enter her heart, which by degrees worked so effectually with her that at the time appointed she must be gone.

When Christiana saw that her time had come, and that she was the first of this company that was to go over, she called for Mr. Great-heart, her guide, and she told him how matters were. So he told her he was heartily glad of the news, that he could not have been more glad if the Post had come for him. Then she asked that he should give advice as to how all things should be prepared for her journey. So he told her, It must be thus and thus, and we that survive will accompany you to the river side.

Then she called for her children and gave them her blessing, telling them that she had read with comfort the mark that was set in their foreheads, that she was glad to see them with her there, and that they had kept their garments so white. Lastly, she bequeathed what little she had to the poor, commanding her sons and daughters to be ready when the messenger should come for them. And when she had spoken these words to her guide and to her children, she called for Mr. Valiant-for-truth and said to him,

Chr. Sir, you have shown yourself to be truehearted in all things. Be faithful to death, and my King will give you a crown of life (Rev. 2:10; James 1:12). I also would beg of you to keep an eye on my children. And if at any time you see them faint, please speak comfortably to them. For my daughters, my sons' wives, have been faithful, and the fulfillment of the promise on them will be their end.

But she gave Mr. Standfast a ring. Then she called for old Mr. Honest and said to him,

Chr. *"Behold an Israelite indeed, in whom is no guile!"*

Hon. I wish you a beautiful day when you set out for Mount Zion, and I shall be glad to see that you go over the river dry-shod.

Chr. Come wet, come dry, I long to depart. For however the weather is in my journey, I shall have time enough when I get there to sit down and rest and dry myself.

Then that good man, Mr. Ready-to-halt came in to see her. So she said to him,

Chr. Until now you have walked with difficulty, but that will only make your rest that much sweeter. Only watch, and be ready, for at an hour when you do not expect him, the messenger may come.

After him came Mr. Despondency and his daughter Much-afraid. And she said to them,

Chr. You should remember your deliverance from the hands of Giant Despair and from Doubting-castle with thankfulness forever. The effect of that mercy is that you have been brought safely here. Be watchful, and cast away fear, be sober, and hope to the end.

Then she said to Mr. Feeble-mind,

Chr. You were delivered from the mouth of the Giant Slay-good so that you might live in the light of the living and see your King in comfort. Only I advise you to repent of your aptitude for fear and doubt of His goodness, before He sends for you, lest you should be forced to stand before Him for that fault with blushing when He comes.

Now the day drew near when Christiana was to depart. So the road was full of people to see her take her journey. But, behold, all the banks beyond the river were full of horses and chariots which had come down from above to accompany her to the City gate! So she came out and entered the river, with a wave of farewell to those that followed her. The last words that she was heard to say were,

Chr. I come, Lord to be with You, and bless You!

So her children and friends returned to their place, for those waiting for Christiana had carried her out of their sight. So she went and called, and entered in at the gate with all the ceremonies of joy that her husband Christian had entered with before her. And her children wept at her departure. But Mr. Great-heart and Mr. Valiant played on the well-tuned cymbal and harp for joy. So all went to their respective places.

In the process of time, another Post came to the town, and his business was with Mr. Ready-to-halt. So he searched him out and said, I have come from Him whom you have loved and followed, though upon crutches. And my message is to tell you that He expects you at His table to sup with Him in His kingdom the next day after Easter. Therefore prepare yourself for this journey. Then he also gave him a token that he was a true messenger, saying, *"I have broken your golden bowl and have loosened your silver cord"* (Ecclesiastes 13:6).

After this, Mr. Ready-to-halt called for his fellow-pilgrims and told them,

Ready. I have been called, and God will surely visit you also.

So he asked Mr. Valiant to make his will. And because he had nothing to bequeath to them that were surviving him, except his crutches and his good wishes, he said,

Ready. I bequeath these crutches to my son that shall walk in my steps, with a hundred warm wishes that he may prove better than I have been.

Then he thanked Mr. Great-heart for his guidance and kindness, and he then addressed himself to his journey. When he had come to the brink of the river, he said,

Ready. I shall now have no more need of these crutches, since yonder are chariots and horses for me to ride on.

The last words he was heard to say were,

Ready. Welcome life!

So he departed.

After this, Mr. Feeble-mind had news that the Post sounded his horn at his bedroom door. Then he came in and told him, I have come to tell you that your Master has need of you, and that in a very little time you must look upon His face in brightness. And take this as a token of the truth of my message, *"Those that look out at the windows shall be darkened"* Then Mr. Feeble-mind called for his friends and told them what errand had been brought to him, and what token he had received of the truth of the message. Then he said,

Feeble. Since I have nothing to bequeath to any, to what purpose should I make a will? As for my feeble mind, that I will leave behind me, for I will have no need of that in the place where I go, nor is it worth bestowing on the poorest pilgrims. So when I have departed, I desire that you, Mr. Valiant, would bury it in a dunghill.

This done, and the day coming on which he was to depart, he entered the river like the rest. His last words were, Hold out, faith and patience! So he went over to the other side.

When many days had passed by, Mr. Despondency was sent for. For a Post had come and brought this message to him, Trembling man! These are to summon you to be ready for the King by the next Lord's day, to shout for joy for your deliverance from all your doubtings. And the messenger said, To prove my message is true, take this for a proof and he gave him a grasshopper to be a burden to him (Ecclesiastes 12:5).

Now Much-afraid, Mr. Despondency's daughter, when she heard what was done, said that she would go with her father. Then Mr. Despondency said to his friends,

Despond. You know what my daughter and I have been, and how troublesomely we have behaved ourselves in every company. My will and my daughter's is that our desponds and slavish fears be not received by any one, from the day of our departure forever. For I know that after my death they will offer themselves to others. For to be plain with you, they are ghosts which we entertained when we first began to be pilgrims, and we could never shake them off afterwards. And they will walk about and seek entrance into the pilgrims, but for our sakes shut the doors on them.

When the time had come for them to depart, they went up to the edge of the river. The last words of Mr. Despondency were, Farewell night, welcome day! His daughter went through the river singing, but no one could understand what she said.

Then after a while, there was a Post in the town inquiring for Mr. Honest. So he came to the house where he was. And he delivered these lines into his hand, You are commanded to be ready a week from tonight to present yourself before your Lord, at His Father's house. And for a token that my message is true, *"All the daughters of music shall be brought low"* (Eccl. 124). Then Mr. Honest called for his friends and said to them,

Hon. I am dying, but I shall make no will. As for my honesty, it shall go with me. Let him that comes after be told of this.

When the day that he was to depart came, he got ready to go over the river. Now the river at that time overflowed its banks in some places. But Mr. Honest in his lifetime had spoken to one Good-conscience to meet him there, and when he did, he loaned him his hand and so helped him over. The last words of Mr. Honest were,

Hon. Grace reigns!

So he left the world.

After this, it was reported that Mr. Valiant-for-truth was taken with a summons by the same Post as the other. And he had this for a token that the summons was true, *"That his pitcher was broken at the fountain"* (Eccl. 12:6). When he understood it, he called for his friends and told them of it. Then he said,

Valiant. I am going to my Father's. And although I have gotten this far with great difficulty, yet I now repent of all the trouble I have been at to arrive where I am. My sword I give to him that shall succeed me in my pilgrimage, and my courage and skill to him that can get it. I carry my marks and scars with me, to be a witness for me that I have fought His battles, He who now will be my rewarder.

When the day that he was to depart came, many accompanied him to the riverside, into which as he went he said,

Valiant *"Death, where is your sting?"*

And as he went down deeper, he finished, *"Grave, where is your victory?"* (1 Cor. 15:55).

So he passed over, and all the trumpets sounded for him on the other side.

Then a summons came forth for Mr. Standfast. This Mr. Standfast was the one that the rest of the pilgrims found on his knees in the Enchanted Ground. And the Post brought it to him, open in his hands. And its contents were these, that he must prepare for a change of life, for his Master was not willing that he should be so far from Him any longer. At this Mr. Standfast was put into a muse. No, the messenger said, you do not need to doubt the truth of my message, for here is a token of the truth of it, *"Your wheel is broken at the cistern"* Then he called Mr. Great-heart to him, he who was their guide, and he said to him,

Stand. Sir, although it was not my lot to be much in your good company during the days of my pilgrimage, yet from the time that I knew you, you have been profitable to me. When I came from home I left behind me a wife and five small children. Let me beg you when you return (for I know that you will go and return to your Master's house, in the hope that you may yet be a guide to more of the holy pilgrims), that you send to my family and make them acquainted with all that has and all that shall happen to me. And tell them of my happy arrival at this place, and of the present and late blessed condition I am in. Also tell them of Christian and his wife Christiana, and how she and her children came after her husband. And tell them of the happy end that she had, and where she has gone. I have little or nothing to send to my family, unless it might be my prayers and tears for them. Of these, it will be sufficient for you to tell them, if perhaps they may prevail.

When Mr. Standfast had thus set things in order, and the time had come for him to haste away, he also went down to the river. Now there was a great calm at that time in the river. So Mr. Standfast, when he was about halfway in, stood a while and talked with his companions who waited on him there. And he said,

Stand. This river has been a terror to many. Yea, the thoughts of it have also often frightened me. But now I am standing easily. My foot is fixed on that on which the feet of the priests that bore the ark of the covenant stood while Israel went over this Jordan (Josh. 3:17). The waters are indeed bitter to my palate, and cold to my stomach. But the thoughts of what I am going toward, and of the conduct that waits for me on the other side, lies as a glowing coat at my heart. I now see myself at the end of my journey. My toilsome days are over. I am going to see that head that was crowned with thorns, and that face that was spit on for me. I have formerly lived by hearsay and faith, but now I go where I shall live by sight. And I shall be with Him in whose company I delight. I have loved to hear my Lord spoken of, and wherever I have seen the print of His shoe in the earth, there I have coveted to set my foot too. His name has been to me as a perfume-box; yea, sweeter than all perfumes. His voice has been most sweet to me, and I have more desired His face than those that have most desired the light of the sun. I used to gather His words for my food, and for antidotes for the time of fainting. He has held me and has kept me from my iniquities; yea, He has strengthened my steps in His way.

Now while he was saying these things, his countenance changed. His strong man bowed under him. And after he had said, Take me, for I come to You, he ceased to be seen by them.

But it was glorious to see how the open region was filled with horses and chariots, with trumpeters and pipers, with singers and players on stringed instruments, to welcome the pilgrims as they went up. And they followed one another in at the beautiful gate of the City.

As for Christiana's children, the four boys that Christiana brought with her, with their wives and children, I did not stay where I was until they had gone over. Also, since I came away, I heard one say that they were yet alive, and so would be for the increase of the church in that place where they were, for a time.

Should it be my lot to go that way again, I may give those that desire it an account of what I here am silent about. In the meantime, I bid my reader, FAREWELL!

CPSIA information can be obtained
at www.ICGtesting.com
Printed in the USA
LVHW021224250421
685514LV00033B/1106